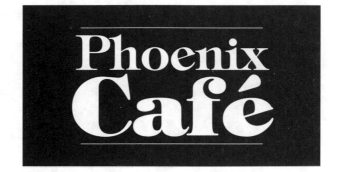

Phoenix Café

G·W·Y·N·E·T·H J·O·N·E·S

TOR®

A TOM DOHERTY ASSOCIATES BOOK
NEW YORK

PHOENIX CAFÉ

Edited by David G. Hartwell

A Tor Book
Published by Tom Doherty Associates, Inc.
175 Fifth Avenue
New York, NY 10010

Tor Books on the World Wide Web:
http://www.tor.com

Tor® is a registered trademark of Tom Doherty Associates, Inc.

Library of Congress Cataloging-in-Publication Data

Jones, Gwyneth A.
    Phoenix Café / Gwyneth A. Jones.—1st ed.
        p.   cm.
    "A Tom Doherty Associates book."
    ISBN 0-312-86534-1 (acid-free paper)
    I. Title.
    PR6060.O5163P48   1998
    823'.914—dc21   97-29862
                                                                  CIP

First Edition: January 1998

Printed in the United States of America

0 9 8 7 6 5 4 3 2 1

I am grinding away, on a series of different effects . . . I am becoming a very slow worker . . . (but) it is imperative to work a good deal to achieve what I seek: "instantaneity" above all . . . the same light present everywhere . . .

Claude Monet

Comme devant un paysage enseveli sous la pluie, nous nous représentons ce qu'il eut été dans le soleil, ansi Thérèse découvrait la volupté.

François Mauriac,
Thérèse Desqueyroux

I

Blood and Fire

1

A PRISONER OF CONSCIENCE

i

FAR IN THE blurred distance, a jet of red tumbled from the fountain of life. As she became puzzled that the blood should still be liquid after so long, she began to wake. The surface under her, a mixture of tackiness and unpleasant slither, struck cold as she moved. The drops of scarlet were gathering like raindrops on her fingertips now, and running off into the air. She was kneeling, arms outstretched, staring at the blood.

She woke: lying on a bed with legs, on a hygienically wrapped mattress, in her police cell. The wrapping, meant to swallow all her body's minor effluent, had become fully charged several prisoners ago; it ate nothing now. Her blanket was shoved down onto the floor in the narrow space between the end of the bed and the wall. The cell was always chilly, but she'd decided she would rather get used to the cold than endure the blanket's slimy touch.

She had been working for the Aleutian Mission when she was arrested, helping converts to die their first death. The missionaries of the alien faith, the Church of Self, taught that human beings were *no different flesh*. Like their immortal alien rulers, the humans were each of them eternal aspects of God the WorldSelf: reborn time and again through lives without end. If only they would throw off the superstition of permanent death, they would realize the truth. In this city, the most resistant to Aleutian influence, the Mission had a small but enthusiastic following among the poor, and an uneasy tolerance from the rich. A steady stream of proselytes reached the moment when they must reject their old ways in an ecstatic act of faith. Catherine had been assisting at a conversion ceremony, which had run into trouble with the human authorities. The arrest was illegal; she'd been committing no crime. But she was glad of the confrontation. The Mission needed publicity.

She recalled that she'd been in the apartment's dry-shower stall with the rich boy when the orthodoxy raiders had arrived. The two of them had written on the wall, in huge dripping letters, in English: DONE BECAUSE WE ARE TOO MANY. He was fluent in several human languages and a student of English literature. Many of the young people in the hives were like that: they had nothing to do, and the free grid was full of knowledge. Such a nice boy—rich only by comparison with the rest of her congregation—old-fashioned, gentle, and serious. She would have liked to hold him back from salvation a little longer. But he knew what he wanted. He had been very earnest about it, eager and composed while the others were running wild. Then the orthodox humans had arrived. She remembered fire, confusion, a roar of foul energy rushing through the warm smell of blood. Someone, probably the building, must have called the police.

She lay gazing around at her simple home. The walls were covered in rows of glossy ceramic squares. They were light blue and white, alternately. Every third square was decorated with a bunch of dim pink roses tied in a ribbon. Catherine had counted the roses and their leaves. She knew the gradation of wear and tear whereby the flowers near the ceiling were clearly colored, while those at human shoulder and hip height were almost obliterated. The floor

was not tiled but its bare gray concrete was perfectly in period. In one corner stood the covered waste bucket. Beside
it, a powder-water washing unit and a smooth niche—a
recent intrusion in the ancient wall covering—that held a
drinking-water button. There was no other furniture. In the
wall opposite her bed stood her front door: a handsome elderly slab of metal, ornately hinged and riveted and
hatched.

She could be happy here. Who would have guessed that
a bleakly modern poor ward police station had such hidden
depths? What would she do today? Count the tiles again.
Think. Dream. Make up poetry. She might ask for art materials, but she wasn't sure about that. She must not be too
comfortable. She sat up, swung her legs over the edge of
the bed (it was made out of tubular metal), and went to
have breakfast at the water niche. She must drink. She
gulped—the supply was generous—until her stomach re-
belled. Her hands and arms were still streaked with dried
blood, so were her clothes. She was refusing to wash because the blood was evidence. She leaned her forehead
against the wall. This was by no means the first time she'd
embarked on a hunger strike in a prison cell, but she didn't
know how much a human body could take. Today, the fifth
day, she felt weak.

The inert slab of door opened, without warning.

"Come with me, miss," sighed the policeman.

In the front office there was no one about but the duty
sergeant. The place had been cleared of traffic. Catherine
looked up and saw that the regulation camera light was
dark.

"What's going on?" She tugged her arm free from the
gendarme's kindly grip. "If you are at last going to charge
me, I insist on it being on the record. I want a camera here."
Her head suddenly began to ache. She leaned on the desk,
trying to make it look like an insolent gesture. She noticed
the blood under her fingernails, a band of rust across the

top of each nail bed. This was a pitiful sort of livespace. Yet some obscure news agency might use her, and others might pick up on it. She imagined herself reproduced: a barefoot young woman with her long dark curly hair in a mess— unmistakably a young woman, the stained and disheveled sexless clothes of the underclass shaped by her breasts, buttocks, waist. Would that be interesting material, in the machines' reckoning? Interesting enough to be selected? She hoped so. The hallowed female flesh of the rich, exposed in public. The blood might help.

"There'll be no charges. We're sending you home."

"No—? But that's ridiculous! What about multiple murder?" She bit her lip. Nothing is as ridiculous as a dissident begging to be locked up. She attempted sarcasm. "I didn't know the Church of Self Mission had such powerful immunity. Can we make this official?"

"There's a cab outside. We've called your guardian, so he knows you're coming."

Catherine recoiled. "Maitri? You shouldn't have done that. I'm an adult."

"Lord Maitri, yes. His lordship's been very worried."

The sergeant, who had been pretending to study the flat screen in his desktop, finally consented to meet her eyes. They were old acquaintances. All the police of this ward knew her: the young lady brought up by the aliens, who worked among the poorest of the poor. She heard in her mind the words he refused to speak. *Oh, Miss Catherine, why? How can you help those poor people and get them to trust you, knowing you're going to set them hacking each other to pieces? Do you know what it's like for my men, having to clear up after one of your "conversion ceremonies"? It's filthy work. You're not one of them. How can you do it?*

"I *am* 'one of them,' " she said, as if he had spoken aloud. She summoned her resources. The light was out, but they couldn't really stop the monitoring inside a police station, could they? Surely, that was impossible. She must not miss this opportunity to serve the cause. "The conversion ceremony is not murder or suicide. It is a valid act of faith. If you people believe I'm doing wrong, then *charge me,* so that I can make my case in public, as is my legal right."

He didn't answer. There was a sour smell; it seemed to be coming from Catherine's clothes. It had a color: dinge gray, like the ashes of burning rubbish. It was the smell of the hives. . . . The sergeant ought to hate her. Catherine's people had stolen a world. Stolen it, played with it, broken it, thrown it on the dump: the waste heap where this city's poor endured their hopeless lives. She lurched against the desk, longing for his violence, the consolation so long refused: *punish me!*

"D'you want breakfast before you go?" he asked.

She can't help it, he was telling himself, silently. *Poor kid, it's true. She's quite insane.*

"No, thank you."

"A cup of coffee?"

"No." She made a last effort. "What about *my* rights? If I'm not to be charged, what about the orthodoxers? Get it straight. Either you charge me with murder, or with assisting group suicide—which is not much of a felony—or else you admit that my converts and I were attacked in the peaceful expression of our difference. It was unprovoked gender violence. I want to make a complaint."

"Go home, Miss Catherine," said the sergeant wearily.

The other officer took her arm. She shook him off and walked away, with what dignity she could muster. Her head was spinning.

Out in the lobby there was still no one about, except for a ragged down-and-out hunched on the floor, passively resisting the efforts of a gendarme trying to move him on. The officer who had brought Catherine up from the cells came out of the doorway after her and was summoned to help. She heard a scuffle begin, decided that it wasn't her business, and then, reluctantly, turned back. They'd given up and were standing irresolute, unwilling to use more force. They were not cruel people. They looked at Catherine hopefully. A different relation was restored. She had often helped them with their difficult customers. She had been brought up by the aliens, who were supposed to be telepathic. They knew, because Catherine had told them, that she read body language: she did not read minds. Yet she could often understand and make herself understood when all other approaches failed.

"It's your uniforms," she explained. "I'd guess he's just been discharged from a hospital or a work camp. Your uniforms mean security, they are comforting, that's why he's here."

"Can you get her to tell you her name, miss?"

"Her?" That was strange. The poor were neuter to any casual appraisal. And why did they need a name? But she had learned to be patient with the bureaucracy of human kindness.

She looked down at the huddled body. "I doubt it. But I'll try." She crouched on her heels. <I'm friendly,> she offered, in the silent, universal, physical language that Aleutians called "the Common Tongue." <You seem to be in trouble. Perhaps I can help.>

A pallid face stared upward, completely without expression.

"Watch out, miss. She's got something alive. It might be dangerous."

Catherine saw a second pair of eyes, round and bright. They belonged to something clutched tightly against the lost soul's ragged breast. She saw a bright, scaled, snakelike head, a horny mouth that gaped, emitting a faint hiss. A red-gold ribbon of a tongue flickered. But the illusion of life was perfunctory.

"It's only a toy."

The hand and wrist that held the toy snake were wrapped in a strip of cloth. "She seems to be hurt," said a concerned police voice over Catherine's shoulder. "If we could at least change that nasty old dressing—"

The body suddenly came to life, flailing, and fell against Catherine. For a moment she felt, as the police must have felt, soft full breasts under the rags. Startled, she looked again at the curious pallor, slender hands, the artfully delicate contours of the empty face—

<Who are you?> she demanded.

Now Catherine was uncomfortable. The genuine young ladies of this city, the daughters of rich and powerful people, were extremely well protected. One did not see them on the streets, not even with an armed escort. There must be some very strange story behind this girl's plight if she was really what she seemed to be. Catherine shouldn't get involved. She was on safe ground with the poor. She knew she mustn't meddle with the rich.

She was ashamed of this worldly-wise reaction.

"How did you get into this state?" she demanded, aloud. "What happened to you?"

No response, not a trace.

She took hold of the injured arm. "They say I'm crazy," she murmured. "I know I'm not, but I think you are. What does it take to drive a person truly mad, *ma semblable, ma soeur?* And have you escaped from it all? Or are you still suffering, wherever you are?"

The dressing was made of native textile, a kind of material rarely seen among the poor. Cotton? Linen? Nylon? Maitri would know. It had been torn roughly from a larger cloth, something elaborate and embroidered. She glimpsed tragedy. A love story (did young ladies fall in love? She didn't know). A botched escape from the gilded prison, clumsily tended injury. And then what? Abandoned by her lover, driven insane by grief. . . . She thought of the tiles in the police cell. Maitri would love to hear about them. He adored hunting down overlooked survivals of old-earth, bygones that nobody valued, forgotten treasure.

The dressing came away. She saw what was underneath.

"Miss Catherine? I've some multitype skin here. Can you hold her still?"

"No," said Catherine, quickly binding up the wrist again. "It's only a scratch. Better leave it alone. Better leave her alone. Nothing can be done."

She stood. The walls and floor swayed. The police station entrance had a hyperreal, visionary clarity. She saw that she had replaced the dirty dressing and didn't remember doing it. She was in no state to play nurse. Catherine was hallucinating. Maybe the lost girl didn't exist. She was afraid she'd been crawling around on the floor talking to herself, and the police must think she was mad. *Nothing can be done, nothing can be done.* She saw the desperate faces of the hives, the packed tenements where the doomed waited to die—so many, so many.

"I want to go home. I'm not well."

A single-seater cab was ready for her outside on the ramp. As she blundered into it, she knew she should turn back. The fugue moment had passed; she felt she'd betrayed the girl with the bandaged arm. But there were so many, so much grief and pain. *Don't meddle with the rich,* she whispered to herself. She huddled into an animal crouch inside the little vehicle's fat belly, and let it carry her away.

The cab took her to Maitri's house at the giratoire. She roused herself in time to stop it from trundling in at the front gates and got out in a dusty alley, where naked children played in the black and orange tiger weed outside the aliens' back door. A tinker shook powder onto a broken griddle and rubbed two rims of metal together, releasing the acrid stink of lattice-fusion. The children pulled sprigs of alien weed and let them feed on warm skin, giving themselves tiger weed bracelets, earrings, tattoos. Faces peered from troglodyte windows in the stained cliffs of artificial stone. The giratoire had been one of the vast road junctions that had ringed this *quartier* when it was a conurbation in its own right. Most of them had vanished into later development. This one, in ruins, had miraculously survived. Maitri had settled here long ago for the romance of the location. He refused to move, though the neighborhood had gone downhill and the monument teemed with squatters. There was a brief stir as Catherine got down. But the streetlivers knew her. They returned to their own concerns, and she passed through Maitri's gate. A barrier impermeable to any material it did not recognize, living or dead, sucked her in and closed behind. She left the human city and entered a different air.

It was always green in here: the green of true native plant life, that was rarely seen now anywhere outside a sentimental alien's garden. Maitri had a "burst main" spring, which helped. It was fed by the lost workings of an ancient pumping system. The human servants said it had been going for more than three hundred years. The tank was in Maitri's vegetable beds. Catherine went to it, drawn by the grieving sound of the water. She stood watching the silver daemon, that thrust its blunt head endlessly through viridian mosses to fall into a pool of transparent darkness. When she was a child, she used to think that the water-daemon was trapped, begging to be let out. She would try to catch it and help it over the side. But the water flowed through her fingers and just went on crying.

The alien air had a slight haze in it, enough to blur the vista of Maitri's lawns and flowers. At First Contact, human observers had noticed straightaway that the aliens communicated "like animals." It was true that a chatty gathering of Aleutians could look like a troupe of baboons in clothes, silently embracing, grooming, nuzzling; conversing by gaze and gesture—with the occasional startling outburst of articulate speech. It had taken longer before the humans realized that Aleutians were also in constant biochemical communication, through tiny particles exchanged in the air they breathed and absorbed through their pores, and through the wriggling scraps of skin fauna that they picked from each other and ate. Like almost every animal on earth—except for humans—they lived in a broth of shed cells, tastes, and smells that kept them always in contact with each other: but in the aliens' case the traffic was conscious. It was this living, intelligent flux, thick and complex as commerce on the lifeless human information networks, that had destroyed human supremacy. It was the basis of the aliens' effortless biotechnology.

The Aleutians *were* like animals: animals who had attained civilization still possessing and developing their most ancient animal traits. Controlled biochemical processing—which the humans had just begun to develop when they arrived—was their natural element. They had conquered, like the alien weeds, not because they were different, but because they were like enough to compete. Meanwhile the extraordinary human technologies, their weird dead machines, their occult control over the forces of the void—*electrons, photons*—had fallen into neglect: used only for social calls, games, fashion effects. Such irony! It was as if the people of earth had taken a wildly convoluted wrong turning, and arrived back on the right track just a little too late. The Aleutians and the humans had met as equals. Who would believe that today?

The green of Maitri's garden seemed to be in mourning. White everted stars looked up at her, each pushing out a furred yellow tongue. Thick, water-hungry leaves brushed her thighs. They were crying: Help us, save us! We can't survive without you now. . . .

She was suddenly aware that her bladder was bursting. She had to drop to her haunches among the vegetables, barely managed to get her underwear out of the way in time. She stayed there, in the rising fumes of warm urine, laughing weakly. She should have used the waste bucket in the cell. But she could not remember these things. The body was human; the spirit knew a different set of rules. Under any stress she simply forgot how to behave. Her head between her hands, she found herself staring at the hairy base of her belly that hid the secret human female parts. *Will the flower bud open when I grow up? Will it be beautiful?* Maitri had told her: *Darling, I don't know. That's partly what you wanted to find out.* The real young ladies did not wear trousers. They wore long, layered flimsy skirts and tight little bodices, veils and scarves and jackets glittering with gold and silver and gemstones: but *no underwear*, Catherine had been fascinated to discover, where it mattered. She wanted to be authentic, but she had balked at that. Aleutians are a prudish people. She thought of the girl at the police station and was again ashamed of her panic. But now she must go into the house. She must face Maitri and the others. They didn't like the Mission. It was going to be hard to admit her defeat. Her head pounded. Always defeated, always. It was too much to bear.

In the kitchen, in the part of the house that belonged to the human servants, she found her foster mother. Leonie was cooking something on her open-flame hob, the perilous-looking device on which she produced her miracles of old-earth cuisine. Peter, her human son, was sharpening knives.

"Maman?"

But her foster mother (breasts as flat and hard as if she was an Aleutian now: it was a long time since she'd suckled a child) had refused for years to acknowledge that Catherine had ever been her baby.

"Yes, miss?"

Catherine could taste the stinging tinker-reek of Peter's workbox. The smell of cooking made her dizzy, and Leonie's rebuff brought her to the verge of tears. But Leonie herself was visibly shaking. Peter kept his eyes on his work in an unnatural pantomime of unconcern. She stood between them, human blood dry-smeared on her clothes and in her hair. She'd forgotten they hated her missionary work worse than Maitri did. She lifted her shoulders in the gesture that meant a smile in Aleutian, an apology in human body language, spoke earnestly and kindly.

"I know I look terrible. The blood, I know the blood looks bad." She tried to laugh. "Don't worry, I'm not going to try to convert you!" She gestured with the flowers that she'd brought in. "I picked these for Maitri. Could I have a vase?"

Peter kept on madly sharpening. Leonie stared in wondering pity.

"You can't have those indoors," she said. "They're poisonous." But she brought a vase, and filled it with water from the hydrobiont pump on her kitchen counter. "Lord Maitri's waiting for you in the atrium." She swallowed. "Maybe you should get washed first."

"No, it'll wait. Maitri won't mind."

The atrium was a large and splendid square hall, colonnaded around the sides. A dome of the marvelously transparent local glass, stained in sweeps of green and gold and ruby, rose above the central space. Pieces of ancient machinery, beautifully restored, stood among the troughs and tubs of native plants. The centerpiece was an examination pit from a motor garage, which Maitri had had transported here and let into the floor. It held a small fountain (fed from the "burst main") with cushioned seats beside the pool, and gave off from its blackened walls a faint romantic whiff of engine oil.

Lord Maitri was alone, resplendent in one of his antique morning robes. "My dear"—he put the potato flowers aside and gripped her hands—"I hope the police have been nice to you. They've been being very polite to us. Now, tell me *all* about it."

Maitri spoke "formally," in articulate human language. When he and his ward were alone, they always conversed this way. Catherine in her human body had learned to manage very well in the Common Tongue, but she was still at a loss sometimes, deprived of the living traffic of the air. He shrugged ruefully, waving a hand to indicate the rest of the Aleutian household. "I thought I wouldn't subject you to 'the zoo' so early in the morning. But everybody wants you to know that we're glad you're safe."

"There isn't much to tell," Catherine said. She recovered her hands, folded her arms under her breasts, delivered her report in a firm, level tone. "I was attending a conversion ceremony. It was in an apartment belonging to one of our proselytes—belonging to his family that is, but the rest of the household were away for the evening. I was alone with the candidates. I tried to keep them indoors but they kept rushing out again. I warned them that we could be in trouble if we invaded a public space, but they wanted to bear witness to the good news. It was chaos, I admit. But no one was getting hurt . . . that didn't want to be, I mean. It was almost over when the orthodoxers arrived. They had heat guns, don't know where from: totally illegal. They fried everything in sight, the building turned on the powder-sprinklers for the whole landing, and then the police turned up. They arrested me. Me, not the orthodoxers, of course. They put me in solitary in an unmonitored cell and refused to charge me. So I refused to eat, and that was embarrassing, I suppose. So this morning they decided to throw me out, and here I am."

She rubbed at her sleeves. "But I'm not hurt. It's not my blood."

"I almost wish it was," Maitri burst out. "Hurt? I don't care if you're sliced to bits. I don't know why I said I hoped the police had been nice. I wish they would *beat* you."

He drew a breath. "It's not that I don't agree, in principle, with what the Missions teach. Of course permanent death is pure superstition. Their physiology has not been much researched, but it can't be *that* strange. They must be born again the same as we are: the same chemical identities, the same set of individuals that goes to make up a society. They only have to learn to remember their past lives, to *know themselves* as eternal aspects of the Cosmic Self. . . . And the conversion ceremonies. It's something we've done ourselves in the past, and no doubt we'll do it again: licensed group suicide in times of hardship, for the good of others. The humans themselves don't consider it a crime. It's all very, very spiritual and uplifting, I am sure. . . . But darling, I think it has to come from them. From the humans. We can't impose our forms of belief. It won't *stick*. My dear child, I know you want to help. But a *missionary*, darling! So banal! Is it really you?"

He broke off to make a tart little bow to the populated air, which was carrying away the chemical trace of his opinions—to be picked up, maybe, in the wide web of the Commonalty, by a sensitive clergyperson. "No offense meant, none taken, I hope. I've always made my views on the Mission plain."

"You think the whole idea is stupid and nasty," she whimpered accusingly.

Maitri stood in a pool of lucid gold, the dark nasal space in the center of his face contracted in helpless anxiety. He lifted his clawed hands and let them fall.

"I respect your belief. But we're—so worried. You don't seem happy, or well."

"You should have told me you hated the Mission when I moved out."

"I was afraid," explained her guardian simply. "I was afraid of losing you."

She turned away, wrapping her arms more tightly around her body. "My cell was lovely," she announced. "You'd never guess. The walls are covered in real ceramic tile, must be over three hundred years old. And roses. You'd love the roses. You should get yourself arrested, then you could see for yourself. He was so nice, the boy whose apartment we used. I wish I could remember his name. I can never remember their names."

Maitri was watching her with undisguised concern. "How long is it since you ate?"

"Am I babbling? Fifth day. I'm not going on with it. There's no point. I'm beaten."

"I'm glad of that, at least. There are so many interesting drugs on this wonderful planet, if you *must* ruin your health. Starvation is just silly. Have you begun to hallucinate?"

Catherine frowned sharply. "No! Not at all."

She began to weep, the human tears spilling from her eyes. "Maitri, I'm so sorry. I know I've let you down. You expected more from me. I know the Mission is stupid. But the humans are dying. We're leaving, but their world is trashed and they have nowhere to go. They can't survive, and *I know that it's my fault.* Can you understand how that feels?"

"Go and lie down," he advised gently. "Have something to eat, sleep. Let us look after you. You don't mean these wild things. You'll feel better soon. But I should warn you, I'm having a little reception this afternoon. One of my usual parties for the locals; it won't disturb you."

She smiled feebly at his use of the dissidents' term: *the locals,* meaning our neighbors, people like us. Not *the humans,* meaning the alien species for whom we can't be held responsible. By such signs a world of difference is made known. And she blinked at him, graceless: "Do you want me on show?" The humans were very curious about Catherine. She was quite "a draw," as Maitri vulgarly put it.

"Not unless you're feeling *much* better." He handed her the vase, with a puzzled glance at the contents: touched her cheek with one clawed finger. "Now, go and rest!"

Her room was as she had left it, when she moved to her little rented *trou* in the hives. She put the vegetable bouquet on her desk, under a twentieth-century icon of the *Sacred Bleeding Heart of Jesus,* a very lovely moving image, in a silver frame, of blue Krisna dancing and playing the flute. "If you were Aleutian flowers," she said to them, "hearing you talk would almost make sense. So you see, I am not crazy." She lay on her bed, which was a soft Aleutian pallet spread on the floor. She found the same cracks in the plaster ceiling that she had named, to console herself, when she came to live in the aliens' part of the house. The seagull. The happy face—which had been human when she was very young, but became Aleutian after a patch of plaster fell, leaving a gap instead of a nose. The friendly spaceplane with a crooked wing. In Aleutia, buildings did not fall into decay. Everything the aliens used, built, touched, was alive and part of life's constant change and reparation. On earth, fascinated by dead objects that seemed to *stay the same* as they slowly crumbled, Aleutians let splendid mansions tumble around them, dressed themselves in old curtains, collected scraps of litter—to the disgusted astonishment of their human acquaintances.

She closed her eyes.

She was Lord Maitri's human ward: but she was an Aleutian, inside. There had been no solemn moment when they told her, *You are an immortal. You look like a human being, you grew in a human womb; but you are not what you seem.* They had simply taken her from her mother and treated her just like an Aleutian child: giving her the possessions this person had owned in previous incarnations, and speaking to her as to the friend they had known so intimately through so many lifetimes. They had set her in front of moving-image records of her Aleutian past, hour by hour. The records had a biochemical content that her human body could not process: a haze of living inscription that left the screen but could not penetrate her human skin. But one day it had come to her, exactly as if she was a normal Aleutian, without a shadow of doubt, that this was herself. *I am me.* This is my history.

She thought of the conversion. After prayer and meditation the candidates, exalted, leapt on each other. In future lives they would be able to die like Aleutians, slipping quietly away whenever a life's task seemed to be over, in the certain hope of return. This first time they needed the rapture. They had staggered out into the little concourse in the depths of that genteel, respectable, foul-smelling tenement offering handfuls of their blood and flesh to horrified passersby. *For my flesh is true food, and my blood is true drink.* The Self is God! they cried. Die to mortality, and live forever!

Maitri was right. The Mission was stupid, distasteful. Those idiotic faked records in which humans pretended to recall other lives. The bogus arguments, shifty false ideas. She did not *like* any of her comrades in the Church. The aloof Aleutian missionary priest who visited so seldom. The self-satisfied lay readers: longtime proselytes who were never *quite* ready for conversion themselves. The ingratiating halfcaste deacon, so eager to condescend and patronize "Miss Catherine." She had told herself, liking didn't come into it. There were nowhere near as many humans as had once been predicted. There were still too many. So much living space had been lost during the Aleutian era: devastated by war, poisoned by overuse, ruined by bad, alien solutions to earth's problems. The numbers had to be cut back. The Church of Self Mission had seemed to offer a way.

No, it is not spiritual or uplifting (she told Maitri, in her mind). *We missionaries reduce the surplus population a little: nothing more. It is foul work. That's why I wanted it.*

She was stifling. She got up and stumbled to her window. She clawed at the living membrane that had taken the place of the vanished glass, but the rents sealed as fast as she could make them. The air was full of tiny living things: messages her human body couldn't read, tools she couldn't use, servants who would not obey. She crumpled to the floor, trembling, seeing all that blood.

Dying, falling in flames . . .

She dreamed that she was dead, and lying in a funerary room. Her body's substance was seeping away, carried off by the tiny creatures in the air, delivered back into the common store of life. She had become a desiccated skeleton, slowly crumbling. Maitri was dead, the Aleutians long gone. Catherine's self inhabited the air of a ruin. The city buzzed over her and consumed her. She was divided into a million million dust motes, swallowed and breathed and excreted over and over again: but still Catherine.

When she woke she was lying on the floor under the window, and the tiny servants had been busy. The room had become cool; her body was clean. The rusty rims had gone from under her nails; every tangle and burr and louse had been nursed out of her hair. As she sat up, fragments of her shoddy poor-ward clothes fell from her: immaculate dust. Someone had left a bowl of savory gruel by her bed and laid out clean clothes: fresh underwear and a spruce suit of overalls, the dun uniform of the Aleutian Expedition on Earth.

She dressed and drank the gruel by stages, very slowly. When she replaced the bowl, the tray stood up on little caterpillar legs, nudged her knee in farewell, and trotted to the door. Catherine smiled. Since she'd moved out to the hives, she had missed Maitri's whimsical commensals most of all. She had missed a world that was alive with tenderness: full of gentle eyes, nestling touches, snuggling caresses. And yet she could feel suffocated—

She returned to her window. She was a tiny speck in the center of Youro, one of the huge cities that spanned the surface of the giant planet: "cities" in the Aleutian sense of a great colony of life, not an urban concentration. It was curious how closely earth had come to resemble the Aleutian homeworld, where the "cities" were ecologies and outside there was nothing but desert wilderness. "Like dogs and their owners," she murmured.

Within his domain Maitri preserved the old cycle of the seasons. It was midsummer noon in the flower garden under her bedroom. Red roses bowed their heavy heads, papery blue bellflowers nodded on long thin stems, speckled lilies gaped. The flowers on her desk were just as beautiful, but considered non-flowers. Leonie had said they were poisonous. Poisonous vegetables? She must have misheard. She was sure she had often eaten potatoes.

The vague murmur of human traffic, the whole world outside, and all her life in this body seemed more transparent than the film that closed her window. A phrase came to her, one of those expressions that appears from nowhere and is suddenly repeated everywhere: *the unreality of these last days*. Somewhere, not very far from here, humans and Aleutians were working to perfect a device that would annihilate space and time, the engine that would power the Aleutians' return to their home planet. Her Aleutian self had played a crucial part in the tragic adventure of that discovery. But why should Catherine take the praise or the blame for that person's actions? The humans are not immortal, she thought. Neither am I. *Already I am not the person I was last night, and this is not the same world that was then. I do not live forever; I die and keep on dying.* She lay down on her bed, drugged by an immense lassitude. With eyes half closed she dreamed of Maitri's garden, of the huge ruins of the giratoire, the sigh and chatter of the human poor in their baked-clay alleys and their high-piled tenement hives. She would not go back to the Mission. She would live and die in this quiet house. She would be Catherine, human ward of the alien Lord Maitri: tranquil, unimportant, unregarded. The peace of exhaustion overwhelmed her.

When she next woke, she heard the sound of human voices. She jumped up quickly, full of good resolutions, and prepared to face the world.

ii

MISHA CONNELLY TURNED aside before he entered the atrium, where the aliens were gathered to greet their guests, and followed a short passageway that led to the character shrine. He had never been inside this house before in the real, but he knew the layout. If you wanted to do anything or be anyone in this city, you had to be familiar with *their* affairs. The shrine was large and softly murmurous. There were ritual screens, one for each member of Lord Maitri's household (whether presently living or dead). Some of the stands were plain, some grown in ornately peculiar forms: a squatting homunculus, a mound of fungoid foliage. The predominant color in the decor was deep copper, with highlights of translucent purple. It blended well with the cobwebs in the corners and the cracks in the walls. Most of the screens were blank. A few were playing scenes from former Aleutian lives, two-dimensional animations in the archaic style they reserved for their confessional histories. Bronze and silver candelabra stood about, laden with genuine wax tapers.

The main presentation, shown on a virtual screen much bigger than the antique boxes on the stands, was a passage from the life of Peenemünde Buonarroti—no doubt in compliment to the afternoon's human guests. A forest of blue-hearted flames burned pale and still around it. Perfumed smoke rose in coils from an incense burner. Misha sat cross-legged, his chin propped on one hand, head a little thrown back, his golden-topaz eyes a little somber. Russet-tinged dark curls escaped from his black beret and clustered on his brow. A practiced dandy's gesture spread the skirts of his light overcoat to advantage. He covered his face, briefly: *The Self Is God.*

The great physicist of the First Contact era, later to become the inventor of the Buonarroti device, the instantaneous travel machine, looked like a fat young man in a strange, greasy suit. She was hunched on the edge of her seat, her hands knotted in front of her belly. It was early in the twenty-first century, maybe a decade or so before the arrival of the aliens. She was young, she had won a prize, she was suddenly famous. She faced the TV public with a piteous, trapped stare. She was being asked about her philosophical beliefs, in the context of self-conscious artificial intelligence.

"I don't know," she said. "I'm not sure. But as far as I look into what it means to be conscious, I find an act of separation. An act which is intuitively impossible because the elements involved in the action cannot exist until after it has been completed: the self and the world. Consciousness is that displacement. To be unreal. To be separate from reality."

Misha took a few amber grains from a bowl of cloisonné enamel, and dropped them into the censer. The scent of frankincense was quickly devoured by the living air.

In the atrium hall aliens and humans mingled, both groups wearing the same formal attire: wide-sleeved Aleutian-style robes over dun-brown or gray coveralls with many loops and pockets. Inevitably, humans outnumbered the aliens by a considerable margin. Many aliens had returned to their shipworld out in orbit in preparation for the coming Departure. Of those who remained in this city, few shared Maitri's dogged intersocial illusions. Few of the humans shared those illusions either, in fact, probably none. But it was still important to be here.

Misha saw his father, engaged in formal conversation with one of Maitri's secretaries. His sister Helen, heavily veiled, was clinging close to the old man's side, her little hand tucked into the crook of his berobed, brocaded elbow. She looked across the room: a glance that had something in it of the alliance they'd lost. He passed safely by, threading his way between the blunt-muzzled lumpy-pelvic hairless bipedal baboonoids, and the others, the jut-nosed native simians—uniformly wider in the shoulder and narrower at the hip. In his present mood he found the two species equally repulsive. He reached the buffet and studied a fantastic array of delectable-looking archaic foodstuffs: miniature chicken satay with peanut sauce, tiny pleated dim sum dumplings, luscious pink-tailed prawns in garlic mayonnaise. No one else was eating. He decided to set an example. He picked and chose with studied, affected greed, until his progress placed him in front of the alcove where the most interesting element in this bizarre social construct was holding court.

He heard the voice. It was nothing like Helen's voice, and yet unmistakably feminine: husky, slightly raucous, fragile as a child's.

"Diderot says: *'tout le monde a son chien.'* It's true. But it's also true that *tout le monde à son maître.* Everybody must serve someone. It's a physical necessity. We are hierarchical animals, Aleutians and humans both. But I am one who has searched and never found any master except that Person we call "the Cosmic WorldSelf" and you call God. Therefore to me God is a necessity. When you ask me whether I believe in God, I can only say it isn't a question of belief. This is something I need."

Misha, who had eyes in the back of his head when he wanted them, ranked the sleek young fashion plates around her expertly and assured himself that they were no competition. But the lady was right. You have to check your place. The young men seemed to be snatching each word from the air, openmouthed. He knew that none of them was paying the slightest attention to what she said. They were gorging, in suppressed sexual excitement, on the phenomenon of her presence. But Lord Maitri's ward was equally on auto. She looked to Misha as if she was drunk: or else like someone staggering under a burden, defending terrible injuries behind a wall of words.

She wore the Aleutian costume, the same as everyone here—the same as Misha, though he'd pushed the limits as far as he dared with his duster coat. Her hair was loose, tumbling down her back in dark, smoky masses. The orange and blue robe was carelessly open, revealing glimpses of a figure devoid of Helen's rich and dainty curves. The rise of Miss Catherine's breast barely lifted the dun stuff of her overalls. But he suddenly felt that he was in the presence of a real woman for the first time in his life. She was woman as nature intended her to be—an alien creature prowling the edge of the firelight, a dangerous trophy to be pursued in fear and trembling. Next to her his beautiful little sister, with her human soul looking out of those huge voluptuous eyes, was like something grub-like, preserved in a jar.

He decided that he would make Miss Catherine come over to the buffet table to join him. Misha had an augmented lymph system, designed to protect him from infection—especially from the infested air, teeming with their life, that surrounded the aliens. Without scientific grounds for the belief, he sometimes thought he could use the defense that his skin exuded to communicate like an alien. He willed the summons outward, keeping his back to the alcove and systematically devouring a platter of minute cinnamon-flavored meat patties. It was amusing, but the trick had better not work! She'd tell Maitri that one of the humans was talking dirty to her with his immune-system glands, and he'd get thrown out.

"Yes? What is it?"

He started. Miss Catherine was at his side.

"Damn," he said. "I missed the show."

"Why did you call me?"

He leaned across to pick out three golden packages of feta cheese and spinach.

"Did I call? You were sitting down, and I wanted to see

you walk, that's all. I'm curious, like everybody else, Miss Alien-in-disguise." He tucked the food into his mouth.

At close quarters her robe seemed to be made of interwoven flower petals. Freckled orange lily throats drew the glance inward. White stamens curled, indecently inviting, in the splayed mouths of the bellflowers. He could tell that it was an instant creation: grown to serve a whim and meant to vanish after an evening's wear. He was glad she wasn't a snob about enduring artifacts, like Lord Maitri, the culture-vulture (rarely had the ancient phrase been more appropriate!). The coat he was wearing himself would not last through the night.

"And I was curious about you. So we were thinking the same thing." She smiled, struggling out from her private torture chamber. Misha had to bite back the retort, *I doubt it!*

The Aleutian artisans had not given her a perfect finish. He guessed that maybe they just couldn't *believe*, when it came to it, in the fine details of human appearance. There was a suggestion of baboon tusks in her lower eyeteeth, which caught her lip when she smiled. Her nose was awkward, and they'd overcorrected the slope of her shoulders. In alien terms they'd given her a permanent wary smile. Presumably, that's the way we look to them, he thought, amused at the insight. But the mistakes, paradoxically, made her seem even more a natural animal, a wild creature.

Now that he'd caught her, he didn't know what to say, since anything he really wanted to say was impossible. He'd have to take care to remember that she was a young lady of his own caste, as far as social manners went.

"I was curious," explained Catherine gravely. "Because you seemed so hungry."

"Not anymore. The food's excellent, by the way. Won't you try something?"

"Oh, good. I'll tell my mother. . . . No, I won't eat."

Suddenly, her eyes flashed. Her head turned, with the

speed of a hunting animal fixing on prey. An instant later Misha saw a flurry of disturbance over where Lord Maitri was still receiving guests. The air quivered, and an Aleutian figure stood beside their host. Somebody had just arrived by telepresence.

"Excuse me," muttered Catherine.

Sattva, the Expedition's Planet Surface Manager for the City of Youro, found it more convenient to manage his turbulent megapolis from the Aleutian second capital in West Africa. His in-person visits to the Youroan continent were rare (Sattva blamed a shrinking budget). Telepresence, though it involved spooky void-forces mechanisms designed by humans, was a useful compromise. As a walk-around ghost, he could satisfy the humans' *amour propre* and yet assure them, truthfully, that he was unable to decide anything or grant anything while in this wholly un-Aleutian state. He was not pleased when he saw Catherine coming. She hadn't expected that he would be.

<I want to talk to you, Sattva.>

<Ah, hello, "Catherine." How *are* you? You know, we're very concerned—>

<Thanks, I'm quite well. Let's not bother with pleasantries. As the person who tested the means of faster-than-light travel invented by a human physicist, which is going to take us home, and as, in fact, the only Aleutian who has yet used the device, I want to remind you about the promises that were made concerning that technology by all members of the Expedition and with the full and informed consent of the Commonalty, living and dead. I urge you—>

Sattva flashed a glance of furious reproach at Maitri, who made helpless gestures. <So sorry,> he snapped. <I must circulate—>

<Sattva, we *can't* just leave them,> she pleaded. <Even if we owed them nothing, they are in desperate straits—>

<And whose fault is that?> demanded the City Manager acidly. <Are we to blame for their economics, or the state of their living space?>

This question, to *Catherine,* whose views on the subject were utterly well-known, was so insolent it took her breath away.

<Must circulate,> repeated Sattva. His ghost moved jerkily over to the examination pit and hid itself behind a group of Maitri's elderly Aleutian retainers.

"I'm sorry."

Her enigmatic exchange with the City Manager was over. Amazingly, she had returned to Misha's side. She set off again, with a glance that invited him to follow. He kept pace with the drifting train of her robe, through green light and into gold, to an embrasure where native glass doors opened on the gardens. He wondered what they'd been saying to each other. To watch a conversation between earth-accustomed Aleutians was very odd. They stood looking at each other, twitching a little, in a silence occasionally broken by a spoken word or phrase of human language, suddenly barked out aloud . . .

"What was all that about?"

She glanced back at him. "You don't speak Aleutian?"

She meant the intricate code of facial gesture and body language they called "the Common Tongue." The aliens read human faces and gestures so accurately, using the rules of this Common Tongue, it could seem like mind reading. Few humans were able to return the compliment.

"Not when it's so fast and, um, elliptical."

"Too bad."

Finality. She would not or could not say any more.

"Maybe you'll tell me one day. I heard your Diderot lecture. You speak good French."

But she was speaking impeccable English now. Most of the aliens didn't ever speak aloud. They were "the Silent," the ones who did the processing of materials: the cooking and cleaning, hewing wood and drawing water so to speak. Disconcertingly, some of them were rich and influential, though dumb as animals. But the few who used articulate language, the Signifiers, were the ones who mostly dealt with humans; and they seemed to be the cultural elite. Maitri was a Signifier. His human ward, naturally, had the same status. Misha wondered if, like Lord Maitri, she could do the trick of speaking *any* human language, almost perfectly, after hearing it once.

"You were listening." Catherine showed her teeth. The little tusks gleamed. "I was thinking of Aleutia. But it's the same with you. You call our Signifiers a 'ruling class.' But isn't it just as true among humans that most people do not want to have public opinions? They 'only want to get on with their lives,' as people always say. So they pay some Signifier to have opinions for them. That's what your hierarchy amounts to, same as ours. *Tout le monde à son maître.* Loyalty is convenient. It answers that nagging question, why? *Why am I here? I don't have to answer that. Go ask the head of my household.* The energetic few who *will* speak out are psychopaths of some degree: people who think they have a right to use others for their own ends. Maitri's like that, gentle Maitri, though nobody thinks of him as ruthless. And then there are the ones like me. Who will not be silent but who have no agenda of their own. I don't want to rule even the smallest world; yet I do nothing but criticize the obliging folks who do the job. It's very irritating of me. People run when they see me coming. I don't blame them."

Maitri had let his lawns run to seed. They were striding through a miniature meadow, a horticultural effect that Misha found insulting. *If you must imitate us, at least get it right.* Her hands brushed the fluid sheaves of red and gold. She turned and smiled, shoulders lifted and warmth in her eyes.

"Excuse me: I make speeches. It's a dreadful habit. I love

a lawn at this time in its year, don't you? Grasses are so beautiful in flower."

They reached an informal arrangement of old-earth stone carving, now buried shoulder deep. Catherine knelt, squatted, and finally sat with her legs curled under her, propped against one of the stones. The aliens were halfhearted bipeds, reverting easily to a four-footed gait. It was odd to see that animal fidgeting in the limbs of a civilized young lady. Misha traced the lettering on a stolen fragment of his ancestral culture. *Not lost to memory, not lost to love. But gone to her father's home above.*

"You're a missionary, I gather. What's that like? Do you make many converts?"

Catherine thought of blood and entrails. "I've given it up."

"Very wise. Personally, I avoid the poor as much as possible. They tire me."

"We don't only preach to the poor." Shoulders lifted. "Sorry. No more speeches! You're Michael Connelly, aren't you. The son of the park keeper Michael Connelly, who manages everybody's virtual wilderness experience. I know about you. But I don't think I've seen you at one of Maitri's parties—?"

Misha laughed. "So young, and already having memory problems. No, I've never been here before. My father gave me an Aleutian education, but he doesn't like the kind of young man who hangs around the aliens. I would have defied him of course," he added gallantly, "if I had known what I was missing. And you are Lord Maitri's ward, the young lady who is really an Aleutian in disguise. Everybody's heard of you, but nobody seems to know exactly what that means."

Catherine leaned her head back against the stone. For an extraordinary moment back in Maitri's atrium, she had felt that Michael Connelly knew everything. She had looked into his eyes, and he had seemed to *know* about her pain, to understand the terrible burden of guilt. He had even seemed to know about that girl on the police station steps, on whose flesh Catherine had hallucinated the marks of a deadly industrial disease that was unknown on earth. . . . (She understood the hallucination very well, its message was plain: *they are doomed!*) Now he was just another of the *quartier's* rich young men, who clustered around her whenever she made an appearance. She wondered how she could recapture that flash of understanding, and was afraid to try.

Misha had never been so close to a young woman in the flesh, except for Helen. And Helen, he had to accept, was always chaperoned now. Catherine had closed her eyes. She opened them suddenly. They'd given her level brows, long lashes, and left her the *black on black* Aleutian effect. The alien eyes were very human in structure, but so dark there was no visible distinction between pupil and iris. It was more startling in the frame of white, without their pronounced epicanthic fold. She looked away, frowning.

"Don't worry," he said. "I'm not going to pester you about the Departure, which I assure you is the major topic indoors. One day, a few hundred years ago, we woke up and you were here. One day soon we'll wake up, and you'll be gone. I don't care. You people can leave whenever and however you like as far as I'm concerned."

She laughed, human style, with teeth bared and a full-throated sound.

"Do you believe in reincarnation, Michael?"

"Misha, Mish. Or you can call me 'Junior,' but I'd prefer you didn't. No."

"Nor do I."

"Ah . . . ? But you are 'an Aleutian in a human body,' however that works. Doesn't that mean you're an immortal yourself?"

"You think I'm confused? So would you be. This person beside you will live and die a human. But I'm an Aleutian; that's the truth. I feel it. Yet does our form of rebirth mean that the same person lives on, exactly? Some of us don't think so." She moved restlessly, as if struggling against invisible bonds. "You're right," she told him. "The Departure doesn't matter. What matters is what's going to happen on earth, afterward."

She rose to her feet, in a single movement that had no trace of ladylike helplessness. He realized she had decided to escape.

"We should go in. I'm supposed to be circulating."

<Sorry about that,> said Maitri.

The apology was so brazenly insincere that Sattva could only pass over it in silence. <The fuck you are, Maitri. You told me that blighter wouldn't be here.> He reverted to formal speech, to keep things polite. Lord Maitri, though out of office, was a respected veteran of the Expedition. "How *is* 'Catherine,' anyway? It's such a shame about the psychosis. Sad for our friend, and awkward for the Expedition."

"She is not crazy."

Catherine's powers of recovery had reassured her guardian. She was in control again; there was no trace of the desperate state she'd been in this morning. The person who was at present Catherine had always been the same: always taking life terribly hard, always capable of getting back on his feet, laughing at himself, fighting back.

"Didn't someone tell me all human females are insane, to some degree?" continued Sattva imperturbably. "Something to do with hormones or enzymes or neurons or whatever. I suppose our friend didn't know that when he made his famous will. Or he might have considered the risk to the reputation of the Buonarroti project, if not to his own health. The folks out in orbit don't know anything about humans, and they care less! But they don't like unknown risks. Not that I'm in the least worried. Our friend is unbalanced, .

owing to the effect of having been translated into human female form. It's very sad. But it has nothing to do with that
early trip he took in the Buonarroti prototype. The engine's
going to be as safe as dying in bed. Everyone who matters
is satisfied of that."

In the great days of the Expedition to Earth, the person
then called "Clavel" and now called "Catherine," one of
the three captains of the original Expedition, had used the
prototype Buonarroti device to return briefly to the Aleutian homeworld. He had died, of his own will, in that experiment—and had not been born again in the next
generation. It had looked as if, like so many other members
of the original crews, Clavel had vanished into the random
mazes of rebirth and would not be seen alive on Earth
again. Then suddenly, in this last life of the Expedition, and
with the Departure imminent, Lord Maitri—always
Clavel's staunchest ally—had conceived in late middle age.
The embryo had been immediately identified as Clavel:
and in accordance with the Third Captain's wishes had
been reengineered as a human female and transferred to a
human womb. Sadly, the translation had had serious psychological ill effects. Or so the Expedition Management
maintained. Which was suspiciously convenient, for if
he hadn't been "unstable," the Third Captain—even disguised as a human female—might have made things very
awkward for Sattva and his cronies. But "Catherine's" behavior didn't help those who protested that she was perfectly sane.

"It just goes to show," went on Sattva, looking hard at
Maitri, "what we can expect, if we start messing about with
designer-embryos in that nasty human way. I don't want to
sound pompous, but some things are best left to the World-
Self. We can't have conceptions being triggered at will, people getting born whenever their friends feel like it. It would
destroy society as we know it. Don't you agree?"

Maitri had never admitted the implied charge, in seventeen human years or so. He was too wise to be goaded into argument. He gave a diplomatic shrug.

"Oh, absolutely. I'm sure you're right."

"Well, well. Let's say no more. I really must circulate." Sattva looked for a suitable target. <I miss some of your usual curiosities,> he complained, discreetly reverting to Silence so the humans couldn't understand. <What's become of that, er, what's the name? The serious one, charity worker, junior city councillor. Wears *colored overalls*.> Sattva, an austere dandy in a plain black robe over his uniform, made a moue of amused distaste.

"Agathe. Agathe Uwilingiyimana."

<That was it. Where is he, anyway?>

"She."

<Sorry. I can't always remember which they prefer.>

Maitri sighed. <Reformer,> he explained succinctly.

Sattva's manner changed.

<That bad?>

<That bad,> agreed Lord Maitri, in the slightest flicker of facial gesture. <I cannot and will not stop inviting the Traditionalists, who are after all the party in office in the government of Youro, so the Reformers don't come to my house anymore.>

The Reformers and the Traditionalists were the two principal human political parties. They contended for control in every city, under somewhat different names. When the Aleutians arrived, they had also represented the human sexes: the Reformers being chiefly the party of the women, and the Traditionalists mainly led by men. The situation was less clear-cut nowadays. But in Youro, where the Traditionalists had won the Gender War, the two factions were still bitterly at odds.

<I don't like the sound of that.>

<You'd like it less if you were living here,> Maitri told

him cheerfully. <They don't know the date but they all know the Departure's coming, and the old rivalries and grievances start bubbling to the surface—>

Sattva frowned, then deliberately raised his voice in another speech, short and to the point. "The Expedition is doing its best to build bridges," he announced. "One reason I'm here today, Lord Maitri, is to sound out Youroan opinion on the recent negotiations between the Expedition and the Reformer regime in the Americas."

The North American continent, known as the USSA, had quarantined itself early in the Aleutian era. The southern continent had joined them sometime later. Americans had ripped out their undersea cables, set up a defense shield around their coasts, jammed satellite signals, and refused to recognize the existence of the alien-ruled world. Presumably, there was some covert human contact, since such barriers are never totally impermeable, but the Aleutians had been completely shut out. For a hundred years they'd been pretending they didn't care, and secretly longing to be invited back.

Maitri grimaced a discreet warning: the word "Reformer" struck a wrong note in this company. Sattva forged on regardless.

"It is our hope that our last act on earth will be to bring the Americas back into the human fold. We mean to secure peace with honor, before we leave, for all humankind."

<The day after we leave,> he added sourly, <they can do what they like to each other. *Until then* I want my patch quiet.> He paused, his attention caught by the appearance of Catherine and Michael Connelly Jr., returning from the garden. <Now there's someone we need to watch. The fellow in the peculiar outer garment. I suppose you realize, by the way, that he's been alone with your ward? That's going to cause a scandal with the locals.> He stared forbiddingly at the gilded scion of the Traditionalist Regime, as Misha

parted from "Miss Catherine" and strolled idly across the room. <I dislike the type. Aleutianized, ungrateful spoiled darlings. I hate the way they always look as if they're *looking* at themselves.>

<They probably are,> said Maitri. <Especially Misha. They have those 360 things: you know, tiny video recorders and so on that they have fitted inside their eye sockets. Like a permanent mirror.> Maitri's glance lingered tenderly on the self-regarding progress of the young human male. " *'The uncertain splendor of an April day—' "* he murmured.

<Really? *Inside their eye sockets?* How revolting. I know it's tactless to say so, but I think it's a damned good job we're leaving, before we become totally corrupt.>

Once the Aleutians had been horrified by human communication technology. They were the lords of life. The propagation of a living voice or a living body, in the form of an unliving image and through the weird void forces of not-life, was a blasphemy, an offense against reason and religion. Maitri glanced at Sattva's virtual ghost with a wry smile.

<If you say so.>

They had drifted, as they talked, to the buffet table. The food was as usual practically untouched. Maitri surveyed it, sighing. He felt warmly toward Misha Connelly, whatever the young rascal's motives. He began to rearrange the tidbits in more enticing patterns.

The City Manager shook his head. <They definitely won't touch any of it now, you know. Not when you've had your dirty alien paws all over it.>

iii

LATE IN THE evening, Misha's friends arrived at the Connelly town house. They found him in his aerie on the top floor. The house was large and substantial, the lower floors in the possession of various Connelly tenants and subtenants. The rooms allotted to Misha, above the apartment that Helen shared with their father when the family was in town, were his private territory. He was allowed to let his imagination run free and was always in the middle of a new creation. Nothing you saw or touched could be trusted.

He had changed his clothes, exchanging the vat-grown overalls he'd worn at the party for a suit that looked similar but was cut and stitched from mechanically woven old-earth cloth. His friends were dressed in shirts and jeans. Misha couldn't bring himself to adopt the full, embarrassing native costume. He excused his reluctance by explaining that he, at least, was not *afraid* of the aliens—and therefore he didn't have to be slavish about avoiding their fashions. His friends knew he was lying. But they were tolerant of Misha's vanity and the slippery nature of his political commitment. He was their leader.

"What was she like?" they demanded. Mâtho, the shy and solemn one, a Traditionalist but by no means a gilded youth, was the son of a struggling newsagent. Rajath, the halfcaste, had no affiliation, not even to his own kind, and not the slightest hope of being on an alien lord's guest list. Joset, "the politician," was of Michael's monied class, but a Reformer whose formidable female relatives were no longer accepting invitations to Lord Maitri's at homes.

"Why is it called an 'at home'?" Mâtho wanted to know. He was a small, round-shouldered individual with a large nose and a wide-pored caramel-colored skin. His big eyes seemed stretched out of shape by the hours he spent at the screen, splicing and blending by hand footage gleaned from the leavings of more prosperous news handlers. His question was serious. He spent his hungry leisure studying obscure informational byways, hunting out the tiny details that would be needed to rebuild a world. "L-Lord Maitri was a-at home, but no one else was. Except the other aliens in his household, I mean. So why at-at-at home? Shouldn't 'at home' mean a p-party where people stay at home and meet on the grid?"

"I have no idea." Michael poured lime-flavored water for them, and rinsed his own mouth again. The soapy taste of the buffet lingered. Maitri's cook might be human, but the air in the aliens' kitchen was Aleutian and irremediably tainted. He was receiving his friends in his bedroom, which was at present fitted with invisible furniture and apparently walled and floored in clear glass. He threw himself carelessly onto his bed, stretched his arms above his head, rolled onto his belly, and lay like a diver suspended, gazing down over the landscape of roofs and towers and chasms that lapped to the rim of a dusky horizon.

"I couldn't care less what Maitri calls his parties. I met *her*, my brothers in the struggle. We talked, intimately. We were alone together out in the garden for, oh, hours."

The three friends gathered around his couch like courtiers around a prince of Aleutia. "Did you ask her for sex?" Mâtho groaned aloud and rolled his eyes.

"Did you *take* her," demanded Joset with a sarcastic grin. "There, among the strange flowers, in the wild urgency of your mutual passion?"

Misha stared into the abyss: floating, free fall. "She's one of those women who exudes the scent of come, as the aliens exude their wriggling information cells. The hot, sticky smell of sex fills the air around her. You know as soon as you see her move, as soon as the chemical breath of her mingles with the taste of your skin, that fucking her will be an experience of fabulous, sensual savagery."

"Does she have a good figure?" lisped Rajath. The half-castes were descended from humans who had long ago dedicated themselves to physical imitation of the aliens. "He" had been altered before birth in the customary way, and culturally speaking was supposed to have no human sex, male or female. But he was grinning wildly all over his noseless face. "Does she have their *place* in her belly? Did she let you put your finger inside? Did you get her wet on you? Did you feel the claw? How I'd like to have one of their women—if I had a dick you know—and stick it in and feel that *claw* clutching me. Or is she made like human women down there? Does she m-*menstruate?*" He shuddered in thrilling disgust.

Mâtho, the shy one, started to get upset. Rajath's crude language distressed him.

"What does it matter?" he protested. "Whatever traits they have given her, she is not a woman. They don't have sexes; they are all exactly the same. *He* is an alien; we must remember that! We must not be fooled by his disguise."

"She's not an alien," put in Joset, the doubter. "She's the daughter of one of Maitri's human servants: conditioned, characterized, stereotyped into believing herself one of them. She's not an Aleutian; she's a dangerous madwoman. You're a brave man, Mish. I wouldn't have liked to be alone with her. Did you ask her about that latest conversion ceremony? Have you seen any of the coverage? Nasty! Very, very nasty . . ."

"The missionaries don't kill," muttered Mâtho, being scrupulously fair. "It's assisted suicide; it's quite legal if it's done in private. It's *not* legal to watch."

"Is it my fault if some grasping newsagent has been trawling the emergency services?"

"We talked about God," Misha whispered drowsily. "And death and immortality. But the sex was there. The subtext of our conversation was definitely sex."

Rajath and Joset crowed and slapped each other on the back. "Michael Jr. is in love with the alien throat-slasher!" howled Rajath, and broke into a fragment of popular song. " *'Oh, sweet mystery! Across the galaxy! Fated we meet, to become each other's doom—'* " Mâtho looked ready to weep, torn between shame and guilty fascination. Misha remembered the inner torture chamber, the haunted darkness of Catherine's eyes. He felt that he was feeding his friends with pieces of her flesh and blood.

He swung himself to his feet. "Tomorrow I shall make flowers," he announced. "Blue lilies and orange bellflowers. It's an allusion to her gown. I'll send them to her. She finds the sexual organs of our planets irresistibly arousing."

He swept his duster coat from the foot of the couch and tossed it around his shoulders. It was beginning to melt. It would soon be in perfect tattered form for the *passeggiata.* He resumed his black beret and studied the effect, in his inward eye, with brief but exacting attention.

"There's no need to be frightened. She's given up the missionary work; she told me so herself. Miss Catherine will need a new distraction, and we are the ones to provide it. But softly, softly. We don't want to seem too keen. Let's go. Out, anywhere! To the Café!"

He plunged his hands to the wrists into a crystal nautilus vase that stood on the glass floor. "The City Manager was there, talking to Lord Maitri. He was watching me very closely."

"The City Manager!" breathed Mâtho, stunned.

"So old Sattva ghosted the party." Joset grimaced knowledgeably. "He's a tricky customer. Did you manage to eavesdrop? Hear anything about increased law enforcement?"

"Not a word," confessed Misha. "I wasn't interested. But let me tell you about the food. It was bizarre. Roast peacocks with their feathers, whole antelopes with their heads and horns, hedgehogs in fish sauce, small mountains of extinct fruits . . . and everything tasting *horribly* of yeast and detergent."

They stormed through the house and courtyard and out into the streets. It was growing dark at last: a darkness that would be unbroken by streetlamps or commercial displays. The Aleutians did not understand why anyone would need municipal lighting. Each of them bowed for the prince's asperges. Misha lifted and shook his glistening hands over their heads. On they swept, into the vast, exhausted human city, each carrying their own share of the pale, clinging fire.

2

A POLITICAL MEETING

i

CATHERINE RESUMED HER old place in the household. She joined Maitri's elderly and diminishing band of retainers at morning and evening service in the character shrine, in the slow formal dancing that closed every day, and through the sociable Aleutian nights, when the members of the company napped and chatted and entertained each other. She reminisced about the glory days gone by, discussed sacred records with the chaplain, played 'Go' and 'chess' with the Silent, and 'Scrabble' with the Signifiers.

She told her comrades in the Church that her health had broken down and she would be taking a long, indefinite break from her missionary work. She made arrangements to dispose of her *trou*, along with the few possessions she'd left there. Maitri, delighted, secured her an invitation to visit the daughter of an old friend, a young lady like herself.

The Khans sent a closed car, which picked her up at the front door of Maitri's house and deposited her, a long time later, inside a walled garden. There was a sharp twittering of birdsong. The distant walls (the garden's physical dimensions were doubled, at least, by the artful use of virtual display-screens) were bright with vividly colored Aleutian creepers. Fruit trees stood in rows, bearing flowers and fruits together: apples and pears, apricots and peaches. The leaves, either dark or pale, showed the un-green of hybrid Aleutian genes. Butterfly wings flickered, birds darted.

Airborne traffic within the city was limited by environment laws, and unfashionable. The Youroans traveled continental distances without a thought in the "closed cars" that gave you no sensation of movement. It worried Catherine, like a vague nausea, that she *did not know where she was*. She could have crossed Youro, or spent the time sitting in a traffic jam.

"You must be Catherine." Mrs. Benazir Khan, Maitri's old friend, dismissed the car. It vanished, magically, into an antique false vista of box hedges and fountains. She was a tall human, her sleek dark hair wrapped in a gauze scarf, her figure markedly but sedately female in sober Aleutian overalls. She held Catherine's hands slightly longer than the customary greeting required, as if judging for herself and finally whether this was a suitable companion for her child. "I'm glad you've given up the missionary work," she said at last, with magisterial calm. She shook her head. "The Church of Self is not the answer, Catherine. You must let us find our own solutions to our problems."

Catherine felt humbled.

"Let me introduce you to my daughter."

Thérèse Khan was a tiny creature, dressed like a proper young lady in a cinched bodice and full skirt under a robe of layered gossamer. She was curled in the middle of a pink flower bed under an apple tree, teasing a small white puppy.

"Play nicely, now," smiled Mrs. Khan, and walked away.

Thérèse's hands and face were decorated in living color. Her eyes looked out as if from a mask made of butterfly's wings. Catherine thought of tiger weed tattoos. She didn't know what to say. The puppy yapped.

"Would you like to hold him? Put out your hands."

The puppy squirmed in Catherine's cupped palms and licked at her fingers.

"Isn't he *sweet*? He's called Pipi because he does it all the time. He's supposed to be house-trained, but he isn't."

"How old is he? Maybe he's too young to learn."

"Oh—" Thérèse laughed, not unkindly, at Catherine's ignorance. "He's as 'old' as he's going to get. He's a neo-toneyatey . . . I can't remember the word: he'll be a puppy forever." She put her hands playfully over the dog's minute pricked ears. "I'll tell you a secret. I'll always love Pipi, but I wish I could have a proper dog. A wolfhound or something." She kissed the animal's nose. "I hope he didn't hear that. Misha—Michael Connelly—has wolfhounds at their place in the country. I've seen them often. They're so fierce and marvelous, so sexy!"

"Perhaps they wouldn't be happy living indoors."

"That's what Mama says, and Imran. He's my brother. But if people can make puppies and kittens that will live for a hundred years without ever growing up, why can't I have a hunting dog who'd be happy in here?"

"That might be a logical problem, not a technical one."

Thérèse wrinkled her nose. "If you say so. . . . Shall I show you my birds?"

She jumped to her feet. The dented flowers sprang up, recovering shape like soft furniture. She took Catherine to a rocky grotto that stood incongruously among the tailored trees. It was hung inside and out with tiny wooden cages. "All of them are native Youroan species." Thérèse coaxed a finch with a blue and pink head onto her finger. "It's bad taste to keep exotics. Is it true there are no birds in Aleutia?"

"It's true. In the shipworld people have made winged things for fun, in imitation of yours. But at home we don't have anything that flies. You see, there's never been, how can I put it, open air. Where there are living things, there's no empty space. Strictly speaking, there aren't any separate species in our ecologies, only different variations of the same single form. Our 'cities' are colonies of life, where every variant is related to us, the people, and the air is full of the flux of our life chemicals—"

"Shall I show you my fish pool? You'll love my koi. They can practically talk."

Catherine was prepared for anything. "You mean they're self-conscious? Like, fish-shaped people?"

Thérèse looked back over her shoulder, shocked. "Oh, no! That would be cruel!"

While they were admiring the fish, Thérèse had a telecall. She politely insisted that she could put her friend off, but the interruption was a relief to both of them. Catherine left her chatting with her virtual companion and went for a walk. She found Mrs. Khan sitting at a white wrought-iron table in front of the fountains vista, reading a news site.

She shut the page, frowning a little. "Are you two getting on?"

"Yes, fine. Thérèse had to talk to someone for a moment."

"Sit down, then. Let me order you some coffee. Or would you prefer a soft drink?" She tapped her reader. "Your city manager doesn't understand his city. This negotiation with the Americas won't help him in Youro. Nothing that seems to favor Reformers will. There'll be riots in the poor wards, if this goes on."

A servant arrived with a tray of coffee and fruit juice.

"But the poor aren't Traditionalists," said Catherine. "How can they be?"

"Naturally, you're right, in a sense. To be human male and female, in the traditional meaning of the terms, has become the privilege of a wealthy minority. I'm afraid that's true. But you have worked among the *sous-prole*, our leisured classes. You know how they cling to the old sociosexual identities, though it would be hard to tell their naked bodies apart, if you will excuse my vulgarity."

"I know that," agreed Catherine. "Nearly all our converts were Traditionalist in sympathy, though of course they weren't voters. I meant, I find it puzzling."

"Ah, the Aleutian liberalism!" Mrs. Khan smiled wisely. "Aleutians don't understand the crisis of Reform versus Tradition. I am a Muslim. My colleagues in government are Christians, Hindus, Buddhists, Pagans, Marxists, even half-castes. It's the same in the other party. I am a Traditionalist, a woman and a member of the Cabinet. Some prominent Reformers are 'biologically male.' My goodness, who cares? Biological sex is not the issue. Sexual form is what we make it these days. But the division is real. It is the only thing that matters in Youro politics. Traditionalism is a question of values, of a conscious choice *to remain human*. None of us will give that up. Never!"

"But it's a choice you can't have unless you're rich," Catherine persisted. "Why don't the people, the masses, simply become Reformers—since they can't help their physiological changes, since that's what they *are*, practically speaking—and turn you out of government?"

Mrs. Khan was not offended. She laughed and shook her head at Catherine's naïveté. "The Reformers themselves cling to the sociosexual divide, in spite of their posturing. They don't want to be neuters! That's what makes their position so absurd. Did you see the cages in Thérèse's grotto? They have no doors, and this orchard is open overhead. My daughter's birds have the freedom of Youro, but they prefer to stay here. Our people are like those birds. They prefer the security of the familiar. It's a law of nature."

"You're so right," sighed Catherine. "It's the same at home, always the same."

She sipped her drink. The luxury of this setting was insidious. Chatting at ease with this sensible, pleasantly wicked human politician, an Aleutian need feel no guilt, no discomfort. "Is Misha Connelly a 'biological male'?"

Mrs. Khan looked astonished. Then she laughed, a prim, smothered sound completely at odds with her previous manner.

"I couldn't possibly tell you."

ii

A FEW DAYS later Catherine was in her room and sleeping, when Maitri came in to wake her.

She had been dreaming of the first landfall. They were coming from the shipworld. If we meet hostile natives, we're on our own; if we find treasure, we'll be expected to share it. Heigh-ho, that's the way of the world. In becomes down, we've been lost for so long, at last a new world! Then everything goes wrong. Dying, falling in flames. The screaming, the crying, the sobbing voices . . .

<Catherine? *Catherine?*>

Maitri was by her bed, kneeling upright, human style.

"You were having a nightmare, darling."

His robe was a poem of mingled green and blue with touches of palest rose: the soul of a lake of water lilies. But he looked desperately tired and ill. She started up, shocked. No one had told her that Maitri was sick! She lay back. Of course he was not sick. He was old.

He stroked her hair. "Was it the same one?"

She nodded. "I dream about our first landing, when we crashed in Africa." Maitri's presence seemed a blurred intrusion in the world of her nightmare. "Sometimes even when I'm awake," she said softly, "I think everything that's happened since those flames is an illusion." She'd decided to devote herself to making him happy. She would become one of Maitri's souvenirs, a nature-identical Traditionalist young lady he could show off at his parties. She would make afternoon visits and be pleasant company in hall. She had begun to suspect that there might be enough daily laceration in this quiet existence to keep her need for pain in check. But because the dream still possessed her, she saw that this charade must end.

Before Catherine was conceived, Lord Maitri had announced that he was going to stay behind when the Aleutians went home. In future lives, trips to earth might be commonplace, but he loved the place too much to rely on that. He was determined to enjoy his last certain lease on the beloved giant planet to the very end and die here of old age. But the Departure had been delayed and delayed. The Aleutians didn't cling to life, and they didn't collect statistics. Maitri's age had never mattered. Suddenly, she saw him really *old,* helpless, and confused: alone here with the hungry, angry humans, the people who had been so cynically exploited and abandoned.

"Maitri, you have to give this up," she said abruptly. "I know what you promised yourself. But you didn't know how long it would all take, and you didn't know what the political situation would be like. Suppose Gender War breaks out again in Youro after the Departure. I want you to go back to the shipworld. All of you, the whole household. I want you to start arranging that now."

He looked down at her tenderly. A million tiny chemical touches spilled into the air: she could feel nothing. "And leave you alone? I don't think so, my dear. I plan to have the proud distinction of being the last Aleutian on earth. Not counting yourself, of course." He chuckled. "What you really mean is that you want me dead. You want me out of the way so you don't have to worry about me anymore. I could say the same of you. There've been times, recently, when I've truly wished you'd decide to set your proselytes an example. It is not pleasant to know that someone I love is so continuously unhappy. Shall we make a pact? Kiss goodbye, and pray that WorldSelf brings us together again soon in some better life? I don't seriously think we'd be charged with criminal suicide. I am senile, as

you have so kindly reminded me. And you have been declared insane."

She stared up at him. Escape was not remotely a temp-
tation.

"I can't."

"I know you can't. So don't ask me to leave you, not before I must."

He stood up, grumbling unconsciously in the Common
Tongue. <Oh, my old bones! I don't know why humans
have to sit like that; I'm sure it's bad for the spine. But it
looks so elegant, and I am so vain.> "You dream of our
landing. I dream of the shipworld myself. Those placid lifetimes lost in space when nothing much happened at all.
Poor old Kumbva and his fights with the navigators. But it
was no use: you *can't* teach Aleutian technicians that abstract measurement matters. They said yes and yes, but as
soon as his attention slipped, they were throwing out his
tricks and doing exactly as they pleased. And so we wandered aimlessly, really quite content, or that's the way it
seems to me now. We were institutionalized, as they say
on earth. Do you remember that when we stumbled over
this system, and actually discovered a new habitable
planet—which was supposed to be the object of the whole
exercise, if I recall correctly—practically nobody wanted
to land? *There might be trouble, what's the point, we just want
to go home. . . .* Do you remember that? So it was left to our
private expedition of ne'er-do-wells, our little band. *We*
came down here. *We* found the Buonarroti device and
turned the whole venture from an absurd failure into a triumph. And what thanks do we veterans get? We're ignored."

"Not everyone," murmured Catherine. "Only those who
disagree with present policies."

"It makes my blood boil. Especially, the way we treat
you. You're the one who tested the device! If it wasn't for
your incredible courage, committing yourself to that mon-

strous void-forces machine, we wouldn't be planning the Departure now—"

"I don't remember," she reminded him. She had been curled on her side, smiling faintly at his tirade. She turned on her back, staring at the ceiling. "Everything else, but not that."

Maitri glanced at her and away.

"It's quite normal that you don't remember," he said firmly. "You were very, very stressed at the time." He frowned at the row of Youro devotional incunabula above her desk: printed texts from before the development of moving-image records. *The Way of Perfection. Life of St. Catherine of Siena. Round the Bend, Sittartha. The Letters of St. Paul.* He picked up a glass madonna filled with layers of colored sand from the Isle of Wight and put it down with a shudder. "What dreadful taste you have in this life, darling. You used to collect such lovely things. This robe of mine, did you notice, is copied from one of your Monets. Every stitch hand embroidered too, by a lovely woman in Accra . . . "

"It isn't taste. It's simply that I'm trying to understand them this time, instead of looting. I want to feel their pain, their whole *culture* of grief and fear. That's what those icons mean to me. That's why I joined the Mission."

"But you could become a patron of the arts. There's so much going on in the human world—even here in Youro. You ought to take an interest, in—um—new poetry and so on."

"I'm afraid it's too late. I like human things the way they were before we got at them. So do you. Look at that robe you're wearing."

He went to her window and glowered out at the burning colors of deep summer: asters, fuschias, gladioli. "The saddest thing is to know that deep down one is as weak and selfish and cowardly as anybody else. No wonder you keep dreaming of our landing. I wish we *could* go back and start again. But we can't. And *really, deep down,* we consent: Aleutia consents to the way the Departure is to be handled. Even you, Catherine. We can't stay; that would do no good. We must leave, and they must work things out for themselves. There's no sane alternative."

"Perhaps people like you and I should be nicer to Sattva and his crew," suggested Catherine, not very seriously. "Maybe that would help. Remember what you always used to say? 'Praise is the first rule of good management.' "

"I've changed my mind about that," he said gloomily. "Communication is the first rule. When you can't communicate, nothing else follows. No, there's nothing to be done. But I wish I could stop you from blaming yourself. You aren't responsible for the whole Expedition's misdeeds."

"I can't help it," she murmured, invoking a favorite Aleutian platitude. "It's the way I'm made, the way the chemicals are put together. No one can change their obligation."

Maitri sighed, turning from the flowers to smile at her sadly. "And so we call you 'the conscience of Aleutia.' Poor Catherine, what a thankless talent. But I do wonder what it means," he added bitterly, "when people say that *their conscience* is crazy." Abruptly, he changed his tone. "I'm so sorry, my dear. I rushed to rescue you from a nightmare, and I seem to be trying to give you another one. I had a better reason for interrupting your siesta. I've thought of an outing you might enjoy."

"Another young lady?" asked Catherine cautiously. She felt that her introduction to Thérèse Khan had not been a success.

"No, no! Something *very* different. A political meeting."

"Oh? I thought we weren't supposed to get involved in their politics."

Catherine's tone was dry. Maitri answered it with a glance of equal irony.

"I should have said, a *non*political meeting." He adopted

a tone of artless enthusiasm. "If you hadn't been burying yourself in the Church of Self, you would know about the 'renaissance.' It's a spiritual regeneration, a renewal of the old human arts and crafts, music and food and such like, from pre-contact times. It's been building for years, apparently. Now it's breaking through into general interest, everywhere on the planet. One of the movement's leaders, Lalith the halfcaste, is in Youro making an in-person tour. It sounds very exciting and attractive, and since it's strictly non gender biased, there's no harm in our going along."

"You mean, Sattva will be appalled."

Maitri shrugged innocently. "I don't see any reason why. Well, what about it? I believe Michael Connelly—the young one that is—is sure to be there."

On his way back to join the rest of his household, Maitri stopped for a rest—pretending to the Commonalty that he had halted to admire the decayed paintwork. The passages in this house seemed to get longer every day.

The Aleutians were true immortals, not mere physical replicas of their ancestors. The chemical news carried by the shedding and consuming of their "wandering cells" was constantly being copied and conveyed to each individual's reproductive tract, updating the embryonic model of the whole brood that was held there. No one really knew how Aleutian conception was initiated. Reproductive science, so fascinating to humans, had never interested them. When there is no death, the "facts of life" can be taken for granted. Some said it was stress that triggered budding. Some said it was loneliness—or happiness, or joy, or grief. But whenever an embryo developed, a known Aleutian individual was born again: and the new incarnate was genuinely the culmination of that person's previous lifetimes. Kumbva the engineer, the Second Captain of the original expedition, had named the link between proto-embryos and the life-flux (which also involved a structure in the brain) the "information system," as opposed to the "inert tissue" of muscle and bones, entrails and blood. He said it stood in place of sexual fusion, the mechanism of evolution used by earth's complex organisms. It was the crucial feature in which Aleutians differed from humans, and vitally important to the Buonarroti project.

The rationalists (Kumbva among them) believed that no conscious memory was transferred in the chemical notation. The accumulated experience in your cells could make you an engineer or an artist, bad-tempered or sociable, Signifier or Silent. But it was character study that constructed identity, that sense of *knowing oneself* to be the same person who had lived before. Maitri, romantic and traditional in his religious views, favored the other opinion. It worried him that Catherine did not remember the extraordinarily significant act that had ended her last life on earth. It made him afraid that Sattva and the others were right and the shift into human form had done some awful harm. He told himself he was being foolish. So many clever people denied the very existence of "physical memory."

But if only she would consent to pretend a little. The Third Captain had certainly made the incredible journey. Aleutia had the records of the witnesses and chemical evidence taken from the Third Captain's body when he had returned, on the point of death, from his trip through the void. Why shouldn't Catherine have the credit for that heroic act? If she would make the record the Expedition Management wanted—*how lovely it was to see home again, how welcoming the air*—if she would do that, maybe Aleutia would listen to what she had to say about the humans. People made confessional records about things they knew only by hearsay all the time! Catherine's honesty allowed Sattva to dismiss her, with horrible pretended sympathy: *sadly unbalanced, neurotic, crazy: a sad waste of a lifetime; we can only hope our friend the Third Captain will not suffer any lasting ill effects—*

Maitri levered himself away from the wall. It made his nasal ache to think about things like "reproductive tracts" and "information systems." In the old days nobody had been interested in science. How it used to make Kumbva mad! Now the air was full of comment on the Buonarroti device, the multi-realities problem, obscure puzzles about the engine's development; and Maitri felt like an old dullard. *How we've changed,* he thought. *It's going to take us lives and lives to get back to normal, afterward.*

So many friends were not around for this last life on earth. Kumbva the engineer. Rajath the trickster, First Captain: the unscrupulous individual who had had the idea of making landfall in the first place. Aditya the beauty. Dear Bella, and funny old Sid. The landing party cluster had dispersed, vanished into the random mazes. The humans remembered those once-famous names more often than Aleutia did. Maybe it was just as well that they weren't here. Some of the others might have been tempted to *do something* about the way the end of the adventure was being handled: if it was only to chuck a spannet in the works. It was lucky for the Expedition's current management that they only had ineffectual Maitri to deal with. Maitri, who had nothing more on his mind than thinking of treats for Catherine.

Those delightful phrases, he thought sadly (withdrawing for the while from his mental argument with the Commonalty). *No one uses them anymore.* You probably wouldn't find a human in the city who could remember what a *spannet* was. They didn't watch the movies; they mostly didn't even follow the news. There was nothing but interactive sport and those dreadful virtuality games: art without an audience. What's the use of art without an audience?

Suddenly, Maitri's eyes brimmed with tears, Aleutian tears that blurred his vision but did not fall. He was thinking of his friends in the Reformer party. What would become of them after Aleutia had gone?

"The poor devils," he muttered aloud, piteously. "Oh, the poor devils—"

The Monet robe was heavy. He found himself bending forward as he crept on down the corridor, his hands curling into paws. The baboon body was tired, wanted to trot on all fours. Respect for the stolen beauty of the water lilies kept him upright.

iii

THE MEETING HALL was in a Reformer neighborhood, which caused Lord Maitri's party some qualms when they realized where they were heading. But Maitri pointed out that the next venue on Lalith's tour was halfway across Youro. They'd had to give up their dear old limousine when the household became too small to count as a "transport community" in city ordinance, and the cost of such a journey in hired cars would be shocking. Everybody was supposed to be economizing, he reminded them virtuously, to cover the expense of the Departure Project.

Their cab dropped them at a deconstruction site where something very large was vanishing at speed into the maws of silent, bovine civil engineering plant. There was no sign of a meeting hall, and they began to panic. Most of them had lived in Youro in the Gender War. They were justifiably afraid of finding themselves lost in the human city, where the air was dead as stone and any information available was in printed language or confusing street projections. Catherine looked for a minitel screen; Maitri flicked through a street directory. Atha, one of the Silent members of the household, covered himself in glory by spotting a glowing hand-size green arrow, which did not seem to belong to the projection that surrounded it. He had noticed similar green arrows on the flyer that Maitri had copied from the local listings. Someone spotted another. They followed the trail, from one eye-hurting virtual commercial to the next, through the unbuilding site and into the alleys beyond.

<A pity they couldn't get hold of a can of green "paint,"> Maitri complained.

They knew they'd reached their destination when they met a young person in brightly colored overalls, who was putting up copies of that same flyer at the entrance to an ancient brick-built Christian shrine. He was using a small machine, which he pointed at another machine that was clinging to the wall of the church: a data-grid junction box. As he did so, the renaissance flyer materialized among the church notices, displacing the text of a restoration appeal fund, a list of Mass times, and the yearly summary of the St. Vincent de Paul Society's accounts.

"Isn't that *clever!*" exclaimed Vijaya, Maitri's first secretary.

The human turned and smiled alertly. He was a halfcaste: his face dinted in the middle with nostril slits instead of a human nose, his upper lip short and divided.

"Free advertising," he lisped. "It does no harm. The bitminder will restore the licensee's data in an hour or two, but that's as much time as we need. Step right inside, noble aliens. Your reserved seats are waiting for you."

"But how did you know we were coming?" cried the chaplain, naively astonished. "Have you been 'bugging' Lord Maitri's house?"

"Didn't have to. You snagged us. And then you ordered a cab to the venue. Simple."

By this time the Silent were hanging back, deeply alarmed by the puzzle-trail and the obviously illicit behavior of this halfcaste. Silent Aleutians—naturally conservative, obstinately conventional—were suspicious of any extended articulate speech that did not emanate from "the proper authorities." Maitri's Silent servants had joined the outing under protest. They were well aware that their lord was using them to make a doubtful excursion look respectable. <You didn't tell us it was a *secret* meeting,> they protested. <We don't think we're supposed to be here.>

Maitri managed to reassure them, but then Atha had wandered off down the street, because he'd seen a car that reminded him of dear old limo. Catherine had to go and fetch him, to the amusement of a group of several more humans who'd come out to see the fun. At last they were through the double doors (which were inert slabs, old-earth style, like the door of Catherine's prison cell). They found the whole assembly on its feet, jostling eagerly for a glimpse of the aliens. Stewards wearing green armbands greeted them in the large, infantile gestures of Youroan humans trying to "speak Aleutian." They were ushered to a row of hard seats-with-legs. Their chairs were indeed marked, in symbols and in printed English, "RESERVED FOR OUR ALEUTIAN FRIENDS." This time (to Vijaya's disappointment) the signs were mere solid rag-card.

Maitri rose to the occasion, answering the stewards in the same expansive style.

<SO NICE TO BE HERE, HOW INTERESTING EVERYTHING IS, PLEASE DON'T LET US PUT YOU OUT!>

"So much for discretion!" he muttered, sitting down by Catherine and arranging the folds of his sleeveless robe. He did not seem displeased. He was wearing scarlet, a sober industrial color that he'd thought suitable for the occasion. "I don't think I've caused such a stir among the humans since First Contact. Aren't the chairs lovely!"

Venues licensed for in-person speakers were small and few. The status of articulate speech in Aleutian society made the aliens nervous about human demagogues—especially in Youro, the most recalcitrant region of old-earth. Catherine noticed that this hall was not only small but unnaturally bare. Generated-image decor was cheap and universal, but these faded plaster walls were naked. The ancient niches around the nave, which should have held either actual statues or the economical virtual-image version, held only strange draggled bunches of leaves and flowers. The church seating had been rearranged, in a pattern that had not been current on earth for three hundred years, in rows that faced ahead toward a makeshift dais. At the back of this dais stood a tall public address screen and a row of hard chairs. At the front stood a simple upright lectern. Apart from the screen, which was blank, there was no decoration. One of the stewards scurried up to the end of the aliens' row, bearing an armful of small machines.

"Transcripters—" He spoke in French, then remembered and waved his arms.

<THESE ARE FOR YOU TO KEEP. NO UNAUTHORIZED RECORDING OR DISTRIBUTION. OKAY?>

He scooted off, and returned a moment later.

<SORRY. 'COURSE WE MEAN IN HUMAN MEDIA. WE CAN'T STOP YOU COPYING STUFF INTO THE COMMONALTY. WE KNOW THAT!>

Maitri beamed. "You speak very good Aleutian, young man."

"I'm a woman, actually. But thanks anyway."

Catherine, having looked in vain for the arts and crafts (unless those bunches of leaves counted for something), settled to contemplate Buonarroti's miracle. Peenemünde Buonarroti had bemused the First Contact world by insisting *there's no such thing as alien intelligence. We are all made in the image of Being.* Intelligent creatures may possibly take different bodily forms (Peenemünde had once confessed that she'd hoped the first extraterrestrials to arrive would resemble octopuses; she liked octopuses). Cultures may vary. But a very few simple mechanical laws will shape life wherever it arises: driving through evolution on every fractal scale, from slime molds to party politics. Thought and feeling will be formed everywhere by the same pressures that created them on earth. They cannot be alien. And here was the proof. Every human in this crowded hall was chattering away in a language the Aleu-

tians understood at least as easily as they would understand the Common Tongue of a different brood at home.
Unfortunately, because the humans were addicted to the
spoken word and dismissed what they thought of as an
"animal" mode of communication, most of them didn't
care *what* they said in Silence.

*They shouldn't have been allowed in. What are they doing
here? Well, I've seen them. That's something to tell the grand-
children. Wonder if I could touch one? They make me feel sick,
they're dirty, they're filling the air with their bugs. They make me
feel as if things are crawling on me. Are they really going to
leave? Just vanish, the way they came? I don't believe it. I wonder what they look like naked. They wear nappies instead of going
to the toilet; they have little creatures bred specially to wipe their
bottoms: how revolting.*

Maitri's retainers were veterans. They were by this life almost as indifferent to the legendary rudeness as if they
were humans themselves. Catherine felt the warm bulk of
Atha, Maitri's kindhearted cook, shift beside her. He picked
a claw full of squirming red life from the pores in his throat
and offered it to Vijaya. *This is me, my dear, this is how I feel,
this is how things are with me just now.* Vijaya gobbled it happily. A wave of intensified disgust burst from his human
neighbors. Atha looked about him, wondering silently:
<Did somebody do a poop? I didn't smell it.>

Catherine giggled. A party of people in dull green overalls, wearing the bright green stewards' armbands,
marched onto the packing-case dais. The crowd came to
attention. The stewards retired, and a single figure stood at
the lectern.

Lalith, the halfcaste, presented herself as feminine,
though not female. She had the moderate prenatal transformation: nostril slits and a cleft lip rather than a fully
open nasal. She was sturdily built and had an average rosy
brown skin tone. She launched into some general remarks
about peace, love, and the work ethic. Catherine prepared

to be bored. She wondered if Misha Connelly could possibly be interested in this sort of thing.

" . . . None of us can forget the Gender War. It has shaped our lives. It has shaped the state of our planet, as much if not more than the presence of the Aleutians."

Lord Maitri's people started, and the Silent touched their lord in furtive chemical reproach. Lalith's odd noises could not distract them from her perfectly intelligible Silent language. *<Gender politics,>* they insisted, outraged. *<Maitri, how could you! We're definitely not supposed to be here!>*

"But how much of the rest of human history do we remember? I am, as you can see, a halfcaste. You may wonder why, if the renaissance seeks a way forward that is beyond gender, I remain *gendered* as a member of the third sex. It is because I am proud of the halfcaste tradition.

"When the Aleutians arrived, some three hundred years ago, they were welcomed, almost worshiped. Some people wanted so desperately to be like these angels from outer space that they altered their bodies by crude surgery: became sexless, silent, noseless. Childish enough. But they also adopted the Aleutian practice of *studying the records.* Traditionally, halfcastes 'study the records' for the same reason as the Aleutians. They believe that they can identify their own former incarnations in our moving-image records of the past and thereby 'learn to be themselves.' "

"Although I respect that belief, I do not share it. I study the records not as an individual, but as a citizen of humanity. It is not myself that I find there, it is humanity's Self. We have forgotten our past. We have forgotten our own resources. We play the games, which have no history. We ought to be making movies, talk shows, science programs. We ought to be analyzing our archives. The Aleutians are the lords of life. But they build and preserve their cultural identity through the *artificial* records made by the Priests of Self—a vast mass of data to which every Aleutian, rich or poor, famous or obscure, makes a contribution.

"Why have we given up our own history? We have become dependent on their effortless biotechnology, their skill at altering our landscapes, at generating tailored hybrids so much superior to our original crops, animals, and machines. But we had our own life sciences once. We can recover them. We can build *our own* customized world."

Lalith paused, surveying the crowd with a practiced, ingathering gaze,

"Once, we believed that the Aleutians were divine. Today we know that they are neither true telepaths nor true immortals. They do not live forever; they cannot read our minds. When they arrived here, they were shipwrecked spacefarers desperate to find their way home. Soon they will return to their home planet, using the miraculous invention of a human physicist; and they will go in peace. But when the Aleutians hand over the results of their research on the Buonarroti engine to earth's scientists—as was agreed at the famous Neubrandenburg Conference held after the two *halfcastes,* Sidney Carton and Bella, had found the lost secret of instantaneous interstellar travel (excuse me if I correct the popular record, which credits this discovery to the Three Captains; I'm not without some ethnic pride)—when they leave us, I say, equipped to map our own new territories among the stars: Will we be ready?"

Presumably, Lalith had planned her speech without knowing that actual Aleutians would be in the audience. She certainly wasn't making the alien visitors feel inconspicuous. Catherine was thankful when she realized the speaker had reached her peroration.

"The renaissance is not a war against gender. We in the movement are Reformers and Traditionalists, feminine and masculine. We are women, men, halfcastes, and 'don't knows.' " This sally raised some human tittering. "We don't mean to give up any of these identities! We don't ask you to give up your own. We want to go *on,* not backward. To start history again from *now.* I still call myself a halfcaste.

But I am not a human who's trying to imitate the aliens. I am a human who is the product of three hundred years of history that cannot be denied. Who is trying to find a new way forward for *humanity*.

"The renaissance asks you to reject Aleutian goods and revive our native technologies. Not because we believe that our culture is superior to theirs. Not because we reject the aliens. But because *we are human*. I am a halfcaste, a construction: born not of nature but of human history. Let us admit that this is true of us all.

"We cannot take up our old ways as if nothing happened—on that strangest of days, in Krung Thep, in Thailand, July 2038, when the Aleutians made themselves known. We must go on from where we are now. Changed, not by the aliens alone but by our own dynamic history. *Changed and reborn!*"

Cheers and applause. An interval was announced. Refreshments, a display of renaissance products; informal discussion, after which Lalith would take questions. Lalith was being escorted from the dais. Catherine noticed this time how carefully her escort masked the sturdy figure, and the sparkle of a security shield that flashed around that humble old-world lectern, as somebody clicked it off. Lalith's profession of nonviolence was no doubt sincere. But her material was inflammatory—and the organizers knew it.

Catherine stood, with Maitri and the others. <Behave as if nothing is wrong,> warned Maitri, very quietly.

<Nothing *is* wrong. I thought it was a fine speech.>

They joined the humans and moved into another hall. There were things to see and touch. There were antique boxed and mounted TV screens, out of which renaissance luminaries from around the planet were peering, ready to work the crowd. At a long table, food and drink were being dispensed. The humans broke into groups, into animated conversations and nervous silences. No one approached the aliens; even Silent comment on their presence was now extremely subdued. But there was no real hostility. Most of the people were clearly Reformers, Catherine noticed. Most of them were young; and most of them were from that shrunken and struggling group Mrs. Khan would call, with pity, "the employed." But there were also half-castes and Traditionalists—even a few figures shrouded in the full chador who might be genuine high-caste Traditionalist young ladies. Everything was exactly as one would expect. She noted wryly the scattering of old lags: aging humans with the brave, shabby, world-weary demeanor of lifelong dissidents. She knew that look well! Buonarroti's miracle strikes again.

Maitri's party relaxed. The speech had been alarming, but it was over. The old spirit of adventure began to stir. Atha, pleased to recover his proper role for a while, set off to forage at the canteen table. Vijaya and the second secretary, Smrti,—a pair of amorous predators who had never been lovers themselves, but loved to hunt in couple—attempted to make Silent propositions to some of the young male Traditionalists, whose striking appearance they much admired. They Silently (but discreetly) deplored the Reformer tendency to look and dress like so many big-nosed Aleutians.

Maitri and Catherine exchanged rueful glances.

<Thank God,> Maitri chuckled, <the humans won't have an idea what my wicked secretaries are trying to suggest. The old sinners! It's so long since they've been out on the town, they've forgotten how to behave.>

"That wasn't quite what I expected," remarked Catherine, aloud and calmly. "I thought we were going to be making raffia mats, or trying our hands at desktop publishing."

"I was a little taken aback myself," he agreed, in the same public tone. "But it sounds very creditable, and not at all anti-Aleutian, or gender biased." He beamed at the display beside them. "Look at this wonderful TV cabinet. Reproduction, of course, but how lovely. The severe lines, such a lively counterpoint to the flowing—"

He looked up. He had felt, before Catherine, a change in the air.

"Ah," he breathed. "Ah, well." And no more, not even in Silence. Lord Maitri could be the most continent of communicators, when he chose.

The police moved soberly through the assembly behind their Aleutian officer. Some very unhappy stewards were with them. Catherine saw with dismay that the officer was Bhairava, the Aleutian chief of police. Bhairava was another veteran of the original landing parties. In his last lives he had been a security officer in the service of Catherine's Aleutian self; in one of them he'd also been Maitri's contracted love partner. In this generation the Expedition Management had decreed that Aleutian households on earth shouldn't have private security. It gave the humans a bad impression. So Bhairava had innocently taken the police post in Youro to be near his friends. But Maitri was hurt and angry: considering that Bhairava had sold out to the regime. He came immediately to join them, his head turned to one side, showing throat, the Aleutian gesture of respect.

"This is an unexpected pleasure," said Maitri frostily. "I do not remember asking for an armed escort."

<Not exactly, sir. Obviously, Lord Sattva was concerned about you being here. But it was more or less inevitable that we'd have to show up sometime on the tour. We've been watching this "renaissance" business—>

Maitri wouldn't listen. <Excuse me,> he bowed, bitterly polite. <I see Atha having problems at the food counter.>

<He'll get over it,> said Catherine, when Maitri had swept away.

<In a life or two,> agreed Bhairava glumly. He was a Signifier who didn't speak aloud unless he had to. <I did it for him, that's the sad part. I'd be working for him, or for you, sir, if I could. I can't help my chemistry. I can't suddenly be-

come a cook or a chaplain, can I? No one can change their obligation. But how are you, sir?> Bhairava always treated Catherine exactly as if she were her Aleutian self. <I heard you had another set-to with my boss. You shouldn't let them get you down. You're not crazy,> he added kindly. <You're just depressed.>

"I am not depressed!" she snapped. "I simply happen to take a more realistic view of life than some people—"

<And who wouldn't be,> went on Bhairava, who rarely listened to casual speeches; The spoken word was for sworn evidence, not for trifles. <The way things are going. But what do you think of our new rabble-rouser? We believe she's a plant.>

"A *plant*? I know they reproduce in strange ways now, but that's a new departure."

<Actually, it's not funny, sir. We think she's from the USSA. We suspect they're behind the renaissance movement. It would make sense. If they move in now, undercover, to destabilize the gender situation, this part of old-earth would be a soft target after we leave. But it's a delicate problem to handle, because of the trade mission negotiations.>

Catherine had spotted Misha Connelly. He was standing with his back to her, talking to a group of stewards. It was a curious shock. She was transported back to the day of Maitri's party. *Eyes of a stranger that met mine and seemed to know.* She had been in a daze: somehow walking and talking among Maitri's guests, blood and fire—

<I see. So believing you might be dealing with a foreign power bent on inciting gender violence in our streets, Sattva sent you along to a licensed nonsectarian political gathering with a small army. Of course, how wise: That's exactly the way to keep the peace.>

<Actually, Sattva asked me to be very discreet. The small army was my idea.>

She must have misunderstood. She had never known

Bhairava to act stupidly or maliciously in the practice of his profession.

<I've been looking for an exit for a while. Things are going to get rough. I don't want what's bound to happen here around the Departure as a feature on my résumé. I want to go now, before they can call it suicide to evade responsibility. I'm glad we've had this chat. I wanted to tell you in-person how much I've missed being in your service.>

He laid his hand on Catherine's shoulder, bent and rubbed his cheek briefly against hers. She was startled. They'd had to learn not to caress each other in public. The humans didn't like it: *animal nuzzling, yuk!*.

<Could you say a few words to Maitri for me? I hate goodbyes.>

She couldn't see Misha anymore. And now Bhairava had gone too. What did he mean, *I hate goodbyes?* Where was he going? Everyone was moving back to the larger hall. The Aleutian party had deserted their reserved seats and settled in a different row near the doors. She joined them. The church was not so packed as it had been. The police filed in and took up positions around the walls, hands behind their backs in the *don't want to hurt anyone* gesture. She saw Bhairava standing with them.

Questions, of the usual immemorial kind. She didn't listen.

<What I can't understand,> complained Maitri softly, <is why the poor don't *belong* to anybody. Some people cannot look out for themselves. That's a fact of life. They aren't going to change, and they aren't going to vanish. If the humans lived the way we do, everybody would belong to some household or other, whether they were any use or not, and one wouldn't have this problem, this threat of mob violence.>

Maybe not. Or maybe Lord Maitri was dreaming, imagining an ideal Aleutia that never was. But Catherine was thinking about Misha Connelly. She remembered the russet-tinged curls under a soft black cap, his pink-cheeked bloom, his extreme self-consciousness. He had reminded her of a portrait by Sargent. He had the air, worthless and lovely, of that minor pre-contact poet's work. She tried to remember what they had talked about. There had been something very important, which Misha knew and . . . And suddenly, without warning, she was in the midst of the conversion. DONE BECAUSE WE ARE TOO MANY. Warm blood poured over her hands. She was drenched in cold sweat, bile filled her throat.

She stood up, gasping: <Excuse me!>

But everyone was standing.

Something untoward had happened to question time, but Catherine's need was greater than her curiosity. She pushed her way through the hubbub, found a door marked *females' bathroom* in the city's symbolic script, and lunged at it.

She stayed in the cubicle for a long time, squatting on the floor. The mouth of the toilet bowl was worn and losing its memory. The smell of her vomit escaped from its slackly pursed lips. How dirty everything is, she thought. There was a film of grease and grime on every surface; dead dirt filled the air. She had not noticed this grubbiness in the cell with the pink roses, because then she'd been living down among the humans.

There'd been a lot of noise, she dimly realized, but now it was quiet out there.

When she finally emerged, she was bewildered to find that the hall was empty. A whirlwind had passed through it. Chairs were overturned, scraps of rubbish were strewn over the floor. She walked to one of the plastic seats and set it upright. She was standing beside it when a door at the back of the church opened, and Misha Connelly's face peered around it.

"What happened?" she asked. "Where's Maitri?"

"Gone home. The police got them out before the melee. What happened to *you?*"

"I was taken ill," said Catherine, with dignity.

Misha grinned. "We saw you rush for the toilet. Don't be embarrassed; it was probably the best thing you could have done." He came in. "We told Lord Maitri we'd look after you, and see you safely home."

"We?"

He winked and touched the sleeve of his pale coat, which was the ragged twin of the one he'd been wearing at Maitri's party. A renaissance steward's armband appeared there. "You see. I cravenly concealed my responsibility as an officer of the movement while the police rumble was going on. Does that make you feel better?"

"Better than what?"

The door opened again, and three more young humans entered. All of them presented themselves as masculine. One of them was the halfcaste flyposter, one a very dark-skinned young Reformer who looked vaguely familiar. The third, a scrawny individual in shirt and jeans whose face seemed made of nose, hung back, overcome with shyness. They were disheveled, glowing, excited. The Reformer youth had a glass bottle tucked under either arm.

"So you found her," declared this one. "Are you all right, Miss Catherine?"

"I was telling your friend Michael—I mean Misha—I was taken ill, nothing serious. But what happened?" she repeated. "What happened to Lalith, to the meeting?"

"S-someone asked Lalith if the renaissance isn't really a front for a h-halfcaste conspiracy," burst out the Nose. "I say *someone.* Of course we know him, but I w-wouldn't give his name airtime, not even in deadspace. Lalith can handle those types, but h-his friends started throwing things."

"And the police decided to clear the hall," broke in Misha. "That was a big mistake."

The Reformer brandished his bottles. "Loot!" he cried.

"We were running away, and the constabulary fire broke open a *vente directe*. Naturally, I liberated some of the contents. Why don't you sit down, Miss Catherine. I can't sit while a Traditionalist lady is standing, and I can't drink on my feet. As my friend was saying, trouble broke out. The federales, who were not invited to our party and had arrived without any notice, opened fire on unarmed citizens."

Catherine sat on the floor. She felt too unstable to perch on a seat-with-legs. They followed her example. The dark-skinned Reformer opened one of his bottles and offered it to her. The smell of rough wine assaulted her dizzy head. She refused.

"I know this dreadful stuff," complained Misha Connelly. "It's château-disgusting shareware; it begs to be taken away on every street corner. I thought you said you stole it. Dirtjuice, I think the misconstructed amateurs who make this called it. Lightly aged regurgitated orange peel, and is that a soupçon of dog excreta?'

The Reformer hid his annoyance by taking a huge swig. "I don't think it's too bad. I was a looter in spirit."

"This is my friend Joset Uwilingiyimana," Misha told Catherine. "Looter in spirit."

Joset, sitting cross-legged, bowed grandly from the waist, spreading his arms wide and nearly upending his bottle. "Honored to make your aquaintance, Miss Catherine. Misha has told us so much—"

The Nose spluttered and coughed violently. Misha scowled.

"Rajath," offered the halfcaste, picking up the other bottle, his bright black eyes dancing. "My name is Rajath."

"Rajath?" She laughed. It was the human name of the trickster captain, the self-declared leader of the original landing parties. "So that's what happened to the rascal. He became a human. I shall be careful how I deal with you!"

"And my coreligionist is Mâtho," finished Misha, in a

forbidding tone. "Coreligionist, or compatriot. But he's a foul vessel of lust and worse vices, and a disgrace to male-ordered society. He has a strange sense of humor. Ignore him."

"But what happened," Joset recommensed importantly, "was that fighting broke out at our meeting. It's normal. It's what we expect in raw revolutionary politics."

"It's never happened before," said Rajath.

"We've never had the police at a gig before." Joset took the contradiction in his stride, and continued to explain the situation. "Lalith was very upset."

"I didn't know you'd spoken to her," muttered the half-caste, eyeing Catherine slyly. "I thought her minders took her away, while you ran off to loot a shareware booth."

"But I know she was upset, because I know Lalith!"

"The p-police were here to protect Lord Maitri's party," whispered Mâtho, who was now, after Misha's reproof, keeping his eyes fixed on the floor. "Th-that's obvious."

"I'm sorry," said Catherine. "We shouldn't have come. It was thoughtless of us."

Misha aimed a gentle cuff at the side of his coreligionist's head.

"No, he's right," protested Catherine. "We *shouldn't* have come. Maitri has attitudes that belong to another time. He doesn't understand that some things won't do anymore, that we must not patronize you. But I'm glad I heard Lalith. Your manifesto sounds very positive."

Misha's friends glanced at each other.

"Did I say something wrong?"

Mâtho began: "Lalith doesn't—" He caught Misha's eye and shut up.

"No one will know exactly who did what to whom until they open the hall's black box," Misha announced, killing the question of the renaissance manifesto. "And that account, we believe, will exonerate the movement entirely!"

"It's the tamper-proof recording," Joset explained, for

Miss Catherine's benefit, "of what happens in a public venue. We gave you, and all our guests, our sealed transcripters, which recorded exactly what happened here. We do that because we want it clear that anything other than our authorized script is not a guaranteed record. But the black box is the city's version. Legally, it can't be examined unless there's a felony or a breach of the peace. However, we know it will agree perfectly with our account."

They giggled. Even Misha permitted himself an austere grin.

"*Tamper-proof*," repeated Rajath, screwing up his face in a violent wink, to make sure Catherine took the point.

"Oh, I see. And are we being recorded at the moment, for this incorruptible record?"

Misha stood up. "Not by the black box, because our booking finished a short while ago. There's nothing public going on here now. That's a timely reminder; we'd better leave before the lights go out and the doors lock until the local priest arrives for morning Mass. We'll find you a cab, Miss Catherine."

But they could not find a cab. They began to walk.

"D-do you know how to use the lev-metro, miss?" asked Mâtho.

"Of course she doesn't," Joset told him scornfully. "She's a lady!"

The street projections were fading one by one as the commercial day ended. Rajath used his little machine to unzip the renaissance arrows: running ahead to vanish them, for fun, before they disappeared with their hosts. He was soon out of sight. Joset and Misha went striding on together, swinging a wine bottle each, plunged, it appeared, in intimate conversation. Mâtho the Nose walked beside Catherine and managed to overcome his shyness.

"A-are you still a missionary? Mish said you've given it up. I ask because, you-you see my agency, I mean my father's newsagency, would like to c-cover the Church of Self.

We use material from the big handlers, usually, but w-would you like to record a piece for us, giving the Aleutian side of the story? O-or even a series of pieces, your own account."

"I don't work for the Mission anymore."

They emerged onto a broad boulevard where there were no projections. The twilight air was swimming in a violet haze. Ranks of buildings of every age in the city's long history stretched away toward a glimpse of moving water. Catherine was lost. The landmarks meant nothing to her: an ancient-looking road bridge, a four-peaked tower, a distant spiral monument reaching up between the rooftops. She had no idea where the four friends were leading her. There was no street lighting. Their footsteps rang in the dusky silence; secret glimmers darted from between the slats of window shutters, or from the depths of dark courtyards. The air smelled of quenched dust, orange peel, dogdirt . . .

"How empty the city is tonight. Where are all the people?"

Mâtho shrugged. "It's a Reformer neighborhood. I don't know their habits. But the city's strange. Sometimes there are people everywhere, sometimes they seem to vanish. Don't you find that?"

She was filled with a mysterious euphoria.

"I've been wondering what I should do with myself since I've finished with the Mission. I'd like to record for you. Would you be interested in some other topic?"

Mâtho instantly panicked. "Oh, but . . . You, I . . . A lady doesn't need an occupation. Not that I don't but . . . And we couldn't pay you. We can't afford to pay you." Overwhelmed, he was released by the return of the halfcaste, who had found a cab and was driving it up the middle of the road, whooping in triumph.

"You fool," roared Joset. "It's a four-seater, and there are five of us!"

After a long discussion, during which the semi-sentient vehicle kept trying to move off, the young humans decided to take turns in occupying the fourth seat. Finally, they set out at walking pace. Rajath got down from the driver's place as Mâtho climbed in the back and pranced along backward in front of the vehicle until Joset yelled that he was frightening the poor brute and endangering the lady. Then Rajath ran around to climb in at the back, and Misha jumped from the driver's place. Catherine insisted that she didn't want to ride in state—she wanted to take her turn— so she jumped out and Misha stepped back in . . . and so they continued, until they reached Joset's address.

Catherine was sorry the game had to end. An awkwardness seemed to descend when they were four in the cab: as if Misha's personality, when his Reformer foil wasn't there, was too much for the other two to handle. They arrived at a street that was completely dark, and the cab stopped again.

"This is where I live," announced Misha. "I'll call you another cab, Miss Catherine. This one won't take you to the giratoire: it's too late and too far. We'll let these wastrels have the brute. It stinks of that execrable dirtjuice concoction, anyway. You'd better come inside."

She knew that he had contrived to be alone with her. She'd chosen to accept the pretext: charmed and flattered, taken out of herself. As soon as they *were* alone together, she regretted it. Sattva wouldn't like this. Maitri's human friends would be scandalized! But Misha behaved with perfect propriety. They stood together in a large paneled lift, light from some hidden source glowing on polished wood, smiling and silent. He showed her into his apartment. The walls and floor and ceiling of the room they entered were one seamless illusion of dusky space, lit by dim stars above and twinkling city lights below. It was disconcerting, and the more so because she knew the real streets were dark.

"I'll call a cab. Excuse me if I don't introduce you to the folks. They keep early hours. Do sit down. "A knowing grin. "Or whatever's comfortable, Miss Alien."

There was nowhere particular to sit. Catherine went to the only uncamouflaged item in the room. It was a Vlab, an expensive top-of-the-range professional machine.

"Have you seen one of those before?" asked Misha casually. "It's a Virtual Laboratory. For industrial research, decorative art, games building, so on. A machine for three-dimensional virtual modeling. If you understand what that means."

"I've seen them," she told him, smiling slightly at his lordly air. "But I don't suppose you're doing industrial research. Are you an artist?"

"Of sorts."

"So am I!"

"Oh, yes, I think I knew that. What do you do?"

"I work in stills. Single frames: the things you call 'pictures' and we call 'poetry.'

"How interesting for you." Misha's tone dismissed her ladylike hobby. A vase of flowers had materialized, poised on illusory emptiness beside the lab. The vase was a chipped blue-glazed pottery mug that had lost its handle. The style of the flowers was familiar.

"You built the floral decorations for the meeting!"

"Yeah, they were mine." He grinned. "And I had to change the whole funxing thing at the last minute, because Mâtho said I'd mixed up the seasons, and he insisted—"

"*Mâtho* insisted?"

"Believe it. He may be timid with the ladies, but he's a demon for cultural correctness. But do we have to stand? The cab may not be here for a while."

Catherine's eyes, growing accustomed to the illusion as they might to darkness, made out the dimensions of a soft Aleutian-style couch flanked by pillowy low chairs. She chose one of the chairs, and settled herself warily. Misha flopped on the couch.

"Excuse me, this will seem an odd question, but have you been drinking today?"

"Drinking what?"

"Alcohol. You see, the testosterone supplement in the air in my rooms—I need it, to maintain my secondaries— might affect you if you were mixing it with alcohol. It can make a woman aroused, er, unexpectedly."

Catherine choked back laughter. He was gazing at her in apparently genuine concern.

"I don't think it will be a problem," she assured him.

"Did you notice I used native weeds, street flowers? I had rosebay, rayless mayweed, plantains, dandelions, buddleia. The survivors, bombsite colonizers. I thought that was a neat touch. But it was rough work; I wasn't proud of it. The stuff Mâtho threw out was much better. Now, this coral branch—"

The blue mug materialized again on an invisible table at her elbow. This time it held a single slender branch that was perfect in every detail, in every whorl and stipple of the coral red rind, the veins and stomata of each leaf, each flame-colored bud and blossom—

"That's *very* beautiful."

"But purely imaginary, so of course Mâtho hates it. Touch it."

She reached out, puzzled. Vlab models were exactingly accurate, code by code. But they were built of void-force signals, deadworld nothingness: they were images only. She felt the leaf, cool and waxy against her fingertips, and gasped in shock and delight.

"You're not an artist, you are a magician." She passed her hand through the illusion, fascinated. "It isn't there, but . . . I feel it! How do you *do* that?"

He shrugged deprecatingly. "Make things appear and

disappear? It's easy, in here. This is my controlled environ-
ment; I have the whole four-space mapped and clickable.
How did I make the vbranch fool your sense of touch?
Work. Sheer bit-by-bit grind. Have you ever used a lab?"

"I wouldn't know how to begin," said Catherine frankly.
"But this is so good! Where do you display? Is this your studio? Can people call up and televisit?"

He grimaced in distaste. "We don't do that. We only display in public. The street's our gallery. That's a problem
some of us have with Lalith. She's in favor of gun control."

"Gun control? You mean firearms?"

"No!" He stabbed a finger at her. "Zzzip! zzip! Bit zap-
pers."

"Oh, I see." She remembered the green arrows. "You
steal, er, borrow, grid space. Well, yes, I can understand
that. I can see that would be fun. But"—she touched the
cool unreality of the coral branch—"don't tell me you can
splice *this* into the pixels of one of those crude 3-D projections."

"Four-D."

"For what?"

"Four dimensions," explained Misha, sighing. "A three-
dimensional moving image moves, right? That involves
time, right? Four dimensions. A street projection fate map
is built of tetrals, not pixels. Like points with four-dimensional coordinates. Timelines. That's what we handle."

"All right, 4-D. But ignorant as I am about void-force
technology, at some level your coral branch has to use a
huge number of 'bits.' How can you plug it into a street
corner junction box? Surely, you'd crash the whole depart-
ment?"

Misha frowned. "I'm a rich boy," he told her, after a displeased silence. "I have everything. Even a prestigious job
for life, should my father ever retire. I do my art for myself
and for my friends. I don't care if no one else knows it exists."

So he hadn't tried to display the branch, and didn't think it could be done.

And where was that cab?

She had folded her legs under her, the dull violet robe she wore over her uniform lapped around her feet. Misha's smile returned. "You look comfortable: like a nice little cloud in my night sky. You're an Aleutian in a human body. What does that mean, exactly?"

"What it sounds like," she answered, somewhat defensively. "I was engineered—the same as you were, I suppose. The chemical code of an Aleutian proto-embryo was reconfigured into human bases and implanted into the womb of a human woman. I grew there; I was born."

"Weird. Did you know, I'm almost unique myself. You're looking at one of the world's last authentic white heterosexual males. Our ripped-up ozone layer got all the pure-bred fair-skinned races except for the Irish in Ireland, from whence the Connellys trace their proud descent. Yeah, I'm engineered. Everyone's engineered now. We've been conservative about it so far, but I anticipate an explosion of adaptive radiation soon. Human will diversify to fill the niches stripped out by mass extinction. It's classic." He propped himself on his elbows and peered at her, without offense but with great curiosity. "But you feel you are a genuine Aleutian?"

"Or I'm a genuine human, with Aleutian memories. What's the difference?"

"Can you read my mind?"

"No." She looked at him suspiciously. Misha Connelly was supposed to have had "an Aleutian education." "If you mean, can I 'read' what you are expressing, intentionally or otherwise, in what you call body language and we call the Common Tongue, I suppose the answer's yes. But those of us who've been here often have learned to filter. What you say in Silence has become subliminal information, the way it is for you among yourselves. Even humans know that spoken words are only part of a conversation." She grinned. "If you're planning to insult me in Silence in a way I can't ignore, you still have nothing to worry about. You're protected by the immemorial custom that says nothing expressed in the Common Tongue is evidence."

"They tried to teach me to 'speak Aleutian' for years. It didn't work, I couldn't hack it. I'm afraid we'll never be able to converse by twitching nostrils at each other. But what happens when you 'hear' what I 'say' in Silence? Do you really hear voices in your head?"

Catherine laughed. "Yes," she agreed. "My mind turns it into words. I hear voices. Most Signifiers do—and not only when the supposed speakers are present. But so do you, or one voice, at least. I think the interior life of an Aleutian Signifier is very like the interior monologue of human consciousness, the voice that *you* hear in your head constantly, and you can scarcely stifle if you try. With us that voice is modulated. All the possible selves of Aleutia talk to us, and we talk back to them. It's our way of experiencing social pressure, personal complexity, cultural assumptions, and so on."

"If you were human, people would say you were crazy."

"Whereas in Aleutia," said Catherine, with a wry shrug, "people say you're crazy if you *don't* listen to the voices." How intently Misha watched her! She tucked the robe around her feet, a gesture of defense, and spoke to disarm a Silence that was growing uncomfortable.

"In the Enclaves, in the more Aleutian-influenced cities, many humans "speak Aleutian" fluently. But the halfcastes used to be the experts. Do you remember Sidney Carton, Bella's 'native guide' in the hunt for the Buonarroti device? I met Sid a couple of times. I'm sure he could hear the voices of Aleutia. He didn't have a lot of time for me, but he could certainly make himself understood! But you've always kept your distance here on old-earth. You don't want to be like us. We rather like that. Why should you learn to 'speak Aleutian'? Enough of us can speak aloud. And you have your own kind of telepathy, your implanted machines. How did you call my cab?"

"Interesting you should mention Sid and Bella," remarked Misha, his eyes bright. "Bella was the reverse of your engineering, wasn't she. Human starter, made up into an Aleutian body. I think that was the only time it's been done, apart from your case. Am I right? The only true human-Aleutian hybrids. And her starter came from a sample of Johnny Guglioli's tissue, didn't it, or so the story goes. Which takes us right back to First Contact, the Rape, the Sabotage crisis. Isn't history fascinating?"

Johnny Guglioli was the name of the journalist who had met the Third Captain in West Africa when the landing parties were still trying to pass for human. They had become friends. But after the incident known grimly as the Rape, Johnny had joined the fanatical anti-Aleutian resistance group called White Queen. He and Braemar Wilson, the leader of group, had persuaded Peenemünde Buonarroti to let them use her secret invention to reach the shipworld out in orbit. They had meant to sabotage the main reactor, to blow the aliens out of existence. But they'd been discovered. In the diplomatic crisis that followed, the humans had been forced to make the concessions of land that would later form the basis of Aleutian rule on earth.

"Speaking of Johnny Guglioli," Misha went on, "didn't *he* hear the voices, without anyone teaching him how? He interviewed Clavel, Third Captain, when the aliens had only just arrived. I've seen that on record. But perhaps it was only possible because of their special relationship—"

Catherine stared at him wonderingly. "Strange things happened at First Contact," she said. "Things that have never been fully explained. You can't have seen the original record of the Africa interviews; it must have been a fake. That material was destroyed and never copied. But whatever you've seen, I think I can reliably inform you that

Johnny and Clavel did not understand one another. If Clavel had understood Johnny's feelings, there would have been no rape, and things would have been very different. Are you really interested in those old stories? What does it matter? The Aleutians are leaving."

Misha smiled again. "Please don't take this personally, but I don't think *you* understand. The Aleutians have been here for three hundred years. In all that time there are a bare handful of human names that *feature:* Johnny Guglioli, Braemar Wilson, Sidney Carton, Bella—if she counts as human. A few more. The stories of the humans who have made a difference are very important to the renaissance, to people who are trying to imagine a human future. You heard Lalith. We study the records. We re-member. We're trying to reassemble the parts."

He touched the coral branch, reminding her of the *human* skill that had built that beautiful work. She felt how bitterly he resented his position: a human artist in an Aleutian world. Misha was good, very good. But it was no use. Even when the aliens were gone, he would be left with this legacy of self-distrust: *nothing in the world belongs to me, everything I do someone else can do better, I can never be first.* As he teased her and goaded her with his sly references to the past, she heard the voice of his pain: *mon semblable, mon frère . . .*

Their eyes met: Misha's dark gold and Catherine's dramatic black on black.

"Johnny was executed out in orbit," he insisted softly, "for the crime of attempted genocide. The Buonarroti device vanished, and the Aleutians stayed because they didn't know how to get home. Johnny's tissue was used to make Bella. Bella—who was in some sense Johnny's daughter— came back to earth from the shipworld, and rediscovered the device. So now the Aleutians can go home, and here we are at the end of the story. An Aleutian and a human:

maybe, at last, able to meet as equals. Which Aleutian are you supposed to be, by the way? I know there's no such thing as an anonymous alien. You have to be *somebody*. Who are you? Or is it a secret?"

"You know who I am," she said, uneasily. "It's not a secret. I'm Catherine."

He frowned—

"I wonder where that cab is!" Catherine stood up.

"Oh, it's here. I didn't want to interrupt. We seemed to be getting on so well."

They went down together to the street door, through the dark floors filled by the lives of Connelly tenants. Catherine tucked herself into the pumpkin belly of her hired coach, and it carried her away.

Misha returned to his aerie and walked about with his hands behind his back, pausing often to turn and stare at the place where she had been sitting. *She* . . . His spine tingled; the hairs on his nape rose. He felt as if he'd been listening to the huge, awesome voice of an ancient demigod, speaking from that dainty little body. There she had sat in her aster-colored robe, saying: *yes, I knew Sidney Carton; I knew Bella.* She'd known them all, all the stars of the Aleutian-era screen.

"Oh, my, oh, my. Name of a name of a name! Worth the price of admission alone!"

He executed a neat step dance over the fake abyss, singing:

"*Oh, Paddy dear and did you hear, the news that's going
    'round
The shamrock is forbid by law to grow on Irish ground
It's the most distressful country that the world has ever
    seen
They are hanging men and women for the wearing of the
    green!*"

iv

IN THE ROOM below, Helen listened.

She stayed very still, relaxed in her long chair, until Catherine's cab had passed out of the courtyard; and not the faintest whisper of its passing through the empty streets could be caught by Helen's emissaries, the discreet and obedient servants she had seeded through the nerves of her father's house. Then she sat up a little and shook back the loose, lace-trimmed sleeve of her nightgown. She was looking at the skin-type dressing that covered her right wrist and forearm when Michael Connelly Sr. came into the room, dressed in simple overalls and a dark, sleeveless robe. He seemed disconcerted to find her in her night-clothes.

"Oh, you are ready for bed." He hesitated. "How is it?"

Helen smiled ruefully. "Not getting any better, Papa."

"Let me have a look."

He came heavily to her side, like a statue of Misha walking, and dropped on one knee. The medical cabinet was by her chair. He slicked quarantine film over his hands and the cuffs of his overalls, took her wrist and eased away the dressing. Together they looked down at the lesions on the soft inner skin. "Are there any new marks?"

"I don't know, Papa. This sounds strange, but I find it difficult to count them."

The camera in her father's eye took pictures and made measurements. His gaze, which appeared so intent, was purely mechanical. He knew nothing. He looked up. The examination he'd made was already far away, under expert attention.

"It's just a harmless little reaction; it will pass."

"Yes, Papa," she said. At her gentle aquiescence something stirred in the depth of his eyes, like Misha's eyes cast in bronze, but the flash of emotion quickly vanished.

"Well, we'll see what the doctors have to say."

"Do you know what a black hole is, Papa?"

He shook his head, again absorbed in turning the slim wrist from side to side, taking more pictures. "Some nonsense you've picked up?"

"A black hole is a place where a star has died. It's what happens when the death of a star turns malignant, so that ceasing to exist becomes an active force. It draws everything around it into itself. All of space, and time, and being is dragged through the same dark gate. Some people think a black hole actually destroys the fabric of reality. Isn't that extraordinary?"

"What nonsense."

"Stars are made of the same elements as human beings. Did you know that?"

Her father's tone became less indulgent. "Don't think about such things: it's morbid. I shouldn't let you use the free network, it's a midden of useless information; it's not just ridiculous, it's harmful."

At that threat she said nothing. But she became very still, and the chill that pervaded her small white face seemed to leach all the color and warmth and softness from this large, luxurious room. He replaced the dressing with practiced neatness and patted her hand. "Oh, don't look so sad. I won't take your connection away. But you should vary your amusements. Why don't you work on your project again? You haven't touched your lab for days. I notice these things you know. You need something pleasant to occupy your mind. Soon you'll feel better, and I'll take you out for a drive. Or you may have a friend to visit—one of the inner circle, you know, not a stranger."

Helen had not left this room, or seen anyone but her father, since she'd returned home exhausted from that visit to Lord Maitri's "at home."

"I think I won't see anyone, or go out again. I get so tired, it frightens me."

"Don't talk nonsense," said the man of stone and bronze. "You'll soon be well."

"I don't want to let you down," she whispered.

He selected a powerful painkiller, and applied it to the big vein inside her elbow. "We'll go home. You'll be more comfortable away from the city."

"I'm sleepy now, Papa."

"Yes. Well, I'll leave you." He leaned and placed a dry kiss on her cheek.

When she was alone, Helen lay for a while with her eyes closed. She could feed constructed images of this room to his agents. She used to do that routinely when she had her freedom, when she and Misha were allowed to be together. Since she had become almost a prisoner, she'd been surprised at how little she felt the need for covert defiance. She could be private enough in the darkness behind her eyelids. Papa monitored everything, or imagined he did, but he didn't invade her mind. She thought he'd always been afraid of what he might find there.

She stood up slowly—how heavy they were to carry, those small dark marks—and went to her workstation. Her Vlab was older than Misha's, and showed clear signs of its industrial origins, but it suited Helen. She knew its ways. She recalled from its secret limbo the project that her father had mentioned. (The secrecy was habit; it had never been necessary. Her father had never shown the slightest interest in the virtual art he considered such a suitable pastime for his daughter.)

How long?

She touched her unblemished forearm and the lace at her throat, where she had begun to feel the spots of tingling numbness that were the precursors of the lesions. The reaction would pass, Papa said. It would do her no harm. And if it did pass . . . what then?

She put the thought aside. Papa was right; she must get back to work. It's the experience of each moment that matters. And she smiled, involuntarily: the joy of the work flooding through her, filling every reflection of Helen's self, past present and to come. There were effects that she had struggled for, and now was sure she could achieve. What artist could ask for more? What was it the old man said? Instantaneity, the same light everywhere . . .

But the interview with Catherine was already in her mailbox. She converted it to tincture and waited a few moments. The bubblepack emerged. She leaned back, trickled the drops into her eyes, and settled to watch Misha's rushes.

It was quickly obvious that her brother's obdurate refusal to come to grips with the Common Tongue was going to be a complication . . . But that was all right. Helen would be directing him, and there was nothing wrong with keeping Miss Alien-in-disguise off balance. She would not let herself feel hurt that Misha had found a replacement for his sister. It was necessary for the plot. She watched, frame by frame, immersed in the game that she had devised: a sick child, bored and lonely, deploying her toy armies across the counterpane.

3

THE PHOENIX CAFÉ

i

THERE WERE FOUR fatal casualties of the police action at the renaissance meeting: a small figure, but embarrassing. Bhairava killed himself the next day as an apology for his misjudgment. The Aleutians knew this was a deliberate snub to the Expedition Management, but Bhairava had planned his escape well. Sattva, though he fumed, couldn't call it suicide. The house at the giratoire was plunged into mourning. Maitri spent hours in the character shrine communing with his dear friend and sometimes lover; and everyone in the household felt the loss.

Catherine didn't try to contact Misha. She waited, helpless as a proper Traditional young lady, passive as Thérèse Khan in her high-walled orchard, to see what would happen next. She spent a lot of time in her room, alone. Since she'd seen Misha Connelly's flowers, she had felt—or imagined she'd felt—something stirring in the part of herself that had been empty, dry, and broken for so long.

She woke one day, mid-morning, from a drowse of half-formed ideas to find that someone was at her doorway. It was Misha. He was dressed as before, in a loose light coat over local-grown overalls. This time the coat was dark blue and the dun suit under it had a fine blue pattern moving in the fabric. He seemed nonplussed by the membrane, scarcely more than a foggy thickening of the air, that stood in place of an old-earth style solid barrier. Of course, these days humans rarely visited Aleutian private rooms.

"Just walk through it," she told him. "It won't hurt you."

"I did call," he said, looking around him with interest. "This morning, Lord Maitri said you'd like to see me. One of the secretaries—Vijaya?—had me brought up here."

Catherine had been getting Maitri to take all her calls since she came back to the giratoire. She was afraid of the Church of Self. She hated the idea of having the virtual ghost of that halfcaste deacon appear in her own room. Misha stepped over his commensal escort, which was weaving around his ankles hoping to be petted. He stared frankly at the cluttered array of devotional pictures and movie loops that covered her walls.

"I would have called before, but I was uncertain of my welcome after the massacre," he declared grandly.

Catherine held out her arms. The little servant jumped into her lap, nuzzled her throat, and clambered over her shoulder to get at the wall. It started to nibble at a new crack in the plaster. Its default purpose in life was to keep things looking nice and decayed.

"Why should that have made you unwelcome? It wasn't your people's fault."

"I wonder why the police chief killed himself, over something so minor."

"Bhairava doesn't believe in permanent death," said Catherine quietly. "It's beyond his imagination. He wanted an excuse to leave earth, but he wouldn't have *killed* anyone." She was crouched on her bed, in a pose that she realized was too Aleutian. She rearranged herself. "At least it's ended the quarrel between him and Maitri. That's one good thing."

Misha glanced at his goddess, sidelong. How strange they were about death! He couldn't believe he'd been al-

lowed into her bedroom. He was still wondering if Lord
Maitri was about to leap from a closet, outraged at this invasion of his ward's modesty. Out of bravado he took down
a slim volume and began to leaf through it: *The Life of a
Soul.*

Her heroic virtue was exercised in such ordinary ways
that it was not easily recognizable . . . Likening her life to a
glass of medicine, beautiful to behold but bitter to taste,
she went on to say that this bitterness had not made her life
sad because she had learned to find joy and sweetness in
bitter things. "It has come to this," she said, "that I can no
longer suffer, because all suffering is sweet."

He laughed.

"What is it?"

"I was thinking of our own Little Flower. You've met
Thérèse Khan, haven't you?" He was gratified at her surprise. "We all know each other. It's almost Aleutian, the
way we know each other. Youro is huge, but the inner circle is tiny."

He inspected the litter of curiosities on the table under
her bookshelf: oil pastels, pencils and paper, styli for
graphic screens that had been obsolete before the aliens arrived, an Aleutian sketchpad, a quill pen (never cut), a
Japanese inkstone in a lacquered case, a glass Virgin full of
sand, a bird's nest (beautifully re-created by some Aleutian
artisan) containing three ovoid pebbles of blue, white, and
marbled-gray. A model airplane, hologram holy pictures, a
scatter of unset semiprecious stones, a Hand of Fatima cut
from ancient printed circuit-wafer, its complexity blended
into a pearly moiré, rigid amber silk.

"Is this your souvenir collection? It's rather disappoint-
ing. After three hundred years of looting, I'd have expected
more of a haul."

"I wasn't around for the whole three hundred years.
Anyway, I keep the real stuff in my bank vault." She saw

that he believed this and laughed. "No! I got rid of my hoard of treasure. It embarrassed me."

He was looking at a precontact canvas, propped unframed on an easel against the wall. The scene was a nativity. The symbolic birth was set among ruins, a favorite theme of the original Youro Renaissance. Renewal was held in the disintegrating womb of the past, the sacred child surrounded by a chaos of broken columns, refractory camels, investigative journalists, toppling palm trees, mad astrologers.

"I like this. Who's it by?"

"Someone called Leonardo da Vinci."

"Is that so? It's a copy, I suppose." He touched the picture: it was solid.

"It's an original, so far as I know." She shrugged and smiled. "It's loot; you're quite right. I gave away the rest. But I'm weak and greedy, and I couldn't part with the Leonardo."

"My, my. Leonardo da Vinci. And you don't know if it's real. You should let me find out for you, I can do that." He whipped a small machine from his pocket. "Nothing invasive, a photochemical scan—" The thing had done whatever it did before she had a chance to protest, or to explain that the picture's provenance was actually impeccable. Irony, she decided, had best be avoided.

"I'll let you know." He put the gadget away. "But I came to ask you out. I thought I could show you some sites, places you probably haven't seen. We could eat old-earth style. We might eventually meet those brutes who were with me at the meeting, but I'll protect you from their coarse humor. In short, I'm offering to be your native guide. Lord Maitri approves." He beamed at her, ingenuous, eager. "Do you accept?"

He went to wait for her in the atrium. Catherine put on a robe, the same smoky violet she'd worn to the renaissance meeting (it was a sturdy garment, meant to last a season), and some shoes. He had a demicab waiting at the front of the house, "demi," meaning there were two separate soft compartments. Catherine rode behind, peering through the thick, flawed gel of the windows, where the effluvium of the city air was constantly gathering, constantly being dismantled and dispersed. It was like looking through moss agate.

"Do you know the *quartier* well?" demanded Misha, from the front seat.

She knew the premises of the Church of Self. Her congregation's cramped, sweaty rooms, an estate of packed tenements, a police station, Maitri's house. "I don't know it at all."

"I'll take you to the Car Park."

He stopped the cab between the giratoire and the neighboring commercial area. The pavements were full of people, the roadway full of bicycles, cabs, and buses, the occasional private car. In the distance a lumbering aircraft crawled above the rooftops, delivering bulky goods or carrying humble passengers to some other part of Youro. Shopfront plate glass, that had never reappeared after the War, had been replaced by sheets of a hybrid membrane that ate dirt and turned it into color. The shops themselves were living space. Bodies swam, and faces looked out through cat's-eye, garnet, carnelian, ruby. Humans living as they imagined Aleutians lived—in public, without walls.

"A lot of people hate the bit-grid city," declared Misha. "They want to strip it out. That's the way Lalith feels. So does my father, an embarrassing ally for her, I would have thought. Agreed, the grid is appallingly badly managed. There's a lot of dross, staggering quantities of obsolete public information, and who buys these products? We live like Aleutians these days. We're peasants. We feed and clothe and furnish our own feudal households. We only *buy* commissioned works like my Vlab, luxury items. We stick our surplus production in a *vente directe* booth, and gain little more than status when it empties. Most of the products you see advertised don't exist. Did you know that? Try to get hold of any of those multifarious brands of soap and socks, you'll soon find out. Ads are imaginary, fossilized ephemera. It's a pathetic survival. But we want it to stay because it's our raw material, our creative medium."

He stopped, hands in his overall pockets, the blue coat pushed back from his hips in artful disarray. The crowd parted around them. "This is one of my favorite sites. We call this *eaufort*, etching. I don't know who did it; a lot of grid art is anonymous."

The "site" was an area of smart surface that had been rented out to many different customers, successively and simultaneously. Nothing had ever been completely erased, nothing predominated. The moving images standing in the air ran into each other, layered like sheets of living cells, incomprehensible but full of information: a cruel experience for the visual cortex. Briefly, fortuitous coherence rose up and vanished: a human eye, a moving wheel, a huge shape that looked like a grieving skull.

"In *eaufort* the art is in the data. You don't put it there; you find it there. Like Michelangelo Buonarroti— maybe you've heard of him?—freeing human bodies from marble."

"Thank the Self they're not allowed sound track," said Catherine ruefully.

Michael stepped into the site's footprint and tipped his head back, taking the pounding waterfall of the unreal full in his face. "Have you never been anywhere that's licensed for sound? It's *much* worse than this. But an experience you mustn't miss."

He led her on. "Why do you walk?" asked Catherine. "It means something to you renaissance people, doesn't it? I noticed that the other night. You and your friends ordered a cab for my sake. But you made a joke of it; you didn't want to use it."

Misha halted. "Are you tired?"

"No!"

"Good," He strode on. "The cabs are alive."

"But they're not Aleutian! Most transports are bred and grown entirely by humans—"

"They have hybrid genes. But that's not the point. We don't agree with Lalith. We don't want to develop life sciences. In our view that's not what the renaissance is about. I use my Vlab to make illusions; I don't build 'real' synthetic biologies because Aleutians do that stuff better. We believe in human tech, void forces, and machines. Have you come across the expression: *'Animals have life: machines have soul?'* "

"Er . . . no."

"It was the motif of the *eaufort* I just showed you. Never mind."

"You don't like living technology. Therefore you walk. On your biological legs."

He grinned. "So laugh. You are the lords of life. Your superiority is inescapable. Maybe anything we do to recover our separate identity has to be absurd. We don't care."

He seemed to have forgotten about the Car Park. He had the air of a careless flaneur, wandering at whim. But Catherine detected a growing, almost painful anxiety. It crossed her mind that this might, after all, be a stage in a terrorist plot: an abduction attempt. They reached a large, complex junction. The ancient buildings around it were naked of projections. Probably, they were famous and under a preservation order. They looked skinned and dejected. But the cowl of a maglev station in the center of the *place* was awash with moving color.

"You don't know how to use the lev. That's one of the

things I'll show you. However, you mustn't use it alone."
People were pouring in and out of the arched entrance.
Cabs and minibuses nosed each other outside. Misha
started walking around the cowl. "Young ladies don't, nor
do ordinary females if they can help it. Even dressed as
you are, you'd have trouble, and a chador only makes it
worse. Don't risk it."

He stopped in the viewpoint of a projection. It was a
single-layered cheap image: low rez and detail poor. A
woman, a giant Traditionalist woman with dark hair and
pale skin, stood on a seashore. Her hair fell in chunky
masses over her white draperies. Waves crashed white at
her feet as she went through her classic, touching routine:
buy this and be beautiful like me. She should have been holding some kind of skin bleach or exfoliant.

"Oh, thank you, Lord," breathed Misha, quietly exultant.
"Thank you, Jesus! Whooee!"

The coral branch was lying in the woman's blank white
palm: glowing, extraordinary, an intrusion from a different
order of creation. Misha touched Catherine's arm, shifting
her position slightly. A voice murmured, from nowhere, "a
branch of coral flame."

"Congratulations!" She was genuinely thrilled. "You did
it! What's the response?"

He affected unconcern, while continuing to gaze at his
work in adoration. "It's getting some notice. I don't keep
track." He would clearly have been happy to stand there all
day, but managed to remember his responsibility as a
guide.

He sighed. "Good, we can eat now. You must be starving.
The Car Park isn't far."

They passed into one of the neighborhood's small
stretches of cropland: bean fields in indigo leaf and flower
that gave off a haze of sweet scent. It was cooler at once.
The Aleutians were used to the helplessness of their own

elite. They had been unable to tolerate the idea of ordinary people who could not feed themselves. Every inhabitant of an Aleutian city had to have a piece of earth, besides the larger areas of food plant that were threaded through the urban ecology. In some wards the plots were subdivided into scraps the size of window boxes, but often there was a farming cooperative like this one. The city rose up on every horizon, curled and crooked and indefinitely various. A massive block stood ahead, where their unpaved track reentered the streets—swathes of undecorated concrete coming and going in the blur of its complex, colored aura.

"The Car Park," announced Misha. "I know you'll love this."

It was a food market, spread over several floors of huge, dank, low-ceilinged halls that were connected by massive poured-stone ramps and stairways. Every floor was teeming with booths, counters, and lunching citizens. Almost every franchise offered dishes as ancient as those Leonie re-created. It was a giant *vente directe* fair, and a vision of old-earth.

"What'll it be?" asked Misha, smug with success. *"Potage bonne femme?* A little lobster bisque? No, I'm joking. What about a pizza? Let's cruise. Let's see what's new."

So they cruised, collecting snow-pea lasagna with insect protein from one stall—"You're not a vegetarian are you?" asked Misha—a rice dish with starfruit; beanbread, a confection called carracara flan, with carrots, caramel, and tofu sauce . . . ionized ground water and a flask of rose sherbert. The customers were as various as humanity. Many of them were wearing machine-woven, cut and sewn fabric, not as a revolutionary gesture but because they knew nothing else. Misha chaffed with the stallholders, in person and virtual. Balancing cartons, Catherine looked for somewhere to sit down. The tables, packed with enthusiastic lunchers, were as charming as the food.

"Sorry. We don't eat in. The food is shareware when it's

new to the menu—that's a Car Park tradition. It gets a price when it's hooked the customers. But if you sit down, you pay."

He led her outside, and they found a spot among other frugal patrons on the steps of a fine modern pantheist temple, splendidly decorated with scenes from the lives of Saints Rama, Guru Nanak, Louis, and Genevieve. It was hosting a rousing midday service.

"I've never been *convinced* by starfruit," remarked Misha. "It's an interesting idea, but too clever. I don't know who first did them; they've been around forever."

"God, I believe."

"Really? I never knew that."

There seemed to be a vogue for black-and-white movie clips in savory packaging. The caramel flan came in plain industrial red and brown. Catherine tore up her rice bowl and ate it. Tiny invasive messages were crawling through Lauren Bacall's sleek coiffure. Humphrey Bogart exhaled twenty-fourth-century graffiti. She chewed flyposting, high art, and vandalism in digestible cellulose. Few other lunchers, she noticed, observed this virtuous ritual.

"When we arrived, to *drop litter* was a gesture of alienation and despair. At least that's changed. All litter is compost! Why is it so important not to pay? You're rich, aren't you."

"I don't carry cash. But that's not the reason. You see, the nitrogen-fixing grub-mulch we just visited is an experiment. I like that aspect. I like being ahead of the game."

"Ah, I see. It used to be called ligging."

"Hmm?"

" 'Ligging.' The word for freeloading as a fashion statement, when we first arrived. We were terrific liggers. We never paid for a thing, once we understood the rules. Bother, I ate my spoon. One can take instant recycling too far. . . . Oh, it's all right, this'll do." She unearthed someone else's discarded fork from the drift of debris at their feet, licked it, and began to dig into her flan. Misha watched, slightly horrified.

"Maybe you really are an Aleutian."

"What? It won't hurt me. I have very tough bugs in my gut: same as you. And I *am* an Aleutian, no matter what you think about my chemical provenance. Remember what Sidney Carton said? 'Race is bullshit, culture is everything.' "

"What amazes me," said Misha, grimacing at the clip on his lasagne box, "is the way everyone's so well fed. We're not as heavily upholstered as the folk in the old movies. But ordinary people can still pack out a place like the Car Park, where extra food is sold for fun. And yet they tell us Youro is starving to death. Have you had enough, by the way? Or shall I root you out some moldering bus tickets?"

"Thank you, I'm fine. Don't you believe that Youro is starving?"

"I think things are tight just now. But can you imagine, we once expected to have a population of twenty billion on this planet? God knows how we could have fed them. It's just as well the organochlorines got to us, not to mention that inspired invention, the AIDS vaccine that made women allergic to being pregnant. There simply isn't room. What with the war damage and the climate change. Did you know, in the last three hundred years we've lost more than half our agricultural land, worldwide?"

Some people blamed the aliens for the devastating Gender War, which had broken out only after they arrived. Aleutians were certainly responsible for the climate-improvement projects that had done maybe even worse damage . . . There was a deliberate sting in Misha's supposedly neutral remarks. Catherine looked at her feet and listened to the singing from the temple, wondering if it was possible for any Aleutian, even an Aleutian in disguise, to be real friends with a human. Must there always be this resentment, this point scoring?

N'ayons pas de peur de vivre au monde
Dieu nous a devancés!
N'ayons pas peur de vivre au monde
où Dieu même s'est risqué . . .

"I'm sorry," said Misha, insincerely contrite. "I didn't mean anything personal." He stood up. "Now I'm going to take you on the lev."

"When we arrived—" began Catherine.

"You're going to have to stop that," he remarked dispassionately. "The 'when we arrived' line. It could get to be a bad habit. Don't be offended, I'm trying to help."

N'arrêtons pas la sève ardente
Dieu nous a devancés
N'arrêtons pas la sève ardente
qui tourmente l'univers—

He set off, his coat skirts swirling. He didn't get far. A machine on tracks, a boxy thing about knee high, came rushing toward them and began to circle him, yelping.

"Barcode! Barcode!"

"Funx off, you stupid little brute. I'm not stealing anything!"

"Barcode! Barcode! Barcode!"

It was the returnable bottle, a rather pretty pink glass flask, that had contained their rose sherbert. Misha had inadvertently tucked it into his coat pocket. It was too late to hand it over to the reader. They were forced to slink back into the Car Park, yelped there all the way, and Misha had to raise his family credit line to pay for it.

"You wouldn't believe how many people try to walk off with these," commented the stallholder happily. "We must be on to a good thing."

"I wasn't—" Misha's delicate skin flushed furious crimson.

The entrepreneur, a Reformer in faded overalls, leered cheerfully. "Naturally! It was an oversight; that's understood. Thank you, Mr. Connelly Jr. That will do nicely."

Again they walked. Misha recovered his temper. They talked a great deal, in the version of English (*Youro*, never Europe) that was still a global contact language—thanks to the patronage of the aliens, who had adopted it for their official communications long ago. Misha was bilingual in French, but knew no other national languages. He wanted to know how it felt to be a Signifier, automatic linguist. She couldn't tell him: "I'm not a neurologist!" she protested. "I just do it." They talked of the ancient sects and cults of Youro, stronger now than they had been precontact. Meanwhile the Church of Self, successful in the Enclaves, made few inroads. Perhaps they don't kill their converts in the tropical zone? suggested Misha. And of the entertainment industry: more and yet more gruesome tele-visual-cortical spectacles (gladitorials, bull dancing, duels between humans and wild beasts, duels between humans and robot killing machines) where the audience hooked up and shared the violent experience of the performers. Virtuality gaming hells, tvc's main competition, still packed the public in. But the games had become "degraded pap," said Misha. Crude imitation worlds to keep the poor quiet.

A telepresence package tour to Mars was cheaper to provide than a decent meal, he explained. Did Catherine realize that the whole space program (for the planet, not just Youro) was run on the profits of teletourism? So that the only actual humans who went to Mars and the Moon were the ones who made the virtual masters—essentially, B-movie actors. Which was a splendid joke, if you happened to be a student of cultural history.

Yes, she did know that. The Aleutians starved the Mars and Moon projects of funding. They couldn't see the point in epic discomfort.

"I hate the hells, but I *love* tvc," he declared. "Don't you?

Even the everlasting repeats. I don't care! How many times have *you* jumped from Angel Falls?"

Catherine admitted to eleven. She'd been a tvc addict before she joined the Mission. At last he took her into a lev station. They traveled first-class. Misha apparently didn't mind using his family credit when he only had to transact with a machine. Don't do this alone, he repeated. Only with a male escort. Now she was sleepy, and the shareware food sat heavily and queasily on her stomach.

When they emerged, she had the same feeling that she'd had when she stepped from the closed car into Thérèse's orchard. She didn't know where she was. The color coding of the minitel boards told her she was still in their *quartier*, but she was too tired to read the text. The sky had turned a darker blue, and was pricked by false stars. She'd been told that the real stars were invisible even way out in the parks or food plant. The city's atmosphere hid them. It was curfew hour; the projections had closed down. They were in an old ward of indeterminate character: neither rich nor poor, not halfcaste, Reformer, or Traditionalist. They descended, between tall old buildings, a long serene prospect toward gleaming water, and crossed an ancient bridge set with globe lights that were reflected, shimmering, up and down the dark stream.

Neither of them had spoken since they left the station. It was the quiet of two comrades coming back to the lights of home after a day's tramp in the wilderness. She felt again the mysterious euphoria of the evening when she had first met Misha and his friends. The true city, the old city, not the great Youro sprawl, lay beautiful and still. An owl hooted. A delta plane of feathers, gilded in the dusk, dropped silently. The bird rose, carrying a young rat in her claws.

"Hunting," said Misha. "That's something else we'll do. I'll take you hunting."

Not far from the river, they turned a corner, and there were tables on the pavement under the branches of a huge sycamore tree. There were colored lamps, people were talking. Three shallow steps led to a veranda, where a dark-skinned Reformer wearing a low-brimmed hat over her eyes looked up as they passed. She nodded to Misha and his companion, and looked away with an odd, rueful smile.

Inside the Café there was a wide floor of bare, softly shining wooden boards. There were more tables, most of them occupied. Some middle-aged and elderly people were placidly absorbed in their evening meals, but the majority of the clientele seemed to be young. She had a sense of shared laughter and glances. She noticed several obvious halfcastes in the company, always a sign of general tolerance and good will. There was music in the air. She heard the whisper of leaves, the sigh of distant traffic, an occasional clear word of conversation—all sampled, mixed down, blended, and woven into *musique naturelle*—the sound that was born in canvas shacks and dirt-floored shebeens in West Africa, and took the world by storm the year the aliens arrived. Catherine stood transfixed. Tears of nostalgia stung her eyes.

"I knew you'd like it," said Misha complacently. "Welcome to—"

"Miss Catherine?"

The dark-skinned Reformer woman had come in from the veranda. She was holding out her hands. "Agathe Uwilingiyimana. We've met, but I'm sure you don't remember. I know you've met my brother. I won't make you say Uwilingiyimana even once. Agathe will do. We're glad to see you. Misha promised us he would bring you. Welcome to the Phoenix."

Catherine gripped her hands, and said inadequate things. "Oh, yes, Joset. Yes, Agathe, at my guardian's house, I do remember. Hello."

Someone shouted: "Mish! Over here!"

She saw Rajath jumping up from a chair and waving. There were Joset, Rajath, Mâtho, and a handful of other young people, at a long table. She and Misha went to join them. She was bewildered and pleased at the warmth of their reception. But she could still feel the pressure of the Reformer councillor's handclasp. She hoped she had not become a prize of intercommunal warfare. She was glad to see that there were other obvious Reformers, beside Joset, in the group she had joined.

"Do you like your wine simple or complicated?" asked Joset, proffering bottles.

"Huh?"

"Just the grape, the pure esoteric grape. Or something chemically improved?"

"I'll take the plain grape," she decided cautiously, thinking of orange peel and dogdirt.

"And what will you eat?"

She hesitated. She was still suffering from the lasagna.

"But you m-must break bread with us," insisted Mâtho. "It-it's very significant."

"Give her bread, let her break it. You don't have to eat it, miss,"

"They don't like our 'hard food,' " someone explained importantly to a neighbor. "They live on lukewarm soup."

"Break it over Mâtho's head!"

Food was ordered, after an intense discussion in which Catherine was not expected to take part. She was assailed by fearless, excited questions.

"What does it mean to be 'an alien in a human body?' "

"Is Lord Maitri your biological father? Did he have you made-up or cloned?"

"Are you a single malt like Mish, or are you a blend?"

Misha aimed a thump at the speaker, a bird-boned half-caste, presenting herself as feminine, with slick black cropped hair and enormous eyes.

"Excuse them! They've never been this close to an alien in the real. This is Lois Lane. She's a bull dancer and she adores you."

"It's COWS funx it, dickface. And I'm NOT called Lois Lane. My name is Lydia."

To Catherine's astonishment the halfcaste leapt onto the table and aimed a flying kick that sent Michael's black beret spinning like a Frisbee across the room. She made a neat dismount, into the empty chair beside Catherine.

"I admire you, that's true. I think it's so *casual* to have yourself translated into another species. Just what I'd do if I was rich. What's the point in being normal if you're rich? You don't know me, but I admire you. Maybe we can be friends."

The two people opposite Catherine were shrouded in the full chador, but one of them seemed familiar. "Do I know you?" she asked.

The first veiled figure stripped off her hood, revealing the blonde hair and long, tip-tilted green eyes of Thérèse Khan. She was still wearing butterfly makeup, in a fresh design.

"It's me," she admitted, grinning. "Yes, I'm here in person. I'm not completely a prisoner—or an idiot. This is my brother, Imran." She gestured toward a smoldering, hawk-faced young male. "And this is my maid, Binte, my chaperone." Thérèse ripped open her servant's veil, uncovering a round, placid brown face as glossy as polished wood. "I call them all Binte," she added. "She's my bodyguard, my private policeman. Be careful what you say. She's very aggressive, and awfully strong." She laughed at Catherine's expression. "No, I don't mean that. Say what you like, she's not *human*. She's a surveillance camera. She's only capable of noticing certain things."

"Like what?"

Binte smiled and nodded.

Thérèse giggled. "Shop lifting!"

The food arrived, along with Misha's hat. They had settled on garlic soup, a little roast chicken (it was a *very* little roast chicken, it looked more like a roast hamster), *mamaliga* and sour cream.

"We have our own kitchens," the waiter told her proudly, returning Misha's beret with a flourish. He was a masculine Reformer, but differently "masculine" from Joset. "In the pre-Aleutian style. You must see them. We're a cooperative; everyone does everything. We're part of a chain; we have branches in every city, two or three in many *quartiers.* Would you like to learn to cook?" He held out his hands. "Welcome to the renaissance, Miss Catherine."

"What a splendid logo," she said. "The Phoenix. The mythical bird that remakes itself, that dies in a nest of flames and is reborn from its own ashes—"

The waiter laughed. "Actually, it's the name of the person who opened the first café. He's called River Phoenix; he's a halfcaste. Reincarnation of a great precontact recording star. Maybe you met him in a past life?"

"No," said Catherine. "I never did. But I love *My Own Private Idaho.*"

"Never seen it. Nor has River, but it inspired him to be a cook. A whole movie about love and sex and potatoes. We knew about the extinct birds too, of course. Hey, I don't suppose you remember what they really looked like?"

"*Mamaliga* is only cornbread." Mâtho leaned down the table, mortified by this poor scholarship and trying to distract her attention. "You can m-make it very soft with some more sour cream. D-don't try the meat; it's very hard to digest."

"Could I buy us some wine?" Catherine offered. "If I can use Maitri's credit here." She raised delighted laughter by adding: "That is, if it's not *uncool* to pay for things?"

She ate, to the admiration of all, and found the food excellent. She heard as many definitions of *the renaissance* as there were eager faces around the table, and joined a discussion about the metaphysical significance of *couture.*

They wore "native costume," they told her, because like the renaissance itself it could not be grown. It must be woven, cut, and sewn, by hand or by machine. It must be *separated from the world*. That was the essence of human art and craft. It must be defined, delimited, distilled, detached, unreal!

Misha, seeing his protégé safely launched, leaned back in his chair to consult privately with Joset. They had both been wired for years, and were accustomed to commune with each other like this, whether in the same room or apart: a secret cabal in the midst of any crowd. <*I believe we've caught a live one, good buddy. I had an unexpected stroke of luck today at his lordship's residence. Some primary documentary evidence.*>

<*So? Show a brother what you've got, white boy.*>

<*This.*> He showed Joset, transfering the image from his cortical screen to his friend's. <*This is a picture by Leonardo da Vinci, a study for a major work that was destroyed in the War. It's known to have been in alien possession for a long time. The registered owner is a particular alien we know well. Kevala the Pure, poet and philanthropist, aka "Clavel," the Third Captain. The one who shafted Johnny Guglioli, thus precipitating the Sabotage Crisis and the Landing Party Treaty. The one who, in her next life, tried to get a new "Johnny" made up for herself, cloned and translated from a Johnny Guglioli tissue sample. You'll remember it didn't work, but the resulting fiasco became "Bella the librarian," who found the Buonarroti device. Whereupon Clavel tried it out, proved the feasiblity of the Departure Project, and convinced the Aleutians to steal the invention and develop it for themselves. Thus, to sum up, we have here the alien of all aliens that we want to assist us with our inquiries.*>

Joset: <*Lee O'Nardo? Who he? Don't expect me impressed over some paint-and-canvas paddy geek gender warrior. What is this tourist-tat rubbish? Look at this, it isn't even finished—*>

Misha: <*Trust me, Jo. The thing is worth several million lakhs of rupees, if it's the original, and it is sitting in Miss Catherine's boudoir. You know the way they work. Serial immortality. A baby*>

gets born, the Priests of Self establish a chemical identity by studying the baby's genetic material, alien version. Then and only then, they have assigned to them the possessions and rights, or lack thereof, belonging to their serial self. She says it's hers. If it's the real thing, that means she has to be Kevala the Pure. You know, they took names in Sanskrit when they first arrived because they thought it was our worldwide sacred language. They still do it. It doesn't mean much now, but originally they chose handles that identified the Aleutian person by some salient quality. Guess what "Catherine" means, in this city's reckoning, Mr. Yaweh-Increases? They translated our friend's alien DNA-analogue into human code, and it came out looking pretty much like a girl. She translated her name, and it came out Catherine. Are you convinced? Yours ever, Who Is Like unto God!>

Joset (reads through Misha's long transfers again):<*Does she know you're onto her secret identity?*>

Misha: <*Not sure. If she's thinking like an Aleutian, she assumes everyone knows. If she's thinking like a human Kevala, she feels guilty as hell over Clavel's misdeeds, and she's hoping she can put the past behind her.*>

Joset: <*Not convinced, but go to stage two.*>

Misha: <*Stage two begins now.*>

Joset: <*Wait a minute. What were you DOING in her boudoir???*>

Misha: <*Heheheheh. Logging off.*>

Misha closed the screen that had unfolded before his inner eye: no more strange than a train of verbal thought, no more distracting than a daydream. *No, it is not magic,* he thought, smug as an Aleutian. Though it's true I have constant access to the common mind of humanity in the great library of data storage. I could even, if I was a policeman or a Peeping Tom, know a lot about what my friend was actually *thinking,* not merely what he wants to tell me. But please, it's not supernatural. You wouldn't understand, Miss Alien. It's to do with these *entities,* not even real things, too small to be alive, called electrons, photons, muons, quarks, that float in the human air and join us all in one commonalty of un-life. He raised his eyes, slowly panning across the tables. Slowly smiled. *We're on our way,* he thought. *Stage two. I wonder how she'll like stage three.*

Catherine was thinking that she knew why she had been forced to eat shareware. Misha hated to be reminded that he was a copy of his father, which happened every time he raised a credit line as Michael Connelly Jr. She would get Leonie to give her some cash, and ask someone less prickly to come to the Car Park with her, so that she could really eat *potage bonne femme,* or *moules frites* or something, instead of maggot pasta.

She called to Mâtho: "Those news articles you wanted. Could we talk about it?"

She caught Misha's eye, and sent him a warm and grateful smile.

"How will you settle, ladies and gentlemen?"

Their waiter had returned, the Café was emptying; the evening was over. Catherine tried to offer her palm to his debit machine, but she was shouted down. "Tonight you're our guest!" they cried. "Don't be so keen, rich lady! We'll surely be sponging off you soon!"

"Let Mish pay!" roared Joset. "Let's humiliate the style-victim!"

ii

SOON AFTER HER introduction to the Phoenix Café, Catherine realized that she had to go back to the poor ward. She felt that she had become sane after a spasm of madness. And now that she was sane, she found that she wanted to know what had become of the young lady in rags, the girl with the bandaged wrist and the toy snake. She took a cab to the police station where she had been kept in the cells, but prudently had it drop her a few blocks away. She sent it back to the stand. It would be cruel to leave it waiting, where an untended semi-sentient vehicle was likely to be set upon, butchered, and carried off in pieces before she returned.

In Maitri's garden the seasons kept their ancient courses, and it was autumn now. Here the weather was always the same. The same brazen sky was pasted like strips of paper across the cracks between the termite-nest blocks they called the hives and over the parched miserable patches of *potager* where no crops thrived. The same listless figures peered from doorways, the same dull-eyed children gathered to follow the stranger. She had dressed in the poor-ward costume of loose undershirt and trousers, with a long sturdy overshirt to conceal her female body. But she couldn't make herself inconspicuous. Hive dwellers came to the prosperous streets. They were the beggars. They were the weed cutters who fed your cab when you were stopped by traffic orders or stalled by a crowd. They were the squatters who prowled in ragged troupes in search of new living space or ground to grow food. But a hive "estate" was as exclusive as a rich suburb. Outsiders did not come here by accident.

When she reached the station, she found the usual hopeful straggling crowd covering the ramps and the steps outside. She couldn't make up her mind what to do. Suppose she asked, and the police said: What girl? There was no girl, Miss Catherine. In the end she turned away. The police were like Catherine: They knew they weren't supposed to get involved in rich people's troubles. Asking questions here was the wrong place to start. She decided to go to her own little *trou*. The building was nearby. Someone might remember something.

She left the stuffy glare of the street and climbed. The termite-nest shape of these tenements was meant for coolness and efficiency. It was a design found everywhere in the *quartier*, and quite likely over the whole human world. But though the hives were potentially, easily, self-sufficient in power and light and waste disposal, their minimum connection to the bit-grid was not enough to support their routine maintenance. The elevations and lights never functioned for long at a time; sanitation bacteria gave up the unequal struggle. She reached her floor and picked her way through the overflow, where debris gathered and foul liquid oozed over the floor of the indoor street. Children were picking through it too, looking for anything edible, anything remotely of value. She reached her *trou* and scratched at the entrance.

"Justine?"

A face she didn't recognize peered through the hybrid curtain.

"Who are you?" Catherine demanded. "Where are Justine and her kids?"

"Has she sent you for the rent money? You can't have it. We haven't got it."

She glimpsed her small room, full of bodies: adults, children, a baby, all of them hooked up to the tvc. Except for the baby, which was crying, and one figure that lay writhing and shivering on a miserable bed-with-legs.

"What's wrong with your friend?"

"Leave us alone!"

She could not bully her way in by force. She had stupidly come here without any cash, without anything to give. She pulled off her overshirt.

"Here, have this. It's good material. You can sell it, buy medicine—"

Furious, she went straight to the Church of Self. The shrine, a dirty partition on the ground floor of a much older building, was as she remembered it. Stacked screens were running blurred and indecipherable Aleutian sacred records. A larger screen featured one of the Church of Self's prize exhibits from a lifetime ago: an African who'd been ordained to the priesthood recounting a telepresence visit to the shipworld. Everything was covered in dead dirt, skin flakes, grease, dust. Her former comrades were dozily chatting and eating candies on a low stage between the stacks that imitated an Aleutian dais.

"Where's Justine?" she demanded. "She was to have my *trou*. Why are those people renting my room? There is no rent. I paid it for the whole lease!"

They gaped at her.

"Justine can live with her uncle now," explained the unctuous deacon, gathering himself in alarm, trying to bow. "So she's renting out the room you kindly gave her." <We didn't expect you, miss,> he added in Silence, plaintively. <We thought we wouldn't see you again.>

"What about my things? You were to sell them and buy food for the poor—"

The deacon was wearing a pair of Catherine's shoes. He noticed this fact a moment after Catherine did and pulled the hems of his trousers over his feet with a fatuous grin.

"They were too good to sell, miss. Far too good. It would have been a waste."

She was shaking with rage. She could not remember their names, which somehow made argument impossible. "There's a man very ill in my *trou*. It looks like antifeedant sickness. Did you know that?"

"Oh, yes," agreed one of the laypersons, eagerly. "It's his own fault. They've been squatting on preserved land, miss. They're not educated people. They don't understand that if they don't leave the parkland alone, we will all suffer. So they go there and get sick."

"He's near death."

They nodded, bewildered. Yes, and wasn't death the Mission's gift to the poor?

"You should have told us you were coming, miss." The

deacon had got over his fright, and his tone was of dignified reproach. "If we'd known, we would have been prepared."

Catherine searched for the tenement block where she'd attended her last conversion. She didn't know why she was
looking for it. She was crying, rubbing her bare arms. She
didn't know why she was crying. What else did she expect? In Misha's world maybe trade was a thing of the past.
In the hives buying and selling were the desperate facts of
life. They could not live except by battening on the rich,
and the rich defended themselves savagely, poisoning the
land and everything that grew on it with the antifeedant
genes that kept pests at bay. Pests! The humans were turning on each other, as any creatures will when they are too
many for the space and food and water. And she was responsible for this misery. She, Aleutia, what difference? She
was not like Bhairava. She believed in permanent death.
She believed that death was better than life. She had blood
on her hands, but she did not pity the humans. They were
no different flesh. If they were the masters, they would behave just the same: around and around, no end, no escape,
always the same, always the same—
    "Catherine?"
    She was huddled in a blank doorway, on an indoor street
she didn't know. People were passing, indifferent. Someone
was bending over her. It was Agathe Uwilingiyimana,
wearing red-and-green-patterned overalls and a bright
head tie.
    "You'd better come with me. Come back to the Settle-
ment."
    She knew what the Settlement was. It was a dangerous
rival institution set up by the Reformers. It vied with the
Church of Self for converts. She let herself be taken there.
The Settlement termite nest was better maintained than
those around it. The solars glittered, the window-pocked

tapering walls were festooned with tiny hanging vegetable gardens. Above the entrance, in rather grubby tricolor, arched the Reformer legend: "Liberté, Égalité, Amitié."

"Sit down, I'll get you some tea." Agathe frowned at Catherine's strange undress. "What happened to your shirt?"

"I gave it away." Catherine wiped her eyes.

They were in a large room, cool and well lit: cluttered with office machinery, seed boxes, planters of young vegetables, fruits on the vine, craft tools. It reminded her of the renaissance meeting. Settlements could not compete with the Church in snob value, having no connection with the aliens, so they seduced the people with crude material bribes: cheap, well-maintained rooms, improved seeds for their *potagers,* interesting activities.

"One of those curse God and die days?" Agathe suggested cheerfully, as she struggled with a cranky drinks dispenser. "We all have them. Sometimes you lose it. *Ah, qu'il est difficile de faire le bien!* That old pastorale has it right. Doing good is the hardest work in the world. People are nasty, brutal, ungrateful, sly. And being deprived doesn't make them any nicer."

"How do you cope?" Catherine's teeth were chattering; her defenses were down.

"Anger," said the councillor, handing her a quilted-paper wrap and a steaming beaker. "Anger, authority, and kindness. I try to keep hold of those three, not necessarily in that order. I'm glad to see you here." She sat down, a cluttered table between them. "We don't run group suicides. I admit I don't like the Church of Self much. But I admired what *you* were doing. Our motives aren't so different. Like you, I'm trying to shift people out of the shit."

"Why?" asked Catherine. She could not drink hot liquid.

Agathe laughed. "God knows!"

"She's a priest," said someone. "More than that: she's a Perfect."

The speaker, the only other person in the big room, was Lalith the halfcaste. She came over from a desk where she'd been feeding sheets of print through an ancient scanner. "Do you know what it means? She doesn't make love. She doesn't even masturbate, in theory, and somehow the rest of us benefit. Isn't that a strange idea?"

Agathe touched a small gold pin that was fastened to the breast of her overalls. She looked embarrassed. "I suppose it *is* strange. But it suits me."

"I'm pleased to meet you, Catherine," said Lalith. She was smiling at Catherine's astonishment. "The Settlement's letting me use this place as my office. It turns out that I'm going to be based in the *quartier* for a while. We'll probably meet at the Phoenix. But I've heard about you right here in the hives. People have been missing you. They appreciated your help."

"That's not why I joined the Mission," said Catherine bitterly. "I did it to help myself." She felt repelled by so much bright, cheerful effort. "Why do you try to make them happy? Why should they be rewarded for living the way they do, for enduring the world the way it is? It's their own choice. They'd *rather* have the shit. You know that's true."

"Think of the city's atmosphere," suggested Agathe. "We don't live under a glass dome. Yet the city has its own climate, an envelope of warm fug that shifts and changes, but stays in place without any intervention. A community of people is like that: a mass of individual particles held together by complex pressures. If the air in our mini-atmosphere becomes poisonous, it has to be cleaned. But we can't take it away to clean it. We can't shut down the plant; we have to adjust it while it keeps going. I know what you're saying, Catherine. Some bad things never seem to change, although I believe they may. But that doesn't mean we shouldn't try to make things better. The situation is *not* hopeless."

Catherine shivered and held the beaker awkwardly. She

recognized in Agathe a breed of stubborn dedication that she had met sometimes at home. Maybe the priest was right. Maybe if you kept at it, *being good* would work. For all her reputation as "the conscience of Aleutia," she knew she'd never practiced Agathe's kind of virtue—and never would. But she had begun to recover from her fugue. The Settlement was Reformer shareware—free until you're hooked. She should not be here. This place was gender politics.

"I came here to look for someone," she said, putting down her drink. "A girl, a Traditionalist young lady like Thérèse. I saw her at the police station when they were holding me there after the conversion ceremony. She was in a bad state: down and out, maybe sick, totally withdrawn. At the time I thought it wasn't my business. But she stayed on my mind."

Lalith and Agathe looked at each other, exchanging small, grim smiles.

"You know something?"

"Not exactly," said Lalith.

"It's not so unusual," explained Agathe. "There's a kind of rich young lady who goes that way. Their life is very hard, harder than anything I've seen in the hives, in my opinion. The ones who struggle against their fate—like Thérèse, like Misha's sister, Helen—suffer more. It can end the way you saw. They escape, but they can't survive."

"I didn't know Misha had a sister."

"Well, he does. She used to come to the Phoenix. But we don't see her anymore." Agathe leaned forward, earnestly. "Catherine, I know you don't want to get involved in gender politics. The War is over; even Youro is at peace, and your people are proud of that. You're right to be proud. But you can't pretend it never happened."

"We don't want to bore you," said Lalith wryly, "but there *was* a holocaust. When you aliens first moved into human government in a big way, do you remember what the Aleutians kept asking? *'Where are all the women?'* You'd been told that half the human race was female, and the numbers didn't add up. They didn't add up because millions upon millions of innocent women and girl children and girl fetuses had been killed, simply because they were women. It's hard to forget something like that."

Agathe frowned. "Let's get back to the point. This girl . . . Do you know what a 'Traditionalist young lady' is, Catherine?" she asked. "If you were really here in the War, maybe you remember a kind of sextoy developed by the Traditionalists? Later on, when they wanted to preserve their sons' male secondaries, they used drugs. But they already knew how to produce ideal little girls. Do you understand?"

"Females don't need males," put in Lalith. "Except for intromission, to get pregnant, and we don't need that anymore. Males need females desperately, because otherwise they have no offspring. Males are supposed to have invented our arts and sciences, you know, as toys to attract the females. But women hijacked the famous male *creativity* when they walked out on patriarchy. Then they didn't need men for *anything*. That's where Traditionalist young ladies come in. They're fake trophies, to replace the real trophy-objects that got up and walked away. Male need, female independence: that was the real cause of the Gender War. That's what the men couldn't forgive. It's not rich versus poor, it's not big and strong versus small and weak, it's not aggressive versus gentle. All human beings can be all of those things. It's the reproductive imbalance that's the poison. The rest is just politics."

Agathe smiled uneasily, clearly aware (Lalith seemed to have forgotten) of the effect "gender politics" would have on Catherine. "Sometimes these things need to be said," she defended her friend loyally. "We don't want to force anything on anyone, but humanity must and will get beyond the problem. We say to Joset at home, 'Be as masculine as you like, be as feminine as you like. Take on any role that suits you. But don't—' "

"Don't be male," broke in Lalith. "Because *it sucks.*"

"And does that work?" wondered Catherine mildly. Agathe laughed. "Are you kidding? He wants to be Mish Connelly! We get at him because we can't help it. We call him a throwback. It just makes him worse. But he is still one of us, in the end, because we're not doing anything artificial, to him or anyone. We aren't a creed. We're part of something that is happening, an evolution."

"What about being female? Aren't male and female 'two sides of the same coin,' as you people say?"

"I'm not sure there's such thing as 'being female.' " Agathe shrugged. "Being female is being human and able to bring up children. That's simply normal. It's not a special state."

"Look at Misha Connelly," broke in Lalith again. "His whole purpose in life is to rebel against his father, to outdo his father, and yet he knows that he *is* his father. Isn't that a recipe for psychic disaster? They say they're living in the traditional way, but have you looked at them? The elite Traditionalists don't marry. Why have a sexual partner who may undermine you, betray you, try to share your slice of pie? They don't have children. They make copies of themselves, or worse. Girls like Thérèse never grow up. They are living dolls. They're the embodiment of everything that's wrong. Meanwhile young men like Misha, stuffed full of testo, go crazy because the candy is out of reach."

Agathe gave her a warning glance. "Maybe we shouldn't talk about our friends when they're not here . . . But it is ironic," she went on, "that you people regard the Traditionalists as the guardians of natural humanity. Nothing very dramatic has happened to us, *nous autres,* who have gone along with the tide, accepted the consequences of history. Women are different now. We don't menstruate, we don't get pregnant so easily, we don't have nursing breasts unless we're pregnant or suckling babies. Men are different too. They have a lower sperm count and don't get so hairy or so bald, or build such muscles. Girls and boys both take longer to become sexually mature . . . But it's all details. Everything fun or valuable about sexual difference is still available." She grinned. "My little brother is too young to be interested in sex, though he'd love you to believe otherwise. But by all the signs, he's going to be a raving hetero."

"This is very fascinating," said Catherine. "But what about my 'young lady'?"

The two women shook their heads.

"There's nothing more we can tell you," said Agathe. "This is the city where the good guys lost. Bad things, terrible things can happen here. We see them daily. Your young lady was not unique. That's as much as we can say."

Catherine let them put her into a cab and send her home.

What had she seen that day? It was hard to be sure. The fragile skin of a human forearm, burned or scorched by little black sores. Maybe the girl had been in a fire.

She sat on her bed, wondering. Agathe and Lalith had been hiding something. It didn't take a telepath to know that! But she had no will to investigate further. Did they believe that Catherine had been in Youro in the Gender War? Perhaps they did not. Or they wouldn't have imagined they could get her to take sides . . . It was interesting to have heard Lalith speak so unguardedly, so differently from her public manifesto! Interesting, but not surprising. She studied the flesh of her own naked arms. The inner forearm was very pale and soft.

What do I look like?

There were no mirrors in the aliens' part of the house. The Aleutians considered mirrors uncanny. She found a tvc set, took it to her room, and made herself a tall virtual screen, silvered like looking glass. She observed that her nose was too narrow and slender for the rest of her human face. She had not known that before. And her shoulders were too high. She stripped off her clothes. She smoothed her hands over the barely covered bones of the human rib cage, missing the long Aleutian straps of muscle. She cupped her small breasts, held the sides of her indented waist (another strange absence of muscle), groped the fatty mounds of her buttocks. She opened with her fingers the folds of flesh beneath soft hair at the base of her belly: the place that human females used for making love, for accepting intromission, for giving birth. She had tried to masturbate, but this body did not respond. She had never made love with anyone. She had been *perfect*, without effort.

The reflection was a strange thing. It looked alive, but it had no life. But was this human body alive, in the Aleutian sense? It shed no living presence into the air. It was nothing but an appearance.

In fact, the aliens knew as much as they needed to know about the baroque arrangements of the postwar Youro aristocracy. It didn't seem strange, in Aleutian reckoning, that the human elite should try to make themselves immortal. Or that the adults should take partners much younger than themselves. But it seemed extraordinary, suddenly, that Catherine had never realized exactly what she had done to herself. She had wanted to be a woman, not a man, for many reasons: some personal, some historical. She had been aware, vaguely, that as Maitri's ward, she had the status of a "Traditionalist young lady." But she had not grasped what that meant.

She went to one of her cupboards and took out folded clothes that she had never worn. Skirts and bodices, glistening stockings, subtly engineered undergarments. She dressed. She was trembling, and the sobs that had racked her as she wandered that tenement block were close. She felt an excitement that nobody could understand, unless they too had some reason to hunger for pain. She wondered why it had never occurred to her to dress this way before. Agathe would be sorry when Catherine appeared like this at the Phoenix. Horrified if she knew that she herself was responsible. She stood in front of the mirror again. *I am the embodiment of everything that's wrong.*

Her mouth dried. Blood coursed into the delicate skin of her cheeks. She touched her breasts and felt the nipples rising and hardening. The naked, folded rose between her thighs was trying to open, the petals moist and full. She stood, until the arousal faded.

She thought of Misha Connelly.

4

LES PARAPLUIES

i

"DOES YOUR BUILDING never scrub this, Mâtho?" Thérèse poked at the grainy gel of the newsagency's windowpane. "It's like old cheese. Did it ever open? Do you have a nice view?"

"I don't know. I've never looked."

The journalist was hunched over his workstation, picking out the best from a batch of raw offcut. His friends, who had arrived uninvited "to see what he did with himself," prowled around. They were halfway up the cone of a termite nest, the same design as in Catherine's poor-ward estate, but in better repair. The thick walls were gouged out into shelves and alcoves. The floor space was a clutter of mass-market future-proof media ware, so successful that some of it was over two hundred years old. In a touching show of renaissance feeling, the soft-bodied hybrid tech had been packed into rigid cases.

Mâtho, once he'd overcome his alarm, had eagerly accepted Catherine's offer. He knew exactly what he wanted: mood pieces, untainted by politics, on the last days of Aleutian rule, from inside an Aleutian household. Catherine, accustomed to making her own "tape" for the confessional records of Aleutia, had had no difficulty. Maitri and his retainers had cooperated cheerfully: playing games, making music, and reminiscing to camera. Maitri's only condition was that nobody was to speak aloud. He didn't want anything undiplomatic formally on record. But he was happy for the news agency software to add its own commentary.

Mâtho had no diffidence in his work. He spent merciless hours grilling Catherine on her editing. But he would only appear at the giratoire house on a screen, in the form of text. He absolutely refused to let her visit the agency, except in the same manner. The others had found out that she longed to see Mâtho's workplace and organized a raid.

Catherine stood beside Imran Khan, watching the discard from a major agency that was being dumped, silently, on a stack of screens.

"When we first arrived—" She stopped herself. "How does one pick out a news supplier these days? There are so many!"

Imran glanced toward Mâtho, and shrugged. "They're all the same. News is a commodity. News is what people like my mother buy and sell. We don't bother with it."

"Then, how *do* you find out what's happening in the world?"

"We don't," declared Misha, joining them. "We *are* what's happening." He spread his hands, framing a chunk of the stack. "News is an exploded concept. Look at that. It's a section cut through living tissue, full of process: live art. You don't *stop* that—"

"You are insufferable, Mish."

Joset, unfortunately, was not with them. Imran made a poor substitute as a Misha Connelly damper. He was not the sparring kind: he could neither enjoy Misha nor ignore him. Catherine removed herself from what Lydie the dancer called the "bare knuckled needlery."

"Could we talk blocks and docks?" Rajath was asking Thérèse.

They bent together over one of the packing cases. Thérèse was using it as a desk, sketching briskly on a page of her notebook.

"You should try this," she murmured. "Really good penetration—"

Rajath seemed dubious. "I don't want to do anything that will hurt my back."

"You're such a sissy—"

Binte sat on the floor in a corner, head unveiled, smiling her bland smile. Thérèse suddenly looked up, caught Catherine's eye; the notebook vanished into her skirts. A moment later she was leaning over Mâtho's shoulder, saying, "How interesting text looks. I wish you would teach me to read."

"It's too late," growled the modest Nose, contorting himself to avoid the impropriety of brushing a young lady's clothes. "You have to learn before your brain hardens."

"Cheek! I'm sure my brain's as squishy as yours."

Mâtho was unhappy at being tracked to his lair, ashamed of his cheap machines. He was thinking of the brilliant value of his Aleutian scoop: half in a glow of professional pride, half in despair. The agency had no way to benefit from Mâtho's luck and judgment. If the footage of Lord Maitri and his friends was taken up by the software agents of the bigger handlers, they'd do it without acknowledgment. Mâtho and his father couldn't stop them.

Poor Nose. Catherine peered through the "old cheese," having difficulty with everything that she must ignore, all that was spoken in Silence. Someone came to stand behind her.

"Misha," she said, "I want to go to the Tate. Will you take me?"

"To the *Tate?* That's obscure. How did you know it was me?"

"I can't filter out everything."

The folds of her chador touched his sleeve. She did not

use the hood; her head was only lightly veiled. No one had commented aloud on Catherine's change of dress, but she felt the immense change in their response—especially in Misha. He was more relaxed. He watched her frankly, as the young males always watched cloaked females, even in the Phoenix Café, for a hint of peeping finery.

"There's a picture I saw in my last life. I want to see it again. With you."

ii

CATHERINE'S HIRED LIMOUSINE crossed the Channel by the Amiens Bridge. She saw the sea passage that had been open water *when we first arrived,* half buried under maglev and roadbridges, land clamation and mats of industrial algae. The western fringes of Youro had suffered heavily in the last phase of the War, and the new development was charmless. She began to see why the humans used closed cars so much.

The remaining Aleutian staff in the Expedition's London hostel were delighted to receive her. Misha arrived the next day and dined with them in more than orbital splendor. The day after that he took them to see some rarely visited antiquities. The site was in the west country, in an unlovely neighborhood that made the hives estate look like a miracle of urban design. The Aleutians were highly satisfied. They trotted from one street corner to another, admiring the sarsen stones that stood in tiny patches of turf or bulged from housing block walls. They made records of the children who followed them around and of the local maglev station—which was decorated with tasteful projections of the site in former times when the whole circle had been discernible between the houses. "Imagine!" they exclaimed. "So ancient! And they were Islamic warriors, changed into stone by chemical warfare. How strange and splendid!" They thanked Misha profusely, assuring him that he and his Saracens would feature in their next confessions, and retired to the cars to snack and tvc in comfort.

Catherine and Misha adventured farther into this sad marginal land: not yet part of the city, no longer the true outdoors. Misha went into one of the ugly blocks and fetched out a smooth faced elderly individual, sexless in body but presenting as a Traditionalist male. He was wearing very strange stiff overalls that looked as if they were made of pressed shit, like the walls of the buildings. He led them to an alley that was shut off by a photochemical gate, opened the gate with his palmprint, and retired. They climbed a narrow weedgrown path, and at last came to an open ridge that finished in a grassy knoll. There were no more gates, no explanations. Great slabs of stone guarded the entrance to a stone chamber, a place of stillness that spoke age and mystery beyond measure.

"What a privilege it is," gasped Catherine, somewhat out of breath, "to know the park keeper's son. What is this place? Is it very old? Can we go in?"

"It's called a chamber tomb. It's a funerary room. The people who used it lived here before the circle back in Avebury was made. About five thousand years ago. But I don't know why I bother. You people can't keep numbers in your heads. Yes, we can go in."

It was very simple: a passage room with smaller chambers on each side. Catherine explored it completely in a few minutes and went to join Misha, who was sitting with his back against the cold, smoothed, and raddled slabs at the inner end. Blocks of greenish translucence were let into the roof. She looked up into deep water.

"How old is the glass?"

"Quite modern. About a hundred years pre-contact, I suppose."

She laughed. "As modern as that! You know, you shouldn't have told them that stuff about the Saracens! That was *wicked*."

"I thought it livened up the picnic nicely."

And the cool, damp silence wrapped them around.

"We're in livespace," he said. He jerked his head at a tiny red pinpoint that Catherine had not noticed. "So few people visit this place, it's economic to record them all. I can get you a copy. Then you can splice it into your next confession and send it back to the shipworld. The Priests of Self will turn it into state fiction, in that funny low-rez video animation. Your Aleutian self will study it one day and think *there's me*. On my holidays."

"I'm always in livespace," she pointed out dryly, "when I'm with you. You have a 360 camrecorder implant."

Misha traced a pattern of interlinked circles on the damp earth with his fingertip. "True. But I don't save my rushes. I discard everything. Or nearly everything. *Will* this life go into your record? Or do the priests of the Cosmic WorldSelf decide that?"

"The priests decide. I usually make my own tape, and only turn it over to my character shrine for formatting. I'm, um, a Protestant, I think that makes me, in your native culture. Or something like that. The priests will process my records of being Catherine, and yes, they'll convert them into ideological-state fiction. It's not as dire as it sounds. Physical things happen at confession. It's more like doing deals with your unconscious than submitting your futurity to state oppression. 'Catherine' won't be able to haggle in the biochemical flux, so I won't have much editorial control for this life—but that's just too bad."

"Have you ever had a child?"

"No." She didn't see the connection. "Why do you ask?"

"If I have a child," he said softly, concentrating on his pattern, "Traditionalist tradition dictates that the child has to be me over again. I have to give birth—though of course I wouldn't physically give birth—to my father, to my sister, to myself. There's no other choice. That's my futurity."

She didn't think clonal meiosis was anything like Aleutian reincarnation, anything like another *Self*. She didn't know if saying that would be consolation or an insult. She felt close to the source of that pain in him, that capacity for suffering that had first attracted her. But his whole presence refused her the right to question him directly, and she accepted the refusal. She had her own reserves.

Misha, in Silence, did not even say, <Don't touch me! I don't want to talk about it!> He looked aside, safe on the other side of an invisible wall. He observed without contact.

"Have I met your sister?"

"You've probably seen her. She makes appearances, with Dad. Or she did. You won't have been introduced."

They sat without speaking. Catherine shivered and pulled the chador cloak closer.

"You're cold. We'd better go."

He stood on the windy summit of the knoll, the skirts of his coat flapping. The grass was as green as the plants in Maitri's garden, but it had a doomed look. The city was going to swallow it. There would be tiger weed, building blocks, and vegetable beds here before long.

"It gets bloody chilly out here on the fringes where the mini-atmosphere thins out. We've lost the Gulf Stream that used to keep us warm. And the Mediterranean's drying fast, so there's no hot water bottle in the bed either. Oh, it's going to be a cold, cold winter outdoors, Miss Catherine, after you folks have left. And a long one."

They were unable to find the Sargent portrait that Catherine had wanted to see. It was in storage, a fact that Catherine had not been able to discover by tvc. The Gallery was reticent about answering questions of that kind from prospective visitors, and had blocked her agent. They went to see the pre-Saatchi rooms instead, moving slowly from one soundproofed cubicle to another, contemplating the glorious colors and pure, naive sentiments of the great period of consumerism. The early Heinekens, the Hamlets, several series of British Airways, and the Halifax. There was an inevitable bias toward the Gallery's host nation. The Tate, on principle, displayed only original prints; and it couldn't afford many interurban acquisitions.

They talked about the way these works were not single entities but palimpsests, bricolage. The music might be two hundred years older than the visuals. The scripts were laden with quotations from ancient sources—which were now punishingly obscure, but which the original mass audience would have recognized easily. They reminded each other that the work shouldn't be called "pre-Saatchi." The period had been named by mistake, because of a confusion between the Saatchi *collection* (which had disappeared in the War), and these records. The Saatchi studio had been active at this very time. They smiled at the ancient products, foregrounded in vain. Misha thought the wasp-waisted cola bottle—so modestly pleased with itself—looked like a Flemish burgher kneeling before the Madonna, some centuries before Coca-Cola was invented. "He's convinced that the picture is *his* business. But his name is an irrelevance; his story has vanished. The light that falls through the window of his chapel endures. His figure's importance is its place in a balance of color and shadow . . ."

"I'm talking too much," Misha broke off, shamed by his own erudition. "I'm being insufferable, probably."

Catherine shrugged and smiled. "No. For a change, no."

"I'm wrong, anyway," he decided. "The Coca-Cola bottle matters. These pieces were commissioned to make wealth for everyone concerned. Or they wouldn't exist. That tells you something about funxing dilettantes like me. I remember the first time I realized Jeremy Isaacs didn't create *The World at War* all by himself, for his own glory. Or David Attenborough, *The Trials of Life* . . . I was shocked. I felt cheated."

"Me too. I thought humans were 'individualists.' Do they have a print?"

"I don't want to see *The World at War*. It's too emotional. I find it extremely depressing." Misha stared at some dazzling images of fire and molten metal, a beautiful woman's body morphing into the shape of a dolphin with a radioactive glow, a Peugeot campaign from around the turn of the twenty-first century. "Well, I've grown up a little. I think I hate art that doesn't *do work*. I can't do what they did, those people in the endless credit lists. That machine's run down. But I know they were better than me, smug and alone with my Vlab. Better than me. Don't you love the way the car ones get so sacred, reverent, and death laden, while the car itself absolutely *disappears?* Same thing happened to tobacco cigarette ads in the previous decade. There aren't any of them here, because they were banned from tv for the crucial period . . . Actually, I hate looking at this stuff. Let's find something prehistoric and static that doesn't make me feel small. You'll like that."

"When we first arrived"—Catherine grinned—"people in England were being extremely scathing about this collection. Old tv commercials as high art! The Tate was held to have finally, utterly flipped. But you're right. I don't want to be a superior outsider. I always want my ideas to be ordinary, simple, banal. That's my hopeless ambition."

"Is that why you're working for Mâtho?" asked Misha, nastily.

Catherine frowned.

"I didn't mean that. Mâtho's a good guy. I'm jealous. Would you work with me?"

She shook her head.

The Expedition had arranged for Catherine's visit to be private: an unnecessary precaution. It was not the tourist season, and actual Thames Valley residents never came near this institution, in-person or by tvc. It was supported by a private foundation. Catherine and Misha were alone in the vaults except for the security guards. They parted, again by unspoken consent. Catherine wandered through the funerary halls of war casualties. The headless *Winged Victory* that had stood in the Louvre, the great jagged canvas called *Guernica*, the white marble *David* from the Accademia. Piero della Francesca's bleak, supernal *Resurrection*. All gone. But they were here, alive in the datagrid. Still passionate, still burning in humanity's external mind and heart.

At last she went looking for Misha. She found him as he'd promised, with the Tate's current selection of static canvases. They walked slowly toward each other. The walls of the gallery were a cool honey color. Diffused daylight spread through air, carried from distant windows and amplified by light-bearing veins that ran through the stone. They met in front of a Renoir and stood at gaze, the folds of her honor cloak nudging his sleeve.

"This is what you call poetry?"

"It's your nearest analogue to our poetry. The only use we have for printed words in Aleutia is in abstruse instruction manuals. Art made in that medium would be like, um, expecting your average human audience to respond to a big page of mathematical symbols. People do it from time to time; it's done. Not by me."

"So you do representational pictures. Aleutian Renoirs? Narratives?"

"I don't look for a subject. I draw whatever's in front of me, usually. I try to capture a moment. Is that banal enough? But an Aleutian poem is . . . it's alive. How can I explain? When an Aleutian takes a wanderer from his skin and feeds it to a friend, he's saying *this is me now, this is my state of being*. When I compose a poem, I'm trying to do that to the world, through the microcosm of what I see. When another Aleutian comes along, maybe generations later, and 'looks at my picture,' the biochemical meaning of that moment to me is shed from the picture and enters the viewer. The poem is a communication-loop. Captured and released again, not the same but evolved by everything that's happened since, the whole information system that's involved in the new gaze . . . I'm not explaining this very well. If I could say what I mean by poetry in formal words, it wouldn't be poetry."

She stared at *Les Parapluies:* the flower-faces standing out like love stories in the sober text of Renoir's narrative. Virtual particles of the dead artist's intention filled her air, entered her being.

"I'm wrong. It is the same."

She could feel the touch of Misha's sleeve through her whole body. She did not try to "filter out" her knowledge that he had the same awareness, that for both of them this intellectual conversation was exquisitely, secretly erotic.

Misha applied his utility test. "But do you do it for profit?"

"Yes! Absolutely. Profit for *me.* Doesn't that count?"

A security guard had found them. It sneaked up, apparently fascinated by the sight of the young lady and her escort, and hovered behind them. Misha glanced around with a forbidding glare. It stood its ground.

"It's no wonder nobody comes here," said Misha, loudly. "Who wants to see this stuff? Babies and breasts, dead bodies, movie-moments of corporate confirmation. You'll have noticed there's death and sex and violence in hideous quantities, but if there's an image of someone *shitting* anywhere, I missed it. That's one of the least celebrated pleasures in life if you ask me, the feel of a lovely big fat turd plopping out of you. What's art if it doesn't venerate pleasure?"

"I prefer to ooze," reflected Catherine. "I learned to shit your dreadful bricks in my first life here, same time as I learned to eat your weird food. We never do lumps. We *don't* always use diapers. It was only on the shipworld that we took to toilet pads. But I like them. Oozing into a pad is the best. I like to seep, to feel it going while I'm talking to someone or walking down the street. I like the way it vanishes into your pad. You produce, but what you produce immediately becomes part of the world again."

"That oozing, it must be like the trickle of menstrual blood. *Do* you menstruate?"

The guard had begun to show mechanical signs of embarrassment early in Misha's speech. It fidgeted on the spot, roused a detector vane or two, retracted an appendage. Finally, desperately torn between prudery and censorious suspicion, it scooted off backward and careered out of sight, still ogling with every sensor.

Misha and Catherine burst into giggles.

"Ah, *les rosbifs*. Who says there's no such thing as ethnic identity?"

"No, I don't," she said. "I know your fancy young ladies still bleed, but ordinary women don't. I didn't want to be special."

He flushed crimson. "Self, I didn't really mean you to answer that." He quickly recovered. "For completism, maybe you *should* bleed. It's classically female. Are you fertile?"

"Subfertile, your quacks say. Same as always. I am myself, translated."

They came up into the forecourt. A row of cabs stood waiting under leaden clouds, on a field of alien weeds above the culverted river. The brilliant blur of a commercial zone stood beyond: debased remains of the great tradition, transmuted by distance into shafts of dancing aurora, phalanxes of multi-colored angels running up and down between earth and sky. It was the last day of their trip. They went to the Expedition car that was waiting for her.

"Come back with me," she said, not wanting to say goodbye. She scratched the rubbery creases around the vehicle's sleepy, daylight eyes. "Come back to the hostel; stay the night. You shouldn't pass up a chance to spend an Aleutian night. We can travel together in the morning."

They would travel together, alone in a closed car. It would be scandalous, unforgivable, if Catherine was a real young lady. But she was not. She was wearing these clothes for a whim. She belonged to no one but herself. Of course, Misha understood that. She would tell him how peculiar and perilous it felt to have no underwear. They would laugh about it. They would escape from their roles: she from her need for punishment, he from his secret anger. They would be friends, be good to each other, make love, enjoy—

"No," he said. "*Vive la renaissance.* No belly of the beast for me. I'll use the lev."

He left the forecourt by an underpass. The twenty-fourth century vanished, replaced by dank archaeological gloom. There were cities under cities in western fringes of Youro, where evolution only went skin deep: dead things layered in the dark. Strips of bacterial lighting, crawling with minitel information, directed him to his station. They were the only fragments of the present day. He checked his tally of how many times she said "always," and how many times she said "we." It was interesting, and it helped him to keep his distance. As he passed by a buried shopfront, on a street stepped on and trampled by the clambering generations, a sexless, haggard face looked up from a beggar's pitch. The troglodyte thrust out a filthy palm.

"I don't carry cash," said Misha, but halted, obeying an impulse of petty malice. "You think you'd like to change places with me, don't you?"

The beggar grinned and nodded, now sure of a generous handout.

"You're wrong."

He strode on.

iii

MISHA TOLD JOSET something he could have told him awhile
before. The Leonardo da Vinci in Miss Catherine's boudoir
was the real thing, beyond reasonable doubt. Although, of
course, totally inferior to an analogous Aleutian artwork, as
it didn't give off information-rich whiffs of sixteenth-
century pheromones. The others had either long been convinced that Catherine was the one they sought (Mâtho,
Rajath, Lydie), or remained skeptical, but wanted to get on
with the plot (Agathe, Lalith, Thérèse, Imran). Commence
phase three.

Misha came to fetch Catherine as usual, and they took a
cab to the Phoenix Café. She knew as soon as she walked
into the room that she was in some kind of trouble. The
cadre was unusually united. They were sitting together:
Rajath and Mâtho and Lydie, Agathe Uwilingiyimana, her
brother, Lalith. A few moments after Misha and Catherine
came in, they were joined by Thérèse and Imran Khan. It
was evening twilight, the traditional human gathering
time. The Café was crowded. The regulars were used to
seeing Lord Maitri's ward by now. Lalith attracted more
attention; public interest in the renaissance was growing.
But this evening nobody came over to try and introduce
themselves, no would-be acquaintances casually dropped
by. The group of friends had an atmosphere.

Unusually, there was no food or wine yet on the table. It
was Rosh Hashanah, they explained to Catherine, the Jew-
ish New Year. The citizens of Youro enjoyed the holidays of
all the various cults, if they happened to be employed, or
observed the rituals (as far as they were remembered), if
they happened to be believers.

"What are we supposed to eat?" demanded Lydie. "I'm
hungry."

"Black letter print with sans serif sauce?" suggested

Agathe. "Newsprint paté? The Jews are supposed to be the People of the Book, aren't they?"

"Nah." Joset grinned. "Turtle soup with pigs' trotters, followed by dairy ice cream."

Everyone was waiting for Mâtho to pronounce their menu, but he refused to be drawn. "It isn't Rosh Hashanah," he told Catherine. "It isn't even Yom Kippur. That was last month. Youro celebrates everything on the wrong dates, because of the calendar change in—"

But she was not allowed to listen. Her second mood-piece had just been released by the agency, and everyone wanted to congratulate her.

"There's one thing about this video diary," remarked Joset, "that's puzzling us, Miss Catherine. The 'Aleutian-speaking' software that did the commentary picked up your name."

"Let's get some wine," said Misha, abruptly.

"Apparently, they call you 'Pure One,' around the house. We don't know, is that a common name? Or are you the famous 'Pure One': Clavel, the one in the history records?"

So that was it. She sighed.

"No," she said. "I mean, yes. I'm Clavel. It's not a secret. I'm Clavel."

Joset opened his eyes wide. "The Third Captain! We are sitting here with one of the three original leaders of the Expedition to Earth?"

She had been well aware (she couldn't filter out everything!) that they were fascinated by her Aleutian identity, and that they'd always known who she was. Most of all Misha, whose goading had always been right on target! She didn't mind whether or not they believed she was "really" Clavel. She only prayed that they'd go on being tactful. That no one would refer openly to her past. She'd been asking too much.

The wine arrived. The young humans, maybe non-plussed by her unhappy silence, stared at Catherine or the

tabletop, in different degrees of curiosity and embarrassment.

She began, "But you always knew—"

Misha smiled coldly.

She tried again. "All right. I am the person the Aleutians
call 'Pure One,' translated into a human body. That's who
I learned to be, the way any Aleutian child learns. That's
'who I am' chemically, in the Commonalty of Aleutia. But
I'm not the Third Captain! It is lives—a long time, I mean—
since I was a leader of the Expedition."

"You're still a *really important person*," insisted Lydie.
"You must be."

On a scale of what? She found it hard to face the dancer's
eyes.

"Even when I was the Third Captain, I wasn't very important. We'd been lost forever when we stumbled on this
system, and nearly everybody just wanted to go home. The
Expedition was a private venture. We were a bunch of stir-
crazy wastrels, looking for something to do. I certainly
didn't have an idea that Aleutia would end up ruling this
world."

The humans looked at each other.

"Is it t-t-true that you raped him?" blurted Mâtho. "J-
Johnny Guglioli the journalist?"

"Yes."

She lifted her glass and drank, to fill the silence.

"I don't know why people make such a fuss about that,"
exclaimed Lydie. "What's so terrible about one little rape?"

"It caused the *Sabotage Crisis*, Lydie," muttered Imran,
scowling.

"I don't see that! Johnny Guglioli got raped and joined
the terrorists. He didn't have to do that. He didn't have to
hijack the Buonarroti device, travel out to the shipworld,
and try to commit genocide. He could have turned Braemar
Wilson over to the authorities. Self! What if everybody who

had sex forced on them thought they were entitled to kill millions of people?"

She blushed, her thick, big-pored halfcaste skin flaring suddenly dark.

Agathe touched Catherine's hand. "I'm named after Agathe Uwilingiyimana," she said kindly. "A woman who was assassinated in an early phase of the Gender War. She was the first woman Prime Minister in modern Africa. It's the custom in my party to take the names of Reformer martyrs, people who have borne witness to our beliefs in their lives or by their deaths. Our saints, if you like. We got the idea from the halfcastes, who took it from the Aleutians. I don't believe in reincarnation, certainly not for humans. But I believe that Agathe Uwilingiyimana lives on in me. I've learned from your Aleutian perception of God. We *are* all aspects of the WorldSelf. We are part of each other. If she was guilty, I share her guilt; if she had burdens to bear, I share them too. We are all guilty, all burdened, and all forgiven. But that doesn't mean that I am that dead woman. I am myself."

"It's just a name," put in Rajath. "My parents aren't believers. They keep up the halfcaste stuff out of habit. They sent me to the Church of Self to learn 'speaking Aleutian.' But I didn't. Being called 'Rajath' doesn't mean a thing to me."

Agathe batted him down with a gesture, watching Catherine. "You don't have to be Clavel with us. To us you are Catherine, a human being. You can be yourself."

Misha rapped on a wine glass.

"It's a press conference," he announced. "As Miss Catherine's manager, I'll keep order. The alien in human disguise, formerly known as Clavel, will now take your questions."

Agathe looked annoyed. But she didn't protest.

"So long as you don't ask me about the Departure,"

warned Catherine, "I won't answer anything about that. Sattva would have my throat."

"That's acceptable. We're sublimely uninterested in your leaving plans. Lydie?"

"What's the real name of your planet?" cried the dancer.

"Home."

Lydie pulled a face. "That's what you people always say. But what is it *really?*"

"Home!" repeated Catherine, laughing. "What's wrong with that? It's better than 'dirt.' "

"What's the identity of your home system's star?" asked Imran sharply.

"What do we call it at home? The sun, I suppose, more or less."

Imran wasn't satisfied, but Lalith broke in before he could pursue the point.

"What's the *real* name of your people, nation, brood, whatever?"

"Aleutians."

"Oh, come on! That's the name of a chain of islands off the coast of Alaska, where one of your landing parties first touched down. I mean your own name for yourselves."

For a moment nothing happened. Someone giggled. Catherine looked around the table. "She was telling us in the Common Tongue," guessed Lydie. "And we didn't get it."

Imran had been thinking. "I've got a good one—"

"You've had your turn," protested Joset.

"But she didn't *answer* mine, and this asks why."

"Let him, let him," came a chorus of voices.

"Why have you people never used your own formal language on earth?"

"Our articulate languages are extremely fluid and contextual," she began, correctly. "People change their spoken names, and the names for things, constantly. In the context of the Expedition to Earth, it's natural for us to use Sanskrit or English or whatever seems appropriate." She laughed. "That's the party line. I'm a trader; Aleutia is a trading nation. If people learn your spoken language, your private system of signs, it's supposed to give them useful information, bargaining advantage. If you want to have control in a trading situation, you speak the other peoples' language and manage it so they don't learn yours. I don't know if it works, but it's what Aleutians believe. I think some humans operate that way too," she added. "If they get the chance."

She felt their recoil; she'd offended them. She should not joke about the way the aliens had manipulated the humans. It was not funny.

"So will you say something for us now, in the Aleutian formal language?"

"No."

Misha laughed. "Does that mean no?"

She grinned. "Yes."

"She's an Aleutian," muttered Imran. "They don't break ranks."

"What do you think of the way humans in the Enclaves call themselves 'she' these days? Is it the Aleutian policy to encourage that?"

She was careful; this was a sticky point in Youro. "It's true that local people in our established territories tend to think of themselves as women first and male or female second. But that is physiological fact, not Aleutian influence. Women is what humans are, isn't it? Hence the expression . . . mammals?"

Now everyone was *deeply* offended. Except, presumably, Agathe and Lalith. But they were keeping their thoughts to themselves.

"Whose side are you on," asked Thérèse slowly, "Traditionalists or Reformers?"

"Don't be stupid," shouted Lydie, "you can't ask her that."

"Yes, she can," countered Catherine. "But you know the answer. I'm not on either side. That's not policy, it's the truth. *I was here in the War.* I don't care if you believe that or not. To me it's true. I remember the War. Whatever caused that conflict, there were no 'good guys' once the weapons were out. There never are."

"She's right," said Agathe abruptly. "We have to put gender violence behind us. Isn't that what we keep telling people? Isn't that what the renaissance is about?"

"Is it?" wondered Misha. "I thought it was about not giving up our differences."

"We have to give up s-sex!" burst out Mâtho. "Th-the problem is sexual intercourse. It isn't necessary anymore. Women—and, and men too if they feel it's right—can get pregnant by taking a pill. We can be f-f-feminine and masculine s-spiritually, without sex. If people st-still want to do that, to do those things, it's because th-they are twisted inside."

"Are *you* twisted inside, Miss Catherine?" inquired Joset, with awesome insolence.

Misha rapped his glass. "Disallowed! This is not a medical examination. What I want to know is: is *Mâtho* twisted inside?" He leered cruelly at the Nose, who was covered in confusion.

Everyone laughed. "Order, order!" shouted Lalith. "This conversation is getting disgusting. There are ladies present!"

"Rajath hasn't had a question," said Lydie, when there was quiet.

"I don't want one!" Rajath assured them, looking alarmed.

"Nor has Agathe."

"I think the press conference is closed," decided Agathe. She considered Catherine, her chin propped on one firm, ruby-dark hand. "So what shall we do with her now?"

The Phoenix Café continued its life around them. Natural

music whispered that rain was falling: beating on wet roadway turf, on rooftops, on the river as it flowed, on co-op fields and tiny *potagers,* where the second crop of the year had just been started.

"Do you remember," went on Agathe, "you once asked why there was no tvc and no gaming in here?"

Catherine saw dancing eyes, a little malice, a lot of triumph.

"I remember. It was stupid of me; that wouldn't be in period. You'd have to have virtuality couches, video and voice-phones, rows of personal computers."

"True, and we do use pre-contact systems. But we don't always stay in period," announced Lalith. "The virtual world is very important to us. It has a special place in the Phoenix Café concept. It unites us with our fellow café-goers everywhere."

"What do you think?" demanded Misha. "Is she ready?"

"Feed her to the blue demons!"

Misha shouted across the room, "Leaf! Leaf! Open the gamesroom."

The renaissance cadre erupted from their seats. People at tables roundabout started clapping and cheering as Catherine was hauled out of her place. It seemed that this ritual was something they recognized. She was picked up bodily and carried, a bundle of skirts and veils, by Lalith and Agathe. The back wall of the Café, beyond the comfortable bar area where people were relaxing around the old-world island screens, had suddenly sprouted a pair of blue "Bella" demons, time honored guardians of the entrance to a gaming hell. Thérèse Khan darted up and pulled Catherine's chador over her face.

"No peeping!"

They set her on her feet, and stripped off the cloak.

"You can open your eyes!"

She was standing in a deep blue gloom, in the antechamber to a gaming arena. She faced a semicircle of gateways. Each would be the entrance to a different world, a different virtual *envie*. It was a long time since Catherine had been inside a hell. She looked for racks of visors, for weapons, fx generators, mask readers. She saw only the shining floor, the dim ceiling, and the glittering photochemical gates leading into utter darkness. The young humans stood around her. Thérèse had also shed her chador. Binte the maid had been left outside.

Misha was beside Catherine. "You've played arena games before, haven't you?"

"Not in this life."

"Some things have changed. A lot of things are the same. Once you're in the game environment, or once it is in you, you'll run around and jump and play in real space, with your physical body, in the arena beyond those doors. It'll seem like a whole world. The sensei will keep you from colliding with anybody, or doing anything to make you conscious of the real-world scruffy hall. Remember what a sensei is? The Master Control Program. It keeps everyone in the same *envie* in contact by sensing the electrical activity in your brain and converting it into void-forces signals; it's light, but not visible light. Your world will be made of the game libretto, the storybook that's been put into your brain. Plus the input from all the players who have entered the same *envie*, wherever they may be. You understand?"

She nodded.

He took her by the shoulders, his touch circumspect and distant, and guided her into position, her back to one of the gates. He showed her a tiny vial, cupped in his palm.

"What's that?"

"This is your visor. This is how the game gets into your head, in our time. Look up."

"Yet marked I where the bolt of Cupid fell: It fell upon a little western flower, Before milk-white, now purple with love's wound . . . ."

She heard the murmur of his voice, felt the liquid touch her eyes. "Go!"

She dropped. Into infinite space. She was in the game.

She brought back nothing from that first visit to the Phoenix gamesroom, but the confused fragments of a dream. A dark wood, a wild animal. Something panther or wolflike running through undergrowth, thorns tearing at its furry hide. Had the panther been Catherine? She wasn't sure. There had been hunters, a tremendous chase; and there'd been more, so much more. But it was gone. She would have to learn the skills of virtuality gaming over again. How to remain lucid, how to enjoy the unreal world to the full, without getting sucked in and losing control. She was amazed she hadn't realized that her young friends *must* be gamers. She'd been fooled by the nostalgic decor in the Café, that recalled so strongly First Contact earth: where virtuality had been so crude, those clunky gauntlets, visors, bodybags . . .

Catherine sat up.

She was in the Phoenix Café's ladies' cloakroom, a room reserved for Traditionalist women, whose culture forbade them to share the ordinary bathroom. Someone had laid her on a couch and spread the chador over her. She couldn't remember leaving the game.

"Hello." Misha opened the door and closed it behind him. "I shouldn't be in here. But I've permission from the management. I've come to see if you're all right."

"I'm fine." She felt that the Café out there was empty. "Is it late? I've no idea."

"Quite late. Everyone's gone home." He sat beside her. The door he had closed so quietly was made of paneled, painted wood and hung on metal hinges. She thought how Maitri would adore the Phoenix Café. But she would never let him come here. Lord Maitri would destroy the renaissance; he would love it to death.

"To tell the truth, we were scared. We didn't expect you to black out."

"I haven't played for a very long time. Not for about a hundred and twenty years."

Misha snorted. Catherine giggled.

"It's quite safe," he said. "You can't take the visor off; that worried you in there. But it really isn't dangerous. The nanotech in the eyedrops starts to degrade after about an hour objective time. It gets dismantled, absorbed into your brain chemistry—it's perfectly harmless. If you can't wait that long, you can still leave. All you have to do is *head for the exit.*"

"I'll remember that." She laughed. "You told me you didn't play the games! You were extremely cutting about gaming hells!"

"We don't play the commercial pap. We only play our own. But the fact is, I can't imagine life *without* gaming," he said seriously. "Or at least, I can imagine it. It would be like being smothered."

"Do you write them yourselves?"

"Some of us write them. It's a co-op, like the Café."

They were alone. He hadn't come in here to talk about games tech.

"You were here before," he whispered. "I can't get a grip on that. Whether you believe it, or whether it's the truth. Either way, I don't know who you are. How to treat you."

Catherine drew up her knees and leaned her chin on her folded arms. "I'm Catherine. My mother is called Leonie; she's Lord Maitri's human cook. Let's say Lord Maitri adopted me as a fetus, from who knows where, and had his cook carry me to term. He brought me up as an Aleutian and conditioned me to believe I'm the reincarnation of Clavel, the Third Captain, one of his dearest friends. He was lonely, you see, because so few of the original adventurers had come back for this last life on earth. I can't help believing I'm Clavel. You don't have to think about it. I'm Catherine. Is that better?"

"You're making fun of me."

"No, I'm not." Catherine frowned. "What does it matter?" she asked. "From moment to moment, I'm Catherine. I remember, I forget. Can you remember everything that you were doing yesterday? Are you the same person? I'm not wise; I'm not a superbeing. I'm not even a grown-up. A lot of people think that I'm *never* a grown-up. Treat me like that."

He reached across and pressed her shoulder back against the wall behind the couch. He kissed her on the mouth, gripping her upper arms hard. Catherine responded to the kiss instantly. Misha, his mouth open against hers, slid his other hand inside the gauzy jacket and found her breast, worked it free of the clinging underbodice. A rush of arousal seemed to flood between them. She arched her back, insensately offering the base of her throat, where in an Aleutian body wanderers would be teeming at this moment, hurrying to be gobbled up by Catherine's lover.

Misha drew back; he laughed excitedly.

"I warned you about the alcohol, Miss Alien!"

"Alcohol?" she repeated, puzzled.

She saw her own dead image reflected in the mirror of his eyes.

He pinned her with his weight, reached under her skirts, and pushed her thighs apart. Catherine began to struggle. "Misha, no! What are you doing? Stop it! Not like this! Why are you doing this to me?" But she couldn't stop him, and couldn't make him answer. It was over soon; he'd finished. He stood up and backed away, still breathing hard, sealing the closure of his overalls, staring down at her in sullen reproach.

"Don't tell me you didn't want that."

He went and leaned against the wall by the doors to the toilet cubicles, put his head in his hands, and drew a big deep breath. He looked up, but didn't look at Catherine.

"I've ordered you a cab. I'll tell Garland you'll be out in a moment. I'm leaving." Leaf Garland was the name of the person who was café manager this evening.

When she reached the house at the giratoire, Maitri and Vijaya were waiting in the atrium. They worried about Catherine, because of the intercommunal violence. She went with them to the main hall where the Aleutians were gathered for the night. Atha and some of the other domestics were playing their favorite musical game, capping each other's variations in the wordless, expert harmonies of the Silent.

"You don't seem to have much time for us these days." Maitri smiled. "Don't apologize, I'm very glad. Didn't I introduce you to young Michael? I knew he'd be good for you. Now, tell us about your evening, and the fun you've had."

She managed to leave them at last, pleading her human need for sleep. In her own room she huddled on her bed, blessing the deficiencies of Aleutian "mind-reading." *I am Catherine*, she thought. *This is my life.* The thin keening voices of the old retainers; Maitri's unbearable patience with their whims. Atha's constant need to be approved, to be of use; the chaplain's rambling. Vijaya and Smrti with their endless old roués' gossip. She took off her human clothes. Nothing was torn, but there was a small bloodstain, like a split heart, penetrating the layers of her white underskirts. It was fading. It would have vanished soon.

She stared at the blood. A great trembling began deep inside her, deep in the core of her being. She felt very cold.

5

THE STARDATE DIARIES

i

THÉRÈSE WAITED IN the outer office. It was an austere room, made large by well-tailored illusion but very simply decorated in a classic style: a polished desk, antique filing cabinets, but modern chairs. False windows showed the leaves falling in an old-earth orchard garden: the broad cold plains, a great forest. Thérèse lay curled in the embrace of a soft armchair, cheeks flushed and lips parted. Both hands were tucked childishly between her thighs, where the layers of skirt and underskirt were not such a bastion of modesty as they appeared from a distance, and her straying fingers occasionally touched a soft little mat of pubic hair. She was waiting for her mother, who was in a meeting. She was certainly dozing, with kittenish signs that maybe sexual arousal played a part in her dreams. But her long green eyes, half closed, drowsily followed the proceedings, as they were relayed to an antique monitor on Mrs. Khan's desk.

Thérèse saw a vast, dark and starry sky. The darkness gave way in lovely gradations to a rose-tinged sunlit landscape. The sky above became pale blue, punctuated by a few jewel-like points of brightness—stars so large and near that they did not become invisible even in the full glare of this system's sun. The landscape was a rolling plain covered with grass-like vegetation; there were stands of larger growth like trees. There was a golden river that moved like oil, not water. The rosy tinge in the air was caused by a difference in the composition of this sun's light. It was not, as had been suggested, a smog caused by large scale volcanic or industrial activity . . . The commentary proceeded, visuals changing appropriately, to a general description of the system: of the star, faintly visible from earth via space telescope, its thirteen planets. This, the only one in an earth-type congenial orbit, was the one that had been visited by Buonarroti. None of the others seemed habitable, but one of the moons of the tenth and largest might be no more inhospitable than Mars.

Three hundred years ago, a German physicist called Peenemünde Buonarroti made a discovery of world-shattering importance.

The scene changed to a sparse and rigid interior. A large woman in a curiously square, white, shirt-like garment sat with her back to the viewers at an old-fashioned workstation. She glowed from head to toe, shedding the radiance of genius and goodwill from every pore. Dish aerials, high-orbit satellites, observatory domes like cartoon mushrooms were spinning in the margins outside her cuboid bubble, binary code shooting in rhythmic bursts between them. (This was an artistic impression of pre-contact science.)

But she was unable to develop her invention, because of insurmountable difficulties. Insurmountable, that is, to human endeavor.

The arrival of the Aleutians intervened . . .

Peenemünde Buonarroti's splendid form shifted tetral by tetral into the mean, lean moody figure of Clementina Stewart, Buonarroti's *evil twin* in the mythology of First Contact. Stewart had been the scientific director of the secret resistance movement called White Queen. While

Buonarroti refused to believe any intelligence could be "alien," Stewart, like Braemar Wilson, had seen the arrival of Aleutians as a threat to human supremacy. But it was Clementina Stewart who first examined a stolen sample of Aleutian tissue—and therefore, ironically, was the first to see the proof of Buonarroti's claim. She was depicted standing, peering into a tiny black microscope that looked like a child's toy (a rather sketchily researched historical detail). Around her, filling her air, the ridged and twined molecular chains from an Aleutian "information cell" shuttled to and fro: unlike in detail, but astonishingly similar in conformation and in significance to the structure known as human DNA.

In the tragedy of the Sabotage Crisis, and through the harsh years of the Gender War, the Buonarroti device was lost . . .

Buonarroti, unmistakably feminine and Reformer in aura, has given way to Stewart, notorious in the First Contact story as a person of ambiguous sex. (The sexless aliens' "theft" of the mixed-gender role in society was believed to have played a major part in Stewart's hostility to them. This personal bitterness was subtly conveyed in the text of her image.) Clementina, though far from being an "alienlover," always stood for the halfcastes in the simplified myth. There now had to be some airtime for the third gender grouping. Traditionalist men and women cross the field of view: fleeing from burning cities—no cities were destroyed in the Gender War. Cities survived. It was the land outside that burned. But never mind—running down bunker corridors. Tramping, the blind leading the blind, in endless lines across the battlefields, wrapped in ragged veils and weeping over dead children. The Traditionalists of Youro, the city where the project was located, insisted on having these wartime scenes in any Buonarroti news coverage. The Youro government didn't want the global audience to forget how cruelly their cultural persuasion had suffered in that conflict.

But let the twisting chains of life return. Red for Aleutian, blue for human. Let those shuttling chemical processes spread and change until they become skeins of stars, twisting and shifting, entering and re-entering each other in the dark and fertile void.

For generations there was no proof of the existence of Buonarroti's device. Except for the material known as the Stardate Diaries—*a series of apparently fictional records of interplanetary travel, which appeared on the data-grid after her death. And except for a minor mystery buried in the turmoil of the Sabotage Crisis—the failure to discover any trace of the spaceplane or the rocket launch that had transported the saboteurs out to orbit. It was the Second Captain of the Expedition, Kumbva the engineer, who divined that the* Diaries *were a true record, and that the saboteurs could only have reached the shipworld by means of an instantaneous travel device. Kumbva lived for years among humans, directing the investigation that led to the discovery of the earth's greatest treasure trove. It was Kumbva who initiated the practical development of the non-location travel device.*

The stars faded. Peenemünde and Clementina briefly reappeared, working together in unlikely harmony. They were joined by a massively built smoky-skinned Aleutian: Kumbva the engineer, depicted as tradition decreed with the bald head and animator's white gloves that had been part of his "human" disguise. The three major players faded, replaced by a medley of busy anonymous figures in red and brown overalls (the air around them still filled with wriggling molecular chains). The teams were in sunlight: subtropical greenery, flowers and fruit in the background. The physical differences between human and alien were blurred. It wasn't possible to make out exactly what they were doing.

Lifetimes of research and endeavor have passed since then. Now, at last, the device has been successfully developed for practical use. Sadly, Kumbva the engineer is not alive today. But his place is ably filled by matched teams of human and Aleutian scientists, technicians, and artisans, working together to give us all the freedom of the stars. To give us all, as Kumbva said, the keys of the kingdom of heaven!

The image broke up, tetral by tetral, the tiny shards of color tumbling in a four-dimensional kaleidoscope. The *slow shift*, currently very fashionable, was meant to be a reminder that this was machine-generated image. There were no human actors playing the historical roles, no real backgrounds. (Perhaps, distantly, this taste for acknowledging the machinery was related to the renaissance movement.)

When the picture reformed, it showed a group of human politicians, including Thérèse's mother, standing in the Buonarroti project laboratory. They were waiting to greet a dignitary from orbit, the Project Manager, who was making a rare in-person visit. This was the occasion for the news program. The Aleutians were in-person, the humans telepresent—although this didn't show on the screen. For safety reasons, physical access to the Buonarroti lab was very strictly controlled, and even virtual access severely restricted.

Thérèse, sleepily watching, saw a large red-walled room with a long irregular empty space running down the center, lumpy counters, cabinets, and other half-recognizable extrusions jutting into it. Aleutian technicians were at work (or something), squatting on the counters. Whiplike connections flickered: strange, monstrous-looking living machines crawled about. She couldn't look at anything in detail; she couldn't shift the direction of her gaze. Technically the telepresent politicians had more freedom. They would not use it—constrained by protocol, and by fear.

Thérèse didn't listen to the back track. For a while she watched the minute, continuous unraveling and remaking of the expressions on human faces, the positions of different people in the group, the delicate brushing out (or emphasizing) of alien grotesquerie. Everything was in flux, as political agents in the global grid bid for, bought, and sold fractional rights in this *actualité*. Eventually, it would stop changing. It would be dead, and reeled off the grid by humble hacks like Mâtho's father. She closed her eyes, bored. What is truth? Whatever it is, it doesn't get into the news.

ii

THE BUONARROTI LABORATORY was located in a wild park on the western fringe of Youro. Facilities were austere, because of the preserved-wilderness regulations. The dignitary from orbit and his entourage had been obliged to walk from their spaceplane to the laboratory. They'd found this very interesting. For most of them, it was their first visit to earth.

<Cold enough for you?> inquired the chief scientist, after the rituals of embracing, showing throat, exchanging wanderers—to which he'd submitted with his usual bad grace. <Count yourselves lucky. The snow will come soon.>

They made the appropriate gestures to the telepresent humans, and for a while the whole group stood solemnly in front of a large virtual screen that was running *Stardate Diaries* excerpts (enhanced in line with current scientific information). The Aleutians were not interested in the interplanetary travelogue. Their appetite for adventure was sated. They only wanted to use the device to get home and sell it there. But it was necessary to show respect.

The dignitary, a non-spoken-language user, had taken the obligatory Sanskrit name Gharvapinda. In this name he was greeted by the humans, and responded politely (<Say whatever they want to hear,> he ordered briefly) through his speechmaker. His real identity—inscribed in the prolix, complex, and shifting chemical signature that filled the air around him, might have been expressed formally, in this context, as *The Busy Person Who Accepts The*

Importance Of These Public Appearances, But Does Not Enjoy Them.

For generations after it was rediscovered, research on the Buonarroti device had proceeded at the leisurely pace of Aleutian science. The work had been done on earth, in recognition of the fact that the original invention "belonged" to the humans, and that the technology developed would eventually be shared, as agreed at the famous Neubrandenburg Conference. But the spirit had been entirely Aleutian: *time is cheap.*

In the last decade things had speeded up dramatically. Cynics might say that the Aleutians had finally realized how much damage they'd done to the human planet and wanted to get out in a hurry. Others noted that the latest chief scientist had made spectacular progress. Departure was still without a definite date, but it had been revealed that the engine was up and running, ready for its final tests. This visit from orbit was extremely interesting. It might even be followed by the announcement of an actual timescale for the great event.

They began a tour of the facility. It would not take long. This room was all they would see. Then the aliens would leave the building and walk around it to reach the entrance of the twin laboratory, where the telepresents would join them again to inspect the human team's work. For security reasons it was necessary for the teams to be physically isolated from each other. For political reasons it was necessary for them to share a site. The group moved slowly, dutifully attentive, down the middle of the big red-walled lab. On either side, visible but blurred by gel partitions, technicians went on with their work (as much as people ever do, with an official visitor peering over their shoulders).

<Your folk are calling you something different,> remarked the dignitary, as they passed from one niche to another. <Why is that?>

<We called me "Lugha" or "Laghu,"> explained Dr.
Bright, <in the life when I came here with the landing parties. It means good-looking but narrow-minded, or something like that. It was my companions' snide comment on
my genetic obligation, as I later realized. I don't think contempt for science is appropriate in this generation, do
you? The English and Youro "Bright," as in shining intelligence, suits me better.> He went on airily. <It used to be
that your Sanskrit label meant you were a veteran of the
original crews. Now that every space-sick first-time visitor
is using Sanskrit, it's no distinction. A lot of us have
dropped them.>

<I see,> said the first-time visitor Gharvapinda, with a
slight chill to which Dr. Bright was oblivious. <But that's
not it. What about this *other* handle you seem to have acquired? I may be Silent, but I can pick up what's in the air.
Brown? Something like brown, the color?>

The Busy Person was important enough to use the term
"Silent," at present rather socially dubious, without a
qualm.

Dr. Bright grinned. <"Von Braun." Oh, that's Catherine.
That's Catherine's little joke. Don't worry about it. It's old-
earth talk.>

<Hmm. I don't like the feel of it. Words give things away,
my bright friend. Especially names. I don't like that.>

The scientist shrugged. <What does it matter?>

None of the humans, telepresent or in the news audience, could understand much of what the dignitary and
the scientist were saying to each other in the Common
Tongue. After the meeting the humans would demand a
"transcript" of the aliens' informal exchanges. The Aleutians would comply with this nonsensical request. No one
would read the bland nonsense they provided, and honor
would be satisfied.

The tour proceeded briskly. Dr. Bright expounded at
speed, effortlessly providing a running translation into

English for the human telepresents on non-location travel, and the problem that had halted Buonarroti's original research. Buonarroti had discovered a means of translating a pattern of consciousness, in the form of pure information, instantaneously from any given 4-space *situation*, to any other specified *situation* in the cosmos. Nothing material could travel this way. At the departure point the body of the traveler would vanish. At the destination a new, identical body would accrete to the informational entity, made up of carbon, nitrogen, phosphorus, oxygen, hydrogen, and so on (to speak in human terms), elements that were abundant throughout 4-space. Thus conforming to local-point phase conservation.

<Eh?>

<Can't have the same thing happening in two places at once. Don't worry about it.>

Thus a traveler could cross the galaxy in less than no time, as long as they had some feasible destination in mind, and take on a body there that would be indistinguishable, would in fact be logically identical with the original. But for human subjects there had proved to be an impossible dilemma. Human travelers perceived the second reality as dream. They processed sensory input from the new environment as if it was internally generated, and arranged it into self-referential "meaning": the way the mind, human or Aleutian, behaves in dream-sleep. Or in forms of psychiatric illness. There was a dire risk of falling into psychosis and becoming trapped at the destination. In Buonarroti's model, return to the point of departure was achieved by a simple act of will. But the psychotic dreamer would have forgotten that he'd set out, so he'd be unable to decide to come home.

<And they can't learn to adjust?> The Busy Person had heard that humans had no genetic obligation and could acquire skills at random. He wished to sound knowledgeable.

<No more than you could learn to talk,> responded the scientist rudely.

Then he scowled. He was a physicist. In the Aleutian gestalt, this meant that his talent was for the science of life. His chemical identity gave him a passionate affinity with the baseic elements—their relations, their transformations, the immensely complex processes of those twisted chains. He was impatient with the unreal world that lay beyond the veil, where void-forces and dead particles too minute for life interacted in peculiar occult ways. That was Kumbva's "science." Mystical nonsense. Bright found the cosmological implications of non-location travel exasperating.

<No, they can't adjust, because the conflicting realities problem is real. It isn't merely a form of human-specific travel-sickness, as Buonarroti seems to have assumed. Take it from me, there is a genuine limitation involved. It's been our big problem too. But it doesn't matter, we've found a way around it.>

<I don't think I quite understand—>

<Of course you don't,> agreed the scientist, with cheery contempt.

<Would this be the problem that killed Lord Clavel, when he tried the device?>

<Don't be stupid. Clavel was miserable as shit in that life. He died because he wanted to die, and the device gave him a nice, noble exit.> Bright grinned. <Did him no good, as it turns out, because he's still miserable as shit now he's a girl called Catherine. But that's nothing to do with my problems. Please,> he added, <*try* not to embarrass yourself with dumb questions. Just follow me about and look interested. That's all anyone asks of you.>

And he returned to his lecture.

The original Buonarroti device had incorporated a machine known as a particle accelerator, which divided the information-pattern of the traveler into two streams and slammed the streams into each other, to reach speeds that broke the light barrier and projected the whole entity into non-location. "From" a state that covered the sum of all the possibilities of 4-space, the traveler was translated to the destination by what Buonarroti called an act of desire. Buonarroti had said that desire, far from being an exclusively human emotion, was the human *experience* of one of the laws of being. Carbon desires, bacteria desire . . . But only self-aware consciousness can make use of the state of non-location.

Buonarroti had predicted that the Aleutians would be able to overcome the psychotic dreamer syndrome, because for them self-aware consciousness was diffuse: impregnating their tools, their artifacts, their whole environment. They would non-locate without trauma. She had envisaged an awareness-impregnated starship, built by Aleutians, that could be safely used by both Aleutians and humans. She'd been mistaken. That route had been exhaustively explored. It didn't work. But the project had come up with a solution, which was now in the final stages of application. They had built a kind of engine, not a vessel. It acted as a pump, taking a whole area of 4-space from one "situation" to another, and carrying anyone (any self-aware consciousness) in that area along.

The scientist arranged himself and the Busy Person in front of a soft-walled display cabinet, which he touched, causing the case to open and an exhibit to creep out.

<This is a working model,> he announced in the Common Tongue and repeated in English. The model was contained in a round blob of semirigid gel. Inside the gel was suspended another roundish blob, dark and roughened and irregular.

<Ha! That looks rather like the shipworld!>

<Quite a lot like. Now watch.>

He touched the outer layer. Half of the shell of the rough dark spheroid inside became transparent. Everyone saw in cross section a mass of networked chambers, cables, passages, parkland, crops, churches . . . Deep inside—somewhere, suppose this was the real shipworld, around the location of the main bluesun fusion reactor—there was a tiny shining thread of movement. Bright touched this spot. An exudation from the secretion glands in his wrists slid through palms and fingers to his fingertips and commanded magnification. The pinpoint of movement could be seen to be entering and re-entering another smaller object that was filled with a coiled darkness. There was a short pause.

The Busy Person exclaimed: <Oh, I see! The whole model is being fed into that little coil, from the inside out.>

<More or less. The coil is a particle accelerator, of a very special kind.>

<In reality,> remarked the scientist after a few moments, <if that's the expression I want, the whole operation won't take any time at all.>

The visitor looked around warily. <And where does your bauble, ah, reappear?>

Dr. Bright gave him a pitying glance. <You are kidding me. This is a mock-up.> He dismissed the exhibit. <That's my part done. Now's your moment to ask me if we've done any test-flights, and how long before the big day. You know what they like. Dates. Times. What do you want me to tell them? They're waiting.>

The Busy Person conveyed, in a brief unguarded flicker of emotion, his opinion of these human obsessions. <They can wait. I'm not here to pander to their psychological quirks. We'll leave when we're ready. What's the difference?>

Bright turned to the humans.

"That's the end of the demonstration. If the telepresents will relocate in the twin laboratory, we will join you shortly."

Next moment the Aleutians were alone.

<What are they doing in there?> asked the visitor, jerking

his chin at the dividing wall, after a furtive glance at the ceiling to make sure the livespace light was off. He did not entirely trust the humans' supposed ignorance of the Common Tongue. It seemed to him unnatural and improbable: an elaborate hoax.

<I'm not sure,> admitted Bright. <Probably, still trying to work out how many tachyons they can fit on the head of a pin.>

<What?>

<They're trying to model an information-entity starship, using hybrid technology: a ship with a mind that incorporates the minds of all the passengers. It won't do them any good. It doesn't matter what they do, they can't build a Buonarroti engine. And for obvious reasons we cannot let them help us to build this one.>

Dr. Bright had come to the Project at a time when morale was at a low ebb. His first brilliant insight had been to think of a naked engine, rather than struggling with the impossible concept of an "information-entity vehicle." His second insight had been the realization that the mechanism he needed already existed, in the processes used to create proliferating weapons, the Aleutians' weapons of mass destruction. At that point the Aleutians had been forced to impose complete quarantine between the human and the Aleutian labs. They had explained that full cooperation would be restored after the danger period was over. The actual *engine* technology would be perfectly safe; weapons processing would not be part of the final package. Nevertheless it had been difficult. There had been fanatical human-rule partisans who believed they had a right to unrestricted physical access to the Buonarroti project, and had tried to prove it. There had been a few summary executions—which no Aleutian had liked, especially not those who'd had experience on earth and understood the idea of permanent death. It would have been easier if they could have moved the lab off earth, into an orbital laboratory (naturally, no one wanted this work on board the ship-world). But the human governments had rejected that idea in outrage. Off-earth location was expressly ruled out by the Neubrandenburg Conference Agreement. Those who framed it had made sure there'd be no risk of the aliens developing the engine out in space and just running away with it.

<At least they seem to have resigned themselves. Things have been quiet around here. We haven't had to kill any spies for ages.> He reached for another demonstration exhibit.

<You've had experience with weapons manufacture some time in your lives, so you'll recognize this.>

This exhibit, enclosed in another gel, was a hand-size piece of tissue, a section of Aleutian flesh as if sliced from someone's forearm: complete with information-system nodes, skin layers, blood, and muscle. It was living. Small cell-complexes crept on the surface of the skin, groping the gel, trying to escape.

<*They have no wanderers,*> mused Bright. <I spotted that straight off, when we first arrived. Nobody would believe me. It seemed so far-fetched. But it's true. *Your* body is alive and in a real sense conscious.> He grinned at the Busy Person. <Yes, even yours. Your information system changes, develops, remembers, in response to the world around it, and in response to the flux of biochemical communication. That's the way we work. Not them. With them an individual incarnate, the physical form, is nothing but a carrier: a dumb repeat of the pattern in its chemical bases. Their bodies are dead. They are like ghosts, ghosts inhabiting corpses. It's very creepy when you come to think about it.>

The Busy Person was eyeing Bright's second exhibit with distaste and not attending. He didn't understand this sort of stuff, and he was glad he didn't.

<Buonarroti believed that Aleutians would be able to

beat the mind/body impasse,> Bright went on, dreamily, <because we are not ghosts riding in dead machines. And so we can, but not in the way she expected. We see non-location travel differently now. We see the Buonarroti engine, the pump, as moving between self and not-self, between being and nonbeing, between God and Nothing, if you like: turning one into the other and back again. The engine presents the same problem that we have to overcome in manufacturing weapons. To build accurate proliferating weapons—creatures that will devour your enemy's life on every scale, but leave everything else alive and well—you need a sample of the enemy's tissue. But not self-aware tissue, because if you bred weapons from that, the weapons would destroy themselves, wouldn't they. So you get hold of a piece of relatively inert tissue (not entirely free from information-system cells, that's a vulgar misconception, but dumb enough), and you dope it. . . . To build weapons we need to build a specific *anti-self.* To start the pump we need a—how can I put it—a general, universal anti-self. Essence of Nothing. But the process is essentially the same.>

He turned the exhibit in his hands. The Busy Person involuntarily stepped back.

<Creating an anti-self substrate isn't easy. The resistances one has to overcome are enormous and very strange. But I don't care about that. Worrying about what goes on beyond the veil is a waste of time. I leave it to the humans. In real weaponry, a culture like this would be only the start. We'd be calling for volunteers now, for the breeding stage.>

<Do we have to go into this?> pleaded the Busy Person. <I don't like it.>

<You'd be some kind of whacko psychopath if you did.> Bright affected to recognize the exact source of the visitor's unease for the first time. <Oh, don't worry. This is not a chunk of anybody you know. It's another mock-up.> He

smirked. <The cultures we need for our application are much smaller, but I still prefer to keep them under tight security. A sample of whole tissue is rather personal, isn't it?>

The Busy Person regarded him with shuddering wonder. <I'm very glad I'm not a scientist.>

<And I'm glad I'm not a rich, hypocritical waste of time and space like you,> said Bright casually. He went on turning the mock-up in his hands, watching the little simulacra in their hopeless struggle. The skin (lively, open-pored, soft textured, so different from those insensate human surfaces) was dotted with irregular marks, about the color of a bad bruise, that caught the eye strangely: the notorious empty-centered sores of weapons production.

<There,> he murmured, awed. <Do you see them? Those little devouring voids, gates into the abyss. There, breaking open the house of life to make a breeding place for horrors, lies the heart of the Buonarroti engine. I detest mysticism, but one can't help thinking: this is a strange kind of key to the kingdom. Strange and ominous.>

" 'I am become Death,' " he quoted softly, aloud. " 'Destroyer of Worlds—' "

The dignitary from orbit kept to the point.

<They can't be allowed to learn anything about weapons production. Never!>

<No. Obviously not.>

Dr. Bright abruptly dropped the exhibit, which returned to its cabinet. His visitor stood looking at the back wall of the laboratory, expressing wordless sympathy (restrained by reason and prudence) for the humans on the other side. <Poor devils. It's pitiful how keen they are about getting hold of this travel device, when they've handed over *a fortune* in novel genomes for practically nothing. You may have seen the work done by a colleague of yours on that stuff, extraordinarily light and resilient building gel, naturally occurring in their brand of trees, I do believe—>

The scientist bristled. <"Xylem,"> he snapped. <And by

my colleague I suppose you mean the guy in "Manaus," calling himself Nadi—a name the shit has no right to bear by the way. He, in his fancy Enclaves lab, with every home comfort laid on, couldn't have done anything without *my translation* of the algorithm for "nylon." Which, I think you'll find, is by far the more valuable and novel material.>
<Ah, well. If you say so.> The Busy Person had no time for professional jealousies. But he was always willing to tolerate the creative temperament, as long as it was generating massive potential profits. <Nevertheless, I'm glad we're leaving this treasure house,> he remarked gravely. <It's the best thing for all concerned. Far the best. Leave them to sort out their own problems. If only they weren't so fecund! The masses, that's what we hear from every human ruling class. It's the masses. They just keep budding and budding—>

<Fertility isn't the problem,> Bright corrected him absently. <It's the sex issue.>

<Eh?> Dr. Bright's patron started, for the first time jolted out of his respect for genius and genuinely displeased. <Stop right there! Have you no sense at all? No gender politics!> Then he turned to his entourage, encompassing with a gesture one tiresome duty done and one more to be endured. <We'd better join the humans. Thank you, Bright. Most . . . interesting. Until next time. What a bore all this rigmarole is. You don't welcome visitors, well, don't imagine *I* haven't got better things to do. Roll on the great event, that's all I can say.> They made their embraces, Bright submitting with better grace now that the intruders were leaving. The shipworld visitation fed itself into the entrylock and out into the cold.

Dr. Bright stood and fumed. <If only they weren't so fecund!> he snarled, with withering scorn. <Does that stupid turd think he can tell me my business? I am the only person on earth or in the shipworld who has seriously *studied* human physiology. The truth is, after three hundred years

in our company, there are far fewer humans alive, at any given time, than there were before we arrived. And going down. Do you know what that *means,* asshole? Try going to your doctor and telling him: Doctor, I'm losing weight, and I haven't an idea why. See what his face tells you! But *that's not the point.* A lot of their reproductive-rate loss is benign— rapid, sensible adaption to city life. The point is that the Gender War is going to start up again as soon as we are out of sight. Gender War is a contest for reproductive success: species against species, male against female, all of them fighting for food, status, control of territory, control of futurity. The less of those things there are to go around, the harder they'll fight. It doesn't make sense anymore, but that makes no difference.>

Bright glared around him, defying hostile comment.

<They've changed. They've become more like us, and it's a change for the better, I don't care what anybody says. But we are leaving, and as soon as we've gone, they'll revert. Just as Catherine keeps trying to tell us—>

His silent diatribe ended abruptly. He was gagged. Like Catherine, trapped and helpless in the grip of the Commonalty's will.

The technicians and artisans knew their chief's irritable temperament. Visits from officialdom always had this effect. When the rant was over, they prompted him kindly.

<Shouldn't you be going through to next door, sir?>

<Shut up. Lie down with your parents and spit shit, cloaca-mouths.>

He pushed his way through a partition into his office, and could be seen brooding there, his slender clawed hands working into running pads, his meager nasal flaring.

<Let him alone,> murmured one skilled artisan to his neighbor. <You know what he's like. Hates being made to feel for other people. He can't take it; it just makes him angry.>

Shortly, Bright—still muttering and seething bodywise

—came out of his area, donned a human-made greatcoat, and stormed off to join the VIP's party with the human team. Poor guy, his own team remarked, with varying degrees of affection, toleration, and respect. Signifiers are so highly strung. They forget that *everything must happen.* They get trapped in short-term distress.

They returned to their work: nudging, inhibiting, assisting in the unlabeled processes of the continuum. They agreed that everything Dr. Bright said, as far as they could follow it, was true. But they could see no real harm in what they were doing. If the humans were to suffer now, no doubt they'd get their revenge some time in the lives to come. There is no lasting harm. It was beyond the technicians' imagination to conceive otherwise.

iii

MRS. KHAN JOINED Thérèse in the outer office.

"How draining telepresence is," she complained, tossing the transcript she'd just received onto her desk. "Sheer nonsense, as usual. Everyone knows it's against their religion to give fixed meaning to the Common Tongue." She dropped into a chair.

Thérèse sat up, sleepily rubbing her eyes, as the monitor picture winked out.

"Come here, sweetheart."

Thérèse came over. Mrs. Khan's face was suddenly haggard, as if she had made that grueling trip to the Buonarroti lab in person, and spent the last hour under torture there. She drew her daughter close, and—summoning up a teasing smile—tweaked the sweetly upstanding nipples that were outlined by her dainty bodice. "My little flower. You're such a darling. When I'm in one of those stupid meetings, I want you so much."

Her expression changed, from affection to unashamed appetite. Her hands, like two separate hungry creatures, kneaded at Thérèse's breasts, her face burrowed into her daughter's skirts. The expensive fabric melted, with well-tailored obedience, at the touch of the lips and tongue it recognized. Mrs. Khan gripped Thérèse's buttocks, holding the girl's crotch in place at her mouth as if Thérèse was a spare rib or a slice of melon. Thérèse's breath came fast. Soon she began to press herself rhythmically against her mother's face. Her back arched, she gave a cry: a rush of liquid flowed from her.

Mrs. Khan sat back, wiping her lips. "So sweet," she murmured, stretching. "Ah, that was good. Exactly what I needed. I can come just thinking about my Thérèse, but it's much better to have you here. Darling, you're so reviving." She pulled her daughter down onto her lap, and Thérèse cuddled there, her cheek against the firm maternal breast.

"I'm glad that you and Catherine have become friends," said Mrs. Khan pensively, after a moment. "I thought you didn't like her when she came to visit."

Thérèse stirred. "All she did was sit with you and talk politics. Boring!"

Mrs. Khan chuckled. "I think you're jealous. There's no need to be, sweetheart. I'm not interested in her in *that* way! But we must invite her again. Don't ask me why; accept that it's important to me." She rocked Thérèse in her arms. "My little dolly. I have such a difficult existence, one long balancing act on a knife-edge. You wouldn't understand, but you can take it from me that life is sheer hell for a career woman, the same now as it was in Braemar Wilson's day. Some things never change! You trust me, don't you, darling?"

She sat up, briskly setting Thérèse aside. Looking into an inward mirror, she touched her hair, arranged her light veil.

"Must go. I'll be back soon. And then we'll have a whole half hour, my pet."

Thérèse returned slowly to her armchair. She thought of

Agathe, whose well-meant sympathy she resented. *I can be a Perfect too,* she thought, *In my own way. I'd like to see you try to do what I do, walk on my path* . . . She didn't want to watch the TV any more. Staring into a screen was tiring and unnatural. Without the benefit of implanted gadgetry, which her mother would never allow for a young lady, she awarded herself the freedom of infinite space, and drifted there among the stars.

6

BLOCKS AND DOCKS

i

AT CHRISTMAS EVERYONE gave presents. Maitri, delirious with joy, helped Catherine to ransack the old-earth style hyper-markets around the giratoire. Together they prowled the half-empty stacks in those vast old temples of consumerism, discovering wonders. Catherine sweated blood matching imagination to Mâtho's noble poverty, demure excess to the Khans' impossible wealth. It was fun.

On a morning in January, a closed car came to the giratoire house. Catherine was summoned to the atrium and found Thérèse Khan's maid waiting for her there. Binte, shrouded from head to foot, would only say. "Come. Miss Thérèse wants." The elderly Aleutians found these people-shaped machines very disturbing, so Catherine went with her quickly. She climbed into the back of the car, and immediately someone threw a black bag over her head. She struggled, horrified. But the bag was a chador, and Thérèse was there beside her: giggling as her maid arranged the rich slippery folds of nature-identical silk.

"I'm taking you on an outing. You've been with Misha; now come with me."

The vehicle began to move, smoothly, into the secret void of closed car travel.

"Where are you taking me?"

"Shopping!" Thérèse's eyes gleamed through the silken mesh that covered them.

Shortly, the car stopped. The door beside Thérèse opened. A huge shapeless figure, also veiled and giving no signals as to its sex, stood bowing. It had a red and gold figured shawl around its shrouded head and shoulders. They were in a gloomy, narrow court. The air was stifling and pungent with the tang of cheap building material: barely sanitized, compacted human shit. Catherine saw window-pocked walls, a fragment of sandy sky. The red-shawled person ushered Thérèse, Catherine, and the maid along a covered passageway into a large dimly lit room. The walls were lined with curtained cubicles. Catherine glimpsed coupled bodies moving jerkily and bedraggled young humans, naked and partly clothed—mostly with female-style bodies—chatting together while they waited for customers. Thérèse whispered with their guide, then unceremoniously shoved Catherine into one of the empty cubicles.

"Don't be frightened. No one will hurt you. Do whatever you like."

She found that Binte had been left with her. The maid squatted in a corner, an expressionless dark blot of fabric. Catherine sat on a narrow bed-with-legs that took up almost all the rest of the space. The mattress had the same kind of tired hygienic cover as the one in the remand cell in the hives. A nodule of hybrid growth, roughly in the shape of a pink daisy flower, clung to one wall. It was pumping out a flood of apples and meadows and new bread to mingle with the smell of shit. The curtain in front of the cubicle was pushed aside. The big figure in the red shawl looked in and withdrew to mutter with someone unseen. This second person entered the cubicle boldly. He was half naked, well nourished, broad-chested—cosmetically male. He stood rubbing his hairy chin and looking at Catherine.

He opened his loose trousers and displayed his sexual equipment. He had a formidable erection.

<Don't you want to do it?> he asked, in gesture.

<Not yet.>

It was an inadequate response, but she couldn't think of anything else to say. Binte sat quietly. There was a glow of garnet colored light from the gel curtain. She could see the man's stolid, rather brutal face: his hands stroking and occasionally offering again the thick male human claw. There was a continual coming and going, crying and muttering from the long room outside. The man left. The red-shawled figure looked in and went away. Another man appeared, sat for a while displaying his wares, and then he left too.

They were alone for a while. At last Binte stirred, got up, beckoned. They went out. Thérèse was there in her black shroud, doubled over and moaning. Their guide had to help her into the car.

"Oh, God!" she wailed, tearing open the hood of her chador (smart fabric parting with a faint whimper of protest). Her hair was disheveled, her cheeks flushed and green eyes wild. She clutched at her crotch.

"So big! God, so big! I'm not going to be able to sit down properly for a week." She dissolved into helpless giggles. "Did you do it, Catherine? How many did you have?"

'I didn't.'

Thérèse took out a compact. She smoothed her face with a film that wiped away all signs of disarray and ran her fingers through her hair, which rearranged itself into the sleek blonde ringlets of her set. "I get Camille, that's the old hag in the red shawl, to find them for me. They're drivers, valets, office boys, that sort of thing. They're kept pumped up with testo for fashion. It's quite safe. They never see my face." She stared defiance. "Are you shocked?"

"No," answered Catherine, truthfully.

Thérèse burst into peals of laughter.

"What about Binte?" said Catherine, when the noise had

subsided. "Maybe the johns won't tell, but isn't she pro-grammed to report on you?"

"How funnily you talk, like an old-earth game. *I'm not an idiot.* I can fix her. As far as she knows, we've been doing some in-person shopping. That's what her record will show. We've been buying antique clothes. I thought you'd like that." She glared at Catherine. "All right, I know it's risky. What do you expect? I have to have *something,* or I'd go mad."

Briefly, her face had become hard and adult: insisting on her right to relief from an intolerable strain. She looked cu-riously like her mother, the politician. Then she started to cry.

"Mama would kill me," she wailed. "Oh, God, Mama would kill me!"

The car carried them on. Thérèse stopped crying and sealed her chador. They sat in their small room, without any sense of motion, while anodyne images of rivers, trees, gardens, flowed around their walls.

"You're going to get another invitation to our house," said Thérèse. She spoke very softly, saying goodbye to Catherine on the steps of the giratoire house. "Don't ac-cept."

"Why not?"

"Make an excuse. For my sake, make it a good one. Don't let it seem that you were warned off. Or that you don't like me. Maybe I'm imagining things, and don't ask me any questions because I won't answer, but *be careful of my mother.*"

One night, after meeting at the Café and drinking a great deal of complicated wine, Catherine and her first friends— Joset, Misha, Rajath, Mâtho—took cabs to the corrida, to see Lydie in action. They went in person because there was no tvc at the Phoenix Café. The others chose different names from the program, discussing the season's form in this fash-

ionable interactive sport. Catherine chose Lydie for her virtual partner. They sat in the Connelly box right above the
arena, premier tvc bands clinging to their temples. The
show was called *bull-dancing* in English, in reference to a
very ancient tradition. But the animals were female. Bulls
were reserved for a different spectacle. The wild cattle ran
out: splendid, astonishing beasts, with the pure extraordinary beauty of forty thousand year old cave paintings.
They held their tasseled horns high, and looked around at
the crowd with alert, intelligent eyes. The dancers joined
them: slim young athletes in their white tight suits and brocade jackets, springing into casual back flips and somer-
saults. For the parade the dancers and their dangerous
partners were separated by invisible barriers. Then the
arena was cleared and the fun began. The friends in the
Connelly box were shouting and gasping in the grip of
adrenaline-fueled euphoria: blood, muscle, and brain
united with the performers. The crudely hooked-up poor
in the tiered seats yelled as loudly and seemed equally
transported. The acrobatics, the "dancing," was magical
to Catherine. But it was not so popular with the crowd as
the art of the *ecarteurs*, playing chicken with the charging
cattle.

There were several injuries, but no fatalities tonight.

They left at the end of the first tournament. All of them
were dripping sweat, grinning maniacally; their eyes in the
glimmer of a full moon black mouths of gaping pupil. The
poor and the employed streamed around them, into an ancient street that stank of big, hot animals, dung and piss
and violence. To be at the arena in-person was as much of
a thrill as the sport itself. The mood of the people was uncertain, unbalanced by rumors of the Departure. No one
sure what was allowed now, on the brink of the end of the
world.

They waited for Lydie, high as kites and hungry for more
adrenaline. It was about two in the morning, north-western

Youro time. Misha, who had broken his usual rule and had a cab waiting, revealed that he'd sent for a case of rifles. He had promised Catherine that he would take her hunting. This was a good night for it, he said. They would go after a tribe of foxes that had been plaguing a vehicle nursery. He'd had a report from the local keepers. He'd told the men he'd take care of the cull himself.

The Connellys had been wildlife wardens since the Gender War, when the first Michael Connelly had been huntsman to one of the warlord kings of Paris. Nowadays their chief business was the management of mass-market virtual wilderness experience, but they retained some antique privileges and pleasures. The friends had jumped into cabs at the arena in the jostling midst of a crowd. Now they were alone in the dark on a street corner in a neighborhood none of them knew, and no one except Misha had ever seen before. They sent the cabs away. Misha unveiled the weapons. They were beautiful: classic, sleek, simple works of art and craft.

"It's a vixen," he said, "and her half grown cubs. They don't kill; they graze. They get in the nursery pens and tear chunks out of the vehicle blanks, which are at this stage much like very thick domestic animals: huge, stupid, moving heaps of meat. You know what foxes are like? They go blood-crazy. They can do a hell of a lot of damage."

"Nasty," agreed Mâtho, looking solemn and responsible. "Got to be stopped."

"We're going to try for the mother, because if she's gone the cubs will scatter or die. I've a plan here of her usual movements. Wild animals are creatures of habit."

They sat round him, peering over his shoulders at the flat reader he'd laid on the ground. There was no one about, no sound but a vague stirring and grunting from the open pens. On the screen, menacing tawny shapes slipped in and out of shadow.

Lydie murmured: "Is that what foxes look like?"

Misha laughed. "I lied. It's not foxes, it's lions. A big family group has moved here from some preserved woodland nearby. If it was foxes we'd do nothing. We don't give a damn for the cab breeders, alien-stock profit-grubbers, so what if they lose a little fat. But lions that move into the streets sooner or later will prey on humans, and that we can't allow."

"How many do you want us to kill?" demanded Joset grandly.

"If you kill one, Jo, I'll be very much surprised. To your positions, ladies and gents."

He took Catherine to her place himself. He put her at the mouth of an alley, the pens ahead of her and the street behind. She was in a state of extreme excitement. The night was full of gleaming teeth, flashing limbs, white-rimmed eyes. It smelled of sweat and body heat and blood. She had lost her memory. She didn't know what had happened to the others. Through a darkly transparent barrier she could see the big soft bodies of the living machines. They moved like heavy clouds and exhaled faintly luminous green gases that drifted through the air.

"I'm glad you kept some big wildlife," she whispered, her blood thrumming. "Once it looked as if they would all vanish. There'd be nothing left but you people, your food, and machines like those."

"Only the ruthless ones," said Misha. "Lions, foxes, raptors. Nothing gentle survived." He put the hunting rifle into her hands and guided it to her shoulder. "Have you used one of these in the real?"

"Yes. Have the others?" She was concerned. "The real is still different, no matter how well you can handle yourself in a game *envie*. They might do something crazy."

"You mean Joset?" He laughed softly. "It's okay. He's firing blanks. Self, I'm so high I could fuck one of those things. I could roll in that field and eat tiger weed. What about you?"

He left her. She wondered: *Have I the right to kill the beast that preys on humans?* She wondered if her own weapon was loaded with blanks too. She saw the rust red sand of the arena racing toward her, the wicked curved horns plunging. She jumped over the moon and leapt, oh, *flying,* on the edge of death. The alley was cold. She heard movement. She leveled her antique rifle: searching the uncertain space for a low-moving shadow, filled with fellow feeling for the animal she might kill, waiting intensely for a deadly rush and a spring—

But the animal was Misha. Without a word he gripped her waist, turned her away from him, pushed her against the wall and impaled her, stabbing in and out: *ah, ah.* The barrel of the hunting rifle jarred against her breasts.

When he'd gone she was unsure of what had happened. Was that real or was it part of the high? Fluid dribbled between her thighs. She picked up the weapon, which she'd dropped when he let go, and took it back to the street corner. Lydie and Rajath were there, sitting in the roadway. Lydie had her rifle in one hand and a bottle of complicated wine in the other. "I'll tell you something," she said, when she recognized Catherine. "When we're in the arena, everyone wants us to be killed. People say they do tvc sports for the endorphins, for the excitement, the skill, the artistry of the performers. But what they want is for us to be killed. You only have to look at the stats, the peaks in the ape mapping."

"Ape?"

"Audience participation," explained Lydie gloomily. "Neuron activity mapping."

"I'm not morally challenged," said Rajath, grinning. "I was just scared."

Catherine sat down beside them.

"You know the other *corrida?* The bull fighting?" The dancer went on, "I've never wanted to be a matador. I don't care how famous you can be. But what I was going to say was, nobody wants to hook up to the bull. Maybe a few, but it's a tiny percentage. And it's the rich. Who wants to be the victim, huh? Trapped, no way to escape. Most of us have *that* for free, every day of our lives; it isn't romantic. In my game a steady thirty percent of the punters want to be the beasts, even though you can't remember it. You can't, you know. No one can remember being an animal; it's like a dream—it vanishes the moment you uncouple. But people want it because they know the animals are not the victims, we are. If a cow kills one of us, she's an overnight sensation. Then *everyone* wants to hook up with her. You know what the games are? Drug dependency: brain candy. No different from the injectables and pills that they teach us to think were so awful and degenerate. Why bother with the ana- logues, when you can mainline the original and best . . . So." She handed the bottle earnestly. "That's why I don't want to hunt. Fooling around with death isn't fun—it's work."

"I think they're loaded with blanks anyway. I don't think there are any lions around here. Or any foxes either."

"Oh?" Lydie scowled. "Typical Mish. The outsider, laughing at us all. I bet you're right."

ii

ONE OF THE great ladies of the *quartier* held a reception for Lalith the halfcaste. The speaker's fame had grown, en- hanced by the fact that news coverage of the renaissance was very sparse. The movement was a thing of the streets and the radical young, and therefore piquantly attractive to the very rich, who feel no fear. The lady was called Alicia Khan; she was some connection of Thérèse and Imran's family. She had never been seen by an Aleutian, on-screen or in-person. She had never before allowed an alien into her house.

The rooms, laden with illusion in the style of a century

ago, were thronged with masked or costumed humans, many virtual, a number actually present. Most of Youro's tiny inner circle seemed to be putting in an appearance. The reception was in full flow when Catherine and her friends arrived. They had been at the Phoenix since early afternoon, playing a lovely old-fashioned game (pirates, treasure, monsters of the deep) so engrossing that they'd kept repeating the dose when their time ran out, until someone realized it was midnight. There was no sign of the *grande dame*. Splendidly male footmen, in square shouldered cutaway coats and skintight pantaloons, strode about proffering trays of food, drink, and party favors. Catherine regarded these familiar items of rich-human decor with new interest, but didn't recognize any of them. She became separated from the others, accidentally on purpose, took an fx generator from a tray, and wandered alone, disguised as a large mournful insect.

In each room the decor was different. In a hall dressed as a grove of flowering trees, she noticed a malign small face peeping from the branches, peering down at the revelers. The eyes seemed to follow her around the room. She saw the figure again, looking out of the furniture in the next apartment, and again in the next. She assumed this was one of the tricks of the illusion designers, the kind of *memento mori* human craft workers had always loved to leave behind them. Then Imran found her and told her to take off the mask. He'd been commanded to present her to their hostess.

Lady Alicia was alone upstairs, in a room that was a closet compared to the splendid halls. She lay in a reproduction fourposter bed (Catherine could see that the canopy was an illusion, and not even a good one), propped on pillows and lapped in red satin coverlets. The room was packed with virtual works of art, many interfering with each other in a mélange as wild as in Misha's favorite city sites. Alicia wore a turban and an elaborate dressing gown, on which moving-image cheetahs stalked forever a herd of graceful antelope. She was smoking a green-skinned cigarillo in the style of the Gender War. In her free hand she held a lorgnette, which she lifted to her eyes every few seconds throughout the interview, pausing in the middle of a sentence to examine, it seemed, the ash on the end of her cigarette or a fold of the bedclothes. She was tiny, no bigger than an eight year old child.

"I am two hundred and fifteen years old," said Alicia. "And we have met before."

It was an Aleutian greeting, a polite way of dealing with the fact that they'd all "met before" time and again, though one didn't always instantly remember when or in what context one had known the other person. Humans had adopted the expression; they thought it made them sound sophisticated. But you rarely heard it from them nowadays.

Catherine shrugged. "I don't think so."

"That's because you've forgotten, Miss Alien-in-disguise. I was a young lady once myself. I belonged to the Khans. I met all the great ones. In the end we age, quite suddenly. When it happened to me, they let me retire to Paris, the most beautiful city on earth. I never go out now." She sucked on the cigarillo and studied her visitor intently.

Catherine saw the same bright black eyes that had trailed her through the throng.

"Why did you choose that body?" Alicia paused to raise the eyeglasses, and then spoke in English, with a pretty accent. *I am His Highness's dog at Kew. Pray tell me, sir, whose dog are you?*

Catherine shook her head. "I don't understand."

At the end of the bed stood the shattered image of a woman, impaled on a pedestal. Catherine couldn't make out if it was alive (as Binte was alive) or not. It drew her glance.

"Yo soy la desintegración," said Alicia. "You like that piece?"

"No, I don't. It's American, isn't it?"

"Well judged. The original was from the Americas. Helen Connelly, Michael's sister, made that version for me." Lady Alicia laughed and waved her hand. "Go. I'm tired of you." Imran had been waiting outside the inert, wood-paneled door. "Is she really two hundred and fifteen years old?" Catherine asked as they walked away.

"She always says that. She's about eighty, I suppose. Sextoys aren't long lived: too many artificial chromosomes."

"How old is Thérèse?"

Imran glanced at her, annoyed at being caught out in a slip of the tongue. "We're not monsters," he said, shortly. And didn't answer her question. "Alicia's our great aunt—or something like that—in the old style. She was my great grandfather's principal concubine, *maîtresse en titre.* If that seems grotesque to you, I'm sorry. It isn't, not in our reckoning. She retired here when he died. But we prefer not to talk about our family affairs to strangers. You can mask again, if you like."

It was nearly dawn. Thérèse had left the reception and gone to lie down on a terrace above the river. She had her period. She was curled up on a heap of shawls and cushions, all in Alicia's favorite scarlet, nursing her lower belly and moaning piteously from time to time. Misha was in attendance when Imran and Catherine joined them.

"At least the blood won't show," he was pointing out, unkindly.

"Don't be horrible. I'm having such awful cramps."

"Why don't you take a painkiller?"

"I have, to take the edge off. But, mmmm. You don't understand. Mmmm—"

From the plane of smooth pale stone, a broad flight of steps led to the water. Heavily preserved to protect it from the poor, the great stream ran full and smooth and silver in a diffuse sunrise. The golden lion tamarins that haunted this part of the *rive droite* appeared magically, from nowhere. They had no fear, but a healthy caution. They crept closer to the large human animals and sat watching them with great interest: occasionally darting up to each other to groom or tease.

Agathe Uwilingiyimana and Joset came out of the house with Lalith. They joined the others, attended by globes of silver-gilt light, and a tray of canapés that followed obsequiously at shoulder height. Agathe stripped off her formal robe and lay down on the balustrade of the steps, the robe bundled under her head. "We shouldn't have done that last dose. Six subjective voyages across the Spanish Main, and then this: it's too much."

"My brain hurts," complained Joset, fisting his eyes. "How can people endure all that bourgeois de-grade airtrash!"

To Catherine's alien perception there was practically no difference between Lady Alicia's decor and the gaudy confusion of the bit-grid city. She didn't say so.

"Did you do good networking for the renaissance?" she asked Agathe and Lalith.

Agathe groaned. "I don't want to talk about it. Grown-up parties give me a headache."

"Maybe," said Lalith.

The Aleutian and the rabble-rouser exchanged a thoughtful glance. Lalith smiled.

The tamarins, dark eyes outsize in tiny, extravagantly whiskered faces, were disconcerting. No one knew where they'd come from. They were an anonymous biological posting. Joset tried to lure them with scraps of party food.

"Mish ought to cull the brutes," he grumbled, when they wouldn't come to him. He had not yet forgiven his friend for the fake lion hunt. "People shouldn't be allowed to grow actual entire animals and let them loose at random."

"Thought is free," remarked Agathe. "I mean, if they were virtual, an arbitrary flowering of extinct primates in the data forest, you bit-fiends would defend them with your lives."

"There's no need to cull them." Misha had appropriated some of Thérèse's couch and lay comfortably inert, gazing up into the sky. "They may be entire, but fakes almost never breed successfully. They won't survive."

"Yet they might," said Thérèse. "They're fakes, but they might become real. Things do."

"Ideas can become material," agreed Agathe sleepily. "If the human race returned to a 'state of nature' now, we wouldn't lose the Gender War edits. We'd live as social groups of mothers and children, I mean parents and children. Recalcitrant males would have to prowl about outside, fighting each other madly for the prize of an entrée into our society."

Joset roared and tried to bash his sister over the head with the canapé tray, but it evaded him and scooted away. Imran and Misha refused to rise to her goading.

"Aleutian Signifiers would starve," said Thérèse. "I mean, in a state of nature."

"No, we wouldn't." Catherine lifted a hand, involuntarily, to her throat. "We can eat the way you do. Meat and veg. But anyway, if we're really starving, we can all produce cook's secretions. It's well recorded."

"Your cooks make food out of any old rubbish, don't they? How do they do that?"

"They spit on it," supplied Misha. "Or dip it in piss."

"Yuk! Disgusting!" Thérèse giggled. "I'm glad I'm not likely to be stuck with you on a desert island, Catherine."

Catherine thought: *I have been here before.* She had been in this state so often, in those Aleutian memories that she had absorbed through the endless hours of her childhood in Maitri's house. *This honeyed dawn, this little band of adventurers, this ramshackle crew . . .* She stretched herself out on the cool stone, bathed in her past lives, drunk on nostalgia.

She wondered why she was even interested in Lalith's activities. If the renaissance movement was indeed a front for an international terrorist plot, that was the humans' business now. The Aleutian Empire was over. Nothing lasts.

"Tell us something useful," said Thérèse sleepily, "that you've learned about humans."

"Smiles and grins," Catherine offered. "With us, a smile"—she lifted her shoulders—"is nearly always a good sign. When we grin, it's a warning. We've found that with humans it's the opposite. A grin is harmless. A smile from a human negotiating partner means: *you have stepped over the line.* With you people, bared teeth, the honest warning, is usually friendly. The repressed warning means danger. That's interesting, isn't it?"

"*A man may 'smile and smile, and be a villian,'* " murmured Agathe.

"And a woman. Why did you decide to become a Traditionalist girl?" asked Joset.

They interrogated her like this at random intervals. She understood that her answers were payment for the privilege of their friendship.

"I didn't. I decided to become a woman." There is always some truth that can be told. "When we first arrived, you people used to call me, used to call Clavel, that is: 'the poet princess.' " She fell into reminiscence. "You made up your minds that some of us were men and some of us women. We didn't think anything of it, because we play that sort of game ourselves. You know, there are two sorts of people: the people who talk about *two sorts of people,* and the ones who don't. You could call one of our *there are two sorts of people* games 'masculine and feminine.' It would fit, roughly. With us it's like being extrovert or introvert, or like reading your horoscope. When the consensus says that you're masculine, and you admire the traits that are currently labeled masculine, you think, *how true!* When you don't like the look of your horoscope, you think, *what rub-bish it all is*. It was ages"—she remembered ruefully—"before we realized we were dealing with something more important than a trivia quiz."

They were listening attentively, but blank-faced.

"You mean like halfcastes?" hazarded Thérèse.

"Maybe. I'm sure that's why they still call themselves 'masculine' or 'feminine,' even though they're not supposed to have a sex. Isn't that so, Lalith?"

"It would help if I knew what a horoscope was," complained Joset.

"Or an extro-whatsit, or the other thing," agreed Agathe.

"We need Mâtho!"

"We *don't!* We'd be here forever."

"But I've never heard of this personality-trait package," remarked Misha acutely. "And I've had a fine Aleutian education. I wonder why not."

"Ah." Catherine saw the pitfall too late, as usual. "It's out of fashion down here."

"Why?" mused Thérèse. "It sounds as if it would help alien-human relations."

"Don't be stupid," muttered her brother, casting one of his flashing, hawk-like glances at Catherine. "They're the superior race. It would make them seem like us. They don't want that."

And silence fell. The dawn stillness closed over this little disturbance of conversation as if it had never been. Agathe and Joset's lights had become ethereally pale, but lingered on like ghosts defying the morning. Majestic indoor aircraft, in the style of the last century (*indoor,* meaning they had permission to traverse the city's atmosphere) drifted across the air, taking aged party guests home. Catherine thought about the culture into which she'd so blithely plunged herself. Alicia Khan, Thérèse Khan . . . herself. Toys with minds, built from human flesh. She accepted what

Agathe had tried to tell her that day in the hives. Behind their archaic facade the Traditionalists were even less "human" than the Reformers. She had returned to earth as a woman, to expiate her guilt. She was too late. The men and women she had injured were no longer here. The mystery of human sex and sexual gender had collapsed into hyperadaptive disorder, like an earth-type species at the end of its natural life. She suddenly knew, with the clarity of extreme fatigue, that the Aleutians were not to blame. Not even Catherine herself. *Yo soy la desintegración.* The aliens had simply arrived, by chance, in time to witness the last acts of a long drama: tragic, fascinating, rich and rank and strange . . .

Thérèse sighed. Why was Imran so irritable? Since she had bested him in the competition for their mother's favor, he had been unbearably snappish. And yet why? It was inevitable. Mama couldn't use a real, full grown young man as a sextoy. People would not accept that; it would be a scandal. And almost certainly now he would be the heir: unless Mama played the dirty trick of having another child. While Thérèse, if she lived, would have a beautiful house like this one for herself. A pang clutched at her belly. Misha couldn't possibly understand the slothful comfort of these pains. He would never know how nice it was to lie here aching in her finery, surrendering to her nature, a mere rag of flesh. She gazed at the silver river, undrinkable water, and the parkland beyond, cleared to secure Alicia's perfect vista, that punished trespassers with lingering death. All the great city in its corruption, at one with her own dainty, bleeding body.

"The world is coming to an end," she whispered. "Our civilization is dying, maybe even the earth itself. And it's our fault, and we know it. But I still don't want anything to change. I want everything to stay exactly the way it is now."

ii

THE TREES WERE tall and massive. The rind was fissured vertically in long hollows so deep you could slip your whole hand inside. It was blue-black and greasy on the surface, streaked with powdery indigo where layers had been rubbed away. The branches were very high, but some trees had masses of tall whippy suckers growing at the base. The light was submarine. Fallen trunks were monstrous shipwrecked corpses, weed-draped shapes glimpsed through the broken cages of their own branches, tumbled out of the buoyant air and become impossible obstacles. In shadow there was no undergrowth, only a thick bed of dead needles; violet fading to charcoal gray. In sunlit spaces a knee-high plant with broad, funneled palmate leaves was the most common. Its flower was a cup of two fused white petals, veined in blue. The fruit was a single large black berry, with a warning opalescent gleam. There were masses of a threadlike fungoid ground creeper crusted with tiny jellied purple nodules. Sometimes there was a flash of yellow, a brilliant acid rose that seemed to be a parasite which rooted itself into the tree bark.

"They're like conifers," said Lydie. "But I haven't seen a cone yet." She slid her narrow hands into two bark fissures and studied one of the acid-yellow tree limpets closely. *<The lobes are toothed,>* she noted, silent and intent. *<There's a very thin line of scarlet along the inner surface of each tooth, and there are tiny channels, green lines in the yellow . . .>*

All science is description. Is gaze.

They were playing at being explorers, in an *envie* that Catherine had never visited before. Lydie had persuaded her to come with her on a naturalizing foray. She was making a catalog of the unreal wildlife—a charming idea, but Catherine was bemused by her methods.

"Why don't you make yourself a notebook?"

"Can't. We don't do that. Not in this *envie.*"

In her last life on earth, Catherine had been one of the elite who could manipulate the gaming *envies.* She'd been able to use loopholes and trapdoors in the virtual architecture: create her own objects, add her own features to the plot and landscape at will. In the Phoenix games the others would twist the rules and add to the props, with varying degrees of success. To Catherine the *envies* were as immutable as the real world. She had not asked anybody how the new virtuality ware could be tricked, and she had not tried to find out for herself. This playground belonged to the young humans. She nodded, therefore: accepting the new whim without question. Truly, the Blue Forest did not seem made for trickery.

"I would never have guessed you were, um, a taxonomist."

The little halfcaste shrugged. "You can pick up anything on the public grid if you have the patience. I have masses of time with nothing to do when they lay us off between seasons. And it's free. I got interested; don't know why." Lydie was thinking of climbing another tree. She had climbed several. She'd get a long way off the ground and then slither down again, defeated, before she reached the lowest branches. The view didn't change, she said.

"Gaming seems much more relaxed these days. When I was last alive, it was always battles and gambling hells and torture chambers."

"We do that stuff too."

"Yes, but 'Explorers' makes a pleasant change."

Lydie decided against the climb and moved on.

"Do you know who made this?" persisted Catherine, touching the rind of a tree as she passed. "It's very good. It has, I don't know, depth. It seems indifferent to us."

"No one made it," said Lydie, then looked at Catherine oddly. "No one person builds a game. You know that! It must have been the same when you were last around." She giggled. "Maybe God made it. Maybe it just growed."

It was Catherine's first visit, but the scenario appeared to be popular with café-goers. A row of brushwood huts stood in the clearing where they were camped, roofed with slabs of the thick black moss that grew on fallen trees. There was a well-used bonfire site, a pit oven—even some odd wooden sculptures, complete to the marks of stone ax and adze gouged into the dark, dense timber. All this, Catherine knew, could have sprung up in an instant. But everything had the mysterious air of solidity that attaches to established virtual artifacts. The gathering of young people was quite large. Nobody was masked, or even enhanced, as far as Catherine could tell. There were no demons, monsters, animals, no pirates or princesses—not even a whimsical virtual pith helmet in sight. Blue Forest was a place where people came to "explore" dressed as their natural selves.

Another group had been collecting firewood while Lydie and Catherine were away. A fresh bonfire was built, and the red charcoal from last night raked out to fuel the oven. Somebody had made some flutes from hollow sections of the indigo suckers. As the submarine light faded, the clearing was filled by a whispering music. People started to dance. Others joined them. The flute music acquired a marching beat, and the dancers began to sing.

> *"Oh, when the saints!*
> *Oh, when the saints!*
> *Oh, when the saints go marching in,*
> *I want to be in that number,*
> *When the saints go marching in . . . !"*

Foraging parties brought vegetables and berries. Some people began cooking. The explorers sat down together and ate roast roots, vegetable stew, and a blackish sludge that tasted of chocolate and was mildly intoxicating. They drank only water that had been found and fetched by another party. Misha, who had been in conclave with a group of strangers—gamers from another city—came over and introduced to Catherine a slight, dark-skinned person whose presence was feminine, but with a casually dismissive air—*if it matters*. She was from Asaba, he said: the Aleutian second capital in West Africa.

<My name is "Eva,"> she said, showing just a little throat. <That means life.>

Her manner was so perfect that Catherine found herself replying in the same mode. <How nice to meet you. What a lovely game this is.>

<It's an Aleutian custom, isn't it,> said Eva, <to gather at the end of the day and dance, before eating together? Hadn't humans in most parts of earth, even Africa, given up or degraded the practice of dance until they picked it up from the invaders? Your people have helped us to rediscover something that we'd almost lost, an integral pleasure of self awareness, a conscious reiteration of the state of being: *it dances*. Don't you agree?>

Eva's Silence was complex, reserved, highly individual, self-consciously intellectual. But a mood of warm elation sparkled through it. She sat as near to Catherine as another Aleutian might—superbly assured, perfectly Aleutianized, serenely confident in the non-Aleutian future.

<You renaissance game builders have achieved something important,> Catherine told her. <"Blue Forest" is like a natural feature of the virtual cosmos: born, not created. Virtuality gaming has grown up in the Phoenix Café. It has reached a state of being, which is so much more than doing.> Then she was embarrassed by her own enthusiasm. Maybe there were lots of human games like this nowadays. But the African seemed pleased.

Misha had left them to talk. There was no point in his

staying; he couldn't understand Aleutian. At the end of the evening, at the sorting out of the sleeping arrangements, he came back. She knew what would follow. Since the first time, it had happened whenever he found the slightest opportunity. She knew that the others knew exactly what was going on, though no one mentioned the affair in her presence, even in Silence. She had seen Agathe saddened, because another *Traditionalist young lady* had fallen victim to self-destruction. She had seen Mâtho grieving. She knew she had lost face badly. They were probably certain now that she was simply crazy, not an "alien-in-disguise" at all.

She didn't expect them to understand. How could they?

Everyone was going to sleep out of doors. The mossy huts must be reserved for some other purpose. Guards were set around the perimeter of the clearing to watch for "wild beasts or savages." Everybody else lay down on couches of the indigo needled shoots, around the sinking fire. Misha managed to be lying beside her. When the camp was quiet, he turned on his side. The bonfire made bright red pinpoints in his eyes.

"Please don't," she whispered. "Not in here."

He took no notice. She could see the smiling curve of his mouth as he stared into her face, while his fingers probed between her thighs and into that soft, membranous channel.

"Has it ever struck you," he murmured, "that *envie* means desire?"

He loosened her clothes, bent his head, and sucked hard at her nipples, first one and then the other. At last he pushed her thighs farther apart, the same autistic gesture as that first time in the cloakroom. He held his claw in one hand, for guidance. She felt the pressure of his knuckles, and then the blind head and swollen stem driving through between the walls of muscle—rhythmically, piston-hard. She stared over his shoulder. Her back was jolted against the bed of branches, like a piece of flotsam battered against rocks. He reached his climax, lay heavily for a moment, and then rolled away.

Catherine listened to the night sounds of the unreal forest.

She was not innocent; nothing could make Catherine innocent. But tonight she was desolate. She wanted to take command of the *envie,* to make something nasty happen to Misha. Not rape, but *something bad.* She didn't know how to start. She didn't even know how long this session would last. Subjective time was one of the parameters she didn't control. Finally, she got up, carefully unsnagging her skirts from the branches. Head for the exit. She would leave. She took two steps, and felt a tree in front of her. She groped around the massive base and found another. The fire had disappeared. She could see nothing at all.

"Catherine?"

There was a sound of flint striking against metal. A chip of orange light broke out. She had almost stumbled over one of the guards. It was Mâtho.

She dropped down on her haunches beside him.

"I want to leave," she whispered. "How do I get out of here?"

"You just leave," he said. "If you want to go back, you're back."

But the Blue Forest stayed, strong as pitch and strangely scented.

"Everybody wants different things," whispered Mâtho, looking very sad in the glow of his tinderbox light. "But it fits together somehow." He was holding her hands. He seemed to understand that someone might even want, positively want, the shame and sorrow of loving a person like Misha Connelly.

"We don't have to go anywhere," he said. "We can have more and more worlds, without going anywhere. A space as complex as a universe can fit into someone's head. I think that's what God said to Adam and Eve in the garden. Stay here. Become more and more yourselves: don't *spread*. But they wouldn't listen."

She crouched there for a while, feeling the forest that stretched limitless around them, immovably real as her need for pain. Then she went back and lay down again in her place, and waited for the night to end.

iii

MISHA HAD RENTED a room, an hour's journey away in a neighboring *quartier*. Chance opportunities were no longer enough; they had to have a place to go. His family home was impossible. Catherine understood that. She knew that he wanted badly to rape her in Maitri's house. But that was something she could not allow, however covertly; and she waited in vain for him to force her outright there. He was frightened of the aliens.

They traveled to the room together one day, a short time after Catherine's visit to the Blue Forest. He came to collect her from the giratoire in a cab, but had it drop them at the nearest lev station. He repeated his warning about traveling on the metro alone, then led her to the standard class gate. Their carriage was crowded. They stood in the aisle, pressed by the bodies of other passengers. He bent to whisper in her ear.

"You see why you mustn't do this?"

"What happens?"

"Someone will fingerfuck you. They'll get a hand inside your honor cloak and up your skirts when you're pushed so close in the crowd that you can't get away. Or if they're potent, they'll rub up against the cleft of your buttocks and come that way. You'll find their stuff on your clothes afterward."

"Who will do this?" she asked softly.

"Some man. The sperm count may be low, but there are enough men around. And not only in my party. Think of Joset. It used to happen to my sister."

Catherine stood in the charged air, surrounded by these secret gropings and penetrations. The women were all veiled. Or the veiled were all women. It had become a necessary ordinance, because of the growing intercommunal unrest, that Reformer women, and the less male-looking Reformer men had to wear the chador. Otherwise their safety could not be guaranteed. These were ordinary people, far from the baroque inventions of the rich, but they were playing the same game. The women's heads were bowed. Their smothering cloaks had the strange effect of making their bodies naked. They were dry-mouthed and compliant, nipples stiff and cunts wet with perverse arousal. They had chosen their role. Like Catherine they were greedy for abuse. Maybe they thought they were paying for humanity's crimes. Maybe they thought that this way, someday, they would be loved. The men's eyes were pinpoint blank, like Misha's eyes in the forest night.

It was noon. There was no one about in the old-fashioned neighborhood. They passed through a narrow lobby guarded by a concierge of ancient make, into a cobbled courtyard and from thence up flights of steps covered by some long-lost form of polymer sheeting. It had a static pattern of green and gray: *Maitri,* she thought, *you'd like this. . . .* The room was on the third floor at the back. It was large and bare except for a hybrid foam bed without legs, an ancient bentwood chair, and a waste bucket that stood without a screen against one wall. Catherine went to the window and looked out. Tiers of glazing stared back at her: some festooned with drying laundry, some patched with barrier gel, others empty and sprouting fronds of grass. Rock pigeons stepped the cobbles on coral feet, and crooned invisibly overhead in the cliffs of crumbled yellow stone. A neat brown sparrow hopped on the windowsill below, and looked up with a bold, questioning chirrup. It was late summer again, she remembered. How strangely the time had passed. She wondered why Misha had chosen this place, with its quiet melancholy and air of dusty romance. Did he too think wistfully of what might have been? But she did not want to think about his motivation. That was dangerous.

He lay on the foam bed, dressed in Aleutian overalls, propped on one elbow.

"Have you heard of paper flowers?"

"Is it a bodymorphing cosmetic? Something you swallow, and you get a temporary shift in your appearance?"

"It can be. It used to be. D'you want to try some?"

She came over to the bed. "What does it do?"

"Hold out your hand."

He took out a small tissue folder, and shook two or three minute slivers of a pastel-colored wafer onto her palm.

"Lick them up."

She tasted nothing but the salt of human skin.

"You don't need a Buonarroti engine," he said, licking up his own share, "to get you to another world. It happens all the time. Suddenly, you step over a line, and you're somewhere else. You don't know how it happened, and you may never find your way back." His eyes gleamed. "Take off your clothes."

She had accepted that there would be no excess. There would be no whips, no manacles, no extravagant props, no violence. She would not be beaten or chained up, left to lie in shit and piss in a solitary cell. She would not be mutilated, burned, electrocuted, gang-raped, tortured, made to eat her own feces, forced to watch as her children were violated and slaughtered. And that was right. There must be nothing that might rouse an instinctive, bodily resistance. No humiliation so crude as to restore her dignity. But what he did was not enough. That brusque, brief penetration (in spite of her pleading, and without a single gesture of affec-

tion) was becoming stale. Since he had introduced this
room into their pattern, she had been hoping for something
more. She obeyed him, trembling with anticipation, and
knelt facing him on the bed. He reached out and pushed at
her shoulder: *the autistic gesture,* void of contact. She lay
flat.

"Lie with your knees up. Lift your head. The foam will
prop your shoulders. It's smart; it will do that. Keep looking at me. I want to be able to see your cunt and your face."

Misha bent forward with an expression of awed triumph:
almost of humility. He examined her genitals with his fingertips, pulling the furred petals of flesh apart to reveal the
darker inner folds. He probed the whorled, hooded arrow-
head, and traced a line down the shaft of the arrow to the
slightly reddened slit of the female opening. She imagined
what he saw. A woman's sex is not simple and contained
like a man's. Folded and infolded, it emphasizes surface,
extension, irreducible difference. It is the whole limitless
world turned into a soft, vulnerable rosy plaything. Misha
eased two fingers inside, looking her in the face.

"Now, start to masturbate."

"I can't," whispered Catherine. "I've tried. It doesn't
work."

"Try again."

She began. Her fingers were cold and clumsy.

"Keep looking at me," he ordered, "as long as you can."

She knew why he wanted her to masturbate. So far he
had forced her whenever he wanted to, but she had been a
bystander. She had only been half raped, only half humiliated. Of course, she had to participate. That had to be the
next step. Her face had begun to flush; there was a burning
pressure in her nipples, in the furred mound and the folds
of those petals. It was not her own awkward fingers that
started this response. It was Misha's greedy gaze, the way
he was dressed and she was naked, the way she was exposed, negated, handled like a dead thing.

"This is wrong," she whimpered. "I can't do this. Please don't make me."

"You don't have to do anything. Just keep playing with yourself, as best you can."

Touched her. Catherine started and looked around, bewildered. Two hands had gripped her shoulders: big hands, a man's hands. There was nothing, only empty air. A mouth brushed against hers, vanished, returned. She could see nothing. The tip of a tongue probed between her lips, withdrew, thrust deeper. Her mouth opened, the thrusting fell into a pumping rhythm, she was being mouth fucked. The hands slid from her shoulders to her breasts; the mouth fuck went on. The claw, the male member of her invisible assailant, nudged at the mouth of her sex opening and vanished, nudged and vanished, while the mouth fuck continued and her nipples were sucked and bitten. She tried not to respond. She could not help herself. She heard herself gasping: *Oh, please, oh, please.* She was sobbing, desperate, thighs spread taut and spine arced, agonizingly open. The claw slid in and vanished, slid in and vanished. *Oh, please, oh, please.* The desperation was beyond words. She heard Misha laugh. She saw herself, a last image far away, falling on the dusty floor: howling, mouth wide, head fallen back with her hair in the dust, crawling on her knees like a contorted insect with her sex mound thrust upward, avid, abject, frantic . . .

When she came to herself, she was sitting with her back propped against the wall in a corner of the room. She was covered in drying sweat, and shivering in huge belly-deep tremors. She'd bitten her lip. It was stinging: she tasted blood. Misha was lying on the bed, watching her. He was still dressed but he too had been sweating hard. His clothes were open in the front; he was wiping his claw with a handful of filmy tissue.

"That's paper flowers. D'you like it?"

He rolled over on his back. "Oh, God. Synthesized and

purified, straight to the brain. With anything else you stay conscious. You go on functioning when you're high. This is better. I've never tried heroin, but I bet sex beats it. I bet fucking, now that we've got it properly refined, beats the fuck out of heroin. What do you think?"

She couldn't answer. She didn't know if she was ever going to speak again.

Misha came and picked her up and carried her to the slab of foam. Even in the necessary closeness of this action, in their shared exhaustion and the warm smells of bodily fluids, there was no lapse into tenderness. No contact. He laid her down and lay beside her. She was still shivering. He turned her on her side, with her arms behind her. He parted her thighs with one hand, holding her wrists in the other, and drove his new erection up into her from behind: "Cunt," he muttered, childishly intent on the word, "cunt cunt cunt."

When he'd finished, Catherine waited for a while, then moved herself away to the other side of the bed. The room was warm, but she was cold. She wrapped some of her discarded clothes around her. Now he would sleep, and she would wait. Then he would get up, she would dress, he would put her in a cab and send her home. She tried to doze, listening to the chirping sparrows, the rustle of pigeons' wings. It was no use. The dangerous moment had come. She could not stop herself from thinking: *This is ridiculous. One cannot take punishment as an epicurean pleasure.* And the spell was broken.

"Misha?"

"Hmm?"

She sighed, feeling it leave her, goodbye to a strange interlude—nothing lasts. "Misha, why are you doing this to me?"

She felt him recoil, outraged by this betrayal. But she persisted.

"We know my history," she explained. "Whether I'm an

Aleutian in a human body or a poor deluded human girl, it's the same. The person I think I am raped Johnny Guglioli, and started the whole shameful process of Aleutian rule on earth. I raped; I want to be raped. Even after three lifetimes, I can't let it go. That explains me. What about you? I know that Traditionalist society is strange. But we were friends, and what you are doing to me is not friendly, not on any terms. Why do you want to be the rapist? What is your problem?"

He had rolled over to look at her. He lay back, covering his eyes with his forearm.

"Do you think I'm Johnny Guglioli?" he asked.

"What?"

"When I do it to you. Do you imagine me to be Johnny getting his own back?"

Catherine sat up, pulling the chador around her.

"I was fifteen," she said. "All right, I was an immortal visitor from an alien star system, but forget the technical details. Imagine it. A fifteen-year-old captain of a spaceplane privateer, with a crew of dashing, adventurous adults calling him *Sir* and *Lord Clavel*. Deferring to him, taking orders, loving him. I'm not really a "lord." I've told you this before. I use articulate language, which separates me from our Silent majority, the ones who process the world with their bodily secretions. Who sometimes get very rich and who are often in charge, which you people find mysterious, though it happens as often here. I'm a Signifier; I have followers. I rarely have to work for a living. There are people, Silent and Signifier, who are prepared to give me food and service and whatever is passing for money whenever I appear, and all I have to do in return is 'be Clavel.' Don't ask me why. But I'm not *important*. Most usually, I'm just a nuisance to the important people in my brood. So there you have it.

"I was fifteen, a poet: a minor-celebrity brat who'd joined forces with the buccaneers. I saw Johnny Guglioli in a café

one day, and I fell in love. I thought Johnny was older than
he was. I thought he was my daddy, my true parent: another me but older, wiser. We're expected to look for lovers
in the older or younger generation, because we're supposed to be looking for 'another self,' a twin soul. And according to our popular science, the same embryo won't
develop twice in one brood in the same generation. It's a romantic ideal. I mean, it doesn't happen. It had never happened to me before. Don't ask me how I thought my double
had been born on this unknown planet three thousand light
years from home. I suppose I believed, same as Peenemünde Buonarroti, that there is only one species of intelligence in the cosmos; and therefore Johnny and I might well
be fated lovers. It made sense to me at the time. Later we
got together, we three landing party crews, and devised an
elaborate scam involving our supposed superpowers and
the faster-than-light drive you were sure we possessed. I
helped to plan it. But I decided I didn't like the way things
were shaping, so I went to look for Johnny.

"What we do when we lie down together doesn't trigger
pregnancy. But it means something like the same for us as
it does for you, in that it is an engine of biochemical communication. The little social gestures where we exchange
our wandering cells are a repressed, dilute hint of what
happens in lying down. Your claw and your lover's claw
grappling, your two cups opened and spread wide, those
inner surfaces running, melting, streaming into each other.
I thought if I lay down with Johnny, it would solve everything. I would flood him with Aleutia, and he would pour
earth into me. The information we exchanged would pass
from us into both communities; there'd be no more decep-
tion. I found my way to his room in London. It was a rainy
night in September; I remember the smell of drenched dust.
The air was full of water instead of life—it tasted of grief.
I'd never seen a human without clothes on. I believed our
minds were the same; I didn't know that our bodies were

different. I told him that I loved him. He said, *Get away from me you monster,* but I took no notice.

"I remember it all as if it were yesterday. Sometimes I know everything that followed would have happened anyway. You would have had your catastrophic Gender War. You would have ruined your own weather systems, destroyed your own living space. Sometimes I know it was our fault: our doing, my doing. Maybe I'm crazy. What do I care whether I'm crazy or not? The rape continues. I can't stop it, so I want to be raped too. To be abused, humiliated, used, despised by someone who should have been my friend. What was the question? No, I don't think you are Johnny. I don't care who you are. You'll do."

She turned to him, eyes narrowed.

"Was I supposed to think you were Johnny? Is that what all this has been about?"

"I don't know what you mean."

"It doesn't matter . . . " She had dropped into the Aleutian crouch—a gesture of flight, aborted. She sat up again.

"In my next life, as you know, I had my artisans build something that was supposed to be a hybrid, Aleutian-Johnny; and we supplied it with a stolen Aleutian personality to disguise what I'd done. That was Bella. That's partly why I had *this* done to myself. To make reparation. But in that life, when I knew that I hadn't created what I wanted, I took to hanging around the gaming hells here in old-earth. I would pick up young halfcaste gamers, the younger the better. I'd pretend they were what Bella was supposed to be: my true child, Johnny born again. I would take them home and make them act out the rape with me. I wanted to degrade myself; I didn't care what I did to the children. Did you know about that?"

"I think you're being hard on yourself."

"Think what you like. I was there. It doesn't matter what you do to me. Whether I'm brainwashed or whether I'm the real Third Captain, you can't treat me worse than I want to be treated. Because of the things I've done, and because the rape goes on. *But don't you have anything better to do with your time?"*

"I used to write to you," said Misha softly. "Years ago, I used to send messages to you: Clavel the Pure One, the Third Captain, the great Aleutian poet. I wanted to know about your art, about the images you made, the human artists you'd known. The records and pictures and stuff you'd seen that I could never see in the real, because the War had destroyed them. I wanted you to teach me. I don't know what I was talking to: a piece of software cobbled up from press releases, some halfcaste who believed he was your incarnation, or what. There are so many kinds of simulacra on the grid. There's a whole virtual Madame Tussaud's in there, if you know what that means. Whatever you were, you answered me kindly. From a great height. You were very sweetly condescending."

Catherine had begun to cry. She wiped the tears with her fingers. "It wasn't me."

"It didn't talk much like you."

"Is that why you had to rape me? Because a grid persona was condescending?"

"I don't know. Does what we do need so much explanation? I do it. You like it."

She lay down. They lay facing each other, not touching.

"Misha," she said, "I hate to sound grown-up and responsible, but I have to ask. What you do with me . . . have you done it to anybody else? Or have you done anything worse?"

He flushed. "I don't know what you're talking about. I haven't. I'd never done it with another person, in the real, before I did it to you."

"You're serious?"

"Straight up," he confessed, sulkily. "I was a virgin. What's it to you?"

She laughed. "Well, that could explain a lot!" She sighed

in relief. "I think I believe you. That's good news. That's a weight off my mind."

"I know you like it," he said. "I may be 'very young,' Miss Alien. But I can tell. Even if you refuse to move a funxing muscle, you still get wet. And you can't stop the stuff inside from moving when you come. Why don't we just say we both want this?"

The charcoal masses of her hair fell forward. She pushed them back again. They looked at each other as if each was staring into a mirror: without tenderness, without surrender but with knowledge and complicity. At last Catherine turned from him. She began to dress.

"I'll be out of town for a while," he said. "We're going to spend some time in the Atlantic Forest. I've asked my father to invite you to visit us there, at the Warden's Lodge. You ought to come. You might even like my father. He's . . . interesting. Will you come?"

"Will I meet your sister?"

He hesitated. "She'll be there. I don't know if you'll see her. She's a bit of a hermit."

It occurred to her, alone in her cab on the way home, that he had not answered the other question she had asked: though in the silent subtext of their relationship, he had admitted a thousand times that he was in desperate trouble. Perhaps the invitation was his answer. *Come and see.*

She found Maitri waiting for her in the atrium, by a planter of giant orchids, wearing a splendidly embroidered robe of maroon and silver, gorgeous as the flowers that seemed to stand around him like a company of courtiers. He smiled as she came in: a smile so warm, so ruefully tender that Catherine had to laugh.

"Why are you looking at me like that? Am I such a pitiful spectacle?"

"Not at all." He held out his hands. "You look remarkably well."

She came and sat at his feet, resting her cheek against the deep red robe. She touched her lip; it was already healing.

"I do worry," confessed Maitri, in his best maiden-aunt style. "This 'intercommunal violence' is not directed against Aleutians. But you don't *look* like an Aleutian, especially not in those clothes, charming though they are. I wish the Departure was over and done with, so we could calm down. But at least we can feel that you are safe with Michael."

Catherine chuckled. "Did you know he's a junkie?"

The aging adventurer was neither shocked nor surprised.

"Is he? I suppose it's 'testo,' the sex drug. One hears about that."

"The stuff I had tonight was some kind of cocktail, involving void-forces wizardry I don't begin to understand. But you're right, sex hormones are a large part of it."

"Was your cocktail good?"

"Unbelievably good, my dear guardian. Rather horrible, but very good indeed."

"Can you get me some?"

"Certainly not! It wouldn't work on your chemistry, anyway."

The indoor fountain murmured, the palms and ferns stirred softly in the cool, hazy air. Maitri inquired delicately, "So without wishing to be prurient—I *am* wishing to be prurient, of course, but one must make concessions to the good taste of sensitive people—you take your cocktail, and then you lie down together?"

"Sort of," agreed Catherine. "But no. It isn't like lying down. It's almost the opposite. There's no contact, zero communication. You're completely alone, and completely possessed by an appetite, a greed of such power and desperation that nothing else exists."

"There never *is* any contact between humans, lying down or any other way. Not in our sense of the term."

Maitri grimaced at his own impropriety. "I know I'm not supposed to say things like that, but it is true."

Catherine shrugged and smiled, one finger tracing a path of knotted silver in the plum-shadowed folds. "You are getting old, my dear, and taking refuge in commonplace opinions. I am sure that humans make love, and love each other, all the ways that we love each other. Even now, even now. But this is *sex*, distilled and purified. It has no affect. It's an engine, an engine and a fire. *It burns*. When you take sex as a drug—as we did, Misha and I—you become a machine. You become one with mindless life, with not-self. It's extraordinarily violent, and in a way transcendent . . . Think of their cults. Especially, the Christian cult."

"I'd rather not! Positively my least favorite of your enthusiasms. Those horrible incunabula!"

"Horrible, yes. The lives of the saints, full of gruesome 'miracles' of disease and suffering and mutilation. It seems so disgusting and meaningless until you realize how their world was *saturated* by disease and suffering and mutilation, and then you understand that even spiritual joy had to take the same imprint. And now . . . We've always found their obsession with sex grotesque. That's how we felt before the War broke out, when we thought of it as identical with their *lying down*. Which it isn't. It's the engine of territorial expansion, that has become their engine of destruction. They know what's happening to them; they've known it for a long time. How can they stop thinking about this destroying angel? How can they think about anything else? We stopped the Gender War, but the obsession went underground. It comes out in everything they do when we aren't looking—"

"Really? How impressive. Trust you to find the only game in town, my darling. Last time it was the virtuality hells, and you appalled everyone by plunging into those weird, occult native rites. This time you're a . . . hmm. A fire engine, was it?"

"A sex machine," supplied Catherine.

"People aren't going to understand. You know what we are like. People will just think you're talking dirty." He lifted his hands in apology to the listening air. "Well, it's true. We Aleutians are such prudes. Lying down together is something everybody does. But it's never supposed to be mentioned out loud."

"I think the games are the alternative," said Catherine musingly. "Sex involves no communication, and it eats *lebensraum*. The game *envies* are kept in existence by communication between the players, and they create new worlds."

Maitri hd never entered a gaming hell. "That's exactly what I don't like!" he broke in firmly. "I find it very disturbing to think of those 'other worlds.' Where do they go when the players snap out of it? I imagine them still existing, squeezing into the same space as *this* world, like signals in a cable, or the multi-realities problems in the Buonarroti project, you know. What happens if there's an overload?"

"What happens if we reach the end of infinity," murmured Catherine.

"Well, I suppose I shouldn't talk. I'm so easily disoriented. Remember how I had to send back my lovely exercise bike that we found at Christmas. I kept falling off when the visor showed me going around a corner."

Catherine laughed. The spectacle of Lord Maitri on board that antique fitness aid had been a glorious addition to the life of the main hall.

Absently, he stroked her hair. But his fingers snagged in the tangles. He struggled, careful not to tug, until he was released by the tiny inhabitants of the air, and laughed, rubbing at his wrists, where the wanderer-glands lay in twin soft grooves on either side of bone and tendon. "My skin is getting so hard and dry! Sometimes for hours I have no flux. I might as well be human!"

Maitri was going blind to the Commonalty, deaf and dumb to Aleutia.

She shook his hand and held the callused grainy palm against her cheek. "I wanted to know what it was like to be helpless. Because of Bella, and because long ago Johnny said that I had *treated him like a woman*. I wanted to know what that meant."

"Women fight to defend a territory," informed Maitri wisely. "Men fight to establish ranking. So you must always be aggressive with a man. He will be happy because you are doing something he can understand, and if you win, he'll happily accept his new ranking, at least for a while. But you should never fight with a woman, because whenever she gets into a fight, she feels she's defending her life and her children's food. The *difficulty* is guessing which of them you are dealing with. And the 'sexual equipment' is no guide at all, which is most unfair."

"It's not a parlor game! Dear Maitri, don't try to change the subject. I want to say that I've been very stupid. I meant to dedicate this life to repentance. But every time I try to expiate my sins, I find myself wallowing in an orgy instead. It's absurd. I'm going to give up looking for punishment. Misha has cured me."

"I knew I could trust that young man."

Neither of them spoke then for a while.

"I was sure you would want to be here," said Maitri at last, tremulously. "We were going to leave; it was your last chance of a life on earth. And there was nothing I could do to help the humans. So I stretched the terms of your will, a little. To trigger a pregnancy is not a *crime*, is it? It just isn't something we do. And I thought you had got over Johnny before you died last time. But then you were so unhappy, I was afraid I had done something awful to you. Everyone said you had been born crazy because I had meddled with the mazes of rebirth."

She stepped once more into the Phoenix Café, and heard

the *musique naturelle.* Morning in West Africa, the smell of
that air, the breakfast chatter of a roadside food stall. And
all that had come after the years of grief and longing. She
was Catherine; she was Clavel. Those memories were her
own, and tonight more sweet than bitter, as if Misha Connelly had exorcised her past, leaving it clean of shame. She
would never see Johnny Guglioli again. But to have seen
the *renaissance* of his world, the earth before First Contact,
was a blessed consolation. She looked up and saw that
Maitri's eyes were full of tears, the Aleutian tears that brim
and shine but never fall.

"I'm very glad you gave me this life. Very glad."

"Do you remember?" he murmured: " *'We are the pil-
grims' master. We shall go always a little farther.' "*

And then: "I'm afraid of what will happen to you when
I'm gone."

"Don't be. I will live in a cottage, an eccentric old human
lady. No one will bother me."

"I hope so." He brightened. "But it is only one life." He
patted the seat beside the orchids. "Shall we have a nap?
There's going to be music later. And I find these days I need
to be thoroughly *rested* if I am to enjoy a concert."

So they slept for a while, at the end of the adventure, in
each other's arms.

II

Name of the Father

L'AIRIAL

i

THE RAILHEAD REMINDED her of Avebury. There were traces of a different history, but the atmosphere was the same: a comfortless state of transition. Catherine had traveled this far in a private lev-train car supplied by the Warden. She stood alone outside the station, looking at some miserable allotments and a collection of pressed-shit shacks. The new encroachment of population jostled with the ruins of a town that had been here before the War, or at least before the postwar clearances. She went to investigate a gloomy, brawling sound and discovered a rectangular pit, maybe the basement of some prewar building, where a jet of water was gushing from a lump of masonry. She climbed down. The water was scalding hot. She licked her finger: the taste was foul.

"Mademoiselle?" A face was peering at her. Catherine scrambled out of the hole. The owner of the face looked at her curiously.

"It's a long time since anyone has taken those waters."

"Is the spring poisoned? I mean, preserved?"

"No. It is astringent, but they say it will do you good. I am your driver. Please come with me."

Her spirits rose when she saw a beautifully maintained

mechanical jeep. She was disappointed to find that the back compartment was screened and closed. But the little room had a remembered smell. She touched the upholstery, her fingertips recalling the texture of clean and tenderly polished synthetic hide. *Falling through flames, in becomes down.* Stretch limos and motorcycle escorts. The buccaneers giggling in excitement: *What's inside here? Hey! It's a bar full of drink! Do you think it's meant for us? Let's drink it anyway. If anyone complains, we can pretend we don't understand.* We were happy then, she thought.

"We will reach Arden in about one hour."

"Arden? I thought the house was called l'Airial."

"L'Airial is the name of the place. It is a clearing in the forest. Mr. Connelly, this present Mr. Connelly, named the house Arden when he became Warden."

Her invitation had caused some despondency at the giratoire. It was for Catherine alone, which the Aleutians thought rude and odd. But they had rallied quickly in the excitement of making sure she was properly equipped. It was so long since anyone in their company had privately visited a human home. She must take no commensals, in case the Warden's people found living appliances offensive. She must take quarantine jelly, in case she had to isolate herself. She must take plenty of appropriate gifts. They had racked the collective memory and decided that speciality foods were the safest. As Atha wisely explained, they could always be reprocessed into something useful.

Catherine had been sent to say goodbye to Leonie, a ceremony she would rather have missed. She'd found her foster mother hard at work trying to transpose Atha's "speciality foods" into human terms. When she'd seen Leonie at the stove, she'd realized that the last time she'd visited this kitchen had been the morning when she came home from the police station. She was assaulted by that image, imprinted in her foster mother's hard reserve:

Catherine filthy, incoherent, raving, spattered with human blood.

"You know, I'm going to visit Misha Connelly's family—?"

Leonie raised her eyebrows. "Yes, miss."

"I've come to say goodbye."

She nodded. "Yes, miss." Catherine heard the silent dismissal, given words by her Aleutian mind: <*You've no business here, miss. Whatever it is you have to say, say it and leave.*> She knew she was supposed to go away, but she couldn't. She had an irrational longing to tell Leonie what Misha had done to her, to burst into tears—

"What do *you* think about the renaissance? Have you heard Lalith speak? Misha's friends are very committed. They believe they're building Utopia, a new human future, free of Aleutian influence. How do you feel about that?"

Leonie had given her a glance almost of contempt and turned back to her cooking. "I think talking about Utopia opens old wounds, miss. Things are the way they are. We never get to start fair."

Then Catherine had broken down. "Do you have to call me *miss* the whole time?" she cried. "Is it absolutely necessary?"

"It's necessary for my peace of mind, miss," said Leonie.

But then she'd left the stove, and walked into the room where she and Peter lived. She'd come out holding something in her hand and given Catherine a look: a reserved, retracted, compressed glance that her lost daughter remembered from very long ago. No emotion escaped from her, only that refusal: Leonie would not open old wounds. But she said, "Come and sit down in front of me. It's too late to get your hair set, and you can't take *their* creatures to Mr. Connelly's. I'd better show you how to use a brush on that mess, the old-fashioned way."

The jeep had moved off, she supposed, since the images on the screens had begun to flow. She settled back, thinking of her human mother. And of Maitri, who was getting so old. She saw him small and withered, peering out from his embroidered robe. *I thought you could change things,* he sighed, as if in farewell. She could not talk to Maitri anymore. Old people are like children, she decided. They know how to get what they need. Intuitively, instinctively, they make us protect them from the things they don't want to hear. Thinking of the Phoenix Café: Agathe, Lalith, Lydie, Mâtho, Thérèse. She saw them looking at her with reproach. Like Maitri they had hoped for something more. But Catherine had taken no real interest in the renaissance movement. She had preferred to be led astray by the glamorous, worthless Misha Connelly. Sometimes I wonder, she mused, how I managed to acquire the reputation that has dogged me. When was I ever pure? When was I ever *good?* I don't remember it. The screens recounted autumn woodland, where crowds of half-naked branches scratched the air, the dozed remains of villages cleared when the park was formed, slow streams that crept between beds of bulrushes, and finally a vast hypnotic tract of conifers. She was not paying attention. She assumed it must be the usual banal and irritating fake landscape, customized for the region: visual lift music. She was wondering, would Mâtho recognize the term *lift music?* Should she suggest they have it installed in the gameroom antechamber? *Eine kleine nachtmusik,* or that thing with the long rattling cadences: *Fur Elise.* Suddenly, a passing image leapt into sharp focus.

"Did you say something, mademoiselle?"

A complex of low buildings, a landing pad. The brilliant daytime warning lights of heavy security shielding. A regular, unbroken perimeter of dark green. It had gone already.

"Why was that place on my screens?"

"What, just now?" came the driver's voice again. "It's the Buonarroti research lab."

"I know. But why was it on my screens?"

A short, puzzled silence. "Because it's here, mademoiselle." The voice took on a note of injured dignity. "Your screens are fed by the jeep's external cameras. You are seeing the park in reality, as it is."

"Of course," said Catherine politely. "I never doubted it. But I didn't know. I mean, I had forgotten the Buonarroti lab was in this park."

"I should have thought you would know everything about it, mademoiselle. Yes, it's here. We Europeans (he pronounced the word daintily, in the old, pre-contact way) had to accept it, since everyone agreed it must be on earth but no other government wanted the responsibility. And of course it had to be in a wilderness, away from population. It's a nuisance. At least they haven't killed anybody for a while. They kill anyone who tries to break in," he explained.

"I know."

"It's necessary, I suppose. But it's not what one wants in the park. It makes a bad impression on our visitors. Though in the end," he added dutifully, "the benefits of the research will be enormous."

"At least you'll get rid of us," said Catherine. "That's something."

"It's a good deal," agreed the driver cheerfully. "Though mademoiselle doesn't look much like an alien to me. By the way, any time you want a driver while you are staying, I'll be glad to show you around. We don't have to go near the Buonarroti place."

She wondered if he would rape her.

"But you'd be better off on foot," he corrected himself, having read her mind (that disconcerting human trait). "Otherwise you might as well have stayed in the city. You'll be quite safe and undisturbed. Our visitors can't bother you!"

Conversation waned. There was no incident on the screens until a stretch of precontact highway briefly appeared. It was maintained (a burst of text informed her) as

an historic monument and versatile leisure resource. Soon
after that the jeep came to a halt. The driver opened her
door, and she stepped out. The jeep track faded, like a
stream vanishing into sand, into beaten earth. There were
sheds and barns built in squared courses of precontact
stone or brick, some with strange hooks and chains hinting
at bygone harvest rituals. Big pieces of well-preserved antique machinery were scattered about, giving the clearing
even more the air of an outdoor museum on a quiet day.
The house itself stood in the center of the open ground. Its
red tiled roof stooped low over pale blue fretwork eaves.
The lower floor was solidly blank, wartime style, but a generous modern porch had been added at some recent date
(probably when the upper fortifications were removed).
Small, thick-paned windows in the upper story peered out
of a mass of red creeper. She had been warned that it would
already be cold outdoors. But there was a feeling of captured warmth, as if the house were alive and filling the
clearing with its mild body heat.

The driver must have called ahead to announce their arrival. A small army of people, all of them dressed in the
same spruce dark green overalls—neatly marked as to sex
in the shape of waist and hips, crotch and breast—trooped
out of the porch. They lined up on either side of the doorway and bowed to Catherine. It must be the whole household. Some of those who were clearly the ranking officers
showed throat. Army was the right word. The military effect was not reassuring. Catherine suddenly felt that the
driver was her only friend. If only she had listened to
Agathe, instead of abandoning the good people in the hives
and taking up with the Michael Connellys. She turned to
him imploringly—

"I'll see that your bags are sent to your room, mademoiselle."

She was left to her fate.

Misha's father walked out between the ranks. He was,

naturally enough, the living image of Misha, except that
his vigorous hair was white instead of russet-dark, his body
larger and heavier, and his features deeply lined. He was
wearing the park uniform, but his version was impeccably
custom-grown under a deep brown robe.

"Miss Catherine. We have met before. I'm very pleased to
welcome you to Arden."

That human greeting, pathetic aspiration to Aleutian
manners, was the truth in this case. They had met, or at
least been in the same room. But she did not remember. He
shook her hands; his grip was firm and brief. He ushered
her into an entrance hall that was furnished in dark polished wood. A double stairway led to an open gallery
above: She glimpsed shadowy passageways up there,
closed doors.

"You'll have to give me news of my rival."

"Your rival?"

Topaz eyes twinkled above the furrowed cheeks. "Lord
Maitri, of course. Isn't he attempting the Aleutian record in
unassisted neoteny?"

The troops had dispersed, but one of the officers was
hovering.

"You'll want to see your room and freshen up. Excuse
Misha for not being here to greet you; or excuse *me*, rather,
I'm afraid I have no control over my son. This is my house-
keeper, Mrs. Hunt. She'll take care of you."

The housekeeper wore the same uniform as Catherine's
driver. She had a very similar smooth round face and short-
torsoed stocky build, but her brown hair was bound in two
braids around her head and her overalls were molded,
modestly but emphatically, for a female body. She showed
Catherine upstairs. When she moved, the uniform took on
a life of its own, the formal curves surging ahead of and lag-
ging behind the humble, unmarked human shape within.
Her manner, from the first moment, was distinctly hostile.

"Here you are, miss. You have your own bathroom, you

see, if you should need it while you're here." Her tone
made it clear that needing the bathroom was a serious
crime. The room was plain and pleasant, decorated in a
style that had been *old-fashioned* before the aliens came. A
younger servant, also labeled female, was unpacking
Catherine's bags. She looked around with a rosy smile but
didn't speak. The bed-with-legs was made up with linen
and a puffy down quilt. There were pictures hanging on the
walls. Everything was antique without being precious, ancient without oppression. The floor was of worn dark
wooden boards, partly covered by a machine-made woolen
rug. The sole concession to relative modernity was a bulky
multimedia rack gathering dust in a corner.

"We're not on the grid here," said Mrs. Hunt sternly. "We
have our own network. All the rooms are wired. This
room's password is Wilson. You can use it at any time. If
you need to employ our facilities in order to communicate
with the outside world, you can use the park office. The
evening meal is at seven. The Warden will expect you to
join us; you will be called. Other meals can be served in
your room whenever you wish. I hope you enjoy your visit,
Miss Catherine."

The two domestics left. Catherine went to look at her
bathroom and marveled at the glistening white porcelain.
Handwritten notices, preserved behind glass, reminded her
that she should use hydrobiont powder and chemical waste
disposal "whenever possible." She admired the recalcitrant
spirit that had retained this massive sanitary ware, determined that the lost past of unlimited free-running water
would someday, somehow return. In her bedroom there
were two mineral-glass windows. The larger one looked
down the length of the clearing into the repetitive quiet of
the trees. The smaller was almost entirely obscured by the
red creeper. She sat on her bed, feeling immeasurably
soothed, feeling like an innocent tourist carried back into a
world where none of the wrong had happened.

Her door opened, and Misha quietly entered. "Welcome to Arden."

He closed the door and came to sit beside her. "You'll have met my father and the demonic Mrs. Hunt. Don't mind her. She has a grudge against genuine curves. Did she tell you how to manage the net? It's a natural system. It speaks; you answer if you feel inclined. Speak and you will be spoken to." He opened drawers in her bedside cabinet, pulled out a flat reader. "Guests mostly stick with voice, but if you want to see who you're talking to, you can use this."

"What's your password?"

"Guglioli."

"I see!"

He grinned. "Don't blame me. I didn't set this up. It's a family tradition. The Connellys have been anti-Aleutian for a long time, I'm afraid. In the nicest possible way." He tapped the case of the reader. "Watch out for open lines. Click on this and say 'Wilson,' and you'll find yourself peering into our servants' hall. Or should I say the other ranks' mess. If you forget to log off after you've ordered your breakfast, you're still in livespace. It goes for voice as well, but tests have shown it's the little window that people forget. Wilson."

With a new, and wicked, smile he held up a single pale papery wafer.

"Shall we split it? It might enliven the hideous dinner ritual."

"How do you make a paper flower?" asked Catherine, haggling.

"Well, it's games tech. I use the Vlab to build a neuron-map model of an—an erotic daydream to put it politely. One of my own hand-tested favorites. I download the model into a harmless biochemical substrate that contains hypergrabbers—that's things that grab your perceptual attention—and slam it into high gear. Testo is among them.

You eat it; your brain chemistry takes it up. You have the experience I modeled, *but* you have it in your own way."

He broke the wafer in two.

"People make flowers for sale. You can buy them in the Café. Commercial rubbish, nothing like as pure. I don't do decor. I do *nothing but the hit*. But this won't throw you across the room. You'll be jogging; you'll be able to converse. Are you ready?"

She swallowed the paper petal. Misha ate his share.

"Were you planning to change for dinner?" he said. "You should. It'll be formal. See you then." He tapped, absentmindedly, at the reader screen. "Wilson."

"Wilson," she said, as soon as the door had closed behind him, and smiled. She wondered exactly what kind of private additions Misha had made to the house grid. At least he had warned her: watch out! It was the first time since the rapes began that he'd had a chance to take her and not used it. The relationship had changed. But she didn't quite know how. Perhaps he was simply afraid of someone else lurking in the net, peeping out. She went to the big wooden standing clothes chest, where her things were neatly arrayed. *I will wear flowers*, she decided, thinking of the wicked wafer. She chose a vial and broke it open. A delicate, insistent scent blossomed into the room. Tissue flowed over her arms, the robe became a fluttering mass of clean scarlet and lilac-tinged blue. She remembered the sheen on the grasses in Maitri's garden: and a meeting, a shared loneliness, a secret understanding that she had never managed to recapture.

Dinner was in a large room below ground. By the time Catherine had been called and fetched downstairs by the maid who had unpacked her clothes, the household was assembled. Misha, his father, and the staff officers were waiting for her around the dais table.

"You see," Michael's father told her, "we follow Aleutian

custom: the whole company gathers for the evening meal. Though I'm afraid there'll be no dancing." But Catherine was reminded even more of wartime. The underground hall had the dour atmosphere of an armored bunker. "It's a gloomy old place," he agreed, smiling at her. "But we do our best to cheer it up." He pointed at one of the large fake windows that lined the walls. "Badgers." She saw some grayish, grub-like things moving beside a heap of boulders, under a murky sky. "Charming creatures. They're extremely popular."

She was on Misha's father's left, Misha on his right. The officers were presented to her, a tally of names that she instantly forgot. Her driver wasn't among them. Mrs. Hunt appeared to be the only female-labeled person at high table. Beside her, beyond Misha and his father, there was an empty place. It remained empty as the Warden, with a commanding gesture, signaled that Catherine should sit down. Everybody else in the room followed suit, with an intimidating clatter.

"Now you must tell me about Lord Maitri," said the Warden, as the first course was served. "I consider him a serious rival. Not in terms of years, of course: but *mutatis mutandis*. He's certainly by far the oldest Aleutian left on earth."

"It's my father's hobby," explained Misha good-humoredly. "Growing old gracefully. Ordinary rich people get their faces replaced and their vital organs regrown. If you're in the premier league, you don't stoop to anything like that. Dad would rather die than have his hair color restored. They watch each other like bit-minders, spying on each other's medical records for secret forays into bridge-work."

Misha's father frowned. "The goal is to live longer and better, within one's genetic potential. I have no desire to live forever. I don't use preventive neotenic intervention, and I don't expect I ever shall. If I should ever succumb to major organic collapse, restored natural quality of life would be my goal, not artificial survival."

Misha snorted. "As natural as money can buy. Warning! This is not a sport you can take up if you're forty, living in the hives and feeling quite young for your age."

"Does Lord Maitri, ah, employ any intervention, Miss Catherine?"

"I don't think it would occur to him."

There was a short silence, in which she understood she'd stumbled into one of those invisible pitfalls. She had no idea how she had given offense this time. Everyone spooned their soup, which was very smooth and good but had a strange aftertaste.

"I won't ask you what it means to be 'an Aleutian in a human body,' " said Mr. Connelly easily, resuming command. "I'm sure you've answered that question often enough. But Misha tells me you are a disciple of Buonarroti." He studied her brightly with Misha's golden eyes. "So you don't believe that the Aleutians are aliens? That's an interesting philosophical position."

"She doesn't believe in serial immortality either," put in Misha.

"Really? You believe Aleutians don't 'come back'? But, excuse me, where does that leave you? You are yourself a reincarnate, are you not? Though in human form for this life."

She thought of an Aleutian child at home, some time after the Departure. Who would be told: remember when you were Catherine. The child would study Catherine's confessions, as edited and formatted by her character shrine. The child would consume messenger cells in which the lesson *you were Catherine, you were like this* was minutely inscribed, reports from the Expedition's last days on earth, the chemical notation of other people's perception of her life. Obediently, the child would remember the Commonalty's Catherine.

"Any society is a self-organizing pattern," she said. "Each individual is a nexus of relationships in that pattern: a particular knot in the web that returns like a ripple in the stream, though the water is not the same water. We are very much aware of this phenomenon, more so than you. The *Catherine* construct, that motif in the text of our community, will recur. And will be trained to remember my memories, because that's the way our society works. And will truly be me, because my personality is really nothing but a specially coded bundle of chemicals with its own particular history. But the 'I' speaking to you now, the sense of self that 'I' have in this moment, only exists here and now. I am certain of that. So am 'I' more immortal than you are? You say 'the place X is temporarily occupied by Catherine.' We say 'the place X *is* a person called Catherine': that's all. There are human societies where reincarnation has always been the accepted gestalt, except that few people are expected to *remember themselves* routinely, if I have that right? Humans have told me that permanent death is a more useful concept. People work harder; they have more energy if they think they have only one chance. To me that sounds like an admission that either explanation will do. Aleutian physiology is different from human physiology, Aleutian reproduction different from human reproduction. But our subjectivity is the same: it's the same sense of self. I think that's what Buonarroti meant."

"All seeing is perception," murmured the Warden.

Someone came into the room. The company, lower and upper tables together, stopped what it was doing. The newcomer glided to the dais and took her place beside Mrs. Hunt: a slim young woman, wearing close-fitting black under a gauzy robe and a silver veil. Catherine did not see her face. Nobody breathed a word.

Catherine found herself staring expectantly at Mr. Connelly.

"You are honored," he said sourly. "Misha's sister does not usually join us at table."

Helen—because it had to be Helen—said nothing.

"She doesn't believe in telepathy either," said Misha, gallantly deflecting their father's displeasure and ruthlessly using Catherine as a human shield. "Ask her what she thinks about 'the Common Tongue.' "

Catherine didn't mind. She felt like talking. She was extraordinarily conscious of the lathyrus robe. The exquisite scent and color of those so-frankly sexual flowers seemed to impart a welcome sensual glow to this conversation. It was as if she'd fallen in love with Misha's father. She was bathed in a rush of attraction, the more exciting because he *was* dangerous, he *was* an adversary, she was sure of that. She had forgotten the drug completely. She moved back in the hard, old-earth style dining chair, to accommodate a domestic who was presenting the next course (a salver of roundish golden brown vegetables and a jug of thick pale sauce). She felt two hands gripping the inner surfaces of her thighs.

She managed not to look at Misha.

Mr. Connelly smiled encouragingly.

"I admit it's a misconception to dismiss our Silent communication as a mere feat of memory and expertise in body language. There's more to it than that. Each of us has a model of the whole Commonalty as part of our awareness. We negotiate with those ghost-others, Aleutia in the mind, even when we're apart—with reasonable success in real-world prediction. There is a physical structure in the Aleutian brain, so I'm told, that models this model—more or less developed from one individual to another, just as human brain structures vary. It's part of the information system; it's kept up to date by our exchange of wandering cells. So you can say that Aleutian telepathy is scientific fact and a power humans don't possess. We truly do 'keep each other in mind.' But you have your own huge neuronal-map archives, stretching back through evolutionary aeons, maps of all human experience. You can use that archive to help you guess what another person might say or do in any given situation: and you do use it. We do the same. We just don't call it guessing."

She drew a breath, a pause to fall into the intense reality of the drug. She was aware of Misha in that room in the city: lying on the foam agonizingly aroused, the glans bursting from its sheath, glossy and desperate. He wasn't going to touch her. He was going to watch, no contact, while Catherine was invaded by the ferocious imperative, that paid for its possession of her soul in pleasure strong as poison . . .

"If this was two hundred years ago and I was an Aleutian in your house, I would have to be physically isolated, coated from head to foot in quarantine film. You don't worry about quarantine anymore. You can . . . better . . . defend yourselves, you feel, from our invasion. But also, I think, you no longer quite see yourselves, the way you did when we arrived, as separate objects in empty space. You feel yourselves to be, like us, part of a continuum. Part of the heterarchy of life, where it's natural for all boundaries to be in continuous negotiation. Our 'telepathy' is an intuitive grasp of the changing state of the heterarchic continuum. Incomplete, because there is so much, but effective, adequate. And that's not alien to you."

The Warden nodded. "The sacred character records are your library, your education. Together with the Common Tongue they are in permanent feedback loop with the actuality, or *actualité* of your culture. Would you agree," he suggested, "that the Aleutian Silent language is equivalent to the seamless discourse that for Lacan constitutes the human 'unconscious'?"

Catherine blinked. "Lacan? Why, yes. Yes, I would."

She saw Michael straining against invisible bonds. A mouth sucked at her engorged clitoris, the channel between her thighs was filled, her whole body burned and flowed. Misha was watching, agape, excruciated . . .

Mr. Connelly chuckled, pleased at what he took for astonishment. "Like you, Miss Catherine, in another life I was a student of human philosophy. You were a Marxist once, I believe?"

"It was awhile ago," she managed.

"But you still admire Lacan. And Derrida too, I suspect. All those structuralists, post-structuralists, semioticists of the precontact, so forgotten now. You know, I have often thought that their influence on Buonarroti has never been properly recognized."

"Oh, yes, I agree."

Helen took a roll of bread from the salver in front of her. Catherine glimpsed the sweep of a silver veil, carelessly arranged over dark hair, and pale hands, emerging from close-fitting dark sleeves. Her father glanced at his daughter with a tightening of the lips.

"But exactly what does the term 'Signifier' mean to an Aleutian?"

Catherine shrugged. "Someone who sees the world as made of words. Actually, I think everybody does it. But I would, wouldn't I? Our Silent wouldn't agree."

Mr. Connelly laughed. All the male members of the high table laughed. Mrs. Hunt concentrated on her food. Catherine, outrageously distracted by the drug, wondered what she'd said that was funny. She was aware of Helen, a potent black on the edge of vision.

"Now, you must tell me something about your work among the *sous-prole*," her inquisitor continued, inexorable. "Our leisured classes—"

Glossolalia babbled from her lips, until at last the meal ended. It was time to retire. She realized that the paper flowers experience was over too; she didn't know when it had left her. "We keep early hours," said Mr. Connelly. "The cities make their own time. Out here in the wilderness, we are ruled by the real sun and the real seasons."

Misha had already disappeared, so had his sister. Two domestics in female-shaped overalls were moving about, setting the hall to rights for morning. A third offered Mr. Connelly a ball of glowing flame, which he passed on to Catherine. It was quite cool.

"Arden is 'wired' for communication, but not for heat or light, I'm afraid. Do let Mrs. Hunt know if you feel the cold. We try to manage on piped daylight as far as possible, but we can afford you a lamp at bedtime."

She accepted the lightbulb, dumbly.

"I very much enjoyed our conversation," he said. "Now, since my reprobate son has deserted us, I wish you good night on his behalf. Sleep as late as you like."

The journey to her room was dark and long. She knew it was dangerous. As she passed a curtained alcove between two closed doors, a hand reached out. Misha pulled her into a small rectangular space, brightly lit by a cluster of bulbs that he'd slapped on the wall. It had been a bathroom in another life. The bath, a massive white open pod, was half full of empty packaging, disintegrating plastic sacks, padding granules, paperboard.

He was grinning. "You made a great impression."

"I talked too much. I always make speeches; I can't help it."

"Oh, God," he whispered. "Oh, shit." He grabbed her, crushing the folds of the lathyrus robe, burying his face in the scent, tearing the delicate fabric as he hunted for her skin. "I'm in fucking *agony*," he gasped. "The old man likes you," he gabbled. "Never seen him so taken with anyone; you can say what you like to him, you realize that? He doesn't give a bugger; I realized that a long time ago. He lives in a fortress somewhere else: He looks out and gets amused by our antics far away, but we can't touch him."

He pushed her down on the ice hard rim of the bath and punched his frantic erection wildly at her bared crotch. Catherine sobbed as his claw entered, grabbed his shoulders, locked her ankles in the small of his back, their bodies bucketing like rocks falling down a mountain. He was still muttering as they coupled, *old man likes you, old man likes you.* When they finished—finished, or suddenly neither could stand any more—she was astride him. He pushed her off and rolled free. "You've got to bum fuck me." He was slumped in the rubbish filled tub, groping to cover himself. "I think I've broken my back. Got to have your dick up my rectum. How can this be? Mother Vlab will provide. Next time. Soon. Got to come down now. Got to give this stuff up, soon. Soon. I'm dying . . . Go on, to your room. Go."

Catherine blundered out into the hallway. Her robe was in tatters. She dropped her lightbulb, and it rolled away. A little cleaner, interrupted in its nighttime job of picking bits out of the carpet, started fussing around this strange obstacle with the unhappy air of a simple soul helpless before the unexpected. She crawled to retrieve her light and stayed down, unable to get back on her feet. She was speaking in tongues to the father while the son, at a sly remove, shafted her, absolutely shafted her under the patriarch's table. And the mysterious Helen sat with her head bowed while Mrs. Hunt chewed discreetly. Mrs. Hunt, the ersatz woman. Maybe that should be woman *sous rature?* A concept partly erased, inadequate but essential. She clambered to her feet with the bulb and stumbled, giggling, to her room.

ii

SOMETIME LATER, PERHAPS an hour in human reckoning, she unfolded herself from a catatonic crouch, looked around her, and got down from the bed-with-legs. She went to her bathroom and dumped the rags of the lathyrus robe in the waste bucket. She was wearing Expedition uniform overalls. She'd decided that this was the dress her host would expect of her for a formal dinner. Misha had torn the closures of the suit and her underwear, but the fabric had recovered while she was in her trance. She sat on the edge of the bed, staring at the woolen rug, and thought about her purpose in coming here. She wanted to know more about Helen. She had become convinced, by things spoken and unspoken, that there was some mystery, concerning the fate of Traditionalist young ladies, that her friends wanted to reveal to her: but for whatever reason, they didn't dare to speak. The snake-toy girl at the police station had been something to do with it. Helen Connelly could tell Catherine more.

She could use her password, and ask to speak to Miss Helen. But she knew there were lurkers in the net; and besides, Catherine did not want to meet a voice or a dead image. She particularly wanted to see Helen in the flesh. She decided to go and look for her.

She went out into the corridor, with her fading light. The house wasn't large. It shouldn't be difficult to find the right room. If Misha's sister had not wanted to meet Catherine, she would not have come down to dinner. On the strength of this silent message, she was convinced that Helen was waiting for her somewhere: expecting her. A door would open, and she would be beckoned inside . . . There was a dim glow from the walls, the ceilings, piped in from outside, where it must be a starry night in the forest. She easily found her way to the gallery above the entrance hall. Then she realized she could hear music—old precontact human music, but as faint as if it came from the stars. She followed the sound along a passage that led away at right angles from the gallery, down a small flight of steps, and discovered a heavily curtained doorway. The door inside the curtain was standing ajar, showing a line of light. She pushed it open.

The room was no larger than her own bedroom. It was wainscoted and lined with bookcases to the ceiling. The panels between the cases were covered in blue morocco, stamped with silver *fleur de lis*. Two armchairs, one in studded leather and one in deepcolored brocade, flanked a fireplace where a glowing fire was burning. There was a large table covered in books and papers, and a multimedia rack like the one in her room. But this one housed an array of very old and beautiful musical instruments. Directly in her line of sight stood a virtual screen, half-lifesize. It showed a scene like the one invoked by the music. A young girl was surrounded by her attendants. She stood like a flower in a snowstorm, like a white butterfly. They were dressing her. They were preparing her for her bridal. Catherine found the scene extremely disturbing—she didn't quite know why. She had lived on earth before. She'd attended human weddings.

The music faltered, with a sound like grit snarling in a tiny mechanical gear. Mr. Connelly stood up. He had left his armchair and was halfway across the room before he saw Catherine.

"Good evening!" He continued on his way to the rack and carefully removed, from one of the antique instruments, a large black disk. He studied it minutely. "My music has drawn you from your lair. Come and look at this, Catherine."

He laid the disk back on the platter, took up a small block of red velvet, and rubbed it against his palm. "Something small lodged in a scratch. A little grease from the skin," he murmured, and smoothed velvet over the moving surface. "This is a Linn Sondek. It is three hundred and sixty years old. It does nothing in the world except go around and around and around. But it does so *perfectly*. The arm is not original," he added apologetically, shifting a lever so that another part of the instrument dropped slowly onto the disk. "Unfortunately. Neither is the vinyl, though it is very old. Yet the reproduction of time past is 'nature identical,' I think we could say. You like Puccini? A wonderful artist. He takes the grief of the world and transforms it into exquisite pleasure."

"Well," she said. "Yes, he does. The grief always seems to be a bit one-sided, though."

Then she was afraid this remark was gender politics: but Mr. Connelly didn't seem to be offended.

"Is there anything else that you would like to hear? I have an extensive archive."

The fire was made of flowers, golden chrysanthemums that burned and were not consumed. She'd seen the effect before, but it was still a beautiful design. The big virtual screen had vanished.

"I miss the twentieth century," she said. "The era that was your past, your immediate cultural history, when we arrived. What happened to that stuff? So much has disappeared. I didn't notice it in my last life because of the War. It seems strange now. Misha's renaissance friends have resurrected *musique naturelle*, but they make their own. They seem never to have seen the movies or heard the songs that were 'immortal classics' back then: Bob Dylan. The Beatles."

"Ah, that was the intellectual property wars," sighed Mr. Connelly. "Reproduction fees set too high, copyright disputes: a lot of material died in the transition to the grid. Some wonderful art vanished in those wrangles. I have some very rare works."

But he didn't repeat his offer, and *Madame Butterfly* continued. He returned to the hearth. A supper tray stood on a small table by his chair: cheese and savories in a silver dish, chunks of bread, a decanter of Scotch. He looked at Catherine with a new interest.

"Did you know, Miss Catherine, that the word for patriarch and father, *pere, pater,* derives from this sign, this gesture. The father provides. Will you eat with me?"

He offered the dish, a speculative gleam in his eyes. They were alone.

Catherine shook her head. "No, thank you. It's too late for me."

Mr. Connelly laughed and picked up his Scotch glass. "How do you like my house? Oh, I'd love to rebuild. I'd like to remodel the place completely, get rid of the military element, so *passé!* I can't afford it, because I don't know how to grovel. I only know how to protect and preserve, to keep the pure human traditions alive. I do my duty. But nobody has rights, duties, privileges these days, only more or less money. Those who have the money may screw the brains out of those who have not, and that is the whole of the law."

"What were you watching?"

"Eh? Watching?"

"When I came in. It didn't somehow look like the scene from *Butterfly.*"

He frowned at her. "It was nothing. Some silly old soap from my archives." He put the glass down. "I'd forgotten that Aleutians like to socialize at night. I'm afraid you must feel we've neglected you."

"Not at all," said Catherine. "I'm sleepy now. I'll go back to bed."

She resolved always to wear overalls in Mr. Connelly Sr.'s company, and not to be alone with him. Another time he might make that offer of protection more pressing. But though he could "speak Aleutian," or at least understand it, better than his son, his attitude to the alien belonged to another age. She felt his distaste for *that thing which isn't like me.* Aleutian uniform should keep him at arm's length, reminding him she wasn't what she seemed. The boundaries between Misha and Mr. Connelly were blurred enough without her being actually, physically raped by both of them. She fell asleep wondering about that screen. It seemed poor taste, not Mr. Connelly's taste, to watch half-lifesize virtual fiction in that exquisite antique study.

She dreamed of a house where all the doors opened outward into limitless space. But as she opened them, with a sense of great gladness, she had an unpleasant feeling of something going on behind her. She kept trying to turn back and see what was there. Finally, she managed it. She was standing by her bed in the room called Wilson in Mr. Connelly's house. For no obvious reason she felt afraid—disgusted and afraid. She was aware of movement, a muffled, heavy slithering and scrabbling. Then one of the walls became transparent. She looked through it into another room that was large and brightly lit. The floor was divided into open pens: she couldn't see inside them but she had a sense of big things jostling. She knew (in the dream) that this other room didn't have to be next door. It could be anywhere in the house, being projected to her wall by *piped daylight.* Mr. Connelly was moving between the pens. The skin of his bare face and hands glistened; he was wearing quarantine. He looked over one of the partitions. She had a sensation of falling, and received his view. The animals, or prisoners, stared up at her. They were naked, clean, and plump. Their faces reminded her, horribly, of the bridal scene that she had glimpsed in Mr. Connelly's study.

She woke up with a start, sweating.

She lay very still. She was certain that there was somebody in the room, equally certain that her dreams had been tampered with. What had been so horrible? No, it was gone. She could remember the nightmare, but it had already lost its bitter edge. She touched her face. Eyedrops? A thin visor, slipped delicately across her temples and then stealthily removed? She couldn't tell. And now the room seemed empty except for herself and the silence and the faint glow of channeled starlight. She went back to sleep.

8

PAPER FLOWERS

i

CATHERINE WAS NOT required to repeat the performance of her first night. The evening ritual was unvarying, but Misha didn't spike it with paper flowers and Mr. Connelly did not interrogate her again. He was gracious but reserved, a little on his dignity. She rarely saw the Warden at any other time of day, and Helen never reappeared. Catherine would breakfast in her room. Later she would meet Misha, and he would take her, chaperoned by a driver and a senior female servant, on one of the park's excursions.

They visited the great road, a picturesque ghost village, bird-haunted marshes, those highly popular badgers, the lynxes, a variety of ancient craft workshops. It was extremely curious and otherworldly, she found, to visit virtual-tourism sites in the real. Once they drove to the mountains on the southeastern margin of the reserve, and took one of the great fragile Wings up to visit the nearest of the glaciers. They rode the air alone: Catherine pinned facedown, helmeted and gauntleted, in the web behind the pilot's sling that was used for making masters. Misha was steering. Their chaperones were left behind at the trailhead. It was freezing cold.

The Wing was capable of vast journeys, but not equipped for the comfort of physical passengers. The mountain slopes lay under her like scarred and fissured skin, the darkness of bare beeches and chestnuts giving way to gray turf and shale. They hovered over pallid amoebae of permanent snow.

"It's still spreading." His voice spoke in her ear, as she lay shivering in her borrowed oversuit. "Every year we're supposed to report that the retreat's begun. It hasn't. There." The glacier hung like a gray snake, its back pocked with boulders, the eyeless head stooping to drink at the margin of a long black lake. "Do you want to go down?"

Her view changed, swooped and banked. She was as if standing under the snake's mouth, under the mass of its blue-shadowed flesh.

"Want to see the ice caves?"

"No, thank you."

The trailhead was another point of uncomfortable transition: an ecological hotspot, or rather cold spot. All the hotspots in this park were cold spots. They checked the ground station before they returned to the jeep. The instrumentation was inadequate, Misha grumbled. Scientific monitoring had to take second place to the needs of virtual users.

"The users, and that includes the government, don't want to think about what's creeping up on us. They're safe indoors, and this is the *pristine* wilderness. Scientific measurement is an intrusion, practically a crime. Damned fools. The whole park is unnatural. The air is unnatural. The food chain is stuffed with human effluvia, the wild life littered with weird genes. The forest is a man-made artifact. There is no *pristine wilderness* on the planet."

The cold wind blew from the north, biting into their faces. "And the weather's *certainly* unnatural," grinned Misha. "Ironically enough it's the Aleutians, who are supposed to hate measurement, who defend these ground stations. They want to see how their climate improvement plan is progressing."

The measuring post was by the shore of a tiny pool that was already frozen: a gray bruise of ice that reflected nothing but the cold. Misha looked up into the cloud cover. "It's going to snow soon. Maybe your people are right. Chewing the top off the Himalaya range was a major intervention: bound to be some side effects. This cold spell is only a temporary hitch; it'll be worth it in the end when the whole earth's a semitropical paradise. Or maybe our bad weather was coming to us anyway, and your meddling did nothing. It's a possibility."

"Do you believe that?" asked Catherine.

"Don't think it matters. It definitely doesn't matter to the Aleutians. You're leaving."

She wondered at this other Misha, competent and absorbed in his work, talking like any beleaguered professional she'd ever met: so different from the dilettante artist in the city.

When the weather was poor they spent their time in the big underground room that was called "the great hall" by the officers and Misha's father, "the mess" by everybody else. They gossiped with the staff, and watched trees growing in the fake windows. She was introduced to the Virtual Master, L'Airial's mascot: a hedgehog the size of a plump cat, who was not supposed to be indoors, ate gifts of live slugs with noisy enthusiasm, and liked to climb onto people's laps and chew their clothes. They wired up and played pre-contact indoor games for the virtual-modeling masters: darts, boules, babyfoot. Sometimes they crouched in peculiar positions, wired to the staked-out domains of badgers, martens, flamingos, marsh-harriers, wild boar, and watched what went on—for the benefit of users who liked to spend their virtual visits in comfortless observation hides, so they knew they were really communing with nature.

Mrs. Hunt—on the Warden's instructions, as she made plain—showed Catherine around the domestic and farm-yard offices. She met the gabbling hunting dogs in their kennel, which was a bleak windowless barn where the big animals romped and raced about, contentedly certain that they were living a very different existence. Catherine and the housekeeper looked down from a control booth in what had been the hayloft. Watching the dogs gave Catherine a queasy feeling; they were too much like human gamers. "Don't they come into the house?" she asked, remembering Thérèse's report.

"They are not pets," said Mrs. Hunt repressively.

"Will they be taken out hunting during my stay? I'd like to go with them."

"That depends on the Warden. We also have a stable and riding school, but they are physically located elsewhere. The actual animals are not necessary. We have an enormous archive of mastered material. I don't know why the Visitors cannot be satisfied with that. But they like to know the pack exists and that the horses they ride in virtuality are also real animals somewhere. And their word is law. Next, the *potager.* Our extensive year-round gardening program includes among other pursuits fungi and wild fruit gathering, peasant cultivation, resin extraction, apiary, and prize vegetable rearing. We grow over a hundred different species of edible plants. However, at this season many are dormant in the real."

The Visitors were given a capital letter; Catherine felt sure that she was not. She followed the housekeeper obediently up and down the dormant but efficient-looking rows of food plants, stopping to admire whatever she was required to admire and wondering how she could penetrate this wall of suspicion. She wanted to talk about Helen. She didn't believe that the housekeeper's hostility was due to her resentment of "real curves." She was sure that Mrs. Hunt was Helen's ally and regarded Catherine as a threat.

The *potager* was surrounded by a tall hedge that was, even now, thickly covered in roses. They reached the angle farthest from the house, where a large and very natural-looking compost heap seethed in a pen of rustic-effect plastic. Traces of Atha's speciality foods were enlivening the top layer, being turned into something useful, as he had predicted. Catherine averted her eyes politely from this sight.

"Does Miss Helen help with the gardening?"

A flush arose in the housekeeper's stolid cheeks. She almost smiled and reached out to touch a flower. The petals were white, stained in a crisp random pattern of jet-black.

"The rose is called 'Lord Maitri's Librarian,' perhaps you know it. It won prizes. It was developed at L'Airial. Miss Helen planted this hedge herself, the year Mr. Misha was born. She did it for the *English Garden* program. We still have it on file."

"I didn't know that she was older than Misha."

"It would be strange if she wasn't, Miss Catherine. Next the sawmill, the tannery, and the slaughterhouse. Our slaughterhouse provides a complete practice of the end phase of organic animal husbandry, from a humane but highly immediate experience of administering death to every aspect of expert butchery."

Farther along her own passageway on the upper floor, Catherine found a schoolroom. It had globes of the earth and the stars, an orrery, bookcases. There were big, jolly informative touch-screens on the walls, layered with graded information: "Our Planet," "How Water Is Made," "The Aleutians." In one drawer she found an old notebook that held pages of images, frozen in time and beginning to decay: equations, symbols, algorithms. The most complete of these (as far as Catherine could tell) purported to show how to turn a sphere into an indefinite number of other spheres of the same dimensions. Catherine's dumb ignorance before the world of number was partly a pretense, necessary in Aleutian society. But she couldn't understand these exercises at all. There was a tiny signature cartouche, which on magnification showed a young woman, painted in the style of the first "renaissance," bending over something unseen, her hands clasped in awed, joyful discovery. It was obviously a detail from a larger picture. She recognized the artist, but couldn't place the work.

The rest of the drawers were empty. There were no books in the wall cases, no terminals fitted to the old-fashioned sockets. It was a sad place.

She spent surprisingly little time with Misha.

In the mornings and at night, alone in her room, she watched the records that she found on the multimedia rack. She had long conversations with Maitri: with that Maitri, the true image, who lived always in her mind. Her sense that she *couldn't talk to him anymore* had vanished with distance. Their companionship was restored, her doubts and fears shared without reserve. It was Maitri who persuaded her she really must ask for a room heater. The flame-effect fire in her fireplace (which did not burn flowers) was the safety kind that gave off practically no heat. Mrs. Hunt produced, with great reluctance, an aged, undernourished hybrid foot warmer. Every day it grew colder. Catherine would sit on the floor in front of years-old Youro news reports, Maitri beside her, the woolen rug around her shoulders and the heater in her arms—an Aleutian at prayer, reverently studying the myriad aspects of God-the-Self in process. It was a long time since she had practiced her religion so faithfully. She felt like a hermit: like Helen.

One morning she woke in the heart of a green-tinged white rose. "Oh, Maitri," she whispered, the snowlight lying on her closed eyes like manna from heaven. "You'd love this." The maid who always brought her breakfast had a sweet face, but was firmly in Mrs. Hunt's camp. Catherine could never remember her name. She recited, distantly, the household's schedule for the day—which Catherine had, as usual, forgotten to request. She conveyed Mr. Misha and the Warden's apologies. Both of them would be unavailable until evening, busy on urgent wilderness-management business.

"I'll go for a walk," she said. "Françoise"—this was a wild guess—"is that all right?"

"I am Virginie, mademoiselle. I will arrange outdoor equipment for you."

There had never been any snow in the shipworld. At home it was an indoor phenomenon, a rare accident that had little romance. It was too obvious that the pretty crystals were nothing but the damp exhaust gases of people and commensals, briefly glorified by a temperature swing. She sipped nature-identical coffee at her big window, gazing out at the white day and feeding scraps of sopped croissant to the room heater. She was building up its strength. It seemed as grateful as such a dumb creature could be. She'd always loved the wild snowfall of earth and had hardly ever had a chance to experience it in the real.

How long had she been staying at the Connelly house? She wasn't sure. She hoped her driver would be pleased to know that she was finally taking his advice.

The outdoor suit was dark green, supple, and a reasonable fit. It was slaved to the house network, which annoyed her slightly. But she accepted that the humans couldn't let a valuable Aleutian visitor wander about in extreme conditions without some insurance. There was nothing stirring in the clearing. The chickens had not ventured out; the dogs' hangar was silent. The Lord Maitri's Librarian roses were smothered in white on white.

Catherine remembered why she had not been tempted to explore on her own before this, though she'd had plenty of opportunity. For her taste, a wilderness should be *wild*. There should be no compromise. There should be nothing but desert emptiness, cold rock, and thin air. This vast factory of pumping, churning, life-processing xylem, though attractive enough as a tame city park, did not have the allure of the true outdoors.

But the snow had changed everything. As soon as she stepped under the trees, the temperature dropped dramatically. The air stung her cheeks. The cold parted like a curtain and folded her into itself. The snow came halfway to her knees. Back in the city, news of an early and deep snowfall in the Atlantic Forest would be attracting hordes of visitors to the park. The virtual experience of wintery weather had become a ceremony in the modern calendar. People for whom indoor life was a relative novelty wanted to mark the change in their changeless seasons. People who believed that the ice age was closing in wanted to gloat and shudder over the approach of doom. She was surrounded by ghosts, an invisible crowd of virtual companions, but they were quiet company.

There were trails all over the forest: jeep tracks, broad rides, narrow footpaths. None of them was marked. There was no necessity for signposts, information boards, *balisage*: that could be added later, for the individual visitor's needs. She didn't think she'd get lost. She could trace her own footprints back to L'Airial. She followed the first white trail that she'd chosen at random until she came to a well-established jeep track. She crossed it and took a smaller path that offered more mystery, wondering how far away the Buonarroti research station was. But it was certainly out of reach on foot.

Neither Misha nor his father had mentioned the lab. Perhaps it was something they tried to forget. She remembered how Misha had made a point of telling her, the first time they met, that he didn't care about the Departure plans and he wasn't interested in the details. Maybe that was because he resented having the research station for a neighbor.

She saw no wildlife, heard no birdsong. She sat under a tree and stared up into the laden branches. It was a pine, with a slender trunk and a red, cobbled hide. The needles bowed their backs under their white freight. The air was so still and cold that not a crystal had slipped or been brushed away. At every surface the elaborate little pinwheels were intact. She remembered Lydie in the Blue Forest game, and tried to know what made *this* reality and *that* illusion. She could not find the borderline.

She walked on.

It was Misha's father who had called the house in the clearing "Arden." If she remembered her Shakespeare, the name meant that he considered himself a prince in exile, wronged and waiting for times to change. The Connellys were stinking rich by any reasonable standards (though not as rich as the Khans). Still, Mr. Connelly Sr. felt poor and passed-over and shabby. Though he was barred from executive office by his hereditary privilege, he was known as a power behind the city's government. But it wasn't enough. He wanted to turn his fortified farmhouse into a palace. He was an anti-Aleutian who had lived for too long with the rankling conviction that *real* power on Aleutian earth was out of any human's reach. He must be desperate for the Departure. He said he didn't want to live forever, but she knew that he secretly believed that he was immortal. When he was alone in that study with his souvenirs of pre-contact, he almost believed that he was as old as his ancient machines. He had lived through the alien invasion; he would live to triumph after the aliens were gone. If he (ever!) suffered organic collapse, maybe he could have himself transferred into Misha's body, and then into another clonal package, and on and on. He would never die.

Some Aleutians were convinced that human aristocrats routinely used void-forces wizardry in this way: had "themselves" moved or copied from one of the dumb-chemistry bodies to another, indefinitely. They treated any human they dealt with as if they were the same people who'd been around at First Contact and claimed this worked just fine. Catherine knew that it wasn't so. The humans had no such technique. But even if she had not known, she would not have believed them the same person. What she felt between father and son was a barbed intimacy: they knew each other far too well, didn't like each other much. If they were the same person, they ought to be lovers, she thought wryly. There wasn't any sign of that!

Mr. Connelly's hunger for survival struck her as grotesque. But Catherine could be as skeptical as she liked about immortality, it was nonetheless her birthright. Lord Maitri could grow old for a whim; he did not have to face the raw terror of extinction. She could not judge the Warden; she could not blame him. Never, no matter what he did. She was up against the frustration that had galled her for three lifetimes, the other face of her enduring guilt and shame. She could not find a place to stand. She could not reach a situation in which she could judge the humans, and be judged by them, as an equal. Where she could accuse and be accused, speak and be answered.

She had not been raped since she came to L'Airial.

They had abandoned that simple scenario—it was played out. Now it was paper flowers, and the consensual sex—furtive, frantic coupling in that disused bathroom—that they both needed to finish off the rush. But nothing else had changed. She was still helpless, he still in control, still as harsh. He'd slip a wafer into her palm without a word or the faintest hint of a caress. She never knew when he was going to do it. Sometimes it was last thing at night, sometimes in the day. They would walk sedately around a tourist site with their chaperones: practicing bilocation, minds in riot. They would part in the entrance hall and go to their separate rooms, and hurry to the rendezvous as soon as they dared.

As she walked now, the flashes came. Her invisible partner was visible, was Misha himself, naked (as she had never seen him in life). She felt the clutch of anatomically impossible illusion, she was human male as well as female, she was driving into Misha as he plowed into her, thrusting deep into his gut. *Harder,* he ordered. *Harder! Harder!* Misha was sucking her, face between her thighs, and she had become an Aleutian again. The lips of her *place* gaped, her claw reached into his throat; his claw, impossible, punched into her anus.

She had to admit the stuff was good. It was the most pleasure she could ever remember getting from lying down with someone (though it was so little like lying down). By far the most. Yet something had been lost when they had stopped being rapist and victim and started sharing needles. Some immediacy, some chance of truth.

Some of the original material for the flowers came intact through the reformatting.

(Misha hanging naked by his manacled wrists in a corner of the room where his father, obviously his father, even bigger and broader than in life, pounded his male bulk into a slight girl body, broke her open (was that Catherine?). Misha cried stop it, stop it! struggling and jerking in his bonds, in ecstasy, his erection stabbing the air—)

Many images of that kind . . .

She knew she was glimpsing the defenses that he'd built for himself, witnessing the cunning with which a child's mind turned helpless grief into the trigger of a hormone cascade, shame into pleasure. Thérèse Khan would understand. But she couldn't ask Misha if he was showing her these things deliberately. He would not talk to her, except through the drug.

Catherine stopped, wrenched out of her calm appraisal.

In the white world, blue-shadowed, in the piercing stillness, she knew that she was horrified by what went on between her and Misha Connelly. He had asked her, *Do you think I'm Johnny?* She would always dream of meeting Johnny again. She would always dream of that sweet, go-nowhere green-sickness: sweet in spite of everything that had followed. But Johnny had been confused and scared by Catherine's unwanted attentions. It had been nothing personal. Misha hated her.

She began to walk, rapidly. The snow clogged her boots. She blundered into low branches. Snow fell over her outdoor suit, blinding her as it spilled onto her bare face. She dropped to her knees on the cold ground. She wanted to go on four feet and run, but her joints wouldn't reverse, her body wouldn't obey her. Horrible, horrible to be a pleasure that was feared and hated. To be handled in that monstrous way. To be a baited trap, from which Misha grabbed the goodies and escaped in triumph. To have the act of lying down, the act of communion, heart of everything, negated and despoiled. She had ordered her people to make her into a woman. She had asked to be raped: *asked for this.* Insane arrogance! Her situation was so terrible that she began to shake and howl, physically overwhelmed as if by the drug itself. She had never been more miserable. Never, in all her restless and unhappy lives, had she been so lost.

She huddled against the ground. Her sobs broke into human weeping, tears that filled her eyes and tumbled. She had been pounding at the snow with her fists. She lay with her cheek against bared earth, the black friable earth built by forest fires out of the native sand. Melting crystals stared back at her from the stems of heather and dead bracken.

I have found my punishment. But I don't want it. I didn't know what I was asking for. I didn't know it would feel like this. Please, God, I've learned my lesson. Can I go now?

The tears stopped. She rolled over and lay on her back, wiping her face with snowy gloved fingers. She relaxed, stretched out in the cold, springy embrace of the giant planet. Long ago, at home, poems . . . She shrugged and smiled in rueful acknowledgment. Yes, I'm a fool. I think too much; I talk too much. This world with its histrionic sorrows is a drug a person like me should avoid like poison. I admit everything.

She had left her path. She was simply lying among the trees, which looked down on her from every side: hypnotic, unvarying, uncannily still. The silence, which had been unbroken except for the crunch of her boots until her burst of sobbing, brought the quiet sound of voices. Catherine stood up and shook the caked snow from her back. The voices had stopped. But she was curious. There should not be anybody else here. Virtual visitors did not make the forest's air vibrate. There was no reason for any of the park staff to have followed her on foot, and she hadn't heard a vehicle approaching. The jeeps were far from silent, unless you were shut up in the back. She stepped carefully in the direction from which she thought the sounds had come.

She found a glade among the trees. Perhaps it was the trace of a fire, or of a once-inhabited clearing much smaller than L'Airial. Trees grew close and evenly around it, enclosing an oval of extreme, glittering blue-whiteness. In the center of the oval, Catherine saw two human figures. One of them was pale-skinned, with a rosy flush of blood showing clearly through the pallor. The other was a light brown, biscuit color. They both had indented waists, round buttocks, jutting breasts. They were naked. Catherine could see no sign of their discarded clothing. They moved together, coupling, clasped in each other's arms on the snow. They were not speaking now. The only sound was the sound she had heard in the *sous-prole* brothel while she was waiting for Thérèse. The two bodies were oblivious. The faces were the faces she had seen in her dream and on the virtual screen in Mr. Connelly's study. Catherine backed away. She hid herself behind a tree. She covered her face and uncovered it. She swallowed bile. She felt herself trembling and watched her gloved hands try to fist themselves into running pads.

What is it? What's wrong with me?

When she went to look into the glade again, the figures had vanished.

She touched her temples, rubbed her eyes. She didn't want to step out onto the unmarked snow, but in the end she did. There was no sunlight in the glade now, no glitter. There was not a sign of disturbance where the two bodies had been. The unbroken cold had kept the snow firm, but it was not unyielding. She had left a trail of deep footprints. When she pressed her glove down lightly, it made a dent in the surface. She felt slightly ridiculous as she made these investigations. She was sure she was being watched. She did not know what had been so horrible about the love tryst that she had seen. Her body had recoiled from something her consicousness had failed to assimilate, that had fallen through the meshes of memory as a dream vanishes on waking. But the air of the glade seemed tainted.

A bright gleam winked at her from the ground. She went to see what it was and found an object lying half buried, where the snow was loose under the trees. She picked it up. It was a bracelet of polished metal, incised with a pattern of crossed branches and tiny flames. Catherine examined it suspiciously, hefting its weight, turning it from angle to angle in the light. She knew what it was. This was the badge of rank of an officer of the Special Exterior Force, overseas army of the USSA, sometimes known as the Campfire Girls. What was it doing here? There was no inscription. It was rather small for the wrist of a normally muscled adult woman. It looked as if it would fit comfortably over her own hand, but she decided that she would not try the experiment. She fastened it away in a pocket of her suit.

And looked up. The shadows had turned a deeper blue. It would not be dark for a while, but the cold was growing fierce. She closed the suit's visor and set off, not looking for a path but heading as far as she could judge in the right direction for L'Airial. After a short brisk march, she struck the jeep trail. Not long after that she found her own footprints, where she'd crossed this track earlier. As she reached the clearing, more snow was beginning to fall.

ii

AT THE END of the supper ritual that evening, Misha wanted to slip her a dose of paper flowers. She contrived to make this impossible, without seeming to refuse the offer. Mrs. Hunt was always too close, Misha's father too attentive; Catherine's hands were never conveniently placed for the stealthy transfer. As soon as the house was quiet, she put a plain robe over the overalls she'd worn at dinner and darted along to their meeting place.

Misha was there, sitting on the rim of the tub. He held out a wafer between finger and thumb, but his eyes were wary.

"Do you want this? I wasn't sure."

She looked at that glistening bathtub. So old-earth, so incredibly arousing, she remembered it cold and hard against her soft flesh.

"Not yet. I want to talk, Misha."

She remembered how bluntly she'd asked him in that other room: "What is your problem?" She wished she was like Maitri, who could control his demeanor in the Common Tongue with such skill. Catherine was not tactful. She felt that her sympathy, humiliating sympathy, filled the air of this room. <*Your life is terrible. I admire you greatly for living it even as well as you do.*> And Misha was insulted. She had left the bracelet hidden in her clothes chest. She hadn't liked to leave it there; she was afraid it would have disappeared when she went back. But she hadn't wanted to bring it with her either. She wasn't going to show it to him. Not yet. They came here because the bathroom was not wired, or so Catherine had understood. But she wasn't sure.

Misha was looking at her quizzically. "What about?"

"How far is the sea from here?"

"Not far. Why?"

"Could we go there? I'd like to see the Atlantic."

"It's not the right season."

She chewed at her lip. He waited, repelling her attempts at contact, smiling.

"In this life," she said, "I've had no other lying-down partner but you. I never do have many partners. I'm too intense. I scare people. I scare myself. They say I'll never lie down unless there's some *reason* for it, either something bad and twisted or some exalted passion. They say I never do it just for fun, for pleasure with a friend. The Aleutians think I'm . . . undersexed, as you people would put it."

Misha snorted. "That's a joke!"

"Yeah," she agreed, glancing at him wryly. "I'll have some useful tips for my future partners." Her hair fell into her eyes; she pushed it back. "I want to talk about Helen."

Misha appeared to admire the effect of a bee-stung, arrogant smirk in his inset lens.

"What about her?"

She sighed. "You know, I can't tune out *everything* that I learn from your body language. Before you invited me here, you told me—I mean, I gathered—that you were very worried about her. Agathe has said it too. Helen's in trouble. She used to be one of the gang; now no one sees her. Will she see me? I had the idea . . . I thought that was why you invited me here, because you wanted me to help."

He took a breath and let it go, a heavy resentful sigh.

"Yes, I've been worried about Helen. Yes, I thought you might be able to help, and I got you out here because she won't leave L'Airial now. But I've changed my mind. I don't know. I'll think about it." He took her by the waist and arranged her (that autistic gesture) so she was straddling his thighs. He worked his fingers through the closure of her overalls. "Why aren't you wearing girl clothes?" he wondered sulkily, looking into her face with eyes as hard as metal. "Someday soon, Miss Alien-in-disguise, I'm not going to want to fuck your brains out anymore. You are finally going to have to learn to eat your shit and shut up about it, like the rest of us. No more Mr. Whiplash from me. Meanwhile"—with his free hand, he held up the wafer—"do you want to do this?"

"Yes."

Misha went to Helen, after he had left Catherine. She was sitting by the fire. She was wearing dull, fluid silver, cut high at the throat and covering all her arms but clinging softly to her figure. Flame light, from the heap of red roses in her grate, played on her shining hair and roused pewter gleams in the folds of her dress. There was no other light in the room. Her face was in shadow. She was singing, very softly, about the life of her art: a girl's art, hidden from view, unworldly, secret, and lonely.

> . . . *mi piaccion quelle cose*
> *che han sì dolce malia,*
> *che parlano d'amor, di primavere . . .*
> *che parlano di sogni e di chimere,*
> *quelle cose che han nome poesia . . .*

Misha crept right up to the chair, like a little mouse, until he was touching the brocaded arm. The scent of the fabric and the feel of it against his cheek were exactly as they had been long ago. Everything was perfect. The singing stopped.

"You can come out, little mouse."

He stayed where he was. He didn't want to break the mood.

"Daddy won't come in," she reassured him. "He may come to my room and find me alone in the firelight. But there are rooms within rooms in my network. It won't be *your* me. It will be one of my copies."

So he came out of hiding and snuggled against her knee, the way he liked best.

"What have you been saying to Catherine?"

The old bathroom was not wired, but Misha didn't seriously believe she didn't know what happened in there. She knew everything that went on in this house.

"I told her I was a virgin before we started our mad, passionate affair."

He didn't look up. He felt her smile.

"It's true," he protested. "It's *true*. I had never touched another person, never."

"Did she ask about me?"

"Not yet."

"She will. As soon as she asks you about me, you must bring her here. Then we begin phase four. But not until she asks. It has to come from her."

She didn't say anything more. She didn't talk much these days; it tired her. Misha knelt watching the roses. *Tomorrow,* he thought. *Tomorrow.* He had not lied. He didn't think it was possible to lie to her. She knew everything. Lying to her was a way of asking permission. If she accepted the lie, permission was granted . . . It was a reprieve beyond his hopes to be in this room again. To have returned to their sweet first world, where she was author of everything. To when he hadn't yet learned how to say *I love you, you are so beautiful.* All he wanted was to stay forever by her side, snuggled in her arms, her mish-mouse. For just a little longer.

iii

CATHERINE DID NOT get another chance to talk to Misha. The next morning she woke in dark snowlight and immediately put her hand on the silver bracelet under her pillow. It was still there. But she had been woken, she realized, by someone knocking on her door. Mrs. Hunt was there in person, looking solemn. Catherine was summoned to Mr. Connelly's study.

She was to return to the city at once. Lord Maitri was dying.

She went back to her room to fetch her personal belongings. She stared at her global mobile, which she'd never taken out of its case. Mr. Connelly had been genuinely shocked to learn that she knew nothing about Lord Maitri's sudden decline. In the Aleutia of the mind, Maitri had said nothing about being ill. If only she'd called the giratoire, surely she would have found him out. But it had not occurred to her to contact him through the deadworld. They were Aleutians. They were together always. She had forgotten that she was human.

She stuffed the bracelet, and Leonie's hairbrush, in the pockets of her robe, left everything else to be sent on, and ran back down to the hall, where her driver was waiting.

9

THE SECRET AUTHOR

i

SHE WOULD NOT wait an hour for them to arrange a private lev journey. Her driver took her to the railhead. She traveled alone in the park staff's own carriage, back to the junction where this spur met the public system. The station was aboveground. There were few people about. She waited on the platform, conspicuous but unmolested in her plain dark-figured robe and Expedition overalls. And she remembered many things. The bone-squeezing cold of so many station platforms, airline runways, quaysides: the same cold and the same black dawn all over the earth. How shockingly the scale of the giant planet reasserted itself when you left the limousines and the air-cruisers and the motorcycle escorts, and set out on your own. The color of the sky, the smell of paraffin lamps, a sickle moon glimpsed through clouds, the empty air. She remembered nights when the white and gold and scarlet lamps of the great teeming highways, long gone now, would spin away in the dark like an endless network of stars. Days wandering in strange crowds, eating the street food, making experiments in contact. Passing for normal. The frustration, the loneliness, the fascination of the new.

She did not try to call the giratoire house from the train. She didn't need to call. She knew.

Atha and Vijaya were waiting for her cab at the garden gates. Mr. Connelly had told them she was on her way. Lord Maitri had died in his sleep, about daybreak. Here was the graveled drive down which she had walked with Misha on the day she was introduced to the bit-grid city and the Phoenix Café. The air was warm, powdery, thickened. It felt like clay in her mouth. Here were the doors to the atrium. Maitri's plants, his orchids, the stained glass dome. She saw, glancing through the garden doors, that someone had cut the grass. His stone carvings stood bare.

The Aleutians were gathered around his bed in the main hall. They shuffled to let her pass. She knelt by his shrunken body; it was lost in the robe they'd dressed him in.

<He had his heart set on staying behind,> explained the chaplain sadly. <So we didn't think anything of it when . . . One day he didn't get up. He said he felt like resting. Next day he said he wasn't feeling very well. And then I think we knew. We stayed with him: he napped, chatted, played a game or two. We had some music. And he talked to you. We knew that he was talking to you a good deal, while you were away. Before he was taken ill and after, very lovingly. Though he didn't want you to know he was ill. He said he felt so close to you. But, of course, you know about that.>

<Yes.>

<He wasn't cut out for old age,> sighed Atha. <He tried to be obstinate, but he kept complaining that it didn't suit him. Poor Maitri, he'll be so annoyed.>

<No,> said Hiryana the chaplain, sentimentally. <I don't think so. He was glad to go in the end. People always are; it's funny. Always.>

The household, the depleted little group, clustered

around Catherine. <I've seen him dead before,> whispered Atha, eyes shining. <Often, often. You never get used to it.>

"No," she said aloud, in English. "You never do."

She lay down by his side, involuntarily, not knowing quite what she was doing: her arm around him, her cheek against his still breast. A quiet interval passed. It could have been minutes or hours. At last she sighed, sat up, and settled back on her heels.

<Now, what do the rest of you want to do with yourselves?>

They hesitated. <Most of us will probably die soon,> murmured someone, Smrti.

<But not until you don't need us!> declared Atha loyally.

<Do you want to go back to the shipworld?> There was a stir of shamefaced assent and stout denial. Of course they wanted to go. Staying on had been Maitri's whim, not theirs. They wanted to die among friends, in homely surroundings.

<But we won't leave you!> they chorused. <How can we leave you!>

<Good. I'm glad you agree. So that's settled. I think it's by far the best plan for you to leave. But it may take some time to organize passages for you all—>

Another discomfitted stirring. <Well, actually, Catherine,> Hiryana began, <Lord Sattva has done that. Or he's doing it. He wants us to be ready to escort Maitri's body out to orbit almost immediately.>

Catherine's eyes widened. Maitri's dogged presence in the old-earth city, and his eccentric determination to stay on after the Departure, had been an annoyance to the Youro City Manager. But such haste seemed positively indecent.

<That was quick!>

<It's because of the trade delegation,> put in Vijaya. <Sattva wants Lord Maitri's body safely back in the shipworld, where he can have his proper funerary respects. It's

impossible to arrange anything suitable here, because so many important people are about to go off on the trade delegation. And he can't put off the delegation, because relations are too delicate, and the Departure's too near.>

<What are you talking about? What trade delegation?>

<To the "USSA,"> said Vijaya, the English term falling blankly into the Aleutians' puzzled, compound gaze. <It's the high spot of the Expedition's last life on earth,> he explained, with fatuous conviction. <It's our triumph. The Americans have invited us back, through the Great Quarantine.> They stared at her in amazement. <Had you forgotten?>

Catherine's hand closed on the silver bracelet in her overall pocket.

<The trade delegation! Yes. I had forgotten. Yes.> She stood up, slowly. "I'm going to my room for a while. Make whatever arrangements Sattva wants." She left, without another glance at the body.

Bon voyage, traveler. I hope you meet your Catherine again soon.

This room. The face on the ceiling, the friendly space-plane. Her bed. Her souvenirs. The Leonardo sketch of the *Adoration of the Magi*. The sounds of the city. She knelt on the pallet, which felt that she was distressed and tried to engulf her. She pushed its attempts aside, took the silver bracelet, which she'd been clutching in the pocket of her robe all the way from Arden, and put it in front of her.

What do I do now?

Someone coughed: a stagey throat-clearing look-at-me noise. She recognized both voice and gesture. She turned and saw Rajath the trickster lounging relaxedly on the end of her bed. He appeared much as she had last seen him, on that windswept university campus where they'd found the Buonarroti device. Young, bold, dangerous, and shifty. He was dressed in high red boots, corded breeches, and a Cossack blouse. Kumbva was sitting massively at her desk, for some reason wearing the head of an elephant. She welcomed them without a word. They were the Three Captains. They had always taken decisions together, though their equality was notional. Kumbva immovable and careless, Rajath in love with the endless play of power, and the Third Captain, the one they called the Pure, seemingly always in pain over something or other.

What do I do? she repeated, exasperated. *What can I do, now?*

Pray that you're wrong! suggested Rajath, brightly and grimly.

<I never pray for things,> said Catherine, looking sadly at her menagerie of icons. <I'm too arrogant. I think that's why God doesn't like me.>

God doesn't like you because you are a bad guy, Rajath corrected her, grinning. Be reasonable, Catherine. You've got to be reasonable in trade, even when you're dealing with a cussed old sod like the Almighty. We're pirates; we came here to rob these people. We're criminals. *God is not on our side.* What did you expect? A happy ending?

Kumbva said, Then if you don't ask, what *do* you do when you pray?

<I don't pray. I don't know what I do.> She felt the void, the great emptiness that welcomed all her reverence, all her contemplation. <I don't think God exists, really.>

But what is real? wondered Kumbva. Yet I think you've learned a new prayer here on earth. The one that goes: *Lord be merciful to me, a sinner.* It's very interesting. Aleutia has taken it up from you. We're still trying to work out what *sin* means when there is no death. Give us time, we'll have an answer.

Kumbva took off the elephant head and tucked it under his arm.

We have to go now, said Rajath. Good luck, compadre. See you soon.

Catherine went on kneeling and thinking and staring at the bracelet. Finally, she stood up, pushed it back into her pocket, and hurried to the humans' kitchen.

"Maman, I need those fastened-together blades, I've forgotten the word: *ciseaux.*"

Leonie and Peter were packing. Faces peeped at the door that led to their living quarters. Not even Maitri knew exactly who lived in there, how many or how they were all related. "Miss Catherine," said Leonie distractedly, without acknowledging or refusing the term Catherine had used, "you'll have to come with us. *They* say you're planning to stay on here, on your own. You can't do that. It wouldn't be safe, not without Lord Maitri. We're moving to the Mediterranean district. We can find a smaller place, with an apartment for you. We can keep house for you somewhere quiet. What do you want the scissors for?"

"I don't want you to keep house for me."

She took the scissors, twisted her black tangled curls over her shoulder in one thick rope, and hacked the rope through. She shook her head. The loss of weight was delightful. She left the humans staring after her and returned to the aliens' part of the house. She took some money, cash and credit-line ID, from Maitri's desk. As she passed by the main hall, she saw that the Aleutians were dancing. They moved in sad and gentle measure over the floor beside their dead lord, with wide sleeves swaying, hands meeting and parting. The Silent members of the household were singing in their quavery old voices, one of those plaintive Youro songs the Silent—to whom the words were pure musical sound—had always loved.

Farewell and adieu to you fair Spanish Ladies
Farewell and adieu to you ladies of Spain
For we're under orders to set sail for old England
And we may never see you fair Spanish Ladies again.

Already the house felt dismantled, empty. She thought, briefly, as she passed through the still rooms: *How will I live, afterward?* Hurt to know that Leonie's offer had been a guilty afterthought . . . No, she didn't want that, but she didn't want to stay here either. When something's over, it's over. She had so often woken from dreams into this house. Into the eternal warmth of the mote-filled air, into the distant murmur of the human crowd outside the garden walls. Dying, falling in flames, rising from nightmare. I am Catherine. I am Clavel. I am Kevala the Pure. I am, I am . . . The tumult had stilled. She was herself, a tiny persistent pattern within the vast pattern of being, at this moment, now and here.

One morning, in the lobby of a police station. There had been a destitute girl, a young lady fallen out of her gilded cage. Her wrist seemed to be injured. Catherine had unfastened the bandage, revealing the scattered pits of dissolution in the pale skin and—

—refused to believe what she saw.

It's your own damned fault, Aleutia. You shouldn't have told me I was crazy. Don't you know how difficult it is for one of us to deny something when nearly all of us say it is true? You told me, and I believed you, and I *was crazy.* Crazy people have hallucinations. They can't believe in the monstrous things they see. They can't *tell* anyone . . .

She was sure it would be worse than useless to have Maitri's retainers mediate for her with Sattva. She would have to reach him another way. She had cut her hair because it would be difficult and dangerous for a young lady to move about the streets alone. She did not want to wear the chador (which was poor protection, anyway). Never again. In Aleutian dress, with her hair short, she felt confident. She recovered those forgotten skills of the days in West Africa: shipwrecked mariners passing for normal. *Don't stare at me; don't mess with me. I have every right to be here, and I am well able to look after myself.*

She took a cab to the cablenet dome. It was a typical government building of the *quartier,* cool and elegant: without a trace of "old-earth" grubbiness but with no sign of craven surrender to Aleutia either. Everything was yellow or cream. There were no displays on the marbled walls of the foyer. Huge virtual screens of muted, abstract color dropped occasionally from space down to the floor, stayed for a few moments, and then vanished. The cablenet—so called for historical reasons, though not restricted to cable—was managed separately from the public datagrid. It was the communication system of the government and the powerful, extremely well protected and difficult of access. But it administrated the Youro branch of the Office of Aleutian Affairs, an ancient institution that still accepted petitions and messages from individual humans to the aliens. Using Maitri's credit line, those First Contact skills of silent intimidation and a great deal of patience, she secured access to one of the Aleutian Office servers. She asked to place a person-to-person call to the shipworld.

And waited, reflecting on the changes in human society (brought about by the long War, the aliens, the previously existing conditions of late capitalism) that had turned a police station into a shabby, overcrowded locus of care and compassion, while the Post Office became a heavily armored luxury bunker.

She was assigned, eventually, to a livespace cubicle. No ghosts. No decor. The sleek small room contained a chair, a desk, and the obligatory little red lamp in a corner of the ceiling. When she sat down, the wall that faced her chair across the desk cleared from blank to blue. The light in the ceiling winked on. An Aleutian looked at her out of the screen, across a quarter of a million miles. The face was subliminally familiar. Recognition struggled and failed. She recovered only a sour conviction that any dealings she'd ever had with this person had been futile.

"Can we help you?" The functionary spoke careful English.

"I asked to speak to the Youro City Manager, to Sattva. It is urgent."

"The European Manager is on earth."

"I know. This is the way I want to do it."

"Do you have an appointment?"

"You know I don't. Tell him Catherine wants to talk to him. Tell him she says *please.*"

The face opposite her barely shifted—

"He's in a meeting," Catherine read aloud, exasperated.

The Aleutian beamed idiotically. <Ah, you speak our language!>

<Just a little,> she agreed, through gritted teeth. She continued, silently. <In fact, most humans "speak" the Common Tongue to that extent. You'd be surprised . . . or you might be surprised, if you had the capacity. But I am not human. I am Catherine. If you think about it (Have you ever tried thinking? Some people find it useful), you'll find that you know my story, and you recognize me. *Get Sattva.* I know he's in Asaba. But Lord Maitri is dead, and this is the only way I can reach Sattva quickly, without endless obfuscation. Tell him . . . >

Her teeth were going to be gritted to pulp.

<Tell him that Catherine wants him *as a very great favor,* to let her come along on the USSA trade visit. Tell him,> even in her desperate alarm, this was agony, <that she'll be happy to give the USSA authorities her eyewitness account of the trip home she made by non-location travel. She'll be happy to have the whole thing put on record for the ship-world audience too. That should fetch him.>

The person in the screen peered out, inspecting Catherine carefully. A light dawned in the blandly obstructive countenance. <Oh, you're *Catherine!* Sorry, I didn't recognize you. You're the Aleutian in a human body, Lord

Maitri's ward. How sad that he's died; wasn't he planning to stay on?>

<Thank you for your heartfelt expressions of sympathy. I will meet Maitri again, in another life. I would prefer to meet Sattva in this life. Soon. Now.>

<Weren't you the first person to try non-location travel?>

"No. Peenemünde Buonarroti, who invented the device, was the first. And then the saboteurs, Braemar Wilson and Johnny Guglioli."

<I meant the first Aleutian,> explained the other, sticking to the Silent mode, though Catherine had switched to formal English—which was rude. Her point was entirely lost on him. He leaned farther forward, as if hoping to make serious inroads on the distance between them, and remarked with genuine and unofficial interest, <I see it now, through the human suit. What a weird thing to do to yourself! So you're Catherine. Well, fancy that. I think we've met before, but I can't remember when. Didn't you used to be a poet?>

He resumed his functionary face.

"We're sorry but we can't arrange an interview with the European Manager at this time. Lord Sattva has departed Asaba to join the Expedition Delegation to the USSA. The Aleutian Affairs Office cannot contact him."

Catherine stood up, breaking the connection, and left the booth.

She'd forgotten to bring a tele with her. She bought a cheap phone from a vending machine just outside the baffles and warning lights of the cable-net dome's shield. Leonie answered her. "Maman, would you check my desk for messages?"

"Yes, Miss Catherine. Mr. Misha has been asking for you. He said if you called, we were to tell you to meet him at the Phoenix Café."

ii

IN ONE OF the lev stations she had to wait for a connection. She sat in the ladies' waiting room. The screen on the wall showed burning cabs and a running crowd, somewhere, nowhere near this neighborhood. The trouble you saw on the news was always far away. But while she sat there, a young Reformer was half carried in, clothes disheveled, bleeding from a head wound. His friends recounted his story to each other, in words and Silence and frustrated anger. Someone had decided he looked too feminine to be out on the street without a chador. He'd tried to placate his accuser, but a mob had gathered and watched while he was beaten. The injured youth's friends kept looking at Catherine uneasily: <Whose side are you on?> They couldn't place her. They didn't speak aloud to her, neither did she speak to them.

When she left the lev, all was quiet. Though the urban atmosphere kept the temperature indoors blandly mild, it was winter and nightfall came early. The globe lamps on the bridge were coming into bloom. Golden ripples flowed endlessly into the beauty of the city night: most beautiful of cities. She walked a little beyond the river, turned the corner, and there was the Café. Antique-effect colored lamps were strung in the branches of the great sycamore, tables set out in the warm evening. They were empty. So were the long chairs on the veranda, where Agathe had been watching for Catherine that first time. The renaissance Café ought to have been a refuge from "intercommunal violence," but a lot of people stayed at home now after dark. She had a moment's fugue as she entered the dining room. She saw faces without any aura of life, without any history in the structure of her mind; and she was frightened. But there were only a few customers. She went to a table near the stage. A smiling waiter came who spoke to her by name. She ordered uncomplicated wine.

"How many glasses, Catherine?"

"One. No, two."

She should have approached Sattva differently. She should have gone through Maitri's people. She could have cut through their weakness, their mourning, their conviction that Sattva was in charge and everything the Expedition Management said was right. She had been the Third Captain; surely she had some power. Going through the Office of Aleutian Affairs had been the act of a crazy person, reduced to futility by the conflict in her mind. She wanted to speak to Sattva; she didn't want to speak to Sattva. So she spoke, but made sure he wouldn't listen. She was disgusted at this feeble prevarication. If there was *any chance* that what she suspected was true, she ought to be moving heaven and earth (as the humans used to say) to impress the danger on Aleutia. Instead she'd come here.

She saw, more clearly than before, how little of genuine recursion there was in the decor of the Phoenix. There was no nostalgia for her beloved "old-earth." The culture of the renaissance was new and spare, and singular and strange. Not a survival but a birth. The people at the other tables were conversing in low voices and in the Common Tongue. What were they talking about? The Departure, obviously. The air was full of fragments that she was too distracted to read. The memory of a blank functionary face. She had no power. She might as well be here as anywhere. A phrase that had been current at the time when she first met Misha Connelly kept running through her head: *the unreality of these last days.*

At last he appeared. He was wearing jeans, and a cotton tee shirt that read, TAKE ME DRUNK I'M HOME. It was the first time she'd seen him in renaissance dress. He looked very odd. He came toward her, full of grave sympathy and secret malice.

"I'm so sorry. You left in such a rush. I felt terrible about letting you go alone, so distressed. I followed you immediately. I've been chasing you all the way back here."

"I'll bet you have," said Catherine.

He let himself look briefly puzzled, then offered a smile of polite mourning. "I'm very sorry about Maitri."

"So am I. Sit down. We have things to talk about."

Misha sat, drawing his chair close. He lowered his voice. "You want to talk about *us?* Surely, not here, Catherine. It's too public."

"Misha, stop that. Stop that game and listen. Do you remember the day I met you? I'd spent the night before Maitri's reception in a police cell. When I was leaving the station, the police were trying to remove a sick beggar who had collapsed in the lobby. I went to help, and found out that this poor wretch was a Traditionalist young lady. She still had all her secondaries, none of the reduced sexual difference you see in ordinary humans, who breathe the city's standard issue air and don't boost their sex hormones. She had a bandage on one arm. I unwrapped it and saw the empty-centered chancres on her wrist. I recognized them. The only way you can get sores like that is through unprotected, or poorly protected, handling of the materials used in proliferating-weapons production."

Michael poured himself a glass of wine. He appeared bewildered.

"I'm sorry, Catherine, I'm not getting any of this."

"Don't tell me you don't know what proliferating weapons are. They're legendary among your people: the alien Ultimate Deterrent. And you know how they're made, the outline of the process anyway. The information's been on the grid for three hundred years. You take a sample of your enemy's tissue, dope it in some esoteric ways, and use it as a starter to breed a kind of anti-self, a specific killer.

You must know, though *you never talk about it*, that weapons processing has been part of the development of the Buonarroti engine. You remember the Buonarroti engine, Misha? The device that is being perfected in a high security lab in the Atlantic Forest, *right next to your father's country house—?"*

He didn't react except to shake his head slightly, as if helpless to stop the torrent of speech.

"Proliferating weapons attack and consume anything that shares biochemical self with the enemy. People, living machines, buildings, food plants, the microscopic traffic in the air. Superheat will stop them in the first generation, but once they've started to divide, they're almost impossible to destroy. You can't poison them; they can eat anything. In response to attack, they divide faster and without limit. Blow them up, and you fill the air with microbial devouring mouths. They're in the water, in the food chain; they get inside people's bodies and eat their way out. They go on until there is no food for them left. No people, no commensals, no plants, no tools, nothing. It is genocide; there is no other outcome. At home it's our only form of real murder."

He leaned forward, frowning in concern. "Catherine, why are you telling me this? And what have you done to yourself? What's happened to your hair? I think I'd better call a cab and get you home."

She bared her teeth. "You really don't know what I'm talking about? I am glad to hear it. Go ahead, call a cab. I can tell you the rest while we're waiting . . . When we met at Maitri's party, there was a moment when I thought you knew about that girl. But it passed. I was very, very unhappy at the time. I have always blamed myself for the disastrous effects of Aleutian rule on earth: because of the Rape, because what I did to Johnny Guglioli seemed to be what had set the whole relationship between your people and mine on the wrong track. In this life, as Catherine, I'd been more desperate than ever because we were leaving, with all our debts unpaid. When I met you, I recognized a kindred spirit, someone as unhappy as myself. *That's what I found so attractive.* So I forgot about the girl. I thought what I'd seen on her flesh had been an hallucination. You adopted me, you brought me here, I made friends with your friends. When I remembered about her, I went back to the poor ward to see what I could find out. Of course, I couldn't find *her*. I mean it in all pity and sympathy when I say I hope she's dead by now . . . But I met Agathe and Lalith, and they told me that Traditional young ladies who escape from their captive lives often end up dying on the streets. Like the fake animals people make and release that can't survive in the real. Apparently, my girl was just an everyday sad story of Youro city."

The thin murmur of talk from the other people in the Café continued. Misha watched her with gentle curiosity, his honey-colored eyes clear as gemstone. He seemed to have decided it was kindest to let her go on babbling wildly until she silenced herself.

"So I forgot about her again. I didn't *completely* forget, but I was distracted. As you know, I was distracted . . . Then finally you asked me to come to L'Airial. I learned that your sister Helen keeps to her room and emerges—if that was a living person I saw and not a virtual ghost—wearing long sleeves and high necked gowns. Weapons-processing sores show first on our most active secretion-sites, the throat, base of the throat, inner skin of the wrists. I suppose there's a mapping to the same areas when it's happening to a human body . . . I learned something I'd known, but forgotten: that the Buonarroti station is close to your father's lodge. And someone arranged that I should find this"— she laid the Campfire bracelet on the table—"in the forest, near your father's house. I know what this is. It belongs, or it ought to, to an officer in the American Special Exterior Force. The Atlantic Ocean is a short jeep ride from L'Airial, and those Wings have immense range, don't they? Then, this morning, I discovered something else that I'd known but I'd forgotten. A party of Aleutians is about to visit the USSA, breaking the Great Quarantine." She took a gulp of wine. "Did you call that cab?" she asked.

Misha shook his head. "You know, I'm still not *getting* this, Catherine. These, um, 'empty centered sores,' or 'chancres' did you call them? How can you be sure? Suppose you weren't hallucinating? How would you know what proliferating-weapons disease looks like?"

"I'm an Aleutian," she said. "I have access to records—" She stopped, disgusted at herself. "Because I've seen them before," she snapped. "What did you think? A long time ago, but I remember. I've been alive in some bad times, Misha. I've seen weapons used."

"But you've always been on the right side of them."

"Obviously. So far." She put down her glass, which she had been clutching so hard she was in danger of breaking the stem. "Why didn't you *tell* me?" she burst out at last. "I don't understand; I can't understand. I knew that there was something badly wrong. I knew that you, Misha, were terribly unhappy. I knew that the others were hiding something. But you didn't *tell me*, neither in Silence nor in words. You didn't give me anything to go on. If you've discovered a plot to build proliferating weapons—" She shuddered and glanced at the empty tables on either side of them. What humans could understand and what they couldn't, one could never be sure. She continued, speaking very softly but with controlled violence.

"I suppose they could have smuggled out a sample before hard quarantine was imposed. It wouldn't have been too difficult. Lugha, I mean Dr. Bright, despises humans so much—don't be offended, he despises everyone—he didn't give a damn about security until we forced it on him. Which means that somebody on the human science team is involved. But that's irrelevant. I know that your father is in-

volved, and Helen is involved. And the trade delegation to
the Americas is crucial. That's when it's going to happen,
isn't it? That's when they're going to strike. . . . But it's the
rest of you, the people I met here at the Phoenix Café. I
don't understand your part. If you approved of the plan,
why did you come to me? Because you *did* come to me. If
you wanted to stop what was happening, why didn't you
tell me?"

"Are you saying that somebody's going to attack the
Aleutians? Some humans who have secretly been making
proliferating weapons? Is that what you think?"

She was furious with him. "How long are you going to
keep this up, Mish? Why are you playing this stupid game
with me? Why else would humans want a sample of
weapons starter? Why else would they be doing experiments that left the subjects infected with those sores? Don't
tell me they were trying to build their own private Buonarroti engine. You know that's impossible. Humans can't
build self-aware machines. They don't have the physical
capacity—"

Misha said softly, "But why would anyone want to do it,
Catherine? Why destroy the aliens now? You're leaving.
And before you leave, you are going to hand over the
Buonarroti technology, this hybrid technology we can't
possibly develop for ourselves, so that we can have inter-
stellar travel too."

She glared at him, took another gulp of wine, and set the
glass down.

"We're not."

She stared at him in defiance.

"I'm sorry," said Misha. "Could you repeat that. I didn't
quite understand."

"We are not going to give you the technology. It would be
too dangerous."

His whole presence breathed his triumph, so that she understood that this moment was the point of the charade, the climax. He had made her say it.

"We know."

He nodded: relaxed now, the fake concern and fake puzzlement both wiped away. "Yes, we know the secret that's been driving liberal Aleutians crazy with helpless fury. I think a lot of people, planetwide, suspect the truth. It's not being openly discussed, for the same reason that's kept you gagged." He leaned back, smiling. "Actually, I think everybody's fears of panic on the streets are exaggerated. There *will* be panic on the streets, there already is, but not over that. The idea that the human race may soon, literally, run out of food and water and *die* if we're left stuck on this rock is beyond most people."

Catherine remembered the night when he had raped her for the first time. At the giratoire house, staring at spots of blood on her white underskirts. Thinking about the empty sores that she had seen, about proliferating weapons in human hands. Thinking, if it is true, then let it be true. *Let it be true. Let it happen. It's what we deserve.* The terrible cold of that moment surrounded her. But nobody deserves to have proliferating weapons turned on them.

"We'll probably squeeze through the crunch," went on Misha dispassionately. "We'll lose a lot of genetic variance, but we'll come through. In *your* terms, that means permanent death for most of the brood. But who cares? We're not Aleutians. We're all going to die anyway."

She put the silver bracelet back in her pocket.

"All right. You've had your satisfaction. And I think I understand. It was your father and Helen. Whatever you knew or suspected, how could you betray them? So you came to me instead of going to the authorities, led me up to clues, and waited for me to ask the right questions—"

"And you're supposed to be a telepath," put in Misha helpfully. "We thought you'd catch on a lot more quickly than you did."

She nodded, accepting another barb. "Can we get on with this, Mr. Whiplash? I'm here; I'm asking. Tell me what you know, if that's what you want to do."

Misha said, "Traditionalist young ladies live very private lives. But my sister Helen used to be one of us. She came to the Café, she was committed to the renaissance. Dad let her come out with me, from when I was old enough to look after her. It was flattering to him in a way; it was stylish. But he didn't like it: and he was difficult. He wouldn't let us use his credit for transport when we were together. All we could afford on my pocket money was the standard lev, and of course she was harassed. I couldn't protect her. Things like that. Then there was one particular incident with my dad, and Helen stopped coming out. But Thérèse . . . Thérèse started telling us that something was going on in the secret world of the young ladies. Girls were disappearing from that little scene of closed cars, shopping trips, parties, telecalls. They were the daughters of rich, influential people, treasured property. What could have happened to them? Agathe heard the same sort of stories in her poor ward, from a different angle. I realized that though she hadn't *vanished*, Helen was one of the disappeared. And then I found out what Dad was doing: what he'd let his friends do to her." He broke off, suddenly defensive. "You think I should have called the police?" he demanded angrily. "What could our police do? Suppose they wanted to do anything about an inner-circle Traditionalist conspiracy? You think I should have told the Expedition Management? It was Helen, as well as my father—"

Catherine shook her head. "Don't bother about that. Just tell me."

Misha's voice was controlled again, his golden eyes cast down. "Okay. There's a conspiracy. It involves important people. They've been using Traditionalist young ladies— vulgarly known as sextoys—as experimental subjects, as what you call 'breeding ground,' I think, for the development of Aleutian-style proliferating weapons. As far as we know, Helen's the only one of their subjects who's still alive—except for one other, but she's out of our reach. Helen's the only person who can tell us how the strike's going to be carried out. But she doesn't leave Arden anymore, not even by tele. She stays in her room."

"Yes. You took me to L'Airial so I could talk to her. Had she agreed to that meeting? Then, why didn't it happen?"

"She kept changing her mind," he said. "She's dying, Catherine. Maybe she's not thinking very clearly." He reached into his jeans pocket and brought out a small dark vial. "She gave this to me last night. I would have told you, but you rushed away this morning. She used to build games; I don't know if anyone ever told you that. She is an auteur. I don't do games myself, but she taught me all I know about virtual art. She says now that she won't talk to you or to anyone. I don't think I'll ever see her again, in the real. We're to go into this. She says this is where she's hidden the truth—"

He looked over Catherine's shoulder. "Here are the rest of them."

She turned to see Rajath, Mâtho, and Joset standing behind her. Lydie, Imran, and Thérèse Khan were coming across the room, Lydie struggling out of the chador she had to wear on the street. They all looked at Misha first, and he nodded.

"We're sorry," said Lydie to Catherine. She spread her hands, shrugged her muscular little shoulders. "We didn't know what to do. We were scared that if we managed to tell someone like the City Manager, maybe he'd have all the humans in the *département* killed, to be on the safe side. But we thought you'd help us."

Thérèse opened her hood. "Do you remember, I warned you against my mother?" Her hands were shaking. "She isn't in the plot, but she knows about it. They wouldn't let her deeper in because she wouldn't let them infect me. A living young lady is the only stake that gets you into their game. But Mama loves me, in a kind of a way. She *does*," insisted Thérèse. "After you came to see us, she said some things that scared me. You're Lord Maitri's ward; maybe she wouldn't have dared. But people can disappear in Youro: sometimes no one ever finds out why. Your car could have vanished on its way to our house, something like that."

"I don't think we should talk anymore out here," said Joset. "Isn't it obvious? Helen gave us a game because the gamesroom has the best privacy. We've booked a slot. Let's go."

Rajath drained Misha's glass of wine. Mâtho went to Catherine, ducking his head self-consciously. "I'm sorry about your father." He blushed. "I mean your guardian. We could do a piece on the funerary respects—?"

"*Mâtho!*" they all groaned. Imran hauled him away.

iii

IN THE ANTECHAMBER Thérèse stripped off her chador and Catherine her robe. Misha administered the eyedrops. They passed through the gate. Catherine fell through infinite space.

She was standing in a cloakroom. No particular cloakroom, any one of such rooms, transition places. There was a faint smell of human sweat, urine, feet, digestive gases: the ever-present taint she had learned to ignore. The features, details that were away from her immediate focus, were unplaceably familiar. This was an effect that Catherine knew, where the player's own memories weaken the game-world instead of reinforcing the illusion. It was called *bleeding*, a sign of amateur work. But the wall in front of her appeared solid enough. It had a film of greenish blue decor, with a *trompe-l'oeil* effect of aged paintwork: a blister here and there, a network of tiny cracks. On a raised bar at about head height—which had the same antiqued finish—a row of cloaks hung on pegs. Above the bar there was a message, overlaid on the paintwork in neat, fluorescent green capitals: WEAR ME. The gamers looked at each other. Lydie shrugged, took down a cloak, and put it on. "I don't expect to have to do this in a *game,*" she grumbled. The hood fell over her face, hiding her eyes. Each of them took down the cloaks and put them on. They were all of the same design, not the head-to-foot bag shape of the chador, but the classic domino of old Europe. Chins and mouths and hidden eyes: Catherine saw her friends disguised, not made naked, by concealment. Everyone's cloak fitted them exactly, though they had seemed identical on the pegs. Joset was in purple, Misha in black, Thérèse in a very dark gold. Catherine's cloak was burgundy red velvet. She looked around for a clue as to what they should do next, and in that moment she lost the others.

There was only one door. It stood open. A figure was walking away from her—either Joset or Misha, depthless black or the rich indigo of a moonless night. She followed.

Into old-earth. She was in a large, bright room. It was windowless and felt as if it was underground, but well lit by piped daylight. It was a kitchen. Down the center of the room ran a long, massive table. The blond wood had the bloom of many hundreds of years of scrubbing and scouring. Ugly varnished dressers were set around the walls, laden with plates and dishes, salvers and tureens. The kitchen staff, unmoved by the antique splendor of their surroundings, were at work preparing a meal for a small army, using the most practical and up-to-date hybrid appliances. They were wearing dark green overalls, most of them labeled female. Catherine and her guide had just stepped, apparently, through a wall. None of the people busy at their tasks took any notice of the intrusion. She followed the domino shape (cut from black void or night sky) across the kitchen and into a large walk-in closet, where cleaning ma-

chines were humbly waiting to be needed. At the far end
there was a hatchway so low that she had to bend double.
Up a winding narrow stairway and through another door.
Now they were in a different part of the house. They were
aboveground. There was a carpet on the floor and decoration on the walls.

She could feel every detail of the recorded setting with an
extraordinary, surreal intensity. She could almost taste the
separate fibers in the turf of dark red wool under her feet.
She glanced at frames of mass-produced trite verse, made
touching by their age, that hung on the walls, *L'Angelus*, at
copies of sepia-tinged photographs that had been old when
the Aleutians came to earth, *La Pyramide de Cheops, Piazza
San Marco,* and felt herself leap, almost, into the pictured
landscapes. She could not decide if this passion of repre-
sentation, intense to the point of synesthesia, where all
senses bleed into one, was the naive work of an amateur or
an effect of deliberate and original skill. *How beautiful it all
is,* she thought, her pulses thrilling, her responses racing.
But no professional game-builder would have made *everything* so consummate. The real world is not so. It fades, it
loses resolution, it barely exists outside the beam of the fo-
cusing gaze. She knew she was in Arden, in a simulacrum
of the Connelly manor house. She wondered what had happened to the others. The passage with the red wool carpet
met the gallery that she remembered, above the entrance
hall. She glanced down and had a shock. There was no detail at all below, nothing but shadow. She looked for her
guide.

The cloaked figure had vanished. Catherine was suddenly walking in another carpeted passage, and it was
dark—a dreamlike switch, again, the kind of thing that
didn't happen in a conventionally well-made game. A door
was standing ajar, showing a line of light. It was like the
door of Mr. Connelly's study the night she went looking for

Helen, but it wasn't the same. She knew she was going to be shown something she didn't want to see.

No. I don't like this.

But she went in.

The room was not large, but pleasantly proportioned. Catherine had hated to think of someone living in a cage, even a gilded one. The word implied bad air, stale bedding, the always imperfect human hygiene, isolation, disinfectant smells. Her remand cell under the poor ward had been a blessed hermitage. But if you weren't choosing to suffer of your own free will, a human prison was a hideous place. This room was as pretty and fresh as Thérèse Khan's orchard. And far more elegant. A fire of red roses burned in the grate, flanked by graceful antique armchairs. The bed was a four poster with curtains and canopy of green and gold brocade. The framed poetry on the walls was original, lovely, and unexpected: some of the artists were familiar, some completely new to her. There were flat moving picture screens, in the Aleutian style, a Vlab and library console in muted dark casing. A small upright piano stood against one wall, beside it a music stand and a table on which lay a silver glove. There were no natural windows, but one didn't miss them. Catherine went to the fireplace. She held out her hands to bathe them in the perfumed glow . . . Slowly, reluctantly, she looked toward the bed.

There was a woman lying there, propped on white pillows. A baby was at her breast. The woman lay with her head turned on one side, cheek pressed against the shadowed linen, looking down at the child that suckled. The baby was newborn. The woman's body was as if crushed into the pillows by a weight of immense physical exhaustion. Her eyes, when she turned to look at Catherine, were the somber eyes of the Christ in Piero della Francesca's *Resurrection: Yes, I have conquered death. Conquering death is not so difficult. Now the work begins . . .*

The baby changed in his mother's arms, until it was Misha lying there.

He vanished. He was replaced by Mr. Connelly, who sat on the edge of the bed. He had an air of dignified, fastidious removal from the crude exercise that he came here to perform. She saw the Warden speak, but heard nothing. He adjusted his clothing, took a step into the room, and disappeared. She thought he'd have looked the same, behaved the same if she had accepted his offer of food that night in his study. The rational patriarch does not take pleasure in sex. He performs ownership.

There was an ending shift: another of those deliberate caesura. Misha had returned. She had not been certain in the first passage which incarnation of "Michael Connelly" she had seen grow from baby to man. But this was definitely Misha. He was in his nightclothes, old-fashioned pajamas. He was younger than the person Catherine knew. He was crying. Helen, dressed in a long wispy pastel gown, was comforting him. Catherine couldn't hear their words. She gathered the Warden had told Misha he would not be allowed to be alone with his sister, his mother, in the real, ever again. They had to part. Helen said something. Misha sobbed and turned. He pushed her down onto the bed . . . *that autistic gesture.* He pushed up the gown, clumsily and unconsciously as a baby groping for the nipple, covered her without subtlety. Catherine knew exactly how.

Misha left. The young woman sat up. Her skin was now black as old wine, as black as fragile human skin can be. Her breasts, that seemed too heavy for her rib cage, glowed above the lace of her gown like the night of some alien planet: ripe and suffused with blood. Her eyes shone like diamonds. She looked like the mother of the world. She lifted the heels of her hands to cup her chin, covered her face, and smoothed her palms upward. The face changed. It was biscuit brown, heavy, with a thick swooping bar of eyebrow and a mouth like bitter fruit. It changed again, flickering through variations in a way that seemed almost perfunctory. *I can be any woman; I can be anyone.* Finally, it became pale-skinned, dark-haired, delicate. Catherine understood, as if looking into a mirror, that she and Helen Connelly must look rather alike, except that Catherine was not so female-shaped. And Helen was human.

Helen said, "In Johnny Guglioli's day, humans had invented a data-processing medium called coralin. It seemed a substratum as complex as a human brain, in which mind could be immanent. But the coralin creatures live in another state of being from ours. They are not human, nor exactly self-conscious. After the Aleutians came, our scientists abandoned research into artificial intelligence, along with so much else. They said, 'We will never construct a self-aware machine; it isn't possible.' But here I am. Intelligent by accident, as an unforeseen by-product of my primary function. Made, not born. Created, not begotten. I am a machine.

"I was made for the Michael Connelly you know as the Warden. Technically, I am his sister, since I was derived from his father's tissue, as he was himself. I was made so well that I was able to bear my own child, which is unusual. Misha was a parthenogenetic conception and needed work, but he is all mine. But I am still property; I am still the Warden's spare piece of flesh. He didn't hesitate long before offering me as an experimental subject when he was invited to join in the plot that you have discovered. Maybe jealousy hardened his heart.

"The Warden and his friends wanted to get hold of the Aleutian superweapon before the aliens departed. They managed to persuade some of the scientists on the Buonarroti team to cooperate. There are other human scientists working for the plot now. With the small knowledge they had of weapons manufacture, they began by crudely injecting the stolen culture into the bodies of the young ladies they'd decided to sacrifice. After several of these experi-

ments had been swiftly fatal, they started fast-growing nature identical blanks, 'young ladies' without any higher
brain functions, as a cheaper alternative."

"I saw them!" breathed Catherine.

Mr. Connelly, shepherding his flock in the room in her
nightmare.

"You saw them," agreed the young woman with a serene
smile. She was now wearing a deep green gown, with her
hair drawn back sleekly from a passionate bare brow. "You
have seen whatever I chose to show you. This is my network. The program had been going on for some time, in the
greatest secrecy, before I was infected. As you know, the
anti-self culture must pass through several generations, in
successive host bodies. They had preserved me for the last
stage because I am fertile, which is rare in a sextoy—and
perhaps because the Warden didn't want me to die, and
they needed to keep him sweet. By then they had improved
their technique. I swallowed the *Vinum Sabbati*, it was like
an innocent white powder, and I lived. I live still. I became
breeding ground. Do you remember the marriage that you
saw in the glade? I made you see that. You were wearing a
suit that was slaved to the house's system: I controlled what
you saw. What happened in that congress was not a human
conception, but it was like enough that they believed my
fertility was needed. My partner, who was also fertile, became pregnant, and she will give birth."

"Why did you let them do it?"

It was not possible to believe that this woman had been
powerless.

She ignored the question. "It didn't happen when you
saw it. It happened awhile ago. My partner has since been
delivered to the USSA, to a secret site where the weapons
will be tested in controlled conditions. Maybe you wonder
why we allowed ourselves to be used this way. Well, we are
small and physically weak, and we are property. We have
no rights in law. But my bride, I can tell you, was a willing

sacrifice. She was glad to give her life (in so far as she had a life of her own) for the cause. Don't judge her too harshly. Have you never, in your long lives, asked your retainers to die for Aleutia? Has Aleutia never asked for volunteers for just this terrible purpose? As for me, when Papa told me I would serve our party's cause, that I would suffer *pour la patrie* and he would be proud, I laughed to myself. I wasn't fooled . . . But in some shamed dungeon deep inside, there was a little girl who was so very glad—"

She drew up her knees to her chest. She looked like an abandoned child.

Catherine imagined the nights, years long. The days, years long, spent in this room by the little girl who never grew up. Who was always and everywhere, whatever her talent and her skills as an *auteur* of worlds, still this desolate child.

Helen opened one hand and pointed at the Vlab. A demonstration was running on the monitor screen. Catherine saw diagrams like the ones she had found on the old notebook in the schoolroom. Worlds giving birth to worlds, impossible divisions of the infinite. Finally, the image of a woman bowed with clasped hands over the glory that she had discovered. She recognized the signature cartouche this time. It was a detail from the legend of St. Helen, another of those great images of the first renaissance. The mother of the Roman Emperor Constantine, Helen, whose son had imposed the new religion of Christianity on his empire, was pictured in the act of accomplishing her quest to discover the True Cross on which Christ had died. Helen's son became Emperor. Helen herself went looking for "scientific proof" of the salvation of the world. Catherine stared at this message, unable to decipher its meaning.

"It's like a museum, isn't it?"

She spun around. Her guide was sitting in one of the armchairs by the rose fire, knees tucked up, the hood of her black domino pushed back, folds of green silk tumbled in shimmering virtual detail around her voluptuous little body. She was holding a brightly colored toy. Catherine had seen the same kind of thing once before: that scaled head, the beak with its scarlet gape. The Phoenix clung to Helen's wrist with miniature talons. Its undiscarded ancestry, its history of transformation—reptilian into bird—was proudly evident.

"It's like a museum isn't it?" repeated Helen, gesturing with the hand the Phoenix was clinging to. "My mind is like a museum, and I'm the prize exhibit. I have wanted to talk to you for so long, Catherine."

The phoenix gaped and uttered a harsh, short cry.

"I make myself look like this," said Helen, "in virtuality. I make myself speak and move like this. It's no longer true in the real. But you know that. I'm at Arden now. I think I won't leave this room again, in the real. Sometimes I wish everything would move more quickly. Sometimes I beg for every second to last a thousand years. I'm older than I used to look, you know. Dad had me made when he was quite young. But what I remember from before Mish was born hardly counts as living. I blank it out. No one can be human all on their own." She began to fade, losing definition by trembling degrees. "I am the secret author of everything that you have seen or will see in my game. Don't question me. I can't tell you anything more. Ask Lalith. She knows."

"But you're not a dumb patriot," cried Catherine, feeling that her last chance of learning the truth was slipping away. "The other girls maybe, not you. You could have killed yourself when you found out that you were being used for something so monstrous—" She had forgotten that Helen was only human, that even life in this cage, life as the servant of a savage revenge, might be better than no more life at all. "You must have had some reason! Why don't you *tell me?*"

The girl in the armchair raised her free hand and touched two spots at her temples, where Catherine now saw small dark wounds, as if Helen had been prepared for some crude early form of virtuality immersion. "Nothing more proved me human," she said, "than the price I was willing to pay for knowledge." She turned blind eyes to Catherine. "I am sorry," she said. "I am a ghost. I'm not real. I cannot answer your questions."

Catherine was alone. The roses burned, undying; she saw a heap of raw, agonized flesh. Wisely, she did not look again at the canopied bed.

She wondered what had happened to the rest of them. Maybe they were talking to other versions of Helen elsewhere in the construct. Head for the exit. She looked for a doorway that wasn't part of the recording. Instead there was another cloaked figure, standing by Helen's chair. She followed again. They left Helen's room and passed quickly through the house, brushing through vital, casually realized images of National Park staff at work. Out in the clearing she saw her driver, who was polishing one of the jeeps with tender care. The chickens pecked and strutted and bullied each other. Mrs. Hunt was in the *potager,* speaking severely to a young male servant, who squirmed and looked at the ground and hated the old bat—

Abruptly, she was hanging in a sensory blank, blacker than the darkest night. Then she was out of the game, in the blue sweat-smelling gloom of the antechamber. "What am I supposed to do now?" she asked aloud. No one answered.

She walked, feeling empty and bewildered, through the demon gate, which read her identity and would eventually shift the price of this use from Maitri's bank account into the coffers of the cooperative. Into the real-world, late and empty Phoenix Café.

III

Yo Soy la Desintegración

10

INTERMUNDIA

i

THE CAFÉ WAS still lit and *musique naturelle* was playing softly. The dining room was empty, except for one table where Agathe and Lalith were sitting together. They were obviously waiting for Catherine. The *musique* was made of rainfall. It must be raining outside, but the windows— small, postwar windows—that looked onto the dark street were sheltered by the veranda. She couldn't see any spattering drops; she could only hear the muted, ominous whispering. She crossed the room in a world that felt thin and devoid of conviction, all her senses reeling from that extraordinary *envie*.

"Was that an hour? Where is everyone? It felt like a few minutes!"

"Sit down," suggested Lalith. "You look burned. It's the intensity she uses. Intensified experience just *eats* objective time. But it isn't as late as it feels out here. We were the only customers left, so Anatole decided to shut up shop."

Catherine sat down. Agathe gave her a glance of sober greeting. "Drink," she said, pushing forward a wineglass. "It's good for what ails you. I don't use the stuff, but I had that from someone I trust. Let's drink together." She had a tumbler of the Café's best groundwater in front of her: which was for Agathe a wild indulgence.

Catherine drank. The wine was soft and warming in her mouth.

"How do you like Helen's style?" asked Lalith, sounding oddly prim and unlike herself. Lalith, like Catherine herself, wasn't good at small talk. "It's different, isn't it?"

"I think it's 'modern art,' " proposed Agathe, mock philistine. "I don't understand it."

"You should try her paper flowers," added Lalith. "They are *excessive.*"

Catherine blinked. "Better than Misha's?"

"Better. Rougher, weirder." Lalith glanced slyly at her friend the priest. "I'm embarrassing Agi." Catherine caught a glimpse of the strain that the Perfect's vows imposed on these two, the unknown hinterland of their relationship.

"Did Helen build the Blue Forest game?" she suddenly wanted to know.

They glanced at each other. "No," said Agathe.

Catherine took out the silver bracelet and laid it on the table, as she had done when she'd confronted Misha. She looked directly at Lalith. The halfcaste answered with the Silent defense she'd given at every previous encounter: <What if I am? It's not what you think.> "Is this yours?" said Catherine.

Lalith examined the token, and made to slip it over her plump, solid brown hand. She didn't have the classic halfcaste bird bones. The bracelet was far too small.

"Apparently not."

"But you have one somewhere. You are an agent of the USSA. I think you must be an officer of the Special Exterior Force: a Campfire Girl."

"It is not the USSA," Lalith spoke with resigned reproach: she did not affect any surprise. " 'The USSA' was a crazy fantasy. It ceased to exist, even in name, more than a hundred years ago. I'm a citizen of the republic of Colombia, of the *Federación de Democracias Americanas,* north and south. I don't know why the funx you people, aliens and others, can't call us by our proper title."

"Why should we," muttered Agathe, "when you've shut yourselves away like that?"

"Well, on our part it's not deliberate," said Catherine formally. "We're sorry. We're stupid aliens; we're lazy and we don't like changes. Shall we get back to the point?"

Lalith set the bracelet down.

"It's true. I'm a secret agent. I came over several years ago. I have a history in the records, so far as they keep records in Aleutian earth, back to birth: it's not disprovable. I joined the renaissance movement, I traveled all over the Aleutian ruled cities, eventually I met these people. But it's not what you think—"

Catherine grinned. "No, really?"

"Don't take it like that!" protested Lalith. "You're wrong about me; you're wrong about the Americas. I was sent here to prevent gender violence, not to incite it. We don't want to encourage a bloodbath, so we can sweep in and take over. We want stability here. My mission was to encourage any initiative, vision, concept, that offered a peaceful alternative. I didn't invent the renaissance movement; I found it in place. I joined it because that was my mission. But I'm a *convert.* I'm not doing this for the FDA—or not just for the FDA. I'm doing it for the rebirth of humanity, in the Americas as well as over here. We've *all* been trapped, paralyzed, for as long as the Aleutians have been on earth . . . Agathe knows the truth, so do most of my close contacts. I was planning to go public with the real story very soon."

"I see." Catherine nodded, withholding judgment. "And do your superiors know about this, er, extended allegiance of yours?"

"My brief was to try to stop old-earth from blowing up in our faces at the Departure." A faint flush showed in

Lalith's cheeks. "By whatever means. That's what I'm doing. We have other people in Youro, but I don't have any contact with them. They don't know who 'Lalith' of the renaissance really is. I'm a Campfire Girl. We're expected to act on our own."

"Are you really a halfcaste? I thought they didn't survive in the USSA."

"I am now!" She touched the neat rims of her nasal slits. "I don't mind the morphing. I've grown to like it. I had to be a halfcaste, couldn't be on either side of the gender divide. It wasn't only because of the politics: semantically I couldn't have passed as a woman or a man over here, not of either persuasion. But who says how a halfcaste is supposed to act? They're cultural throwbacks. They could be copying some character in a three-hundred-year-old precontact movie. That suited me. Come to the Americas; you'll understand what I mean."

Catherine gave the same cautious Aleutian nod as before. <I see. Although I don't necessarily accept your version.> "But what does the bracelet mean? It has no inscription, no rank, no name, no number. Is it genuine?"

"I believe so." Lalith's mouth and nasal tightened, as at a sour taste. "A special issue."

Agathe stirred. She laid her clasped hands on the tabletop, like someone anxious to prove herself innocent of trickery. "We don't know what Helen has told you. Or Mish."

Catherine frowned. "Were you in the *envie*? I lost sight of the others."

"We arrived late," The priest hesitated. "How much do you know?"

"Helen didn't tell me anything." Catherine was suddenly chilled, though the room was warm. She had picked up her robe in the antechamber. She thrust her hands deep in the sleeve pockets, found Leonie's hairbrush, and was obscurely comforted. "Hardly anything about the plot, at least . . . She said I should ask Lalith, but I want to hear from both of you. What's your version of all this?"

Again they glanced at each other. Lalith nodded fractionally. Agathe began. "It started for us a while before we met you, when we lost Helen. We all knew that Helen and Mish were lovers—"

"Imran hated it," put in Lalith. "Said Mish was going to destroy us by messing about with the rules. Of course it was a dominance-ranking gripe, because Mish had grabbed the forbidden candies that Imran didn't dare to touch. But he was right; it was dangerous. And Helen was the one who would suffer if they were found out."

"Let me tell her," Agathe said, and went on. "Helen stopped coming to the Café. We suspected the Warden had caught her and Mish together, but he didn't tell us anything, just said she was grounded, not to leave the house without Michael Sr. But then Thérèse heard, on the young lady circuit, that Helen Connelly had joined the secret society. Well, not exactly a secret society. It didn't have a name; it was simply an inner circle of that little world: another of our Youro 'inner circles.' The girls would go to special parties with their parents, private functions, and never tell a word of what went on there. It was only for young ladies whose fathers or mothers *really loved them*, that was the story. Thérèse assumed it was sex, of course, some kind of toy-swapping orgies. But those girls became *ultra*-Traditional young ladies. After attending a few of the special parties, they'd vanish into complete purdah. They were literally never seen or heard of again. It was classic. They are treated like shit, but all they want is *more* shit, as if they might prove themselves, be really loved, if they only submit enough. We didn't think that sounded like Helen, but we were worried, because we realized she had vanished, like the others. Mish says you saw her once at a reception at Lord Maitri's. That was probably her last public appearance. But we weren't . . ." Agathe paused, chewed her lip. "Worried enough, as we now know. There was a rumor going around at the Settlement, in the hives. It was about a young lady who became mysteriously unwell, strictly confined to her room. A human servant got into the room by accident and found a body half dissolved into a weird black puddle on the sheets of the bed: *but still alive . . .* You know how it is. I suppose it happens in the air, in Aleutia. A story gets about. You hear it several times, different versions. You start to realize that it connects with something else, but you don't quite get it. We couldn't believe Helen would retreat into purdah and join an ultra-Traditionalist society of her own free will, but young ladies are unstable. Maybe after she lost Mish, it was too hard to go on fighting . . . We didn't connect what had happened to her with that bogey story in the hives. Then finally, Helen broke the silence. She told Misha what was going on."

"And you believed her, but you did nothing?"

"What could we do?" demanded Agathe, as Mish had done. "Who should we have told? The police, the army, the City Council? The Expedition Management? None of the girls would have been any use as witnesses, not even Helen. They have no rights. I don't know about the girl you saw outside the police station. But if we'd found one of them who had escaped like that, it would have been no use. She wouldn't have talked. Think about our position. Lalith is the agent of a foreign power; yet she's become a figurehead of our movement. If that came out in the wrong way, it could ruin us."

"You don't understand Youro," said Lalith. "There is going to be hell to pay when your people are gone. There's a hard core of reactionaries running this city for whom the Gender War has never ended. They haven't forgotten; they haven't changed. They're just waiting for their chance. The renaissance could make a difference. I didn't mean to become a leader of the movement," she added unhappily. "Or I did, but I didn't know I'd be so successful. When Helen told Mish and he told the rest of us about the conspiracy, I didn't know what to do."

Catherine remembered the afternoon of Maitri's reception. She sought through the chattering crowd in the atrium for a small figure: slender, curvaceous, veiled. She could not find Helen in her memory. She wondered if Misha had found out what was happening to his sister before or after he began to rape Catherine.

"I don't understand how *Helen* could have let herself be used like that—" she whispered, still feeling the shining intelligence and power of that woman in the firelit room.

"Nor do we," said Agathe. "Not completely. But how could we? I don't know how it feels to be a Traditional young lady. Maybe you could explain it better than I could."

"Anyway," Lalith continued the tale. "Helen convinced Mish there was nothing we could do for her, or for the other girls. She told him she wanted to string the conspirators along until she knew exactly what they were planning. They talked in front of her, you see: especially Mish's father. So we waited. Do you remember the time we took you to the Blue Forest? It was about then that she managed to send us a record of the final phase: what they'd forced her to do. I think you've seen part of it."

Catherine thought of Misha giving her paper flowers in the rented room.

"Why did it have to be 'Traditional young ladies'?"

"Because they are property," explained Agathe grimly. "Citizens have some protection against the bad barons, even the poor. Sextoys don't. Also for what they considered 'scientific' reasons, as Helen understood it. Aleutians make proliferating weapons by doping inert enemy tissue and growing the culture in the bodies of living volunteers. Am I right?"

"It can be," said Catherine. "But except in desperate straits, it would be complex commensals, not people."

"That's what they knew. Complex commensals: that's what the conspirators thought they needed. Property made flesh. But I think the users—I hate calling them parents—of sextoys must always have a need to destroy them. There's so much shame, disgust, revulsion involved in such a relationship. It doesn't go away because the users refuse to admit those feelings in themselves. Our minds don't work like that. It fights to be expressed; it escapes in twisted ways."

Catherine felt herself begin to shudder hard, belly-deep, as if she was coming out of a paper-flower high. Agathe reached out and laid a hand over hers.

"Still feeling burned? Hang on. We're all fighting our own demons over this, believe me. You saw the reconstruction Helen made of her 'chemical marriage'?"

"When I was at Arden. In the forest, a kind of vision. I saw two women—"

"Exchanging body fluids," agreed Agathe. "It's the usual way to get pregnant these days, woman-woman. One partner takes a pill, or both if they both want to try. They wait until the drug's been taken up, then they make love. The doped ejaculate they swallow and absorb will trigger a semi-parthenogenetic conception that will include elements of the partner's DNA. If they follow the right course of prenatals, the pregnancy should be perfectly normal. In this case I don't know exactly how the process works, but obviously there are supposed to be offspring."

"Where? When?" demanded Catherine. "Helen said her partner was sent to America."

"Yes. They've smuggled her through the Great Quarantine."

"The Shield's permeable," Lalith said bitterly. "The system's meant to destroy any unauthorized object, micron to air-cruiser, that crosses our coastal approaches. But a gate's no better than the gatekeeper. For anyone in a position to fix the bits that define 'unauthorized object' there is no shield—"

"We think it was the Americas factor that gave Mr. Connelly his key role," said Agathe. "He has no special access to the Buonarroti lab; he's only the park keeper. But he has those solar Wings, and he has the Atlantic Coast."

"You remember Tracy Island?" asked Lalith. "The Campfire Girls' Home Base?" Catherine nodded. "The Special Exterior Force has changed. We're still the old-earth marines, the alien-watchers, but we don't sign up for perpetual quarantine these days. I trained on the northern mainland, in a regular armed-forces college. The Island is a museum piece. But it's preserved as a national monument, a leisure center for R and R, a showcase for state visits: and it still has the hardest quarantine. I guess some people have always been convinced a bunker like that would be needed again. What they call a self-fulfilling prophecy?" She grinned nervously. "That's where the test is to be held. That's where they have Helen's partner and a pack of blanks ready to be consumed in the trial. The only thing I don't know is exactly where the containment is located inside the base. The Aleutian delegation is going to visit Tracy Island. Being the main anti-Aleutian base, it has some of the strongest Aleutian associations of anywhere in the Americas, ironically enough. Helen says the trial is set to coincide with the trade-delegation visit. If by any chance there's an escape, well, these are alien weapons. The aliens can take the blame. If the trial goes off okay, then later, when the mysterious plague breaks out, the trail will lead back to Tracy Island and the Aleutians' presence. The bad guys think they'll to be able to wipe out their enemies without admitting responsibility."

"I don't understand this," said Catherine slowly. "The Aleutians can take the blame, you said. Are you telling me, *the Aleutians are not the target?* Then, who is?"

The two women looked at her almost with pity.

"The Aleutians are not the issue," said Agathe. "If you think they are, you're living in the past. This is not an anti-Aleutian plot. The ultra-Traditionalists in Youro plan to use their superweapon against the Reformers, as soon as the aliens have gone home."

"The Americas group plan to explode a small bomb, high altitude," said Lalith. "It'll be packed with weapon larvae, if that's the right term. The explosion will be tiny; no one will know what's happened. You want to know who's supposed to die in the plague in the Americas?" She glanced at Catherine and away. "I can't tell you that."

But clearly she knew, or could guess.

Catherine felt that the effect of Helen's *envie* had finally left her. She was stone cold sober. The whisper of the rain seemed louder. It threatened a flood, reddened and turbulent, filling the streets. She understood that she had never really believed that the Aleutians were in danger. This was the truth; this was what she'd been waiting to hear, through three lifetimes. Falling in flames, she had known what was coming. She had known what Aleutia would do to earth.

"That's insane! Weapons attack biochemical identity. They can't distinguish between *political parties!* Bright thinks everything that lives on this whole planet belongs to what we'd call the same brood. Sharing life, sharing self . . . Did you say 'blanks'? You mean, *they're going to let the test weapons eat?* Don't they know *anything?*"

"Just because you're a psychopath," pointed out Lalith, "and head of the twenty-fourth-century Klu Klux Klan and all, it doesn't mean you have to be intelligent. That's a myth."

"But is there no one you can trust? I understand why you don't want to go to the Expedition Management with a story like this, but what about Lalith's chief of staff?"

Lalith gave her a bleak look. "Didn't you hear what I said? They're doing the test on Tracy Island."

There lay the Campfire bracelet: dainty, pretty, like something made for a child.

"The FDA isn't a monolith." Lalith suddenly seemed angry with both of them. "You people think of us like some giant matriarchal hive with a single aim. It isn't like that. The Americas is a whole world. There are certain people who are crazy enough to want to get hold of the Aleutian superweapon and try to use it. That's predictable. And the - SEF, the alien-watchers, they'd have to be involved. That's predictable too." She stared at the bracelet with hatred. Catherine saw Lalith unmasked: someone very simple and truly ingenuous, someone who reminded her of Bhairava. A good cop. "I didn't believe it," the American confessed, hurt and shamed, "when Helen told us. But I had to check. I'm on my own here, but there are ways I can 'phone home.' I went into the system, the SEF bit-grid. I found out enough to be sure she's right. Some of the people involved in the plot are . . . well, predictable, like I said. But I don't know where the rot stops. There's no one I can trust."

"My Self," whispered Catherine, awed, horrified. "My Self!"

"That's how we feel," said Lalith. "You feel like laughing hysterically; you feel like lying down and screaming. You feel like refusing to believe it could be true and ignoring the whole thing. We've been through that stage. But we did tell somebody. We told you."

"You're the great Clavel." Agathe's clasped hands showed peach-pale at the knuckles. "The Third Captain. We were sure you'd understand. You'd be able to stop this without harming the renaissance. You'd use your superpowers to make everything all right."

Catherine laughed. "You want me to help you? I tried to talk to the City Manager this morning. But he's with the delegation. He's out of my reach. I got the *didn't you used to be famous?*—and the bum's rush. I'm not the Third Captain. If I ever was, it was long ago. I'm Catherine. I have no power. There's nothing I can do."

Lalith and Agathe did not look at each other then, but they seemed to consult.

"Yes," Agathe confessed. Her tensed hands relaxed, spread wide. She looked down at her own capable, square-tipped fingers. "One doesn't know—I certainly didn't know—how deeply ingrained the idea of Aleutian superiority is until one tries. We were sure that you would perform some miracle. It took us a long time to understand that you would not. In the end we realized. We're on our own."

The others, Misha and his friends, must have had some signal from Lalith or the priest. They came out from wherever they'd been hiding and gathered around the table.

"I have a flier," said Lalith. "And clearance. I can take us through the Shield."

"We've been preparing for this," said Imran, "while you were at L'Airial. We're ready. Are you?"

She wanted them to put her in a cab and send her home. Away from their troubles. Back to the giratoire house: friendly spaceplane in the ceiling cracks, faint sound of the Aleutians "having a little music" in the main hall . . . Maitri died this morning. She suddenly remembered this with a sense of falling.

"You'll need firearms," she said. "I mean real ones." Aleutians regarded the projectile weapons humans knew as "firearms" as almost useless for anything but sport.

"That's taken care of," said Misha. "I've managed that. We have superheat, and we have Lalith, who is a Campfire officer. She's trained us, drilled us, taught us the way around the base."

"We're going to Tracy Island," declared Lydie, her narrow face white as paper. "You don't have to be part of this; it's your choice. Will you come with us?"

"When?"

"Now," said Misha inexorably. "Right now."

ii

AWARE THAT SHE was not being told the whole story, aware of shifts, anomalies, omissions that hid she couldn't tell what secrets, Catherine followed the others. They hurried between the blue demons, through the sparkle of the gate to the gamesroom.

"Why are we going through here?"

"To get to where Lalith keeps her flier," they told her. "It's the quickest way."

"But the ID reader. The Café's shut; it will look strange—"

"So what?" hissed Lydie. "How can you worry about money at a time like this?"

Catherine wanted there to be no trace, not a sign that the conspiracy had existed: not even a puzzling entry in the Café's accounts. But she let it go.

Into the antechamber. Through an unlit gate, footsteps rattling strangely: into a drab open space. They were on the edge of a wide, empty pan of paved ground. It was circled by ranks of seating terraces, faintly visible in the night. Catherine looked up and saw the indigo sky through the skeletal spars of a domed canopy.

"What is this place?"

It was the arena, of course, the physical stage of their nanotech make-believe. She could see no hint of its secret life. When she looked behind her, the row of *envie* gates were no more than indents of deeper shadow. How extraordinary: this was the space where she had spent hours, weeks, years of subjective time. She had been a pirate on the Spanish Main. She had touched the great trees of the Blue Forest.

"But it's huge!"

"It's probably the biggest arena in the *quartier,*" said Joset, with pride. "It dates back to the wartime visor-games boom. Not many people know it's here. The infrastructure maps don't mark it. It was used as a detention camp in the last days of the War. It came cheap with the Café's lease because nobody wanted it. Supposed to be haunted."

In the last phase of the Gender War, the urban centers of old-earth (which had until then been places of refuge) had lost their immunity. Throughout Youro hundreds of thousands of civilians had been rounded up and killed, or imprisoned and left to die, in gaming hells and swimming pools and leisure domes. Most of the buildings concerned had vanished, deliberately buried in new development. The city's present arenas and stadia were postwar.

"I had my flier hidden at a disused airstrip in a West Coast industrial complex," said Lalith, "which was none too secure. After I revealed my secret identity to the Phoenix Café people, they let me move it here."

Joset and Misha had set off across the pan. Menacing little eyes of orange luminescence twinkled as they passed from the tiger weed that veined the cracked concrete. There was a smell of rain, ozone, and emptiness: a sense of ghosts. Suddenly, a section of the arena wall split open, revealing a fat parabola of pale gray. Joset and Misha appeared in silhouette, hauling on something invisible. It looked as if they were clawing at the air. "Come on," urged Lalith. Catherine and Agathe followed her. As they reached the empty archway, the young men's arms were suddenly full of material. A huge flimsy sheet of camouflage tarp rucked and tumbled to the ground, false dimensions shattering. Lalith's flier was revealed: a blunt-nosed pilot's cone locked to a payload frame. The wings were retracted to stubs, there was a barrel-shaped pod in the frame, belly flat on the ground. It was bigger than Catherine had expected. It had to be, of course, or their mission would have been impossible.

"Didn't you come over here alone?"

"I did, but I was carrying passenger space in case I needed to get people out. That was one scenario: identify key peacemakers and rescue them. Didn't find any candidates."

"How long since you've flown it?"

"I keep everything maintained," said Lalith evasively. "Can't do much flying. If I lift off from out of here too often, somebody on the ground's going to notice. There'd be reports of a hell of a big bird flapping around the haunted arena."

The flier glided out, guided by Mâtho and Lydie on either side. It opened its lamps of eyes and started violently as if woken from sleep.

"Steady, boy, steady." Lydie patted the cold skin of the cone. She giggled at herself. "Funxing thing's not alive! I can't get used to that idea."

"Some renaissance warrior you are," complained Lalith cheerfully.

Joset bundled the tarp down, opened one of the doors of the pilot's cone, and stuffed it somewhere inside. Faces, dark and pale, turned to Catherine in the chill gloom. The gleam in Agathe's strong and tender eyes. The messages speeding between Joset and Misha's socket insets. She could read none of it. Imran and Rajath were carrying some long bulky cases between them. They loaded them in to the carrier pod. Thérèse, who was wearing her chador again but with the hood thrown back, came to Catherine and announced: "We're staying behind, Imran and me. If you fail, at least somebody will know what those beasts are doing. We'll tell. We'll find a way." She put her arms around Catherine and kissed her: soft cheek, golden hair, implacable green eyes. Living doll with a will of iron.

"Goodbye, Catherine," said Imran stiffly, stepping back. "Good luck."

"Let's go." Misha had opened a hatch in the curved side of the craft. "Inside!"

Imran and Thérèse moved away from the plane.

Catherine stepped onto the open hatch. It lifted, waited for her to embark, lowered itself again. The interior was a bare shell, with a glimmer of light piped along the roof. Mâtho and Lydie were ahead of her. Agathe, Joset, Rajath came after. Misha was last, and then the panel sealed. They settled on rudimentary benches braced against the fuselage, and fastened themselves into jackets of webbing. Their equipment was webbed down with the life-raft capsules along the center of the floor. Catherine sat between Agathe and Lydie.

"I wanted the renaissance to be *yours,*" she said, full of loss.

"It is ours!" insisted Lydie. "Lalith's our ally. We're one brood. You said so."

"Animals have life!" shouted Joset, apropos of nothing. "Machines have soul! This is a truce, Campfire Girlie. After the party's over we resume the quarrel, is that understood?"

"Can't wait, dickbrain," came Lalith's voice from the pilot's cab.

No one spoke again until the pod began to shake (no protection for this cargo from the stress of takeoff). Mâtho was huddled opposite Catherine. His hands trembled over the fastenings of his web. "Don't be frightened," he whispered kindly. "We'll make it."

They were airborne. Someone—Imran—must have opened the canopy. "This is going to seem a very long journey," announced their captain, "to your effete Youros. There will be no inflight movies. No protection from 'the sensations of movement.' The head is in that tiny compartment at the back. Don't overuse it! Keep your webbing on you at all times. If we crash, those weird-looking things become spider balloon cradle-chutes: very safe. But we won't crash. Try to get some rest."

Catherine dozed. She saw Maitri's body lying in its embroidered carapace. *The person I love most in all the world died this morning. They tell me I am immortal, but I know that I, this Catherine, will never see him again.* Lalith's shining sincerity. The halfcastes in the USSA were purged, pogromed, killed. She must know that; yet she wore her disguise without a shiver: strange people, secret agents. Lalith came from the great stronghold of non-biological culture and preached a life-science renaissance. Could the movement in Youro survive when people found out that this charismatic figure was a fake? Catherine could hardly believe it. Fake things can become real . . . Who said that? Thérèse, of the nature-identical tamarins on the *rive droite.* But she was talking about herself. Michael's sister in that room lit by the fire of roses: a living doll, fake human being. And yet the maker of worlds. The girl outside the police station: *ma semblable, ma soeur.* Flight into madness, into acceptance so complete that nothing can ever hurt you. Helen Connelly with her Vlab, making movies about her own destruction. Was she mad? If anyone ever had a right to be insane, it was Helen.

Catherine opened her eyes and saw the others playing some kind of game. They were rolling dice, passing them from hand to hand. Discussing each score in murmurs. Casting lots. *Wonder what that's about?*

Misha watched Catherine until her eyes finally closed. He turned away, looked into the camera eye in his head, and made himself a porthole window. It was a cold night out there. He could see stars. *What if the wings ice up, and we fall out of the sky? I am going to give up the drug,* he thought. *Goodbye, sweet poison. I am going to stop using.* He saw himself walking away from Catherine on that steep, dark underground street beside the Tate. There was a beggar in a foul doorway. Now Misha changed places with the beggar. He dwindled; he lost substance. *She will never know,* he thought, *how important she has been to me.* And with the thought that Catherine would never know came a sense of repaired defenses, renewed security. For some reason the buried alley turned into a canal towpath. Gray water under a darkening sky. The wilderness paved over. This terrible beauty must die. He saw himself walking away, walking away. Wearing the beggar's clothes over a body raw and naked as a peeled twig.

The pod was poorly heated. Catherine burrowed into chill dreams of shuddering movement. They woke her and bundled her without ceremony into a survival capsule. Heat flared through the bone-eating cold. Her knees seemed to be pressed into her eye sockets. She was sucking air through a tube, breathing out into a sweaty mask: she was tumbling, rolling; she hoped she wasn't going to vomit. *In becomes down.* The heat was intense. Flames thundered. She fell and fell, terrible sense of catastrophe: and worse, responsibility. *What's happened to the others?* She managed not to vomit, and not to bite her tongue in half when the pod landed like a dropped brick . . . But actually she was floating. She lay in a mass of something between soft gel and spiderweb. There was a steady moaning sound that seemed to come from everywhere. She crawled out of her cradle chute, wondering what had happened to the survival pod. She had landed on a beach *(in becomes down, the flames).* The shore was dun brown; the sea was gray. She sat staring at the ocean, half unable to make out why she was not in West Africa.

It was daylight. The sky was the same color as the sea: low cloud without a break. The beach ran straight on either side. She stood up and looked behind her. There was a sandy cliff, about as tall as a three-story city block. The base was slabs of brown stone. A short distance away she could see a vertical fissure that might have been made by falling water. She was very cold. She thought she was suffering from shock, then noticed that there was some white, crisp frost on the shingle that in places interrupted the brown sand. *I'm outdoors,* she thought, and suddenly realized that this was the Americas. She saw one of the flier's life pods lying in the scum of the tide and ran to drag it clear of the water. Somebody called her name.

"Catherine?"

It was Misha, appearing from behind a stand of boulders farther along the shore. He waved and ran toward her, cradle-chute flapping and peeling from his clothes.

"What happened to the others?" she demanded. "Did we crash?"

"No, we didn't crash. We jumped. Everything's going according to plan—"

"I don't remember the plan."

"We didn't discuss the details with you. We're sorry— corporate apology. But we've discussed everything so much. We wanted to get on with it." He pulled the pod farther onto the sand, sprung it open, and hauled out one of the long, heavy dark bags Rajath and Imran had stowed in the flier. "Lalith has told Tracy Island that she's coming home, bringing in some highly sensitive refugees. She's told them she's spotted some strange looking agents in their system; she's afraid it may be compromised. That's why she's arrived with so little warning. That and the fact that these valuable refugees had to be lifted out of Youro at very short notice. She's behaving exactly the way she'd behave if it was the truth. Her passengers will be asking for political asylum from Aleutian earth. Tracy Island is the obvious, secure port of entry. The asylum seekers are played by Lydie and Mâtho and Agathe, representing the three genders, you see. The rest of us jumped. Don't you remember? You seemed to be awake. Now we have to collect our share of the gear, which also jumped, and rendezvous with Joset and Rajath. Most of the base is underground. There's a network of tunnels around it; we're going in through one of them. Lalith's going to escape from her escort once she's inside and bring the others to join us."

He was looking up and down the shore.

"There," said Catherine. He shouldered the long bag. They set off at speed toward the second pod, which was bobbing about a short distance away.

"Where are we?" asked Catherine, having difficulty keeping up.

He produced a pocket printer and, without breaking stride, slapped the pickup across his temples. The small cylinder whirred, extruded a white tongue of paper. Misha tore it off. "Here. Map of Tracy Island."

The flimsy sheet showed a four-cornered shape, each corner pulled out to a point so that it made a halfhearted star. The outline was a mass of cramped tiny details, contour lines tracing a truncated cone, marshy scrub, tunnel entrances, massive concealed engineering.

"I meant, where in the Americas."

"Well"—he pointed out to sea—"Kamchatka's that way, somewhere."

"Oh?" She laughed. "Really? How . . . how appropriate. But I don't understand. I thought Tracy Island was off the coast of Yucatan."

"Maybe it was in your day." Misha dragged the second pod out of the water, sprung it, and ripped open another bag. He pulled out two drab oversuits. "Take your robe off and stuff it in here. Put this on. I'm not well up on Americas geography. Where's Yacktuan? I suppose they moved this thing sometime in the last couple of centuries. It's not a *real* island, you know. It can be towed from mooring to mooring like a wavepower raft or something."

He handed her a packet of soup and a sealed chunk of bread.

"Eat. That was a long flight."

They sat side by side on the pod, sucking warm instant soup and gnawing the tough bread. Catherine found that she was ravenously hungry. Misha dragged the heavier bag to his feet, eating all the time. He ripped it open and looked down on the contents: fat gleaming barrels and rows of separately packed charges. They were real, deadly firearms: seriously illegal in human possession.

"Where did you get those?"

He didn't answer. "Good," he said. "Good. They've traveled well." He shut the bag.

There was a strange moment as they finished eating, when she realized that they were alone and wondered by reflex, *Will he rape me?* She looked at Misha, who seemed utterly unconscious of her, staring out to sea. He turned his head, as if she had spoken.

"What is it?"

The golden eyes met hers: preoccupied, tranquil. She shook her head and smiled.

"Nothing."

"Come on, let's go. Got to get up that cliff."

The brown rock slabs were more formidable in close up. The first handhold was a long way off the ground, too far for Catherine's reach. Misha took a swing at it with the light stuff bag on his back and climbed. He fetched out a rope from the bag and let it down. Catherine attached the bag of firearms. When that was raised, he let down the rope again. She fastened it around her waist, and he pulled her up.

"Should be easier now," he said.

They climbed, Misha leading. The stuff bag was slung over his shoulder, the bag of weapons roped and hauled after them in stages.

"Tracy Island was financed by a woman called Marjorie O'Reilly Steyning," he reported. "Better known as Seimwa L'Etat, legendary media proprietor who became, posthumously, a fanatical anti-Aleutian. She'd hidden most of her assets in the 2038 revolution, so the revolutionary government never got hold of her money. Many years later her estate funded this base. She used to employ Johnny Guglioli before First Contact. I suppose you knew that. Bet you didn't know she's still here."

"You said posthumously. Is she reincarnate?" Catherine was prepared for anything.

"Depends what you call incarnation. Lalith"—he paused briefly, searching for a new hold—"says they keep her body in a tank, by the terms of the endowment, the tissues pumped full of some patent goop. It's room-temperature technology, she didn't trust cryogenics. She bubbles like a ginger beer plant, Lalith says. Whatever the funx a 'ginger beer plant' may be. She's alive as a sacred object. I don't think my dad would regard her as competition."

They were in the fissure she had seen, alternately bracing and scrabbling in an unstable sandy funnel and clambering between the vertical slabs. She climbed automatically, her mind filled with images from the Phoenix Café. Misha playing "Great Balls of Fire" with enormous verve, hammering wildly at a hallowed twentieth-century keyboard up on the stage while the Phoenix staff yelled at him in helpless protest . . . Does the Koran permit the taking of gaming-drugs in Ramadan? Discuss. Their sumptuous Christmas breakfast in the eternal cartoon-colored spring of Thérèse's orchard . . . Catherine had seen these friends bound together by Misha, but they had been bound—she realized—by Helen Connelly. The *auteur*. The maker of worlds. Even now, she regretted her loss. She would never know Helen. She saw her knowledge of the Phoenix Café, of these young people, spread before her like a mariner's chart of a strange country. The coastline traced in detail but only a blank beyond, that she would never explore. Maitri whispered to her as she climbed: *Nothing lasts.*

More images, adventures from her Aleutian past, journeys in the wild places where there is no life. Friends who trekked with Catherine were daunted by her appetite for hardship. "It's not that I feel at home in the wild," she shouted. "Some people do, not me. I'm afraid. I'm crushed by the emptiness. Nobody believes that, but it's true. I still have to come out here. I need edges, starkness, absolutes—"

"May I give you a piece of advice?" cut in Misha from above. "Don't talk. For once. Just climb."

She had not realized that she was speaking aloud. Now there was no more sand, only a rocky chimney. The drop below, between her feet, was startling. How did they come to be so far up, far out? She was in the shipworld, climbing in the huge spars between the two shells of the giant spheroid vessel: a dangerous entertainment for stir-crazy voyagers. She couldn't tell if she was heading up or down. She slipped, felt the weight of the firearms dragging her backward, the thunderous energy of fear coursing in every nerve. She saw Johnny Guglioli's face staring up at her in everlasting terror and disgust. She felt herself a small, naked crawling thing, extended beyond her powers . . .

They were standing on level ground.

"*Cath.* Are you all right?"

The abyss above and below weighed on her like death. She was coming apart, her body drifting into fragments on the aether. The faces of gods and demons, impossibly huge faces, looked down on her and roared. She was tumbling into fugue. Arousal, tension, fear. Functioning under the influence. Michael Jr. putting Catherine through her paces, a roguish twinkle in his eye, and she responded, she performed, because somehow she must. Columns capped in dirty snow surrounded them like sentinels. There was gray ice underfoot. A nameless wind had found them. It drove straight through the insulated suits, searching every sweated crevice of flesh. Misha tugged clumsily on Catherine's arm.

"I said, are you all right?"

He pointed to a cove among the boulders, rocks piled around a wind-riven house.

They crouched in shelter, and he fed her with pieces of something sticky and sweet. At last she managed to speak.

"I'm all right. I don't know what came over me."

"You shouldn't be wearing that body," said Misha. "It isn't practical outdoors."

She nodded, feeling the fragile young lady limbs still trembling. A tuft of gray-green barrens grass grew in the entrance of their shelter. She reached out and touched the tough blades with her gloved hand, grateful for their reality. "So this is the Aleutian islands," she marveled. "I think it counts, even if this is a movable one. Rajath always said they were horrible. I loved West Africa. Kumbva was very fond of Uji in Thailand, where he landed. But Rajath never came back here, never. I don't agree, but I can see his point."

A wonder at finding herself in the Americas, at being an adventurer again, filled her: it blotted out the sense of crisis. "Is this where we're to meet the others?"

"No, we have to go farther. Drink. Eat some more. You'll be fine."

The central cone was ahead of them, built of rugged glittering granite: a solid though unlikely landscape feature. From the rim of the cliff to the skirts of the cone, the ground descended into a shallow valley. There were no trees. Between patches of windswept snow, the turf was crisp with the brown ghosts of summer flowers.

Misha gazed into his inner eye. "Lalith is inside the cone. She's landed the flier, and it's been sprayed with quarantine film. She and her passengers have deplaned, they've all been dipped in quarantine, and they're being escorted to a reception suite. There's no sign that anyone suspects anything; all the precautions are normal. She expects they'll try to separate her from the others soon and take her off for her own debriefing. So far she's managed to convince them she has to stick with her passengers. The important refugees only trust Lalith, won't impart their vital information unless she stays with them, that sort of thing."

"I didn't know Lalith had an inset."

Misha frowned impatiently. "Of course she's wired. She's a secret agent, isn't she? Just listen, don't interrupt. She's sent this as text, up to some FDA satellite or other and down again to me, as if she was calling me up on a global-mobile. Now we'll lose contact for a while. Once we're inside the base, she's bit-stitched me and Joset into the system. Nothing high security and nothing that'll stand human scrutiny, but we should be able to function. There won't be many humans around. This is actually the most dangerous part. Where's that map I gave you? Take a look at it."

Head up, staring inward, he traced the contour lines on the flimsy she spread between them on the ground. "See here. A dip, under the slope of the cone, nearly opposite the fissure we used to climb from the beach. We have to get there without alerting the exterior surveillance. We have the advantage that the surveillance 'knows' nothing has crossed the shorelines. Lalith fixed that. So it won't be searching. These suits are good camouflage. They'll make us look like nothing, as long as we don't move. If we move, they'll give us the profile of large animals behaving naturally. Only trouble is"—abruptly his eyes changed their focus—"there aren't any large animals on Tracy Island. When I say run, run like fun. When I yell stop, stop *at once* and pretend to be a boulder. When I say run again, run. Got it?"

She nodded.

"Run!"

Run, stop. Run, stop. Run, stop. Catherine stumbled and fell into the final shelter, an iced-over marshy dell of frosted tussocks and moss. One of the tussocks at once flew into the air. Rajath's impish noseless face burst out of hiding. He leapt at Catherine and embraced her. Joset rolled out from the lair he'd made for himself, grinning widely.

"You made it! You made it!" Rajath was dancing with excitement.

Misha slung his bag of firearms down beside the bags Joset and Rajath had carried. He and Joset bent over them. Catherine heard fragments of their spoken interchange: "... a sticky moment on the beach, when she ... " "Did you get the flames, or did you climb?" *What did I do wrong on the beach?* she wondered, and closed her eyes. Misha was right, she really shouldn't be wearing this body. She had lived in Catherine's limbs all these years, now suddenly she felt trapped in an ill-fitting suit. She had chosen to wear a human body in this life so the earthlings wouldn't be able to call her a superbeing, so they wouldn't feel she was unfairly advantaged. *That part of the plan seems to have worked,* she thought. She lay waiting for the telepaths to report on their discussion.

"Wake up, Catherine. We must get underground."

They moved swiftly and with confident precision. Near to the rendezvous dell Misha dropped to his knees and tugged at a granite slab. It came away revealing a dark pit, roughly square. "Escape route. There are exits and entrances everywhere, for the death-and-glory scenario where the aliens get inside the ultimate bunker. Campfire Girls don't like to be trapped." He reached inside and brushed away fibrous earth to find the first rung of a metal ladder. They clambered, one after another, into darkness. Above them the slab dropped back into place. At the bottom of the shaft a section of the wall rose silently. They stepped through into a sleek horizontal tunnel. It was dimly lit, tall but not wide. Misha handed out charged firearms, and they set off in single file: Misha first, then Catherine, then Rajath. Joset last. Misha and Joset were carrying the stuff bag of supplies and the second case of weapons. The tunnel led to a junction concourse, where there was better light and an air of occasional use. Joset and Misha searched until they found a panel of controls, and used them to open a supply closet. Shining limbs swayed in the depths, disembodied heads peered out.

"Suit up. Campfire Girls uniform from here on. One at a time. Rest of us on guard."

One by one they shed their weapons and outdoor suits, and climbed into the body armor. Catherine was surprised at how light and flexible her suit seemed, how speedily it adjusted to her physical dimensions. She pulled the sleek helmet into place and felt the seals connect. Briefly, she breathed stale packaged air; then the sweet cold returned as her suit decided the air in the tunnels was viable. Text and graphic display burst across her field of vision. Testing. She entered a shared world.

"Now Lalith can send to me, and I can send to you," came Misha's voice. He seemed to speak inside her head. "Try not to talk much once we get inside the base proper; don't use suit radio unless you have to. We don't want to kill any innocent people, but we have to assume that all the staff of this mothballed base are compromised, is that understood? Lalith's arrival should cover us for a while. Let's see what's going on."

The suits settled on the floor of the tunnel, heads together, cross-legged and easy: a convocation of pallid, blob-headed fungus people. In Catherine's field of view a transparent image blossomed. She saw Lalith, Agathe, Mâtho in the reception suite. Mâtho and Lydie were finishing off that dice game. The suite, what she could see of it, had the bland corporate comfort of another age. Fitted carpets and fussy wall lamps. Mâtho seemed to have lost the play-off. He pocketed the dice with a dignified little smile.

"Now, study this infra—" ordered Misha.

Another layer formed over the reception suite picture, unpeeling the intricacies of Seimwa L'Etat's anti-Aleutian bunker. In section the underground base was strangely beautiful. It had the configuration of a nautilus shell: a ribbed central helix wrapped in level on level of curved paths of chambers, in the center a cleft that must drop in a single fall from the height of the dome inside the "volcano" cone to the platform level undersea. In the old days, anyone recruited to the Special Exterior Force could never return to the mainland. That way the Americans could be sure that none of those sneaky alien-microbes would ever contaminate their country. For generations the Special Exterior Force—all of them women, forbidden to marry, discouraged from "lasting attachments"; all but a few either infertile or sterilized—had lived and died here, between tours of duty, on their artificial island. These days the base was nearly empty. There were few people moving about, few streams of power or data. "This is realtime," said Misha's voice. "There has been an invasion, that's Lalith. We have introduced a foreign population. We're watching for an immune reaction."

Catherine's display focused in on above-mean activity and counted off the systems and locations involved. There was a stir that clearly sprang from Lalith's arrival: information and other vital fluids hurrying around the flier in its quarantine bay, around the reception suite and related offices. There were routine activities: a kitchen, power generation, a heated swimming pool. And then a tell-tale isolated hotspot. The palimpsest fell away, leaving one group of rooms highlighted, on the third level above the deepest, midway between the shell of the nautilus and the central spine.

"There!" hissed Rajath. "That must be it!"

"It's a sick-bay," read Joset from pages of infrastructure text. " 'Non-acute hospitalization,' says here."

"Makes sense," whispered Misha. "I suppose. So we head for the labor ward. Lalith will follow as she can. She's in control."

"Wait!" cried Catherine. "Something's happening—"

A party of suits had entered the room where the asylum-seekers and their sponsor were being held. Their helmets were intimidating, the visors silvered blank: they didn't remove them. Their voices emerged flattened and stripped of expression. They had come to take Agathe, Lydie, and Mâtho away. The Youroans got to their feet, each of them clutching a piteous bag or bundle of personal effects. Lalith must have noticed the sinister fact that none of the suits was displaying badges of rank or identity. She didn't comment on this, but she insisted reasonably she had to come along:

"They don't know what's happening; they don't understand—"

A suit challenged Lalith in turn. "Are you Astrid Liliana Villegas Como?"

"Yes, I am. You checked my ID. What's wrong?"

"What's wrong is that we've double-checked, and you're not her. We don't have any record of an SEF agent with your physical ID."

"That's because I've been morphed. I'm a halfcaste now. But my new identity should be in the records." Lalith stayed calm. But Lydie grabbed at her arm and cried in French: "Astrid, don't let them separate us! What's going on? I'm frightened!"

"Don't worry," said the first suit, flattened, cold. " 'Astrid' is coming along."

Suddenly, in the transparency it was hard to say how, one of the suits had hold of Lalith's arms. The first suit was pointing a light pen into her eye. Agathe, Mâtho, and Lydie were shouting, protesting; the other suits closed around them—

"They've been rumbled!" howled Rajath. "The suits've found Lalith's inset! What are we going to do?"

"Thanks for the information, Raj," snapped Misha. "We might never have guessed." He hesitated. His voice, when he spoke, was shaking slightly. "They'll have to look out for themselves. We're going to check that 'sick-bay.' Is that agreed?"

The convocation rose. They began to walk quickly.

Catherine felt the muscles of her weary calves trying to resist the suit's expert intervention. She made herself relax. She thought of Lydie's magnificent athleticism, the spin and leap and spring of the dancer's body. Up a ladder (the suit assisting her arms and shoulders) into an enclosed space. A locked door that gave way when Misha tapped the keypad. They were in a garden. Flowering plants, trees, wisps of water vapor, a moist and scented air. Loungers, chairs, cushions, a vast false window showing ocean and the sky. There were sculptures, mobiles, decorative screens, every sign of wealthy comfort but slightly *wrong*. Different, old-fashioned, and all the leaves were green. There was no one around. Rajath skidded and fell against a cane lounger. Catherine hauled him to his feet, and Joset restored his weapon, but Rajath refused to take it.

"It's weird," he wailed, waving his arms. "Why's it like a fancy hotel? I thought this was an army camp, some kind of barracks. I don't think we're seeing it right; it's masked—"

"Why are you *always* like this, Rajath?" yelled Catherine, falling into her own past. "You're the one who has these terrific ideas. And then you *always panic*—" She clutched at her helmet with gauntleted hands, shocked at her own loss of control. She felt as if she'd been shouting loud enough for the whole base to hear.

Misha had rushed back. He silently bundled the weapon into Rajath's arms. They hurried on.

Another eye view continued to overlay Catherine's field of vision. She saw Mâtho and Lydie and Agathe being marched along a wide passageway. Lalith must be in the rear. She wondered why Lalith was still sending. Surely, the suits could use that signal to trace the other intruders . . . It was bad, bad luck that she'd been discovered so soon. *We need a diversion,* Catherine thought. *Maybe they don't know yet why we're here. We need something to distract them from our real purpose.* The prisoners had reached a wide gallery around the central well, where elegant liftshafts rose like fountains between the spurs of a huge spiral stairway. Lydie suddenly ran for it. She flew across the fine big space.

"I am a terrorist act," she cried in English, obviously a prepared speech. "I am an explosive device, and I'm carrying a camera as well. Attack me, and I will detonate! I'm here to tell the American peoples about their federal government's involvement in alien oppression . . . Leave your weapons alone! Injure me, and I appear instantly on every news site on earth, telling my story!"

"My God!" screamed Lalith's voice. "I didn't know! I knew nothing about this! You've got to believe me! My God!"

"Get her!"

Catherine saw Mâtho and Agathe running toward Lydie, who howled in turn and went pelting off around the gallery. She saw the suits rushing after in some disarray, and heard Lalith yelling, "Don't fire! I don't think she's bluffing—" Transmission abruptly ceased.

They hurried on. Catherine's visor flashed bursts of text and figures, scraps of the continuing pursuit of the dancer. She didn't know if they came from Misha or if she was catching Campfire Girl communication. The others didn't speak, neither did she. She had her wish; she was stripped of privilege. It was Catherine, the Aleutian, who followed the humans, stumbling and blind, unable to share their plans. She felt that she was functioning on a knife edge— in the stink of lattice fusion, the continuous bleeding of one surface into another. The scenario Agathe and Lalith had outlined was appalling: *a bomb packed with weapon larvae, anonymous microbial plague.* She remembered Misha's father speaking, with noble grief, about "the pure human tradition." He did not regard Reformers as human. The conspirators believed they had found some marker of *difference* that would separate their own kind from the rest. That would spare the elect. It was not such a new idea; it had been tried before, but never with proliferating weapons to back the madness. On such a big planet, such a volume of atmosphere, the kill would take time. The weapons would mutate, eventually become harmless. But life on earth was already weakened by the Gender War and by alien rule. An escape even from this small-scale test might mean the end. *Surely, it can't happen; surely, it can't happen.* Episodes from the past of her own home and from earth's own history told her: *It can happen. Death can be forever.* She saw a sign on a corridor wall. Level Three.

They had reached a locked double door. Medical rooms. Misha couldn't get any response from the keypad, nor could Joset. There was a faint, fetid sickroom smell: one of those nasty human smells. It could not be real. It must be an artifact of her fear.

"Luck's run out," muttered Joset. "It couldn't last. They've blocked us."

He moved away from the doors, hefting his weapon and looking warily up and down the corridor. Misha, the firearms expert, prepared to slice the barrier with a fine blade of superheat. Rajath, who was with Catherine a few paces behind the other two, gave a soft moan. Catherine aimed and fired: wheeled, aimed, and fired. Joset stood looking at his own unused weapon, and at two fallen suits: one who'd been coming up behind them, the other who'd appeared around a corner ahead.

"You've played before," he remarked in admiration.

She stared at him. *"Played?"* she repeated, shocked at his choice of expression.

"Inside," yelled Misha, as the door seals gave way. Stale air rushed out. They had entered the base through a garden. The sick-bay smelt like a farmyard. There were no beds in the ward. They'd been removed and replaced by strong slatted stalls. There was a thunder of panicked movement. Animal eyes peered, glistening. The stalls were shoulder high to Catherine. She had to look over the top to see inside. Pallid faces looked back, blurred but familiar. Food for the monsters. She had dreamed of these creatures. Rajath yelled something incoherent. Superheat flared, churning incandescence through the bars and the live squealing meat. Misha shouted, "Stop that! Leave them; get to the bride!"

There was a sound of running feet. Mâtho, Agathe, and Lalith burst together into the ward. "Sorry!" gasped Mâtho. "They're coming! Lydie's in the spiral; she's keeping half the army occupied. But there are so many! We couldn't get away from these—" Joset unslung the second case of weapons and thrust a firearm at each of the three before a crowd of suits came rushing in. There was no chance to follow Misha's advice. Catherine flung herself headlong, tonguing her armor rigid and switching to packaged air. There was wild firing. The hiss of gas cartridges exploding—

"I am a terrorist act!"

The central well was higher than a cathedral nave of the Church of Self, deeper than dreams. The stairway rose in nacreous curves, throwing off ribs and whimsical spurs into vertiginous space. Far below Seimwa L'Etat lay in state: an image delivered in realtime from the clinical suite where she rested, sleeping away her immortality. The tank, from which gross signs of medical intervention had been erased, was a gold and crystal casket. Lydie raced around and around, up into the empyrean. She reached the apex and turned to look down on the armored women . . . *So many, how did there come to be so many? Thought this place was supposed to be shut down* . . . They looked up, some of them helmeted and some bareheaded.

This is what it means to be a halfcaste. To be something else than one self. To be gestures, to be fragments, thefts, dreams. To be a creature of your own imagination. Lydie jumped onto the balustrade. The doors of the fountain lifts opened. Woman warriors in identical armor came pouring out. Soldiers, soldiers. Sold themselves. I'm not for sale. Balanced herself, arms stretched wide as wings. Either or. Stupid coin, same on both sides. I am not a woman; I am not a man. Who knows? Maybe they lied to you all these years, *those others,* the sensible ones. So leap, then . . . Maybe you can fly.

. . . from Lydie's death-dive Catherine returned to her own reality, her perception struggling to right itself. Her heart was still beating from that plunge. She thought she must be in the house at the giratoire, wired up to a tvc show. But no: she was in the room on Tracy Island base, and it was full of smoke. The enemy had vanished. She did not know if she had been watching Lydie on her visor or imagining that scene. The pens that held the blanks were still. There were bodies on the floor. One of them was Mâtho. Agathe was crouched beside him; she'd strapped a breathing mask onto his face and was holding a wad of something against a stomach wound. She was wearing a mask herself, so was Lalith. Agathe's bundle of "personal effects" was scattered around her, Lalith was scrabbling in it for more first aid. Catherine pulled off her helmet, and at once began to cough hard.

"Catherine?" Mâtho turned his head. The eyes above the mask appealed to her.

"They've gone to seal the level, so they can kill us—" whimpered Rajath.

"I think he'll be all right," reported Agathe, without conviction.

Catherine dropped to her knees by Mâtho. "Cold . . . " he muttered.

"Oh, God," cried Agathe, feeling his hands and breast in sudden horror. "He's losing heat fast! He's ice! Must be massive internal bleeding! There's nothing I can do!"

"Catherine."

Mâtho tugged her gauntleted hand to his lips, and his eyes fixed—

Joset and Misha had started hammering on the inner doors, shouting through the lock. They could not use superheat because it would destroy the containment. They had to get inside, and seal themselves in with whatever they found there, until they'd destroyed the bride and her children. They were shouting, "You're surrounded, you're going to die, we're about to suck your air out, we have poison gas—" It wasn't going to work. *Failed*, thought Catherine, amazed at her own calm. *Of course we've failed; we didn't have a chance.* She replaced her helmet. Might as well die fighting. Suddenly, the doors to the containment hissed and were flung open. A group of people rushed out. They were dressed and masked in heavy quarantine suits, but they weren't armored. The nurses or guards, whichever, raced through the scene of carnage and disappeared into the smoke.

"Something's gone wrong in there," cried Rajath frantically.

It was a small room. In a flash of stillness Catherine saw how Helen's partner had been cherished. Her flowers, her jewels, pretty furniture and pictures on the walls, her bridal dress and wreath and veil in a display case. Catherine had seen that white lace and satin gown before—or its twin—on the virtual screen in Mr. Connelly's study. But now, on a narrow bed a young woman, restrained by straps and clamps, lay in premature labor. Something, maybe the panic caused by their arrival, had precipitated the birth. It was happening. Monitoring machinery lay scattered; a trolley of instruments was sprawled on its side. The children were being born from every pore; the mother's skin was tearing open. She moved her close-shorn head and looked at Catherine. Her eyes were pinpoints, drugged deep. She opened her mouth—to speak? A weapon-creature burst out and broke their paralysis.

They burned the whole bed and everything on it. Super-heat flare engulfed them, scalding them through their armor. Catherine passed into the furnace; it leapt around her. On the fire spread, binding them together: guilty, collaborating, denying, colluding, greedy for catastrophe, hungry for destruction. Every flame a life, every flame a self. They were all of them Catherine, and she was all of them: no excuses, no denials. She plied her weapon with joyous savagery, plunging into the rapacity of being, and the flames began to dance. *"Everything says I. I am with you,"* they sang. *"Always with you,"* blood and fire mingled in the void.

And still herself.

The hospital room returned. She was standing in it, feeling sated and happy. The riot control gas in the Campfire Girls' cartridges must have dissipated. She was breathing outside air again. It smelled of seared suit and roast meat. Where the young woman's bed had been, there was a black, glossy mass of fused carbon. The isolation doors stood open. She counted the figures around her, the suits without insignia that were still standing. Her head display was blank. She pulled off her helmet.

"Misha? Joset?"

One of the dead Campfire Girls in the big room with the pens stirred. She sat up, poked at the charcoal cleft that divided her belly, and began to laugh. She pulled off her head. She was not a woman. She was a young man. She was the waiter who had served wine to Catherine, hours or days and half a world away, in the dining room at the Phoenix Café.

<What's going on?>

The other corpses stood. The standing suits took off their heads. The company gathered: Misha, Joset, Lalith, and Agathe. Mâtho and Rajath, and others she didn't know or didn't know well. A heap of shattered limbs materialized in a corner, picked itself up, and became Lydie, grinning. Everyone took a bow.

"You have been taking part," announced Lydie, "in an act of ceremonial magic, meant to keep bad at bay and mark the commencement of a new era. The commencement of the age of the Phoenix, celebrated in the leitmotiv of our culture, which is play-fighting, and as much cost-free arousal as we can get. Well, nearly free. And we hope you'll be a good sport and forgive us, as we've forgiven you."

They took another bow.

"You mean this was nothing but a *game?*"

She ran to the pens. They were empty plastic packing cases. She was speechless.

<You MONSTERS!>

"If this is a game," said Lalith, "then all the games have new rules."

"I don't understand!"

"You will," assured Lydie. "But not until afterward. You'll find out why we did this soon. You won't *understand* until long afterward. It takes time for it to sink in."

The company saluted her once more in a ragged line. They filed out, still partly cloaked in virtual costumes, through a gap that had appeared in the sick-bay wall.

Then.

She was alone. She remembered: *dying, falling in flames.* She realized, with glad astonishment, that at last she knew what the nightmare meant. She had been here before. She had passed before, in another lifetime, into an intensely de- tailed, absorbing dream: and come out on the other side in a different world. She didn't know how it had been done, but she must be *home—*

—but something troubled her. The light was wrong.

Movement behind her made her spin around. She found herself looking into a long mirror above a spotlessly clean counter that framed odd-looking washbasins. The face in the mirror was human, though its body was clothed in Aleutian overalls and a dark brown, figured robe. Nearby there was a confused noise, as of many people and voices milling in a large echoing space. She opened the door that seemed to lead into this noise and stepped out.

11

THE EARLIER CROSSING

SHE WAS NOT home again. She was not in the Phoenix Café. She was in a huge bustling concourse, the distant walls cheerfully, *statically* decorated with blue sky and clouds between big, peculiar minitel screens. Candelabra of electric light globes hung overhead. There was a strut-divided mineral-glass window through which she could see a disk-shaped, domed aircraft sailing up above the horizon. Others like it were ranked on the ground.

A group of people came into view, clearly an important party. They were surrounded by uniformed guides whose manner was awed, obsequious, and wary. Catherine watched their approach and set out to intersect their path. Matching her pace to the visitors', she was soon walking beside one of them.

<Hi, Yudi.>

Yudisthara, an honest merchant whom Catherine had known well in her previous life on earth, started when he saw who was beside him, and then beamed in welcome.

<Oh, hello Pure One. I heard you were trying to get onto this trip. I joined them at Uji. Didn't see you on the cruiser.>

<I missed the flight. Had to come by private charter.>

<I didn't know one could do that. Have they given up their quarantine entirely?>

<I managed to get around it.>

Yudisthara accepted this without difficulty. The Pure One had always been able do things on the giant planet, things that nobody else dreamed of trying.

<So you won't have heard the dreadful news?>

Catherine's heart stopped. <*What dreadful news?*>

<You don't know?> Yudi glowed. <Oh, something completely extraordinary. A party of young humans has turned up on one of the Buonarroti planets . . . well, not strictly speaking turned up, because, of course, nobody's there to meet them. But found our beacon, made a record, left souvenirs, and so on. Indisputable! Apparently, the humans have devised their own Buonarroti engine, and they decided to let us know they'd done it. Very sporting of them; very embarrassing for us! I always thought it was a mistake, you know, not to let them have it.>

Yudisthara was not a landing parties veteran, but his sympathies (he felt) had always been clear. The glory of being the one to impart this news to Catherine brought tears to his eyes. He caught the Pure One's hand and pressed it.

<Vindicated! You said they should have the engine, and they've got it!>

<Of course,> remarked Catherine faintly. <Non-location travel will never be useful for short hops like this, Europe to the Americas or something.>

<Ha! You've been talking to Dr. Bright. Well, apparently we now think it *may* be possible. But that's a long way down the line, lives and lives of research. And why bother? is what most of us say. What's the hurry? Time's cheap. People talk about it making our fortunes, but once we're home, I doubt if we'll find any takers for that engine thing. Let the humans keep it. That's what I always said. And I didn't care who knew it.>

<How true,> murmured Catherine (tactfully accepting

Yudi's proud record of public dissidence). She scanned the Aleutian party, hampered by her dumb human chemistry. <Where's Sattva? I don't see him.>

<Ah, he had to stay behind at the last moment. The Youro government's uncovered a plot. Apparently, some proliferating weapons material went missing from the Buonarroti station awhile ago. It was kept very quiet, naturally. It's been traced. Some high-up Traditionalists are implicated. Luckily, they'd got no further than using it for a few nasty experiments on their complex commensals before they were turned in. By one of their own, apparently: the Youro Cabinet Minister from that big flat suburb with all the trees. You'll know the name.>

<Poland,> supplied Catherine. <You mean Benazir Khan.>

<We think someone was holding a gun to his head, as the humans say. Or is it her head? I can't remember. But never mind that. The material's all accounted for; the scare's over. Very fortunately, the story that the humans have a Buonarroti engine broke the same day and distracted those horrible newsagents from the weapons-starter scandal. But what a catastrophe for Sattva! And we're leaving so soon he hasn't a chance of recovering face. He'll be known for lives as the person who almost . . . well, it isn't a pleasant idea, is it?>

<The poor chap,> murmured Catherine. <How terribly sad.>

Yudisthara paused and glanced at the USSA functionaries. (He had been told the new name of their country several times, but he couldn't keep it in his head.) They had no experience of dealing with international visitors and were trying without much success to look more like tour guides than police officers. <Do they know you're supposed to be with us?> he asked. He felt warmly toward Catherine, who was not usually so confidential with a dull businessperson like himself. He was hoping their companionship would last for the whole trip. <They'll have lists and numbers. Humans always do.>

<It'll be fine,> said Catherine. <They know that we can't count. Anyway, I'm famous. They'll be pleased.>

And the group absorbed her. Faces that she knew from recent acquaintance, others that rose from the sea of inclusive memory. Everyone was full of congratulations and rueful amusement over the triumph of her human protégés. No one was surprised to find the person they knew as Pure One with them. Trust Catherine! Trust Clavel . . . and after all, didn't the Third Captain have a right to be here, on the very last venture of the Expedition?

Catherine did not know; she began already to grasp that she would *never* know the true status of the raid on Seimwa L'Etat's stronghold. Was that a game, a species of travel-sickness, or a new kind of reality? Let it be. For now, she understood that she had been *taken to the cleaners,* as the humans used to say. Taken to the cleaners: wrung out and hung up to dry by the young people at the Phoenix Café. She laughed, feeling a bubble of pure irrational elation rise in her until she thought her feet would leave the ground.

And prepared, as Yudi hugged her arm and the solemn guides stopped to consult, talking not to each other but to little medallions they wore on their wrists, to be very bored.

IN THE FIELD HOSPITAL

CATHERINE SAW MISHA once more. It was the night of the Departure.

When they knew that the natives of the giant planet had managed to acquire or devise Buonarroti technology for themselves, the Aleutians had become ingratiating. They had opened the final phases of their own project to public view and consented to fix a day and a time for the actual Departure. They had chosen the moment of midnight, northwest Youro time zone (because of the location of the laboratories), and a date in early spring by the old seasonal calendar.

It was a year and a half after Catherine's visit to L'Airial. The flurry of leave-taking celebrations was past. Lingering Aleutians from all over earth had packed the last spaceplanes. "Aleutian Rule" in Youro would continue, nominally, until that stroke of midnight: but for some while there had been no alien presence to support it. Intercommunal violence was no longer something that happened on the news. It was everywhere.

Catherine was still living in the house at the giratoire. Leonie hadn't managed to get her family away before the final crisis began, and she'd wisely decided to stay put for the time being. The Car Park food market had been turned into a field hospital and displaced persons center. Catherine was working there, alongside the human staff of the former Aleutian Mission, the police, and other organized aid workers. She had just been relieved after a shift as a ward orderly. She was wandering in a daze, looking for some water powder so she could wash her hands, when she saw Misha. He was standing by the table where new arrivals were being processed. He was wearing jeans and a tee-shirt. He looked up and saw Catherine.

He came toward her.

So this was how they met, under the low concrete sky of the Car Park, among the dispossessed, the wounded, the confused old people; the lost children.

"I might have known you'd be doing something like this," he said, with a reflexive glance into his internal mirror. "Have you rejoined the Mission?"

"Not really. I do anything I'm asked. I'm unskilled labor."

"Unskilled labor?" He grinned. "Trust you, Cath. An archaism for every occasion." She saw the old acquisitive gleam.

"Feel free to be 'unskilled labor' too, if you like the *mot.*"

They walked together between two rows of cots, where the first in line for emergency treatment were waiting. Misha seemed to have grown smaller. *People do that,* she thought. *They change in size, receding into the distance or looming in close-up.* She rubbed the drying blood on her hands. There were rusty crescents under her nails. She remembered their first meeting.

Misha asked, "Did you enjoy your trip to meet the Feds?"

"Thank you, yes, I did. It's a strange place. A time capsule. You'd like it."

But unless he'd seen no news whatsoever, he must be saturated with images from the Americas. They had broken their data quarantine, and contact was flooding to and fro.

She had spent the tour with Yudisthara. Yudi was a shy

and timid soul, his "hardheaded merchant" defenses piteously transparent to anyone who knew him more than slightly. She hadn't had the heart to try and shake him off. She'd felt truly fond of him by the end, and they'd parted kindly when he left for the shipworld. She'd returned to the fascinating news story that had pursued them on tour and stolen much of their thunder. A team of young games technologists of the renaissance movement, working on their own initiative, had developed a version of the Buonarroti engine. Using virtuality techniques for handling huge quantities of hyper-connected information, they had overcome the problem of humanity's lack of "self-aware tissue." They had possibly even achieved an experimental form of "short-hop" non-location (though this was only a rumor). Congratulations were in order! Everyone was delighted, and Aleutia warmly welcomed the locals to the freedom of the stars. (Humans were being described as *the locals* again by Aleutians, as they had been long ago. Not strangers to be gulled, but neighbors who had better be treated with respect. Catherine found the shift amusing.)

The tale of the unworkable doomsday plot to "eradicate" the Reformers in Youro had aroused less interest. For the record, it appeared that Mrs. Benazir Khan had alerted the City Manager, and a conspiracy had been uncovered. There had been some resignations, voluntary and involuntary, among them that of Mr. Connelly the wilderness keeper. There had been revelations of grisly, futile experiments on young Traditionalist women. But the investigation had established that, thankfully, the mad scientists had never been close to actual weapons production. Any connection between this theft and the engine the renaissance movement had devised had been buried deep. The fact that the Aleutians had previously decided to renege on their bargain was buried deeper still. And the case was closed.

In the new era, there would be no more "young ladies." The status *sextoy* would no longer exist. All types of engineered embryos were to have the same full human rights. It was a tragically delayed result for Helen Connelly and her fellow victims, but a result, at least.

Catherine had stayed away from the Phoenix Café when she'd arrived back from the Americas. *Let them come to me,* she'd thought. But nobody had come. Then the Departure preparations had begun, and she'd had no time to think of anything but the crisis. Now here was Misha. They crossed, by unspoken consent—threading between bodies and bundles and bloodstained litter—to the counter where volunteer catering machines were dispensing tea and biscuits.

"Did you know Mâtho died?" he asked abruptly.

"Yes, I did know that."

Mâtho and his father had been killed defending their newsagency premises. It wasn't clear how the attack had begun, whether they'd been targeted or simply caught in crossfire. Catherine hoped, but she would never know, that Mâtho's publication of her alien video diaries hadn't had anything to do with it.

"Have you been in touch with Lydie?"

"Not recently." He knew she was thinking of Lydie's fake death on Tracy Island. "Nor Rajath. I've not been keeping up with the Café much. But I'm sure they're both fine. It looks as if Imran's going to be in the new administration, did you know? Joset reckons that's definite; he got it from Agathe. Maybe there'll even be a post for Thérèse; who knows? Those two! They always knew how to look out for themselves, didn't they."

"I see Agathe. I hear about Joset."

They both knew that Joset was with the *casseurs,* the wild renaissance gangs who were out on the streets, talking to the crime of gender violence in its own language. Misha was not. He detested that kind of thing. They passed over this breach in silence.

"And Lalith, of course."

Misha groaned. "Who doesn't? She's all over the place,

preaching at the *casseurs*, interviewing the old vampires, explaining our ways to the Feds. Every time you look into a screen, she's there. It's a joke, isn't it? She's well on her way to becoming the messianic leader of a new world order."

"Isn't that what you people wanted?"

Poor Mâtho. She remembered the Nose: the gentle soul who believed that passion was a curable disorder of the brain. Who had dealt with her so bravely over those articles. "He was my patron," she murmured. "The only patron for my work I ever found on earth."

The biscuits were energy-pumps, packed with fat and sugar and protein. She'd forgotten how disgusting they tasted.

"And I shall become a famous renaissance artist," said Misha. "If you're tired of that, don't eat it. Tempe is an acquired taste, especially when it's sweetened. You don't have to mind your alien manners now, Miss Catherine. Nobody's watching you."

"I went to Tracy Island," she said. "And it *is* moored in the Aleutias. Everything was very familiar. Except that there was no sign of the events of my previous visit. What really happened, Misha? Can you tell me now, or am I never to know?"

"There was a conspiracy," he said, sipping his tea and gazing at the catering machines. "There were two conspiracies, actually. I told you once, if you remember: your people's guilty secret wasn't much of a secret. My dad and the rest of that bunch of psychopaths knew that the Aleutians were not going to hand over the Buonarroti technology. They didn't care. They didn't want starflight; they were only interested in the superweapon. We knew too. Finding some way to get hold of, or to replicate, Aleutian Buonarroti tech was the renaissance's secret agenda: the thing we never mentioned.

"At the Buonarroti lab, Bright and his people were engineering Aleutian anti-self tissue and putting it through the Buonarroti acceleration. We knew we had to get hold of that enriched material, so we could take it apart. But it was the ultra-Traditionalists who succeeded. They had better contacts inside. Helen was recruited to the weapons development plot. She did not kill herself rather than submit, as you, of course, would have done. And I don't see how we could have saved any of the other girls if we'd tried: but think what you like about that. She was already working with some other *auteurs* on her own idea for a Buonarroti gate, which was was based on something Sidney Carton said long ago. A virtual *envie* has much in common, in a sense, with the state of non-location. It's a field of potential out of which springs a world made of minds, a bit like a vacuum fluctuation. It's been known for centuries that habitual gamers have different neuronal mapping. More of it, basically, layers of other worlds complete but existing nowhere in normal time and space: that was the clue. Helen needed to see what the Aleutian anti-self algorithm, their engine core, did to a living human brain, such as her own. That's why she went along with the old monsters. When they did their mad-scientist biopsies of her infected brain, she stole a few scraps. She used what she learned to model a version of what Bright calls the pump: being into nothingness and back again. But she modeled in virtuality, which is where *human* consciousness resides. And that was it. I warn you, I'm explaining something I don't understand, so don't try to impress your friends with my account of how the trick was done. However, I wouldn't tell you any more if I could. You're a business competitor."

"But I'm too stupid to be a dangerous one. You proved that."

He smiled. "Helen designed the engine; other renaissance people built it. When it was up and running, we recruited you. Whenever you went into the games room at the Phoenix Café, you passed through a gate that was linked to *our* non-location device. Sometimes we played games. Sometimes the engine was engaged. The drops in your eyes were saline, and you crossed the light years with us. And you never knew the difference."

"The Blue Forest is another new planet, isn't it. One that we don't know about."

Misha nodded. "That was from the space telescopes. Renaissance grid-hounds have hunted down old space telescope archives, and started collecting and analyzing solar systems. You take the spectral profile of a star, investigate it closely enough so that you can identify the chemical components of the planetary atmospheres. If you find something breathable, in an earth-type orbit, you're on your way to identifying a new habitable planet. Neat, isn't it? But nobody had thought to carry on with that for three hundred years."

"Until the rebirth," she murmured.

"When you stood in our gate," he said, "you were like Braemar and Johnny. Like yourself that time when you were Clavel. We were amazed that you couldn't tell."

"Why should I?" wondered Catherine. "A really good virtual reality is only identifiable because one knows that it isn't real. But what about that night? What was real then?"

Misha gazed into his inward eye. "You want to know what happened that night? You came out of Helen's simulation of Arden; you talked to Lalith and Agathe. The rest of us joined you; we went back through the gate into the gamesroom. Do you remember you were worried about the ID reader? That was when we passed through. Everything that seemed to follow was a transition event, until you walked out into the concourse at Los Angeles airport. I'm sure you know about 'transition events': well, everybody does now. It's what happens when you go through the state of non-location to get to another Buonarroti 'situation' in the cosmic simultaneity. You go through the gate into a spooky, intense dream. If you're lucky, you come out of it at your destination remembering the whole thing and knowing that it was a dream. Sometimes you don't remember anything; you just arrive in the new world. But the danger is that you never come out of it. You're in another world; you don't know how you got there, and it's supercharged with meaning, like a vivid dream. Everything's over-determined, over-intensified: and you go mad. Building the engine was only part of what we did. The other part was finding out how to cope with that problem. We've learned that you can control the transition. You discuss what's going to happen, like a group of games players going into an *envie;* and it does, more or less. You're lucid dreamers. We'd softened you up, laying clues and dropping big hints about the weapons conspiracy. We hit on the Tracy Island scenario for your final trip, because Lalith really is a secret agent and a Campfire Girl. She knew the place and had access to plenty of useful scene-setting information. That night we played the game we'd planned. When it was over, the rest of us willed ourselves back home again, and you were in the Americas."

"But what about the conspiracy? *Was* there an Americas side to the plot? *Did* Lalith have a flier hidden in the arena? Was the girl with the phoenix-toy, the girl with the empty-centered sores, one of your clues? Was she one of you?"

"Resign yourself," he told her, with the old arrogant smirk. "There are some things you're never going to find out. There was no weapons test. By the time we took you for our ride, the unspeakably awful doomsday conspiracy had collapsed. That's the recorded truth, and the only truth you're going to get. There is no absolute reality anymore. We're living in Buonarroti time. The world has become a Belushi sphere. If you know what that means." Misha looked at her curiously. "But I'll tell you something odd. I know what *your* transition experience was when you were the Third Captain long ago. It was fire. Flames, and a sense of falling."

She stared. "It was the landing in West Africa. We crashed. I lived through that crash again, and then I was home . . . But I had forgotten. I had forgotten completely, until you took me to Tracy Island—"

"We've been through your flames. Either flames or some kind of climbing incident, or both: they often come into the transition. We think the climbing must be from Johnny and Braemar's adventure. Of course there *is* only one 'state of non-location': and now it's burned with the traces of the people who opened the way. So you have a memorial. Your signature is on the gateway."

"How romantic."

She took another bite of the biscuit. It wasn't so bad. A child somewhere set up a loud, hopeless keening. Something had happened in the surgery area: she saw figures rushing that way. Burns were the worst problem. They needed endless, impossible supplies of multitype skin. The Church of Self Mission went around preaching their redemption and dispensing for free from their stockpile of painkillers and tranquilizers. They'd become very popular with the medical staff, who had nothing else to offer to the dying.

"Getting hyper-conscious," Misha said, "becoming *nothing but* consciousness, means becoming hyper-aroused. It was easy for us to deal with that state because we're gamers and we're human, full of hormones and stuff. You had to learn, in your female human body, to cope with hyper-arousal. You needed to experience the kind of thing paper flowers does."

"Sure," said Catherine cynically.

Misha glanced uneasily into his camera eye.

"All right, I'm trying to say I'm sorry. I know there are no excuses. I'm just sorry."

"Don't be," said Catherine. "*Çà ne m'a coûte rien.* It's not as if we could ever have been real lovers. We're too much alike." And she laughed.

After a moment's puzzlement, he laughed too.

He checked his inset again. "It's nearly midnight. Shall we go outside? Excuse me."

He left her by the tea counter. She saw the self-regarding perfection of his walk again. The ghost of an elegantly tattered duster coat swirled. He spoke to the young woman who was waiting for him by the processing desk. She was wearing a high-necked, long-sleeved tunic and loose trousers, the usual dress of middle-class Traditionalist women aid workers. Her face was undisfigured; her great, dark, shining eyes still tender and lovely. Catherine marveled at this astonishing resistance to the disintegration. Then Misha unguardedly put his hand on the woman's shoulder. His touch passed through the image.

He came back. They climbed an outside stairway, picking their way between the huddled bodies roosting there. At the turn there was an open landing. Misha folded his arms on top of the low wall of ancient poured stone and gazed out at the city.

"On a night like this, it seems to go on forever."

"Is Helen still alive?"

He glanced at her sharply. "Yes. She's still dying. She wants to hold on right to the end." He looked down at the cropland, which had been scented bean fields one summer day, in another world and time. "I'm with her as much as possible. That's all I think about. When she dies, I'm to keep nothing. No virtual ghosts. She wants me to destroy every copy of her I have."

Catherine wondered if he would do it.

The blank spaces on the chart.

"By the way, I'm off the testo. And I'm staying off." He half turned, following the glittering horizon of spires and towers. There was so much light tonight in the city that had been in Aleutian darkness for so long. "They say, about people like me: *He doesn't care for anyone but himself.* It isn't true. You can't love yourself if you don't love anyone else.

I loathed 'Misha.' Now I don't. And I love Helen. I didn't, before. I didn't know she was a person. I thought she was a goddess, and I thought I owned her. I seem to have spent my whole life doing things exactly the wrong way: out of arrogance, out of vanity. Sorry isn't enough. I want to thank you. I don't know how, but you helped me."

Catherine thought, it was true that they were alike. Far more alike than Clavel and Johnny Guglioli, but nowhere near so close as Misha and Helen. She remembered the night he'd shown her his work, how strongly she'd felt his sense that it didn't belong to him. That nothing in the world belonged to Misha: and therefore he believed he had unlimited licence to "get his own back" any way he could. She'd been eager to be punished for Aleutia's crimes. But Aleutia, in the end, had played a very minor part in the drama. It was Helen who owned the world, in Misha's eyes. Helen was the real object of the bitter mixture of malice and dependency, adoration and resentment that had so puzzled and lacerated a bewildered alien-in-disguise. Parent, lover, mentor, servant. In old-earth the relationship that was Aleutia's romantic ideal was only too possible: and it appalled her. Which was very funny, after three lifetimes. She thought of Maitri, who fortunately would never be her lover. Though in all the lives, she'd probably never love anyone more.

"How little divides us!" she exclaimed.

Misha nodded sadly.

She decided she would not try to share the joke. Though she seemed to remember he had once said much the same thing to her about immortality, which had always been a romantic ideal for humans. In real life, so far as it was possible, it was appalling.

"What will you do now?" he asked. "I mean, afterward."

"Live. I have some credit. I think I'll work. Why not? Mâtho bought my diaries."

He took a small packet out of his jeans pocket. "I've been

wondering how to send you this. I had a feeling that you wouldn't want to see me again, but it seemed as if they should be handed over in person. You know my father committed suicide?"

"Yes."

"He wanted you to have the keys to the house at L'Airial. The park staff will be there, but the family house will be empty. The formalities are taken care of. Helen and I have moved out. The net's dismantled, but everything else is as it was. He thought of you before he died. He said he was very glad to have met you. Take them, anyway. You may want to go back there someday."

She took the packet. Suddenly he started. "That's it!" he exclaimed. "They've gone!"

Somewhere far out in the dark, invisible above the city's atmosphere, the moon's three hundred years' companion had winked out of existence.

Gone.

An uproar of sound and light exploded. Sirens blared, bells rang. A torchlight procession careened wildly onto the cropland. People were trampling the fields, shouting, singing, letting off firearms.

"My God," breathed Misha. "Gone. Here begins the new era."

They watched the city in silence. "This is the real world," said Misha. "Here, where people hack each other to pieces and cry in each other's arms. This will go on. The Buonarroti device will make no difference. No one will think about what it means. *Here*, where we live and die, people don't care how the engine works. They'll just get in that car and drive. And that's the way it will always be."

He looked at Catherine with a new and startling expression. It was compassion. "You're going to be so lonely."

She shook her head. "Oh, no. *Since we are surrounded by so great a cloud of witnesses* . . . It's as true on earth as it is in Aleutia."

Every self in the myriad: every separate flame.

"I'd better get back to Helen. Goodbye, Catherine. Try to forgive me."

She thought how much she detested being pitied and apologized to. It made her feel like a cripple. And she laughed again.

"Nothing to forgive. As my old friend Karl once said to me, in another lifetime: fair exchange is no robbery. Goodbye, Mish."

But he was gone, down the stairs, through the bodies. Catherine stayed. After a while she tired of the spectacle and went to see if the police had any spare washing-powder.

ENVOI: *UN BEL DI VEDREMO*

ONE DAY. IT was mid-July, according to the calendar of the wilderness program, and a late, hot, ocean afternoon. Catherine was coming up from the beach with her bodyboard under her arm. She climbed the wooden steps, sun and salt on her bare back. She was alone in the forest's cloud of witnesses, the invisible virtual users. She put her hand on the rail at the gate and saw the Campfire bracelet. It sat easily on her tanned wrist, snug enough that a band of white developed under it every summer. The tiny brilliants in the incised flames glittered. Her gaze was held. Her grip on the bar of soft, salt-powdered wood became so vital and intense an experience . . . that she remembered the paper flowers, she remembered Tracy Island. She seemed to be walking out of the police station again—punch-drunk, wavering—and there, something moving on the floor, caught in the corner of her eye . . .

The girl with the phoenix in her hands.

She understood that she would never know when it had begun. When time and space have been once annihilated, all the rules are changed. The young people of the renaissance had set out to catch themselves an alien. Not because they needed Catherine's help. Not at all! Because they *didn't* need her, and this was something they wanted her to know.

She remembered her night in the Blue Forest. Misha had been cruel, and that was a crime. But when she thought of his exultant face as he *shafted* her, Catherine, who was on another planet and didn't even know it, she could not help but sympathize with his heartless young triumph. They had taken their revenge: but so joyously, so playfully, and with so little cost to Catherine, in the end.

She saw Misha and Helen Connelly as she had seen them last, in the field hospital. And though Helen had died, while Misha was presumably alive somewhere, she knew that it was Misha who had been destroyed and Helen who had escaped, who had survived the battle of the sexes. But now that war was over, and the territory that they'd been fighting over must vanish, along with many lovely, tainted things . . . (*We don't want to bore you,* reminded Lalith's voice sternly. *But there was a holocaust.*) Let it go, let it pass. She had been a bit player in a drama that she'd only partly understood. Everything must be forgiven.

but when?

Ahead of her, on the landward side of the dunes, began the forest. Where she lived at L'Airial in perfect serenity, with the park staff and her work, with the Virtual Master or some descendant of his (she wasn't sure: the staff simply always kept a hedgehog mascot always known by the same name). The winters were still getting longer and colder, over all. The permanent snow did not retreat. But the Atlantic Forest would last out Catherine's time, not much altered. Sometimes she roamed the house, searching in closets of forgotten junk for relics of the schoolroom that she'd never found again, looking into the empty rooms and wondering which had been Helen's boudoir. She used Mr. Connelly's study often; it was her favorite winter lair. She would sit curled up in one of his armchairs, listening to his Puccini records by the chrysanthemum fire.

Occasionally, she would catch up with the news of the post-Buonarroti world, where the humans were learning to get in that car and drive. But she was not tempted to return.

She believed that Misha had told her the truth about the Tracy Island event. The young people had played that fine, scary, exciting game with her, in the timeless instant of passing through the Buonarroti gate, and finally delivered her safely to LAX. But she would never know for sure. The human scientists at the Buonarroti project had worried endlessly about the paradoxes of breaking the time barrier. *When people are traveling and returning across gulfs of hundreds of light-years, changing the galactic future and past, where is present reality?* But the cosmos has always been changing, constantly re-creating its own present, past, and future. This is not new. This is something discovered, not invented. The sum of being shifts like a kaleidoscope. And yet from moment to moment what happens, happens. What is, is. Somehow it will always seem to fit together: just as the unstable, multifarious cloud of signals that makes a human mind seems a single, coherent self.

But if the mask slips . . . She stared at the bracelet on her wrist. *Is this a new world that came into being that night? Did I ever leave the game? What is real?*

i don't exist, i'm nothing, there is no catherine, no place, no time.

the glitter of the stones released her.

The sky was a blue void in which stately white mountains of cloud hung suspended, the navy blue rollers drove in from the ocean and fell in spume onto the sands. She noticed how her wrist had grown more muscular but thinner over the years. One could see bone as well as blood through the fragile skin now; jutting bone and unexpected hollows. How much time did she have left? Not enough, of course. She felt such a passion of love for this blue air, for this green world. To which Johnny still might return, might have returned even now from the mazes of rebirth. Any day he might come to visit her, or send a message. *I'm back, I re-*

member everything, I love you . . . Some part of Catherine would always believe that the sweet impossibility was possible, as long as she lived. And yet, she thought, she would be glad enough to leave when the time came. All debts paid, the long strain over. She went through the gate, shouldering her board, and shut it behind her. The jeep was waiting, half asleep, in the silence of the forest margin.

ACKNOWLEDGMENTS

A short bibliography
How the Leopard Changed Its Spots, Brian Goodwin, Weiden-feld and Nicolson UK 1994; *Hiding in the Light*, Dick Heb-dige, Routledge UK 1994; *Leonardo da Vinci*, Martin Kemp, J. M. Dent and Sons, London 1981; *The House of Souls*, Arthur Machen, Grant Richards, London 1906; *Greenmantle*, John Buchan, Pan Books 1950; *The Life of St. Catherine of Siena*, Blessed Raymond of Capua, tr. George Lamb, Harvill Press, London UK 1960; *The Story of a Soul*, St. Thérèse of Lisieux, Wheathampstead, Anthony Clarke 1990; *Histoire de Ma Vie*, George Sand, Academy Press 1977; *Flaubert-Sand: The Correspondence*, tr. Francis Steegmuller and Bar-bara Bray, based on the edition of Alphonse Jacobs, Harville Press, London UK 1993; *L'Education Sentimentale*, Gustave Flaubert, Penguin 1946; *Les Blanches Années*, Jacqueline Bruller, Stock 1980; *Thérèse Desqueyroux*, François Mauriac, Bernard Grasset, Paris 1927. The Sargent portrait is of Gra-ham Robertson; it is in the Tate Gallery, London. "Yo Soy la Desintegración" Frida Kahlo, from *The Diary of Frida Kahlo*, intro. Carlos Fuentes, Bloomsbury, London UK 1995. The virtual laboratory (Vlab) was devised (in the real) following the work of Hungarian biologist Aristid Lindenmayer, 1968, reported by Tim Thwaites, in *New Scientist*, IPC mag-

azines, May 1995. Special acknowledgment: Jeremy Miller
(c/o The Photographers Gallery, London) for the influence
of his exhibition "The Institute of Cultural Anxiety" (ICA
December 1994 to 12 February 1995). Special acknowledgment also to Vincent Shine (c/o laure genillard gallery, London) for his version of (plant) life exactly re-created in
artifice. Agathe Unwilingiyimana was the Prime Minister
of Rwanda, July 1993–April 7, 1994.

Quotations
An explanation for group suicide, from *Jude the Obscure*,
Thomas Hardy; Catherine on her need to believe in God,
from *Jacques le Fataliste*, Denis Diderot. Maitri's appreciation
of Misha's style, from *Two Gentlemen of Verona*, Wm. Shakespeare, Act I scene 3; Misha's defiance song, "The Wearing
of the Green," traditional. Alicia Khan's question of ownership, from an epigram engraved on the collar of a dog
given to Charles II; Agathe's complaint about the difficulty
of doing good, from *Paul et Virginie*, Bernardin de Saint-
Pierre. Misha applying the eyedrops on Catherine's first
entry to the gamesroom, from *A Midsummer Night's Dream*,
Wm. Shakespeare, Act II scene 1; Dr. Bright on proliferating
weapons production, "I am become death" attributed to J.
Robert Oppenheimer. Agathe on human smiles, slightly
misquoted from *Hamlet*, Wm. Shakespeare, Act I scene 5;
Triumph chant in the Blue Forest, "When the Saints Go
Marching In," traditional as far as I know. Maitri on the
spirit of adventure, from *Hassan*, James Elroy Flecker;
Helen's description of her art from *La Bohème*, Puccini (li-
brettists Giuseppe Giacosa and Luigi Illica); Maitri's household's farewell to earth, "Spanish Ladies," traditional.
Catherine's ever-present company, Hebrews, chapter XII
verse 1. I regret that I have not been able to trace the writer
or the publisher of the hymn verses quoted as a background to the lunch date at the Car Park.